# THE MOTH

For Robert Bradley, working in a village carpenter's shop, life was not always easy. Exploring the Durham countryside he had his first strange encounter with Millie, an ethereal girl-child whose odd ways and nocturnal wanderings had led her to be known locally as 'Thorman's Moth'. Then a dramatic turn in Robert's affairs brought him into contact with the Thormans of Foreshaw and especially with the elder daughter, Agnes, who alone of the family loved and protected the frail, unworldly Millie. But this was 1913, and anything beyond the most formal relationship had to face the barriers and injustices of a rigid social hierarchy that was soon to perish in the flames of war.

# THE MOTH

## Catherine Cookson

CHIVERS PRESS
BATH

First published 1986
by
Willian Heinemann
This Large Print edition published by
Chivers Press
by arrangement with
Random House Limited
2001

ISBN 0 7540 1668 4

British Library Cataloguing in Publication Data available

Printed and bound in Great Britain by
BOOKCRAFT, Midsomer Norton, Somerset

To my secretary
Sarah Sables
whose heart, like Robert's,
was touched by
Millie

The caterpillar on the leaf
Repeats to thee thy mother's grief.
Kill not the moth nor butterfly,
For the Last Judgement draweth nigh.
William Blake

# CONTENTS

# PART ONE

## The Move

# CHAPTER ONE

Robert Bradley sat in the front room of 122, Upper Foxglove Road, Jarrow, which town is situated in the County of Durham, being bordered along the whole of its length by the river Tyne. It is as though the town had squeezed itself out of Tyne Dock, through East Jarrow, on past Saint Paul's church and the old monastery which was the home of the Venerable Bede, up the Church Bank and into the main thoroughfare, along which run the tram lines. And if you follow them you will eventually arrive at Palmer's shipyard at the end of Ellison Street. There are other yards along the river bank but it is Palmer's that dominates the town and gives it, as it were, its life blood.

Robert Bradley had worked in Palmer's since he was fourteen years old. He had served his time for four years and one extra for improving. This brought him up to nineteen. Now at twenty-four he was a man and skilled in his work as his father had been before him.

Six hours ago he had helped to carry his father out of this room where he had lain for five full days in a bought coffin. He regretted that. And he had made up his mind on one point for the future, and that was if he ever had a home of his own, not just two rooms and a scullery in which you couldn't swing a cat, but a real home, a house where you went upstairs to sleep and had a shed . . . no, a brick building outside as a workshop . . . well, if that day should ever come about the first thing he would make in that workshop would be his coffin, because he was particular about wood, as his father had been. Oh yes, as his father had been. So why hadn't his father thought about making his own coffin, even in the back yard? He'd had plenty time to think about it for he had been in his trade for forty years. But then he'd had a wife to please and she had wanted good solid furniture in the house. And this his father had made in what spare time he had. He himself had helped with quite a number of pieces. The chiffonier opposite, for instance, along which his uncle was now rubbing his hand.

He looked at his uncle, scrutinizing him through slightly lowered lids. He didn't really know what to make of him. Well, who would know what to make of a man who had stopped speaking to his brother twenty-five years ago, and what's more, had looked upon him only twice during that time? The first was three years ago when, as now, he had come to a funeral. On that occasion, however, he hadn't come into the house, he had just stood in the churchyard and away from those gathered about the grave. But when he himself and his father had together turned away from the graveside his father had looked across the snow-clad cemetery at the solitary figure standing alone and had muttered, 'God in heaven! our John.'

He had remained by his father's side as he walked towards the stiff figure of the elderly man, and what the man said to his father on their approach was, 'Well, you've lost her an' all,' to which his father had answered, 'Aye, John, as you say, I've lost her an' all. Now that should make you happy.' And on this the man had turned and walked away.

It was on that night his father had told him the

reason for the split. It would appear that his mother had been going to marry the elder brother but had in the meanwhile fallen in love with the younger one. John Bradley was thirty-three at the time and settled in his ways. He had courted Annie Forrester for six years. She lived in the hamlet in a cottage a little way from the Bradleys' carpenter's shop and house, and everybody knew it would be a big step up for her when she became mistress of the house that was three times bigger than any other in the hamlet. More so, it had ten acres of freehold land, a big yard and a set of stone outbuildings that any craftsman could be proud of. But what did she do? She ran off with Bob Bradley who was seven years younger than his brother and nearer her own age.

John Bradley lived alone for eight years before his bitterness softened somewhat; and then he married. No one from the hamlet, but a woman from a Methodist family in Birtley, and she in her late thirties.

Robert now turned his gaze on the woman. In his opinion she was what he would call a canny body. She must, at one time, he imagined, have been passably pretty; now her hair was greying and her face was lined, but she looked kindly. He wondered how she really got on with his uncle who was a rabid member of the Church of England, so he had been given to understand by his father.

Then there was their daughter Carrie. Now she was something, was Carrie. She said she was fifteen, but if she had said seventeen he would have believed her because she was developed where a lass should be developed: her buttocks were already moulding her full skirt and her breasts pushing at the bodice of her dress. And she had a bright eye, had this Carrie. And he knew all about bright eyes. Oh aye, he did that. There was one in the kitchen there clearing up after the tea. What would she expect of him for that? You just had to smile at Polly and she took it as an advance towards marriage.

He was getting worried about Polly Hinton and her ma . . . and her da; they had never been out of the house since his father had died. When he had said he could manage, Mrs Hinton had thrust him aside, saying, 'Don't be silly, lad. What are neighbours for at a time like this, if not to take over?' And she had taken over, and in doing so had given him a glimpse of what it would be like to be married to Polly. He had no intention of marrying Polly, but you couldn't get that into Polly's head.

Since last New Year's Eve, when he had let himself go and had a bit of slap and tickle with her up the back lane, no more, no, no more than that, she had never been off his tail. His father used to laugh and say, 'Look out, lad, or you'll wake up one morning and find yourself in bed with Polly on one side of you and her ma on the other.'

'This is a nice piece of mahogany. Did you make it?'

Robert blinked, straightened his shoulders and gathered his thoughts together before answering, 'I helped me da.'

'Anything here you've made yourself?'

'Yes, I made the chairs you're sitting on.' He nodded towards his aunt and the girl, and as he did so the thought came to him that it was funny to think he had a cousin like her and an uncle and aunt like these two. It gave him the feeling of not

6

being entirely alone, although, going on his uncle's manner, the time mightn't be far ahead when he would tell himself it wouldn't be such a bad thing to be without relations for he was stiff-necked was this new uncle. But still, they'd soon be gone, and afterwards, apart from an occasional visit from them, if they felt so inclined, he would see very little of them, he supposed.

He looked at his uncle, who was now examining one of the chairs. Then he started slightly as John Bradley said abruptly, 'You satisfied with the job you've got?'

He stared back at the man for a moment as if considering, then he said, 'I'll always be satisfied as long as I'm working with wood.'

'You fit the ships?'

'Yes. Aye, that's what I do, along with a few other chaps.' He grinned now as he looked towards his aunt, and she smiled back at him but didn't speak. She had hardly said half a dozen words since they had met. She seemed to have been put in her place all right.

'I've got a good business: I'm supplying a shop in Newcastle with high quality chairs and tables. I'm taking on another man. How about it?'

How about it? The offer came almost as a shock. Leave these two rooms and move into the country, into the house where his father had been born, and his father and his father afore him, and still be able to work with wood? It seemed too good to be true. Away from the hustle and the noise, away from the swarms of kids making a racket in the street till all hours of the night. He often thought that the number of children from both sides of the road outnumbered the rivets in the plates of an entire

7

ship, for after the lamp-lighter had been they would emerge like hordes of ants. But then ants were quiet, whereas the noise the kids made outside the doors was sometimes deafening.

He was used to the noise in the shipyard but it was a different noise. Ships were built on noise; but his part in their construction was made up more by sounds, the sound of a saw going through wood, the gentle jabbing of a plane along a plank, and the soft plop as the curl of wood fell among its mates. And there was a kind of music in the sound of sandpaper working along the grain. And that final hidden sound: you knew it was there because you made up the click in your own mind as one piece of wood dovetailed into another.

And to work to these sounds without the background of steel plates being hammered was something to think about, to consider deeply. But there were always snags. How would he like working for this man, living on the spot? As it was now, he did in a way leave his work behind when he was through the gates, but for twenty-four hours of the day he would be near this bloke. And as yet he didn't know how to take him. What he also had to consider was that once he burned his boats the oars would be gone too, so to speak, for he couldn't expect to get another house or another job in the yard; there was always somebody ready and waiting to jump into your shoes, and things at the moment were a bit tricky, international like. But they were always a bit tricky international like.

Then there was the Mechanics' Institute. He'd miss that, and his books. Well, he had more than two dozen of his own that were worth re-reading, and he could always go into Birtley or Chester-le-

8

Street, or even as far as Durham. There were bound to be reading rooms there. But, taking all this into account it still left the man.

'Well, what do you say? You're taking some time to think about it.'

He really didn't know what to say. But his mind at this point was made up for him, for the door leading from the scullery into the living-room was thrust open and Mrs Hinton put her head round it, saying, 'Well, everything's clear and tidy in here, Bobby. Polly's gone to change; she'll be in later to see to your supper and things . . . I'll say goodbye, Mrs Bradley. Goodbye, Mr Bradley.' And she nodded from one to the other. Her last nod she kept for Robert and it was accompanied by an expression of deep sympathy, as the occasion warranted.

The door hadn't closed on her before Robert, looking at his uncle, said, 'I'd be glad to. Aye, I'd be glad to take you up on it.'

When you were between the devil and the deep sea, it was wiser to latch on to the devil, he had more substance.


CHAPTER TWO

'Who would have thought one would ever see the wood loft turned into a home. And it is a home, Robert, isn't it? Homely, at least at this end. And you don't notice the wood stacked along there.' Alice Bradley waved her hand towards the far end of the long room that ran above the workshop.

Robert agreed with her: nodding, he said, 'Aye,

9

Aunty, it is homely. And it's all of three times the size of 122, Upper Foxglove Road. As for the wood, why, I think that adds to me comfort, for there's nothing I like better than the smell of wood . . . seasoning wood, like yon is.'

'And to think it was Carrie's idea. She's got an eye for wood too, you know, Robert.' Alice turned to her daughter, smiling broadly now, and Carrie, her fair head wagging slightly, looked at Robert, saying, 'Well, I thought it was a shame you letting all your nice pieces go and for next to nothing, after all the work you had put into them. I still think your neighbour had a nerve to offer five shillings for this table.' Carrie now stroked her hand up and down the patina of the small mahogany dining table as she added, 'Dad would get ten pounds for a table like this, wouldn't he, Ma?'

'Oh yes, at the least, 'cos this quality would sell in Newcastle at anything up to twenty. It's the big houses that buy such, you see. Of course, for a full dining table of this quality you could ask almost anything, up to thirty pounds. That's if it had two leaves. Well now—' Alice looked around her in obvious admiration—'it looks as good as my sitting-room, this part anyway. And you know, if you like, Robert, you could make a sort of partition here to hide your bed.'

'Oh, there's no need for that, Aunty, because for what time I spend up here I'll be asleep anyway . . . well, most nights.'

'You like reading, don't you, Robert?' Alice's face was now straight, her expression serious, and she moved a step towards him, her voice low now as she went on, 'That's the only thing Mr Bradley's worried about, the lamp,' she pointed; 'he's afraid you might go to sleep and leave it burning . . . and with all the wood . . .'

'Never you fear about that, Aunty'—Robert put out his hand in a tentative motion towards her—'I'm always very careful. And I promise that that'll be me main concern to see it's out afore I even go to bed. I'll make it a habit not to read in bed, so that'll ensure there's no danger of anything happening through the lamp.'

Alice smiled at him now and she turned to make for the door which led on to the landing of the house proper, but Carrie, hurrying to her side, whispered something, and on this Alice said slowly, 'Oh yes.' And then, turning to Robert again, she looked at him and sighed before saying hesitantly, 'I . . . I know from a little you've said, Robert, that you follow . . . well, no line towards God, but . . . but Mr Bradley would be obliged . . . and pleased'—she nodded her head at him now—'if you would accompany us this morning to church.'

Robert looked into the face that he had come to like. She was a nice woman was his new Aunt Alice—he still thought of these relations as new—she had shown him nothing but kindness during the few days he had been here. He had discovered that she had some strange ways with her, such as always referring to her husband by his surname and never sitting down if he was standing unless he told her to do so. These actions made her appear to be very subservient; yet he had noticed, at least on one occasion when she had answered her husband back, that her voice was firm, and his uncle had made no further comment on what she had said.

The matter had concerned Carrie going to the church Bible Class unaccompanied. It would

11

appear that Gladys Parkin, the daughter of their only close neighbour in the small hamlet, had caught a chill and was in bed, and as Gladys's sisters Mary Ellen and Nancy were past the Sunday School age, there was no one for Carrie to walk with.

There were only six cottages altogether in the hamlet itself, but there were farmhouses here and there with their accompanying cottages, and a few miners' rows. Then there was the village of Lamesley and, beyond, the township of Birtley. But of all the residents near at hand, there was no young female among them whom John Bradley considered fit enough to accompany his daughter. And as it would have been slightly ridiculous for him to have been seen taking her to the vestry door of the church, he had therefore ordered his wife to be her companion, whereupon on this particular occasion his Aunt Alice had stated it would be as equally ridiculous for her to take her daughter by the hand, so to speak, the girl coming up sixteen.

So last Sunday Carrie had for the first time walked to the Bible Class and back on her own. A thrilling experience for the poor lass, he thought.

And now here was this kind woman acting as mouthpiece for her husband, his stiff-necked, bigoted sanctimonious uncle, because that's what he was. His word was sacrosanct in the house. There was grace before and after meals, at which unpunctuality was seemingly a sin. And under this same banner of sin came swearing, a simple damn being enough to make him look grim; and should the word God slip out of context his face would turn purple. So much he had learned in the short time he had been here. And now here he was being

12

put to the test. Well, it was really no test, for he did not have to think about it, his answer was a definite no. But he couldn't put it like that to this kind woman, and so he said, ' I'm sorry, Aunty, but I think . . . at least I thought I had made it clear to Uncle that I'm not inclined that way. Never have been.'

'It's not too late to start, Robert.' Alice's voice was gentle and had a pleading note in it, and he bowed his head against the appeal as he muttered, 'It's no use, Aunty.'

'You never know until you try. Have you ever tried?'

'Yes, I suppose in a way, until I started to read.'

'But reading doesn't surely close the door to God?'

'In a way it does, Aunty, because so many people have so many different ideas of God, not only in this country, like the Protestants and the Catholics and the Baptists and the Methodists and so on, but in other countries where Jesus Christ is not even recognized . . .'

'What did you say?'

The door had been thrust open and the side of it caught Alice and would have knocked her backwards had not Robert steadied her with a quickly outthrust hand. And then he turned and looked at his uncle and slowly he repeated, 'I said that in some countries Jesus Christ is not even recognized.'

'How dare you blaspheme in my house! Do you know what you're saying?'

'Yes, and it's true, Uncle.'

' 'Tis not! They are heathens out there. They haven't heard the word of God through the Lord

13

Jesus Christ, and when they do . . .'

'They've heard the word of their own gods, and they are many and of all kinds.' Robert's voice had risen and now he watched his uncle swallow deeply; he watched the colour sweep upwards into the bald patch above his forehead and it even seemed to tinge the sparse grey hair that was brushed flat behind his ears. When he spoke it was seemingly with an effort, and the words came out as a growl, 'You disappoint me, boy.'

'Uncle.' Robert's voice was deep now and his words were slow as he said, 'First of all I'm no boy, and not being a boy, I'm not to be swayed in me way of thinking or intimidated or frightened whichever way you put it. And I'll say this now, Uncle: if I'm to continue working for you, I must be free after working hours to lead me own life. I think we'd better get this straight afore we go any further. Perhaps we should have had it worked out afore I made the move.'

John Bradley stared at the young man who was looking him straight in the eyes. He saw him as the son he had longed for. But as he had just said, he was no boy: he was a man of good height, all of five feet ten, with broad shoulders, a firm short neck and a face made square by his jaw bones; his nose was on the large side and his eyes were round and brown, looking almost black now because there was anger behind them; his brows above them were high as if raised with his anger. His hair like his eyes was brown; it was thick and unusually long for a man, for at the back it came to the top of his shirt collar. That was another thing he meant to speak about, but all in good time, for now, here he was confronted as if by an equal, more than an equal, and for the first time in his married life his wife was seeing his authority being lessened. Even his daughter from now on would view him through different eyes, for her love would be no longer tinged with fear, righteous fear, like that which is claimed by God, who is the loving father of all.

In one movement he swung his body round, then with outstretched arm he thrust the door wide again and went out into the corridor; and Alice, one hand gripping the neck of her outdoor cape, the other pressed tightly over her mouth, gave one glance as though in awe towards Robert before running after her husband.

Robert turned now and sadly he looked at Carrie. But Carrie wasn't looking sad; there was a smile on her face, suppressed, but nevertheless there; and her small babyish mouth was quivering as if it wanted to burst into laughter. And approaching him now on tiptoe she looked up at him and her pointed chin moved slightly from side to side before she said in a whisper, 'You're very brave.' And having said this she turned and ran from the room.

He stood looking through the doorway along the passage that led on to the landing where the four bedrooms were, and he thought, God in heaven, what have I let meself in for now!

Tim Yarrow, his uncle's assistant who lived over in Lamesley village and had worked below since he was a lad, had hinted at something like this on Friday. 'How are you farin' upstairs?' he had said. And when he had replied, 'Fine. Oh fine,' Yarrow had then added enigmatically, 'Come Sunday we'll see.'

Well Sunday had come and he had seen, and so

15

what was he going to do? He walked down the room to his bed, and there, his hands gripping the wooden rail at the foot of it, he leant forward and stared down on to the patchwork quilt. Should he up and go, or should he stay and see what transpired? It all depended on how his uncle would take his stand.

After a moment he turned and walked to the low window that went right down to floor level and, dropping on to his hunkers, he looked out over the countryside.

It was a very warm day for mid-September and the sun was shining on the roofs of the cottages down in the vale. Some distance away to the left he could just see the outline of the old church of Saint Andrew in Lamesley.

This was a bonny place. All around was bonny, that's if you didn't include the pit heaps. But there were plenty of places free from them, and up till half an hour ago he had been looking forward to taking a long dander over the countryside and perhaps meeting up with people that he could talk to, because he had already faced up to the fact that this was one thing he was missing, the talk, the backchat, even the ripe language of men at work.

Down in the shop below there was only the voice of the wood interspersed with staccato remarks from his aunty and grunts from his uncle; grunts were the only signs he made of approval even of a finished piece. When he was giving orders he had little to say: he would sketch what he wanted on a piece of paper and hand it to you, with the cursory inquiry: 'Can you manage that?'

He straightened his back. Well, what was he going to do? What could he do but wait and see

16

what transpired. Anyway, he had the day before him and he wasn't going to waste it.

Five minutes later he went down the bare shallow oak stairs into the little hall. Here he paused for a moment as he looked towards an antlered hallstand with the usual square compartment for umbrellas and walking sticks. There was a walking stick reposing in it now and as he looked towards it he told himself that's what he must make next, a walking stick. He had never thought about a walking stick before. Well, who but a cripple would use a walking stick in Jarrow?

He turned to his left, went through a door and into the kitchen. Everything here was as spruce and tidy as his aunt herself. But there was no smell of Sunday roast cooking. They'd had their hot dinner yesterday. And now he knew why. Anyway, what did it matter? He'd have a pie and half a pint in some inn.

Out in the yard he walked slowly to where the ever open gate gave on to the road; and here he paused and looked to the right and the left. The little hamlet was quiet. He wondered if all the Parkins were at church too, or did some go to Chapel? Whatever they favoured. It was funny when you came to think about it, him saying all the Parkins. Families hadn't really much option when it came to picking a religion, they had to follow the parents'. He was living with a good example of that, wasn't he?

Aw, let him forget about his uncle and his damned religion. It was a lovely day, not a day for thinking below the surface but one for thinking above it, looking up into the sky, breathing deeply, feeling your limbs move. Aye, he liked to feel his

17

limbs move. On this thought he stalked off down the road, and as he was nearing the end of the Parkins' yard which ran by the side of the house, a voice said to him, 'Good-morning, Mr Bradley.'

He stopped and looked at the young woman who had a tin dish in her hand in which reposed two cabbages, and he smiled as he answered, 'Good-morning to you.'

He watched her now moving slowly towards the railings. She walked jauntily, her hips pushing her striped skirt from one side to the other, and when she came within a yard of him she said, 'I'm Nancy Parkin.'

'Pleased to meet you, Miss Parkin.'

'And you too, Mr Bradley . . . How do you like living in the country?'

'Fine so far. It's all very new, but very healthy.'

He drew in a deep breath and expanded his chest and flapped his hand against it, and they both laughed.

'Are you off to church?'

He turned his head to the side while still keeping his eyes on her before he put the question: 'Which denomination are you, may I ask?'

'Oh, me?' Her face mockly prim, she replied, 'The heathen denomination.'

At this they both laughed together again, louder now, and when he said, 'I'll come to your meeting any day,' she bent her head over the cabbages and pressed her hand tightly over her mouth while her body shook; then of an instant she straightened up and, her face attempting to assume a solemn expression, she said, 'Eeh! it's Sunday. Denomination or none, it's still Sunday.'

'Yes, it's still Sunday.' His face too attempted to

18

assume a less jocular expression as he asked now, 'How is your young sister faring?'

'Oh, she's a lot better. But I tell you what.' She now poked her head towards him. 'I bet young Carrie wishes that she won't get well too soon, because our Gladys has had to act as gaoler to the poor lass for years.' As she drew her lips tightly in and nodded at him, he imitated her and nodded back, then said, ' Is that how it is?' And to this she answered, 'Aye, that's how it is. If she doesn't watch out her da will have her into a convent. No—' She again clapped her hand over her mouth; then her tone changing and almost primly now, she said, 'Well, yes, there are Protestant convents of a kind, aren't there?'

'I suppose so.' He nodded at her. 'I haven't been in one yet, but . . .'

His voice was cut off by her laughter, which again came as a gust as if from her belly before she could stifle it, and as he looked at her, his own mouth wide, he thought: We could get on together, we two. Yes, we could.

When a voice came from within the house shouting, 'Our Nancy, you!' she pulled a face; then digging her finger down towards the cabbages, she said, 'Dinner . . . that'll be Mam. I bet her first words when I get in the door will be, "Have you stood and watched them grow?" Ta-ra. Ta-ra. I'll be seein' you.'

'And me you. Aye, I'll be seeing you.'

She turned and ran into the house and he resumed his walk through the hamlet, his step almost jaunty now. She was a nice lass, lively. She'd make a good companion; and she was a surprise to find in this little dump set out on the end of

19

nowhere. Oh, things were looking up; life could be quite interesting after all . . . Did that mean he was going to settle here? Oh, well, he'd see. There was one point in its favour: there promised to be some light relief near at hand and he hadn't expected to find that.

*        *        *

Robert told himself he had never spent a more pleasant day. And yet he hadn't walked all that far from the hamlet, not more than five miles; but the knowledge he had gained of the locality was extensive. In the inn at Lamesley he had met an old gaffer and paid for the history of the district in two half-pints of ale.

The old man had asked him if he was a stranger to the area, and had then said, 'Oh well, there's nothing about these parts that I don't know. I've lived here man and boy for nigh on seventy years. Worked up at the castle for thirty of them.'

'The castle?'

'Aye; Ravensworth Castle. Over there.' The old man had pointed to the rack of bottles behind the bar counter where stood the landlord, one Mr Hardy. 'Fine edifice, the castle. Goes back for donkeys' years. Was a fortress to begin with. The Danes occupied it at one time, would you believe that?'

'No!' He had smiled at the old man. 'The Danes? I can't believe the Danes lived round here.'

His ignorance had spurred the old man on. But when later he left the inn it was not just with the feeling of being weighed down with a great deal of local knowledge; but also with the fact that

20

although nobody had asked his name, all those present in the taproom seemed to know who he was. Even the old narrator.

'If you want a gossip shop,' his da had always said, 'you live in a village. Each village has its own carrier system and it's quicker than anything the new telegraph can come up with.'

Now here he was at six in the evening, dusty and tired and still four miles from home, where he wouldn't arrive before seven o'clock even if he were to gallop. And the last meal of the day, Sundays included, was tea at six. His uncle didn't believe in suppers: kept you awake, he said; besides which they caused stomach upsets in later life.

So it was the prospect of a hungry evening that decided him to have another half-pint and a pie or two when he came in sight of an inn lying well back from the road.

The name of the inn was The Bull, and his entrance into the main bar brought round towards him the faces of four men seated along a wooden settle set at right angles to an open fireplace which even on this warm evening showed a mound of burning logs.

Two men standing at the bar counter also turned their faces in his direction; the only people who didn't show any interest were three men sitting with their backs towards the bar at a trestle table in the far corner of the room. One of them seemed to be debating something in a loud voice which was holding the attention of the other two.

'What can I get you . . . sir?'

'Half of bitter, please, and those sandwiches.' He pointed to a large side dish piled high with sandwiches. 'What are they?'

'Beef, sir, fresh roasted this mornin', sirloin. You won't taste tenderer.'

'I'll have two, please.' He was being addressed as sir. That wouldn't have happened in Jarrow.

The barman drew a half pint of bitter and placed two sandwiches on a plate, but Robert did not take them up and go to the empty settle placed opposite, the one that was occupied by the four men who, between gulps from their mugs, were surveying him from under their separate brows, but, resting his foot on the brass rod that ran along the foot of the counter, he remarked to the barman, 'Been a grand day.'

'It has that. It has that. What you would call a thirsty day.'

'You're right there. Yes, you're right there.'

'Walked far today?'

'Some good distance.'

'You staying hereabouts?'

Robert didn't answer for a moment but smiled inwardly as he thought, Well, here's someone who doesn't know who I am. Now he nodded and said, 'You could say that. I'm John Bradley's nephew, over in the hamlet near Lamesley.'

'Oh.' The barman's voice was loud enough to catch the attention of one of the three men from the trestle table, for he turned round and looked towards them as the barman went on, 'John Bradley's nephew. Yes, I'd heard tell of him taking on another man an' a relation. Well! Well! John Bradley's nephew.'

Robert now glanced to the side to the occupants of the settle. They were looking at each other, their heads moving and their dumb actions conveying as much as their speech might have done.

22

For a while there was silence in the room; even the garrulous man at the trestle table had stopped his jabbering, which Robert had now recognized as drunken prattle for the man had obviously taken on more than he could carry.

Robert was biting into the second of the meat sandwiches, which he was finding very good to his taste, when the barman leant forward and asked quietly, 'Does your uncle know that you're along here?'

Robert chewed on the remainder of his mouthful of meat and bread, swallowed, then putting his hand out to the pewter mug, he took a long drink of the beer and replaced the mug on the bar counter before he answered the question as quietly as it had been asked, 'I don't know.'

'Well—' the barman grinned slightly now and, still in a soft voice, said, 'he's not gona like it when he finds out; he's agen drinking, your uncle. Dismissed John Mason, him sitting over there on the settle, one closest to the fire'—he jerked his head to the side—'a few years back 'cos he got drunk, and it on a fair day an' all, Saturday like, and his half-day off. Dead nuts on drink, is your uncle.'

'Yes. Well,'—Robert's voice was slow now—'I'll not be surprised if that's the only thing he's goin' to find out about me that he's dead nuts on.'

He hadn't expected the gusts of laughter that followed. For the first time one of the men on the settle spoke. He was a man in his late fifties and fat, but his voice sounded like a choirboy's on the point of breaking as he said, 'Like to bet you won't reign long.'

'Shouldn't be a bit surprised.' The laconic

answer set the men laughing again, and there was a stir from the trestle table and the man who had been talking threw his leg over the form and was prevented from falling by one of his mates. When they reached the counter and the drunken man spluttered, 'Give me another, Billy,' the barman said quietly, 'No more the night, Jimmy. No more the night. You have been drinking all day.'

'What the hell! You're there to sell, aren't you? Come on, fill it up, and don't you start on me. I've had enough buggers startin' on me this past week. I never touched her, I wouldn't. If she had been all right, it would have been different, I said to Sam here. Didn't I, Sam?' He turned to his companion, and Sam said, 'Aye, you did, Jimmy. Aye, you did.'

'He's a young sod that Master Roland. Like father like son. Master Roland indeed! Master this an' Master that. God! there'll come a day when I'll be able to spit in his eye. Wouldn't listen to me, he wouldn't. Raised his whip he did. Wish he had brought it down, I would've kicked his guts in.'

'Now, now, Jimmy. Make your way home. Something'll turn up; it always does.'

The drunken man, whom Robert saw was little older than himself, stepped back from the support of the counter and stood swaying with his head hanging and, with maudlin tears now running down his face, he muttered, 'Wouldn't have touched her. She just held me hand. Nobody would touch her, not that way. But that bugger—' He raised his head now. 'I'll get him, I will! I'll get him.'

The barman nodded to the man's two companions standing to either side of him, and they, nodding back, led him to the door. And he went quickly but crying audibly now, and the sound

24

created a quick sadness in Robert, for there was nothing more saddening to the ear than the sound of a man crying, even if he was drunk.

The barman was wiping down the counter now and he said by way of explanation, 'He got the push from Thorman's.' He thumbed towards the fireplace. 'It's Foreshaw Park you know. Or perhaps you don't as yet; but it's about a mile along the road. You can pass the boundary if you take the side road from here. It's the longest way around to your hamlet, but it's a nice walk on a summer's night.'

'Had . . . had he interfered with . . . with a . . . with somebody?'

'No, no. He wouldn't, not with her. It's the young daughter of the house. She's not all there, a bit crazy you know. That's what some say; others that have worked up there say different. Well, to tell you the truth, I've never clapped eyes on her meself. But we've only been here ten years or so. She's around seventeen, and as far as I can gather from yet another source she has spasms when she flits through the wood. Round here they've given her the nickname of Thorman's Moth. Funny isn't it, Thorman's Moth?'

'Yes, it is a funny name to give a girl, Thorman's Moth.'

'Did you find those sandwiches good?'

'Aye, I did. I did, indeed.'

'Would you care for another?'

'I wouldn't mind at all.'

So he had another, and another half-pint, and it was on seven o'clock when he left the bar. No more customers had come in and none had departed: the four men still sat on the settle, only rising at

25

intervals to fill their mugs which they paid for individually. The barman had regaled him with more information mostly about the weather in this part of the country, what it did to the farmers in the winter, and lastly why his taproom was practically empty. It was Sunday night, he said, and men didn't go down on their shift in the pit until two o'clock in the morning. But come in noon the morrow, or this time the morrow night, and he'd find the place packed. But Sunday was a dry day, at least in this part of the world. And he had ended with the quip, 'Makes your uncle happy anyway.'

The twilight was deep and the moon was already up. He had taken the road the barman had suggested and when, having passed through an avenue of trees lining the road he came suddenly on two tall iron gates, he guessed this was the entrance to the house, Foreshaw Park. He also noted that it was some long time since the gates had been painted or rubbed down, and as far as he could see up the drive there was the same sign of neglect for the grass verges were running amok. But as he walked on he reasoned there would likely be another gate because there wasn't a lodge near that one and there was always a lodge at the main gate of such houses.

The estate, he saw, was bordered for quite some distance by a high wall, for the most part ivy-strewn which, he thought with amusement, would help the bairns to clamber over, yet there seemed to be an absence of children round here. But then he hadn't been through the mining villages, for these were set further afield. Yet when he was a lad he had walked miles at the week-end to climb a wall behind which he knew there were apple trees.

Where the wall ended, wooden railings took over, and the further on he went the more dilapidated he saw they became. A long section of them was leaning drunkenly inwards, and further on another section was lying flat, having fallen outwards into the narrow ditch. And they must have been like that for some time because the nettles and weeds had grown through them.

It was the first sign of neglect he had seen during his day's tramping, for he had passed a few good-sized estates and these were all sprucely bordered. Some walls even had broken glass on their tops. Anyway he didn't suppose that this boundary was considered of much importance, for the road was but a narrow lane and you wouldn't be able to drive even a trap along it.

A shaft of white light beyond the broken boundary fencing caught his eye and he stopped and turned towards it. Moving his head from side to side in an effort to see through the many saplings, he said to himself, That's water. The river must run through there. Well, well! And there was no interval between his exclamation and his jumping the ditch and leaning over the railings to get a better look. Yes, it was a long narrow moonlit stretch of water which didn't look more than thirty yards away. He had heard that the Team river started up in Tanfield, and so by now it would have widened quite a bit.

There was no harm in having a look, was there? for as far as he could see, this whole stretch of land, although private, was so neglected he doubted if anyone ever got down this far, because if they'd had an adequate staff this fencing would have been seen to long before this. Why not have a closer look, it would be a fitting end to a good day. And it had been a good day, a sort of happy day, in spite of its beginnings.

He did not even bother to retrace his steps to where the railings lay across the ditch; instead, gripping the top of the fence, he arched his body and the next second he was over, but lying flat in a tangle of undergrowth and on top of the railings he had brought down with him. He lay still, spread-eagled for a moment, his body shaking with laughter. He wasn't as clever as he thought; he had cleared four stiles today yet here he was brought low on a rotten fence.

He had some little difficulty in extricating his boot from where it had become wedged between two palings and some wire. Having managed to do this, he stood up straight and then dusted himself down before walking cautiously between the trunks of the young larches until he came on to a grass bank.

Looking towards the water now, he saw that instead of it looking nearer, it appeared further away. He turned his gaze upwards. The moon was riding high, the sky was so clear it was almost like daylight.

Slowly now and each step deliberate, he walked forward, and as he did so he noted that not only did the ground on which he was walking slope steeply downwards before him but away to the left too, and with each step he took the stretch of water became wider. It was with his mouth almost agape that he came to a stop on the edge of a small cliff, which dropped jaggedly down to a narrow boulder-strewn piece of ground about thirty feet below, representing in a way a beach forming the rim of

28

what appeared to be a good-sized lake.

'My! My!' He muttered the words aloud in a kind of awe because he had never seen such a beautiful sight. Perhaps, his reason told him, in the daylight it would take on the appearance of an old quarry, because likely that's what it had been in the first place, a quarry, which was now supplied by a stream perhaps running from the river Team. But with the moon shining deep into its water it looked like the most beautiful lake anyone could imagine.

A border of trees on the opposite bank, he noted, extended partly around the perimeter to the right of him.

He turned his eyes away from the trees and to the left where the grassland sloped down to lake level. His steps still slow, he went down the steep incline and turned round the last jut of rock, which was no more than two feet high at this point, and found himself standing on a stretch of ground that was free from boulders, being made up of smooth gravel that had been washed up over the years by the periodic flooding of the lake, for here and there a rim of drift scum showed up plainly.

Eeh! He had never seen anything so bonny. The water looked pure silver with the moon a golden ball in its centre. He would travel a long way through life, he told himself, before he would ever again experience anything like this. He turned now and looked behind him. The low rocks near the end of the quarry wall were flat. He walked over to them and hitched himself upwards and sat down.

How long he sat lost in a kind of new wonder he could never remember, he only knew that the scene would be imprinted on his mind for life: this water set in a glade of trees. At least, that is how it appeared to him for apart from this stretch of beach the rest of the lake was encompassed by the dark belt of trees and a much smaller belt of larches and low shrubs like that through which he had come.

It was at the moment he was reluctantly telling himself he had better make a move but that this wouldn't be his last visit here, no not if he knew anything, that his body suddenly stiffened, in fact he felt as if someone had cut off his breath permanently while allowing his mind still to work, for he was asking himself if he was drunk, yet at the same time denying the suggestion. Granted he had had four pints of beer that day and that was twice as much as he usually drank, for he was no drinker, a couple on a Sunday being his limit. But this in a way had been an unusual Sunday, and it was now ending with him seeing things . . . imagining things.

Again his mind contradicted him: he wasn't imagining what he was seeing, and he *was* seeing a thing coming along by the edge of the water. It had emerged from the belt of dark trees and now, the moonlight full on it, it floated seemingly a foot or more from the ground.

God Almighty! He put his hands behind him on the stone as if in an effort to push himself up and run. But there they remained, his back arched, his head lying between his shoulders as if someone had dealt him a blow under the chin.

The thing was coming at him, nearer: it had wings, it looked like an enormous bat, only grey in colour.

It wasn't until the thing was about ten yards from him that he saw it wasn't floating but had feet, and that what he had taken for wings were arms,

30

because they had sort of folded now and instead of being held in line with the body were outstretched towards him.

Again he muttered, 'God Almighty!' And then, the thing or creature stopped before him an arm's length away, and stared at him. And he stared at it.

He was looking into a face peering out of a grey hood. It was so strange he could find no words to describe it: the eyes were oval shaped—he couldn't see their colour; the eyelashes appeared dark and sweeping; the skin of the face was pale; the nose small, very small; but the mouth was wide, the lips thin, but well shaped; they were apart and he could see the tongue resting gently as if it were on her lower teeth. He had never seen a face like it in his life. He couldn't say it was beautiful or pretty or plain, for it possessed some quality that he could not, at the moment, define. And then she spoke.

'Why, hello!' she said. The fact that she had spoken as one would when surprised on meeting a friend in a strange place sent a shiver down his spine, and in this moment he realized that he had never experienced fear in his life before. There was no one he had been afraid of, not even at school among the teachers, and there had been some hard nuts there. And he had never been afraid of physical hurt; he'd had enough fights in his early youth; and even while he was serving his time he had punched out a number of battles behind the sheds after work. Through nothing or no one had he ever experienced the feeling of fear; but he was experiencing it now, as if he were in touch with a creature that wasn't of this world, not an angel or a ghost, but something strange which didn't look as if it belonged here. What was she? . . . Who was she?

31

He was given the answer with her next words, for she said, 'I thought you were Jimmy.'

Jimmy? Jimmy? The name rang a bell. *Jimmy.* The drunk in The Bull that had been dismissed, he was called Jimmy. He had been given the push because they thought he was interfering with the daughter of the house . . . Thorman's Moth, the one who was a bit barmy. That's what he had said, wasn't it? Yet not quite.

'What is your name? Isn't it a lovely night? Isn't the moon wonderful?'

When, with the movement that suggested not that she was walking on legs but was floating again, she came and sat down beside him, he moved as if he had been stung. Bringing his arms forward and his back up straight, he created a space between them on the shelf of rock and was about to rise when she spoke again. 'Please don't be afraid.'

He stared at her fully now. All her features were exposed to the moonlight and he saw into her eyes and the deep, deep perplexed sadness lying within them. And when she said, 'I won't hurt you,' he felt inclined to let out a loud laugh: this fragile, ethereal creature hurting him! Aye, that was the word that described her; aye, he had hit it, ethereal. Yes, that's what she was, without substance. That was the meaning of it, wasn't it? without substance. Yet she was alive: she was a young girl, she had a body . . . what there was of it, because her cape had now fallen apart and to his embarrassment he saw the thinness of her body through a garment that could only be a nightgown.

If he had seen her like whilst in Jarrow, he would have termed her as thin as a shaving . . . a wood shaving. His father had had a name for thin

32

women, bust and arseless, yet even the thought applied to this creature seemed in a way blasphemous.

'Won't you speak to me?'

'Aye. Yes, miss.' His voice had a cracked sound. 'But . . . but I must admit, you kind of gave me a start.'

'Oh.' Her eyes lost their sad expression and the corners of her lips moved upwards and she made a sound which in the ordinary way would have been called a laugh, but it was so unusual that it didn't come under that heading; then she said, 'You sounded just like Jimmy. But . . . but not quite. It was the tone of your voice not the words. Jimmy's words were mumbled. Roland said it was because he was a common man . . . Did you know Jimmy?'

He paused before he answered, 'No, no, miss; I . . . I never knew Jimmy.'

She looked away from him now and over the water; then she said, as if to herself, 'Why are some men called common and others . . . er . . . uncommon?' Then she added, 'Do you know?' And to this he replied, 'I think the word common is applied to workmen, and the other kind are called gentlemen.'

'Oh, yes, yes.' She nodded at him now, a smile on her face again. 'Agnes would have given me an answer like that.'

'Agnes?'

'Yes. Agnes understands most things. She can always explain things; except the moon. She doesn't like the moon. I'm sorry she doesn't like the moon because I love the moon. Look'—she pointed—'it's sunk into the lake, yet it's left its light behind.'

He looked to where the reflection of the moon

lay still in the water and he thought, What a strange thing to say, it's left its light behind. But then she was a strange creature, not quite right in the head; yet not mad, just a bit touched he would say. What a pity! It was a shame unto God that such a creature should be touched in the head.

She was talking again, softly now, her voice scarcely above a whisper, her eyes directed towards the water as she said, 'Agnes once told me a story about the moon. She said, once its reflection touches the water it turns to gold; but you must never try to steal it, for if you did the night would lose its smile.' And she turned and looked at him as she ended, 'It's the only smile the night has, is the moon.'

Eeh! By! What strange talk. Yet in a way it sounded beautiful.

'And you know what the stars are?'

'No, miss.'

'Well, the stars are tears that the moon has shed down the years. Agnes said that; she made a poem about it. Will you hold my hand?'

He jerked to his feet as her fingers clutched his. They were cool and smooth and thin, and he found himself actually shaking, but with her hand still in his he said, 'I . . . I think you should be making your way back home, miss. Don't you think so?'

'No, not yet; there's company. I promised Agnes I would stay in my room. But I drew the curtains and looked out of the window and there it was.' She pointed with her other hand up towards the moon that was now slightly covered by small white scudding clouds, and she went on, 'I cannot help it, when the moon is out I must come out too . . . I am not mad.'

34

He gulped in his throat. 'No, I'm sure you're not, miss,' he said.

'Agnes knows I'm not mad, and so does Dave.'

'Is Dave your brother?'

'Oh, no. Dave is an old servant and Peggy is his wife. She always says they brought me up. Funny that, isn't it? I mean, funny words, brought me up. I think about words. Where did they bring me up to? Up to where?'

Robert stared at her, speechless. Part of her mind might be unhinged, but there was certainly a part of it that did some delving, if he knew anything. As she had said, it was a funny term, brought me up, but it was a colloquial term. It was a shame unto God about this poor creature . . . But he mustn't think of her as a creature, she was a young girl, a strangely beautiful young girl. He was now seeing her as beautiful: the hood had slipped back from her head and was showing hair that was like fine silver threads. Topping another face, it would have depicted age, but on her it appeared like a halo of light around her, for it was loose and the ends of it were lost beneath the shoulders of the cloak.

'What is your name?'

'Robert, miss. Robert Bradley.'

'Oh, it's a nice name, strong.'

'You think so?' He smiled gently at her.

'Yes.' She nodded her head. 'I know a lot about names, at least some names. I have three brothers: they are called Arnold, Roland, and Stanley. I don't like them.'

'You don't like their names?'

'No, not the names, I don't like my brothers.'

What could he say to that? What he said was,

35

'What is your name, miss?'

'Millicent. But people who like me call me Millie.'

'I . . . I should think everybody likes you.'

She stared at him for a moment; then slowly her mouth widened into a smile while her eyes took on an expression that he could only term as sad. And there was a sort of break in her voice as she said, 'No, they don't. My father doesn't like me.'

Oh, dear. Oh dear. Poor soul. On an impulse he put out his other hand and now grasping both of hers he pressed them gently while shaking them up and down and saying with unforced gallantry, 'Well, all I can say, miss, he hasn't any taste and he doesn't know a good thing when he sees it.'

'Oh, you are nice.'

As her body leaned towards him while her feet remained on the ground, he suddenly loosed hold of her hands and sprang back from her, not because of her close proximity but because over her shoulder he could see running towards them from out of the shrub two figures, one carrying a stick. She too sensed their presence for now she swung round, murmuring, 'Oh, Agnes.'

Before he could gather his wits about him he was being confronted by an elderly man brandishing a club-headed walking stick at him, and in a natural reaction he thrust up his forearm in front of his face and cried at the assailant, 'You bring that down on me and you'll find yourself on your back, as old as you are.' And the man hesitated, his arm still held up, the stick wavering in his hand.

The girl was now struggling in the arms of a young woman and crying, 'Don't hurt him, Dave. He's nice. He's nice. I thought it was Jimmy.'

The old man lowered his arm to his side, then growled, 'What are you doin' here?'

What was he doing here? He had come to see the water and this is what he said: 'I saw the gleam of water from the road. I just came to have a look at it.'

'You are trespassing. I suppose you know that?'

He turned and looked at the young woman. She was over medium height and she, too, was thin, but it was a different thinness from the girl's. This must be the sister Agnes. She had a nice voice, although there was a haughty note in it, and he answered her, saying, 'I suppose I am, but I never thought about it. The place looked . . . well'—he jerked his head impatiently—'rough from the road, broken railings and such. Nothing much private about it. And I was sitting looking at the water there'—he thumbed in the direction of the lake—'when the young miss came upon me. And I can assure you she's come to no harm in my company.'

'Who are you, anyway?' It was the man speaking. 'You're not from around here, are you?'

He looked the man straight in the eyes and he answered in a similar tone, saying, 'It all depends upon what you mean by around here. I'm from the hamlet, near Lamesley. My uncle's the carpenter.'

'Bradley, John Bradley?'

'Yes, John Bradley.'

'Oh, well.' The old man's tone seemed slightly mollified, but he went on, 'You're a bit out of your way. And anyhow, you should know what's private and what isn't, even if the boundary's broken.'

'I suppose there's an excuse for me: I've only been in the countryside a week; I'm from the town. But I'll make sure in future.'

'You do that.'

'Are you going?'

He turned and looked at the girl who was still being held firmly by her sister, and he said quietly, 'Yes, miss, I'm going. But it's been nice to meet you.'

Quickly the young woman swung the girl round and began to lead her, not without some resistance, towards the belt of trees.

However, the old man did not immediately follow but stood staring at Robert. 'I'd get on your way,' he said.

'I'm going.'

Robert's voice was almost a growl now, and he added, 'If you're as concerned for her as you seem to be, why do you let her roam in her condition?'

'You mind your own damn business and get!'

He did not immediately obey the command but stood his ground defiantly for some seconds more; then when he did walk away it was with a slow step. And the old man watched him until he was out of sight before he, too, turned and hurried towards the woodland.

## CHAPTER THREE

In the thicket of the trees Agnes Thorman drew her sister to a halt and, looking at her, she spoke in a tone that denied the softness and pity in her eyes as she said, 'How could you, Millie! You promised me. How could you! And company in the house.'

'I'm . . . I'm sorry, Aggie, but . . . but it was the moon.' She turned her eyes upwards to where the

38

moon was apparently being chased by the small scudding white clouds, and she went on, 'I . . . I drew the curtains. I know I shouldn't, but I did nothing wrong, I didn't go on to the road. I promised you, didn't I? I promised you.'

'You promised me you would stay in bed.'

'Oh, Aggie!' The slim form now fell forward and was enfolded in her sister's arms and Agnes Thorman, looking over the girl's shoulder, gazed almost helplessly at the dark bole of a tree as she wondered for the countless time what was to become of her, this dear, dear creature who had not been made for this world but for some place where the spirit could soar freely, where lies and subterfuge were unknown, where one spoke one's thoughts aloud, and one's thoughts were always pure.

She was seven years old when Millicent came into the world and seemingly from that day she had become her mother, for her own mother had had little to do with her upbringing. Even when the child was taken into her presence, she would hold her in such a way as to make her cry. It was as if she were pressing the infant back into herself. Afterwards she would refuse to see her for months on end; and Nanny Watson would have the care of her, have care of them all, of Arnold who was a year younger than herself and of Roland a year younger than Arnold, and of Stanley a year younger than Roland.

From the time Millicent was born Agnes could recall that the feeling in the house changed. Before that she could remember the sounds of gaiety floating up to the nursery from the parties going on downstairs; there always seemed to be parties going on downstairs. And there had been so many servants flitting about both inside and outside of the house that she couldn't remember all their names.

It was many years later when she realized who had paid for all the parties and the large staff. Her mother's father, Grandfather Barrington, had lived with them for as long as she could remember. But he had died three months before Millicent was born and it was this fact, not unlinked with the birth of Millicent, that had wrought such great changes in the house.

Agnes knew now that her father had married her mother not for her beauty alone but because she was a rich man's daughter. What he didn't know, however, was that the rich man had lived up to his income for years, and instead of leaving his daughter a wealthy woman, what he bequeathed to her was a scandal caused by his debts and the revealing of dubious dealings which, had he remained alive, might have led to his being sent to the prison.

She could recall how the staff in the house had been cut: like a scythe going through summer corn, they all seemed to fall away in one day, leaving only Dave and Peggy Waters inside, together with their daughter Ruthie, and little Betty Trollop who worked in the kitchen. Outside, three of the four gardeners went, leaving only Arthur Bloom. Three of the stable hands were also dismissed which meant that Greg Hubbard had to muck out the horses and feed and groom them. But then, the number of horses was greatly reduced. Ben Cullen the lodgekeeper and his wife went with the rest, and their house had stood empty since.

No three men could hope to keep the place as spruce as nine had done. This place where they were standing now had once been a part of the rose garden, but saplings had been allowed to take root until now it had the appearance of a miniature jungle. Agnes sighed as she stood patting Millie's hand. Life was difficult and it would get more so if she didn't make a stand. She must make a stand, and soon, very soon. She was tired of responsibility; she herself wanted a shoulder to lean on, a husband's shoulder. She had been engaged for three years now, and it could go on for another three if she didn't do something soon. It had been her intention to speak tonight, then this had happened . . .

Millie was the stumbling block, but a beloved stumbling block. If only she didn't feel as she did about her; and yet if only others felt as she did about her, then things would be easier. But the only people who saw this piece of strange humanity as she did were Dave and Peggy and Ruthie, and yes, the new addition in the kitchen, Dave's Irish niece Maggie.

It was strange about Maggie but she seemed to see Millie in a different light altogether; in fact she sometimes seemed to be even akin to her, for she was another who, she doubted, would ever conform. She even did not know her place in the hierarchy, for she spoke to all alike, even to her master and mistress, much to their indignation. Her mother had even said she must be got rid of, but, as she herself had pointed out, Irish labour was cheap and nowadays some servants were becoming choosey, especially about serving in the country.

There were times when she herself thanked God

41

for Maggie, for she provided the only light relief in what was a succession of dour days, and what was of more importance still, she could be trusted to see to Millie.

On Dave Waters's approach she turned Millie about, and now the three of them made their way towards the house. Dave said no word about the intruder, and he wouldn't until he got into the kitchen where, she knew, he'd pour it all out to Peggy. And she could even hear him: 'Something's got to be done about the boundary,' he would say. 'You've got to speak to the missis to speak to him. I've done me best. Other things'll have to go, but that's got to be seen to, or else we're going to have trouble on our hands.' She'd heard it all, again and again.

They ascended the steps from the sunken garden. The moon was illuminating the front of the house, the grey stone looking as silver as the moonlight itself, and the rows of windows on either side of the oak front door gleamed like elongated eyes. It wasn't a very old house, dating back only to 1805. The front was plain but the chimneys were ornate. It looked as if there were only two storeys but should you approach the house from the back you would see a third storey made up of the attics in which the nursery and the schoolroom had been placed, and running off these a warren of small rooms, little more than cubicles, that at one time had housed the staff.

The back of the house had its own staircase leading from the passage and also from which doors led into the kitchen, the servants' hall, still-room, and pantries. Under the entire house ran a cellar which was partitioned into parts each given over to the household needs, such as a wine and beer cellar, a part for hanging beef and fowl, and at the very end a huge coal and wood cellar.

From the grass-strewn gravel drive four shallow steps led up to a square pillared portico and under it now, standing silhouetted black against the moonlight, stood three men. They were smoking cigars which, one after the other, they took from their mouths and held between their fingers as if posing for a photograph.

Still holding Millie's arm, Agnes went towards them, while Dave Waters continued along the gravel front towards the stable yard that ran parallel with the side of the house. Before mounting the steps, she hesitated a moment and looked up into the face of their guest: a round ruddy-coloured face topped with thinning grey hair, a stomach that was straining against its waistcoat, and a body appearing altogether too heavy for its legs. As Stanley had said only yesterday, Samuel Bennett was weighed down in all ways, for he was known to have his fingers in most of the industrial pies on the Tyne, and inland too, especially in the mines. It was said he didn't really know how much he was worth. Well, he mightn't know that, but what was known about him was that he didn't loan money unless he was sure of getting it back, it also having gained for itself a nice slice of interest on the way; or, failing cash, he made sure there were bricks and mortar enough to cover the debt.

It was whispered that Samuel Bennett had gained quite a bit of property in this way, and as Agnes looked at him she had no doubt but that he had been surveying her home to see if it was good

43

collateral for the money her father was hoping to borrow from him. Would this be a second mortgage? She didn't know. Even Arnold didn't know and he, being the eldest, was the one who should be in the picture as to how things stood. But it didn't seem to trouble him, or Roland. Both had spent the past two or three years up at Oxford, and even their vacations had not been totally spent here, for apparently they had plenty of friends willing to entertain them.

She turned her gaze on to her father now. His long thin face appeared lint white; the moonlight had taken what little colour there had been in his cheeks; and even his moustache at this distance seemed to be bristling. He was forty-five years old but at this moment he looked to be of an age with Mr Bennett who was in his sixties. Even from this distance she could tell that his body was vibrating with anger. Well, she had witnessed his anger so many times before that she was no longer intimidated by it.

Lastly her eyes lit upon her fiancé. James Crockford was twenty-seven years old, he was tall, his hair was dark brown, his face was on the small side, and as always he was immaculately dressed, which was part of his attraction, and he was undeniably attractive. She often wondered why he had chosen her for she was neither pretty nor beautiful. Yet she wasn't plain. She had long ago taken stock of herself: her figure, she knew, would not stir any man's senses, but she had two assets, her eyes and her voice. Her eyes were large and grey and dark-lashed, and her voice was low . . . except when she was angry and then she could raise it. She had one accomplishment, she could play the

44

pianoforte well.

The men parted to allow them to pass, and as her father, in a voice that was as thin as his features, said, 'You're expected in the drawing-room, Agnes,' Millie, putting out a free arm impulsively towards Samuel Bennett, said, 'Hello. Isn't it a lovely night? I'm Millicent.'

Agnes stopped, her head hanging slightly forward while she still held on to her sister, and Samuel Bennett replied after just a slight hesitation, 'So you are Millicent . . . Yes, it is as you say, a lovely night.'

'Are you going to . . . ?'

'Your mother is waiting for you, Agnes.' Her father's interruption was spoken slowly, each word being stressed, and on this she tugged Millie away and into the vestibule and through the glass doors which gave on to the hall. And there, waiting for them, was Peggy Waters with Maggie standing beside her, and like a mother speaking to a daughter Peggy grabbed at Millie while muttering in a whisper to Agnes, saying, 'Get yourself in there, girl, they're waiting for you. He's in a tear.' She nodded back towards the vestibule, then added, 'And you, Maggie, take Miss Millie up to her room and stay with her until I come up.'

'I will that. I will that. Come along with you, Miss Millie. Did you have a nice walk then? It's a beautiful night.'

'Yes, it is a beautiful night, Maggie. The water in the lake is shining and the moon was right in the middle and . . .' Millie's voice trailed away as Maggie led her up the stairs, and Peggy Waters, turning back to Agnes, said, 'Here, give me your coat, and straighten your hair. And look'—she

45

pointed down to Agnes's feet—'there's grass on your shoes. Here, let me.'

When Peggy went to stoop to clean her shoes, Agnes pulled her up by the shoulders, saying, 'Leave them alone, it'll rub off on the carpets.'

'She was down by the lake then?'

'Yes, talking to a man, a stranger.'

'God in heaven, what next! Did you find out who he was?'

'Yes; I'll tell you about it later.' They were both whispering now.

When there came a sound of movement in the vestibule, Peggy, pushing Agnes slightly forward, muttered, 'Go on, do your pieces for them,' before turning and hurrying across the hall and through a door at the far end.

Agnes did not wait for the men to enter the hall, but hurried now towards the drawing-room and when she entered, her mother, who was sitting on a straight-backed Louis couch, turned her head slowly and stared at her before saying, 'We were waiting for you. Mrs Bennett would like to hear you play.'

'I'm sorry.' Agnes was now inclining her head towards the other woman who was seated to the side of the open fireplace in which a fire burned although the night was warm, and she added, 'I . . . I was detained.'

'I understand you are an exponent on the pianoforte.'

Exponent on the pianoforte indeed. The statement suited the guest for she was overdressed and dripping with ornamental jewellery, and she lacked only a tiara; and if further proof had been needed, her voice would have put the designation

46

'common' to her. In Peggy's language, she was common as muck.

Long ago she had stopped thinking it strange that she should fall back on Peggy's sayings to express her thoughts, because it wasn't strange at all for, just as she herself had mothered Millie, so Peggy had mothered hcr from the day she was born, and so creating enemies of their various nannies.

She was already sitting at the piano when the three men entered the room, and when they were seated she began to play. She had not, as she might have done on other occasions, asked what the company would like to hear but had decided to play something that she felt matched her mood: Beethoven's 'The Rage Over A Lost Penny'. She wanted something loud, harsh, she wanted to crash out the notes, torment the keys, bash at them; she wanted in a way to blot out all softness, the softness that was in Millie, the tenderness that was in Millie, because that softness and that tenderness were like chains that were holding her fast to this house.

She was perspiring freely when she finished playing, and she sat for a moment, her fingers lying still on the keys now and her eyes directed towards them. There was no immediate word of appreciation until, after issuing a short laugh, Samuel Bennett said, 'That was a rendering, I'll say!'

'Yes, indeed, indeed.' His wife was nodding now from one to the other. Then addressing her hostess, she said, 'She could earn her living by that, concert like, couldn't she? I mean, she's got the touch—hasn't she?—professional.'

She didn't hear what her mother's answer was

because her father was talking loudly now to Mr Bennett. But James was standing by her side. Bending over her and touching the music on the stand as if he were about to turn the page, and his voice a good imitation of Mrs Bennett's he said, 'Professional, that's what you are. You could earn a living by it, concert like.'

James, she knew, was a good mimic, and he often made her laugh, although at times she thought some of his mimicry was cruel. But tonight she did not laugh at him, and when, after straightening up, he added quietly, 'Come and walk in the garden,' she rose from the piano stool, while he, bowing slightly to Kate Thorman, then to Mrs Bennett, said, 'You'll excuse us.' It was a statement not a request; but then he very rarely made requests.

As they entered the hall, Maggie was coming down the stairs and Agnes stared at her apprehensively, her mouth half open, until Maggie, her smile broad as usual, said cheerfully, ' 'Tis all right, Miss Agnes, me aunt's with her, an' she's tucked up in bed sound asleep.' At the foot of the stairs Maggie looked from one to the other and dared to add, ' 'Tis a lovely night still, lovely for a saunter, 'twould do your hearts good,' before nodding at them and making for the kitchen.

That there was anything out of the ordinary in the way Maggie had spoken never entered her head, but it must certainly have entered James Crockford's for they were no sooner through the vestibule than he said, 'Why must you employ people like that? The girl doesn't know her place.'

'She means well. She's from Ireland; she's never been used to service.'

48

'You should get rid of her.'

'Oh, James.' She turned her head away.

They walked down the steps in silence and across the gravel and down into the sunken garden before he spoke again; then, the tone of his voice curt, he said, 'Your father's in a fix, isn't he?'

'I suppose you could call it that.'

'Is he expecting a loan from Bennett?'

'I don't know.'

'Of course you know, Agnes, you are bound to know.'

'All right. All right.' She turned and faced him. 'I know, and yes he's in a fix, and he's been in a fix for a long time.'

'Well, all I can say is he wants to face up to it, and he should have done it before now. Sending the three boys to Oxford when he hasn't one penny to rub against another. Living high on borrowed money. Where are they now, anyway?'

There was something stirring in her that went beyond temper and was akin to rage, and she wanted to turn on him, this man whom she loved, who had fascinated her for years, well, since she first met him when she was sixteen. She wanted to turn on him and cry, 'What business is it of yours? What have you done anyway with your life so far? You depend on your mother for everything. If it wasn't for your china and ironmongery shops supporting you, you wouldn't be able to earn your living. And you are only jealous because you were never sent to Oxford, not even to a public school.' But she curbed the feeling the while and she cried at herself, What is the matter with me? What is wrong? But she knew what was wrong. She had known what was wrong for a long time. What she

49

needed and mostly at this moment was understanding, sympathy, caresses, tender caresses: she wanted to hear him say that he loved her, and needed her. But their association wasn't like that. When they were together they held hands and he talked mostly about his horses. He loved horses; he lived for riding. When he kissed her it was without passion. He made her feel unwomanly at times; and they were such times when she felt overwomanly, as she she put it to herself, when she longed for him to kiss her and hold her in a way that was anything but seemly. At such times she felt a little like Millie must feel, careless of what anyone thought.

Once when she had kissed him passionately he had for the moment returned her embrace, but only for a moment; then holding her at arms' length he had laughed at her as he said, 'My, my! you must stop eating rich seasoned foods.' Later that night she had bathed herself and scrubbed her body with a loofah to rid herself of the dirt he had exposed in her.

She answered his question by saying, 'They're staying with friends, at least Arnold and Roland are, Stanley has gone to a show in Newcastle. And you know, James, they're no longer boys. Anyway, only Stanley and Roland are returning to Oxford. Arnold is going to Australia.'

'*What!* When did this come about? Why isn't he staying at home and trying to sort things out? Who's he got in Australia?'

She closed her eyes for a moment and drew in a deep breath, then sat down on a wooden seat that stood by the side of the path before she answered, 'He thinks there is more scope for him there. One

50

of his friends at Oxford has an uncle who has a business in Melbourne. He is going out there and Arnold is going with him.'

'Hare-brained! He took mathematics, didn't he? What good are maths going to be in a business? What kind of business is it?'

'I'm not quite sure. I think it's to do with machinery.'

'Good God! And Roland and Stanley going back? Where's the money coming from to keep them there?'

Now she did turn on him. Her voice seeming to jump from its usual even tone, she cried at him, 'I don't know, James, unless you'd like to ask your mother if she will support them.' And on this she rose to her feet and hurried back up the garden. But she hadn't reached the steps before he caught her and, swinging her round, he held her by the shoulders and looked down into her face as he said, 'I was only trying to help. Surely at this stage of our acquaintance I can express an opinion about the family.'

She stared up into his dark eyes. At this stage of their acquaintance, he said. What stage? How long ago was it since he had mentioned marriage? She felt the urge to cry, but she closed her eyes tightly against it. Tears, she understood, could break some men's resolve, but she knew this man well enough to know that tears would have very little effect upon his reactions towards her. When she bowed her head and leaned towards him, he put his arms about her, saying gently now, 'You're overwrought. And it's no wonder. I've got to say this, Agnes, I know it won't please you, but I feel it is my duty. Most of your trouble lies with Millicent. She should

51

be put in care.'

She pulled herself from his embrace, saying flatly now, 'Don't you start on that, James, please. You know how I feel about her. And anyway, she's not insane.'

'Well, she's not sane.'

Agnes bit down hard on her lower lip, then moved her head from side to side as she stared up into his handsome face, muttering, 'She's eccentric, odd in that she knows no boundaries, as we do, as regards class or time . . .'

'Oh, be quiet, Agnes!' He almost pushed her from him. 'Why can't you stop deluding yourself. You must remember that you are promised to me; have you asked yourself what is going to happen when she no longer has you to pamper her eccentricities as you call them?'

His words, 'You are promised to me,' for a moment made Agnes forget the reason why they were quarrelling, for the words had suggested that soon he expected her to go to him. Her voice soft now, she said, 'I know. I know, James. I have thought about it, and Mother will have to take the responsibility.'

'She should have done so a long time ago.'

She gazed at him for a moment; then again she fell on to his breast, her head to the side, her lips waiting for his. And he kissed her. It was not a long kiss; he seemed to break it up into small parts like a bird pecking at seed. This could in a way have led to passion, but it didn't; it ended with him taking her chin in his hand and shaking her head gently as one would a child one was pleased with. And while her mind told her it was enough and she must be content her body protested hotly.

They returned to the drive hand in hand, there to see the Bennetts departing in the coach. Five minutes later James Crockford made his farewells and mounted his horse and rode the five miles to his home.

*       *       *

It was just an hour later and Agnes stood facing her mother in her bedroom.

Kate Thorman had divested herself of her jewellery and her dress and was sitting in her petticoat before her dressing-table. Agnes stood behind her taking the pins from out of the abundant coils of her hair, and as she did so she looked through the mirror to her mother's reflection as she said, 'I must talk to you, Mama.'

'Not tonight, Agnes, please. I'm tired, worn out; those people were impossible.'

'I cannot be put off again, Mama, and I shall come to the point straightaway. I want to be married . . . I am going to be married.'

'What!' Kate Thorman pushed a coil of her hair back from her face and swung round on the stool. 'Has he named the day?'

'Well . . . yes, almost.' It was a necessary lie.

'You can't do it, Agnes. Anyway, you haven't been engaged any time yet.'

'What! Three years. Did you wait three years to marry Father? From what I've learned, you met and married within three months.'

'That was different, there weren't any obstacles. You can't, possibly . . . well, not yet. Anyway, your father would never give his consent.'

'Mama, don't talk nonsense.' They were glaring

53

at each other now, and Kate Thorman drawing herself upwards, said, 'I'd like to remind you, Agnes, to whom you are speaking.'

'I don't forget, Mama. But you *are* talking nonsense when you say Father would object.' She shook her head. 'He'd rush me off my feet to marry a . . . a—' she searched in her mind for the lowest form of male humanity she could think of, then said, 'a tinker, if he thought it would help him out of his financial difficulties. Anyway, James has money.'

'James has no money.' Her mother's voice was flat. 'It's his mother who has the money and she's as tight-fisted as a miser. And I can tell you this, she no more wants her son to marry you than I do, but for different reasons.'

'Oh, Mama, you are cruel. Mrs Crockford has always been nice to me.'

'Yes, because she's clever, but I know Janet Crockford, I've known her from a girl. She'll have her son marry money. And I cannot understand, not even now, how he came to ask you to marry him, knowing how he stands in awe of her.'

'He doesn't. He doesn't.'

'You are blind, girl, and to tell you the truth—' She paused, and now her voice dropping, she added, 'I would rather see you marry anyone, yes, anyone rather than him. There, you have it. And I'll tell you this also, you needn't expect any happiness from that union, for he will try to impose his will on you and make you into a doormat. What he doesn't seem to realize is, you have character, and you are not an easy person to get along with. You must have hidden these traits from him this long time, for had you shown him your real self I'm

54

sure he would have taken to his heels and run.'

'Oh, Mama, you are making me out to be a—' She was lost for a word, then ended, 'How can you say such things?'

'I can because I know them to be true. And on the subject of being truthful, I will say this as well, you cannot leave me here with Millie. You are the only one who can manage her; if you go she will have to be put away.'

'No! No!' Agnes stepped back from her mother and again she repeated, 'No!' Then uttered, 'You are blackmailing me, Mama. Millie can be managed. You know she can; she only needs loving, and you've never given her any love, nor even attention, not for years.'

'I know, I know.'

In some surprise Agnes now watched her mother's body droop, she watched the breasts that were pushed up above the tight laced corsets heaving; she watched her place her hand underneath her ribs as if to hold back a pain, as she murmured, 'I've . . . I've had my own burdens to carry,' and she watched the hand begin to rub under the ribs as if there was actually pain there, and she was forced to say, 'Are you not well, Mama?'

Kate Thorman lifted her head slightly and said between gasps, 'In the dressing-room, on the third shelf of the wardrobe, at the back, you'll find a bottle, a blue bottle. Fetch it.'

'Yes, Mama.' After an apprehensive glance at her mother, Agnes hurried into the dressing-room, and as she entered it she heard the bedroom door being opened and she knew that it was her father who had come in.

The very fact that he hadn't knocked on his wife's bedroom door suggested to Agnes that he must have added to the drink he had already taken during the evening, for always, after taking a certain amount, he lost all his gentlemanly traits and became a coarse bullying individual.

For years now he'd had his own rooms across the landing, and when, in sober moments, he visited her mother's room he paid her the courtesy of knocking on the door.

But now he was talking, his voice thick, his words fuddled. He was upbraiding their late guests, interspersing his opinion of them with lurid language. That was another thing drink always brought out, the coarse side of his nature. He swore when he was sober but not in the same language he used when he was drunk.

She was some little time in finding the bottle. It wasn't on the third shelf which was taken up with layers of underclothes, nor yet below it on the tray that held nightdresses and corsets, but it was at the back of the bottom tray that was filled with stockings of different shades.

She stood with the bottle in her hand hesitating whether or not to return to the bedroom, for she surmised that the sight of her would likely inflame her father's anger still more. He had a habit of seeking her out when he was drunk, and talking at her; and now her body stiffened as she heard him say, 'Wait till I get my tongue around her. She did it deliberately, walked out without a word. But not without a signal, no. That bloody Peggy, coming and seeing if we wanted more coffee. Has she ever done that before? No. Then what does Madam Agnes do but scoot out of the room after her. And what for? Because that flaming imbecile was abroad again. And I'm telling you this, if Bennett stumps up with the loan she's going. It will be money well spent to have her locked up somewhere.'

'No, Reginald, no; you can't put her away. It would be a sin.'

'A sin? Did you say a *sin*, woman? You talking about *sin*!'

At this point Agnes heard her mother mumble something but couldn't catch her words. Whatever it was seemed to inflame her father's anger more for his voice rose almost to screaming pitch as he cried, 'You bloody well talk about sin! And sin is the word, because who sinned in the first place, eh? Tell me that. Who bloody well sinned in the first place? She's not mine! Is she? Say it. Say it. She's a living reminder of your sin, isn't she? And has been all the years, retribution on you for your escapade with dear Lancelot. Lancelot the knight, Lancelot the romantic Indian Army captain. Think I didn't know, thought I was bloody well blind, didn't you? Lancelot be buggered!'

'It isn't true.' Her mother's voice sounded like a moan, and when she added, 'She's yours,' her father's voice came back at her, crying, 'Don't lie to me, you bitch! I've been quiet long enough.'

'Yes, yes, you have.' Momentarily there seemed to be new strength in her mother's voice and not a little of deep recrimination as she went on, 'Just because I was keeping you and this place, not only before father died, but since with the little Aunt Jess left one, that's what kept you quiet; if I'd walked out you'd have been finished. And it . . . it wouldn't do for me to die, would it, Reginald? It

57

wouldn't do for you to kill me, as you would have liked to so often, for my money dies with me, and you'd be finished too, because you're no good, never have been, no good at anything, work or love . . .'

As the sound of a blow accompanied by a cry came to Agnes, she sprang into the room, there to see her mother crouched on the floor, her arms clutching the sides of the bed. Her father was bending over her, his face almost unrecognizable with the rage suffusing it. And now he swung round in surprise and, after straightening his back, he glared at her for a moment before throwing at her a string of obscenities which made her close her eyes and hunch her shoulders against them. When he was finished, the saliva was running down from the sides of his mouth, and with the pad of his thumb he wiped it across his lips before stumbling from the room.

'Mama! Mama!' She turned her mother's face from where it was pressed against the side of the high bed and she knew a moment of fear when the head drooped backwards. Was she dead? Quickly she felt her pulse: it was hardly discernible.

Pulling the limp figure away from the bed she put her arms underneath her mother's oxters, but she could not raise her, so she laid her gently back on the floor and ran round to the other side of the bed and pulled on the bell-rope.

She was kneeling on the floor, her mother's head pillowed on her knee, when Ruthie Waters entered the room, exclaiming immediately, 'Oh my God! miss.'

'Go and fetch Peggy . . . no wait. Is Master Stanley in?'

'Yes, miss, he went along to his room about half an hour ago.'

'Fetch him quick.'

It was some minutes later when her youngest brother entered the room. He was dressed in a nightshirt and dressing-gown, and going quickly to Agnes's side, he said, 'What happened?'

'I . . . I think it's a heart attack.'

'Heart attack! Has . . . has she had one before?'

'I don't know. But she's been taking that.' She pointed up to the bedside table where stood the small blue bottle. And he picked it up and read from the label: 'Take six drops when necessary.'

'What is it, laudanum?'

She shook her head: 'No, it doesn't smell like that, it must have been prescribed. You had better ride for the doctor.'

He rose from his haunches saying, 'You think it necessary?'

*'Stanley!'* The name came like grit from between her teeth and like a young boy who had been chastised he said, 'Well . . . well, I was only meaning, if she was used to these turns and these drops.'

'Stanley, go and fetch the doctor as quick as you can. But wait, here's Peggy. Help us to lift her.'

Peggy Waters came into the room, only to pause for a second as she looked to where her mistress was now lying flat on the floor, but she said nothing. Then between the three of them they lifted the inert form on to the bed and Agnes, again turning to her brother, said, 'Be quick, will you? Go as quickly as you can . . .'

As she spoke she was reminded of her protestations to James earlier on that her brothers

59

were no longer boys but men. Yet she had to face the fact there was very little of the man about Stanley at the moment . . .

It wasn't until Kate Thorman was undressed and lying like someone dead between the sheets that Agnes, turning to Peggy, and lifting the bottle from the table, said, 'Do you know anything about this?' and Peggy, nodding now, said, 'Aye, in a way, it puts you to sleep, and eases pains and things.'

'It isn't laudanum?'

'No; 'tis a concoction she gets from Doctor Miller. I thought it was harmless, but I knew she kept it hidden. What brought this on? Can you tell me?'

'My father, he went for her.'

'You mean, he hit her?'

'Yes.' Agnes began tidying the dressing-table and as she gathered up the scattered hairpins, she said, 'What do you know about an Indian Army captain?'

There was a long pause before Peggy replied, and when she did her voice was non-committal: 'Just that he was a nice fellow, young and handsome, dashin' would be the word.'

'Did he stay here at any time?'

'Oh aye; he was a regular visitor during one of his furloughs.'

'Was he single? I mean . . .'

'No; he was married. His wife came from Dublin. But his people lived in the Midlands somewhere, had an estate there as far as I could gather. He came here at your grandfather's invitation. The young fellow's father and your grandfather had apparently been friends for years. Why are you asking this, girl?'

'That was what the quarrel was about.'

'Oh. Well, it had to come out sometime, better out than in. It should have come out years ago if she'd had any sense.'

'What do you know about Millie, Peggy?'

'What do I know about Millie?' Peggy sat down on a chair at the head of the bed and took the limp hand of her mistress between her own two before she said, 'Only that she is the light of our days and without her life would be very dull in this house. She's a trial, there's no doubt about that, but all things worthwhile are trials. Life's a trial, it's a battle, it's strife from the day you're born. And that's shared out between rich and poor alike, only the Lord seems to be more generous towards the poor with it, if you know what I mean.'

'Peggy, do you think that . . . that Millie doesn't belong to father, and that's why he is like he is at times?'

'My answer to the first part is, I don't know, and to the second is, that your father was born the way he is and if the silver spoon had turned to gold in his mouth and was there to this day, he'd still be the same as he is, especially when the drink is on him. I've seen what effect drink can have on some men; it alters their characters. But with the master, I've got to say what I feel, an' that is, the drink reveals his true self. He's been master over me since his father died, that is all of thirty years ago, and I've never taken to him because I've never been partial to mean streaks in people. I've always thanked God that there is none of him in you and very little of him in either Master Arnold or Roland. But Master Stanley's inherited a good portion: although as yet he doesn't drink, he's still

61

his father's son, and weak with it.'

Agnes in no way thought this condemnation of her family strange, for was not Peggy her mother, if not in nature then in spirit? She had been in this house longer than any of them. She had been born in the lodge fifty-six years ago and started work in the kitchens when she was six years old. And Dave Waters had been born in the actual house: his mother had been the cook and his father the groom and he'd been brought up in a room at the end of the staff cubicles; he had been put on the pay-roll when he was eight and his wage was a shilling a week, although he had been working around the stables from the time he could toddle. In some strange way the place belonged to them. Together they had run the household in its heyday, and now in its swift decline they were still running it, aiming to hold its head above the waters; so she saw no incongruity in her relationship with them.

\*       \*       \*

The doctor arrived an hour and a half later. He diagnosed a bad heart attack and prescribed utter quiet.

Down in the drawing-room he made no remark on her father's absence, but he said to her and Stanley, 'Your mother is very ill; if she survives the night, she could recover. It all depends on her inner strength and the will to live.'

In her mind Agnes repeated the words: 'The will to live', and she thought that if this was a necessary ingredient for recovery, then her mother would die. For she now recognized there had been an air of weary hopelessness about her for some long time.

62

If she had thought about it before she would have put it down to boredom because of the separate lives she and her husband led, only coming together for appearances' sake when visitors called, or when invited out.

But now it came to her that it wasn't so much boredom as the lack of love that was sapping at her mother's will to live: her mother had lacked love for a long time, from her husband, from her sons, even from herself, for she hadn't understood the need behind the stiff, apparently selfish exterior, selfish because she would have little to do with her daughter Millicent, rejecting the responsibility of her; but she knew now there was a reason for all these things and she felt weighed down with guilt for her part in it.

When the doctor left she returned to her mother's room where Peggy was still sitting. Stanley had retired to bed saying she must call him if his mother got worse. She had wanted to say, she couldn't be much worse than she was at the moment, the next worse would be death, but she simply nodded her head at him and let him go. And again she told herself that there went her father in a younger form.

*       *       *

Agnes had slept fitfully through the long night. Her body was feeling cramped with sitting in the chair. She opened her eyes and looked across the bed to the chair opposite. It was empty. Peggy must be downstairs making a drink. She looked at her mother and with a start she saw her eyelids fluttering and she bent over her, saying softly,

63

'Mama.'

Kate Thorman opened her eyes and her lips fell apart as if she were about to speak; but no words came, and Agnes said, 'You're all right. You're all right, Mama.' And she pulled her chair nearer to the bed; then sitting down, she stroked the hair back from the sweating brow and watched once again as her mother made an effort to speak.

Softly now Agnes said, 'Don't try to talk, Mama, just rest.'

'Agnes.' The name came out on a sighing breath and was hardly audible, and Agnes said, 'Yes, Mama?'

'My—'

'Please don't try to talk, Mama.'

'My keys.'

'Your keys. You want them? All right. All right, I'll get them.'

She knew that her mother kept the keys to her jewel box in her desk that stood to the side of the window, and it was to the desk she went and pulled open the top drawer and took out the keys. There were four keys on the ring and when she placed them on her mother's hand, Kate Thorman's fingers slipped over them to hold the smallest one. Then, as if even the weight of this was too much for her, she dropped it on to the counterpane and after staring unblinking into Agnes's face for some seconds, she said, 'The secret drawer ... bureau ... a box in the bureau.'

What her mother called the bureau was a davenport. It was one that had been made about fifty years earlier when secret drawers were being placed in all kinds of furniture, but mostly in the davenports. The button that worked the spring was in the upper part of the small right-hand drawer. This usually released the narrow top of the upright, allowing it to rise as if by magic to display a small panelled aperture with two similar drawers on each side.

Agnes knew all about the secret drawer, she had worked it so many times as a child. She couldn't remember how old she was when she was told she mustn't touch it again, because the wire controlling the weights was getting frayed. But now, picking up the keys from the counterpane, she went quickly up the room, pressed the button in the drawer and watched, as she had done so many times before, the top of the false back rise in the air to expose its secret compartments. The middle panel itself had its separate secret for it had to be opened by a button underneath the false top. When this was pressed the small door sprung open. It revealed inside a mother-of-pearl box. Having taken it out, she went to lift the lid but found it locked. Of course, this was what her mother wanted the key for. Swiftly now, she opened the box, and there she saw inside, doubled in half, a number of sheets of paper, and these lying on top of an envelope. She quickly took them out; but before going back to the bed she pressed down the top of the davenport into place again.

When she reached the bed she saw that her mother was in a state of agitation and when she placed the letters in her hand, it was the envelope she picked out.

Her fingers quivering, she lifted the flap and turned the envelope upside down, and a ring fell on to the counterpane. As her fingers were groping for it Agnes picked it up and held it out towards her and she watched her mother stare at it for a moment before putting out her hand and closing it around her own and the ring as she muttered, 'For you. Keep it, always. Very precious to me. But . . . but burn these. Promise, burn these.'

As her last words trailed away, there was a slight tap on the bedroom door before it was immediately opened, and Agnes knew that her father was entering the room. In one swift motion she thrust the letters into the opening between the buttons of her dressing-gown, automatically pulling the cord tight around her waist. And when her father reached her side she was in the act of lifting the empty box from the bed.

Her mother now was lying with her eyes closed as if aware of her husband's presence and wanted to shut it out. As if he sensed something, he looked down at the box and the ring that Agnes was now holding between her finger and thumb and, his voice thick, he said, 'What's that?'

'A ring. Mother wants me to have it.' His hand came out and took the ring from her and his eyes narrowed to pin-points. Evidently, he had never seen it before.

'Where was it? Where did you get it?'

'In her jewel . . . in her drawer'—she nodded towards the dressing-table—'in this box.' He now picked up the box and turned it over, then handed both the ring and the box back to her, staring hard at her for a moment before looking down on his wife and saying, 'How is she?'

'She's very ill. The doctor says she . . . she must have complete rest.'

'She's conscious?'

'Only just; she keeps coming and going.'

66

'She brought this on herself. You know that, don't you?'

She knew no such thing, so she did not answer him, only looked him straight in the face. And on this he turned about and as he was leaving the room he said, 'Inform me when the doctor comes again.'

She pressed her hand tightly against her breast and felt the papers crinkle underneath the pressure, then she looked down on her mother, whose breathing now appeared to be very shallow. She was about to put her hand into her dressing-gown and retrieve the letters when the door opened once more and Peggy and Ruthie entered.

Ruthie Waters was very like her mother in stature: she had a short thickset body and plain features, but her face was often relieved by a smile, whereas her mother's seemed set in a kind of placid calmness which belied many facets of her character.

Peggy went to her mistress and bent over her, while Ruthie, looking at Agnes, said, 'You're all in. Look, go and have a wash and get dressed. Maggie's got your breakfast ready: you'll have it on a tray in the morning-room; you'll be by yourself there and the fire's doing nicely. Who would think that the sun was almost splitting the trees yesterday, when this morning there was a frost of all things.'

Agnes nodded at Ruthie, then looking at Peggy, she said, 'If . . . if there's any change, come straightaway for me, won't you?'

'We'll see to that. Go on. As Ruthie says, go and have a bite, because if you ask me, it's gona be a long day, and another long night.'

'What about you?'

'Seems to me I nodded on and off most of the night. I'm like that once I sit down. But you were wide-eyed at six this morning, so go on.'

As she spoke she looked at the box Agnes was holding but did not remark on it, and Agnes went out still holding it.

Once inside her room, she placed the ring on the tray on her dressing-table; then she sat down on the edge of her bed before pulling out the letters from underneath her dressing-gown. Holding them away from her, she stared at them. 'Burn them,' her mother had said, and that's what she would do, but not before she had read them, for she felt that in these letters she would find out the truth of Millicent's birth.

The first she opened and read was the one in the envelope, and both her eyes and mouth widened as she read the first line:

Beloved, beloved, I know we promised that we must not write, but I cannot leave the country and you without one last word. I keep saying to myself, why had it to happen like this? All too late, eight years too late for both of us. What cynic arranged that we should be married the same week and in churches not a mile from each other, yet never look upon each other's face for seven and half years. But the moment we did we knew that fate had made a mistake in the arrangement of our lives.

It is possible that I will never look upon your face again, beloved, yet it is clear before my eyes in my every waking moment and held between my hands in my dreams. I have never hated the word duty as I have during these past weeks: duty to one's king and country, duty to one's parents . . . duty to one's family. Oh, this last duty, a duty that is binding us both in chains. Perhaps it is well we are not in the silly years of our youth for we might then have thrown everything to the wind without thought for others. But even so, I have been tempted more than once to do just that. Yet I never put you to the test, perhaps because I saw your children and remembered my own.

I'm enclosing this in a letter to your loyal Peggy. I feel I owe her much. She was so understanding and so helpful. There she was, a servant, a woman of the common people, yet nearer to us both than any of our own kin. As long as you have her, my dearest, you'll not need other friends.

I'm leaving for Southampton now. We sail at six in the morning. Goodbye, my dearest dear. There is one long night stretching before me; when that dawn arrives we will meet again. Of this I am sure.

Ever yours,
Only yours.
Lance.


Agnes dropped the letter on to her lap where it lay among the others and, putting her hands up, she cupped her face and rocked herself gently. Oh, to be loved like that, if only for a short while, if only for a day, an hour even, to have someone say to you the words that man had said to her mother, must have said to her over and over again during the short time they were together. Their love must

69

have been like a flame. Oh, how she wished such a flame would consume her. But the nearest James ever got to a flame was, 'My dear Agnes', and very often the 'My dear' sounded like a slight recrimination. She opened her eyes and dropped her hands on to her knees and stared towards the door as she thought soberly now, Mama may be dying, but at least she has lived.

Picking up one of the folded sheets from her lap she straightened it out and read:

Dearest dear, I've had to destroy the diary, it was too dangerous. But I must talk to you; and I can talk to you in a way that I wouldn't possibly do were we together. Reginald came to my bed last night. I did not resist him although my body shrank into its core, but his presence there gave me an alibi I'm much in need of this time, for I am with child, Lance, our child. I feel unwell and so alone. Oh my heart, at this moment I wish I could die.

The letter ended abruptly here.

The next one, like the first, bore no date. It began:

Millicent is three years old today. She is beautiful and gay, strangely gay, but so small, she is like a little elf. She has your eyes, so why do I not love her as I should? I purposely didn't make a fuss of her as a baby in case Reginald observed my attitude was different to that with which I received the other four, because as I confessed to you I never really wanted children. I suppose I am selfish, I just wanted to be loved, and I was

70

never loved until I met you. I cling to the memory of our nights together; yet they are fading, like your face. Why didn't I insist on having your picture?

I hear little snatches about you through the Morleys. You are making quite a name for yourself, George Morley said. He also told me that your wife had had another child. This seared me to the heart, while at the same time I understood.

This letter, too, ended abruptly. The next one had been written some three years earlier. It began:

You have a daughter, my dearest dear. She is supposed to be a premature baby. Doctor Miller confirmed Peggy's remarks. I wonder what he knows? He's kind. The child is to be christened Millicent after Reginald's aunt. He hopes that this will be remunerative. He never does anything without a purpose. The baby is a fortnight old and I'm up today for the first time.

I am empty in all ways. Hold me beloved, hold me, stretch out your arms to me, I am so alone. And forgive me, forgive me for last night; I prayed that I had never met you, because before, life was bearable, just. But the light you shone into my existence showed me the drab darkness in which I spent my days.

Oh Lance. Lance.

It was some moments before Agnes picked up the last sheet of paper. She noticed that at some time it had been crumpled as if crushed in the hand and straightened out again. And as she read it, the

71

tears rained down her face, and inside of her was a mourning that reflected the agony that had caused her mother to pen the words that began the letter:

You are dead. For three months you have been dead and I have not known. I received no sign. Your face still remained a blur up to last night at dinner at the Weldings, when they talked about it quite casually, saying, it was a pity: such a sad end to a brilliant career. Strange, they said, for a soldier such as he to die of a fever and not under fire. Then for the first time I saw your face clearly again. It rose out of the decimated turkey that was being lifted from the table by the butler, and you seemed to hover above his head as he made towards the sideboard. Then I heard someone say, 'Oh dear me.' . . . I must have fainted. Whatever Reginald thought, he said nothing when we arrived home. Perhaps he deems it policy as he is depending almost solely now on the small income left me by Aunt Jess which allows me to run the house, and of course allows him to still maintain his mistress in Newcastle. I am so grateful to her who was my one time dear friend for she has relieved my bed of his presence for some years. But that she continues to make him pay for his pleasure I am well aware for we live impoverished lives compared to our friends.

Why am I writing like this? You are gone and I am numb. At the moment I don't even feel sorrow. What is wrong with me? Am I becoming as fey as our daughter? Because Millicent is fey, she is unnatural. Seven years old and can neither read nor write. All she wants to do is to roam the grounds running like a hare, leaping like a fawn. Yes, she is like a fawn.

What is really the matter with me? Why do I go on talking like this? My head seems to be swelling, yet there is nothing in it, it is as empty as you must be now. Where did they bury you? Does it matter? I cannot talk to you in the grave. I will not talk to you ever again. You are no more and I am no more.

The letter ended there and Agnes, bowing her head and her shoulders until she was almost double, whimpered now, 'Oh! Mama. Mama. Oh! my dear Mama.'

When the door opened abruptly her body sprang upwards; then she put her hand to her throat and sighed her relief as she saw Peggy approaching her.

Peggy stood in front of her and, putting out her hand, she gripped her shoulder, saying, 'You shouldn't have read them, lass. The past is dead and buried. Look, put a match to them. Here, give them to me.' And she grabbed up the letters from Agnes's lap and, taking them to the empty grate, threw them into it. Then putting her hand into her skirt pocket she drew out a box of matches and having set light to the paper she moved it about until there was nothing but a small pile of black ash left. And when she rose from her knees Agnes was also standing and after wiping her face she said, 'Do you think Father knew?'

'Yes, he knew.'

'About her meeting Mr Lance?'

'Oh yes. But he wasn't sure about the child, not until the poor dear started to show signs of oddness. And then he linked her up with Mr

73

Lance's aunt who had been in and out of asylums for years.'

'Really! She was . . . ?'

'Oh yes; she was quite barmy at times.'

'What . . . what about his own children?'

'Oh, they're all right, as far as I know. It's years since I heard of them. They're about the same age as yourself and the boys.'

Agnes now took off her dressing-gown and went to the wash-hand stand and began to wash her face; and after a moment she said, 'What was he like, this Lance?'

'Fine. A fine man, a kindly sort. You would never have thought he was a soldier. I couldn't imagine him sticking a knife in anybody or shooting them down. But there, I suppose he had to. But one thing I do know, if she had married someone like him her life would have been different. There might still have been a Millie, oh yes'—she nodded her head now—'but they would have coped. When you're fond you cope; without it life's a burden.'

When you are fond you cope. Peggy was terming the passion, the overwhelming passion that her mother had felt for this man and he for her as fondness. Well, by whatever name you called it, at this moment she knew that she would give years of her life to experience it. For there was a longing in her that was reaching out for something, and the physical need was only a part of it.

The door was opened unceremoniously again and they both turned and looked towards Maggie who, gabbling in her thick Irish brogue, said, 'Ruthie says, come. She's in a turn, the missis. It's the end, I'm thinkin'.'

Grabbing up her dressing-gown again, Agnes

74

rushed past both Peggy and Maggie, and when she arrived in her mother's bedroom it was to see Ruthie Waters aiming to hold her mother upright from the pillows as she gasped for breath.

With one hand pressed now tightly under her breasts Kate Thorman looked into her daughter's face and, between gasps, she began to speak. Her words seeming to jump out of her mouth, she said, 'Don't . . . let . . . him . . . put . . . her . . . away.'

'No, dear. No, never, never that.'

'Promise?'

'I . . . I promise. Oh, I promise.'

Kate Thorman now closed her eyes and, her body going limp, they gently settled her back on her pillows.

Fifteen minutes later with her husband and her youngest son standing on one side of the bed and Agnes and Peggy Waters on the other, Kate Thorman died. She was conscious to the end, but not once did she look in her husband's direction, nor speak a word to him.

After Peggy had closed her lids and led Agnes away from the bed, Reginald Thorman continued to look down on his wife and his expression was not that of someone in grief, but of someone grieved.

# PART TWO

## Carrie

# CHAPTER ONE

It was Easter Monday, nineteen hundred and thirteen, and John Bradley had granted that it should be a holiday. It was a great concession, Robert knew, for in his uncle's mind holidays meant not just drinking but carousing and fairgrounds and their improper side-shows.

There had been a storm after breakfast when Carrie had been foolish enough to ask if she could go into Newcastle to the show on the Town Moor. He had thought that his uncle was about to have a fit at the suggestion.

In the months he had been here he had seen a great change come over Carrie. In some ways she had become pert. Aye, he'd say pert was the word, for she had marched into this room more than once and him only half-clothed, and there had been a look in her eye that he thought was a little too old for her.

His aunt, he thought, was also aware of the change in her daughter, but it seemed that she trusted him wholly with her. Only two Sundays gone, when Carrie had been plaguing to go out for a walk as far as Lamesley with Gladys Parkin, her mother had said no, for on a Sunday the lanes were lined with lads who had nothing better to do.

This had amused him, lanes lined with lads. At the most you might see a couple leaning on a farm gate here and there but on this day his aunt had said, 'You may go with Robert if he'll take you.'

So what could he do but come clean and say that he had made arrangements to meet Nancy Parkin.

Well, well, that had caused their eyebrows to meet up with their hairlines. How long had it been going on? his aunt had asked in a tone of voice similar to that his mother might have used.

A few weeks, he had answered, reducing the time from months, because Nancy wasn't for having it known, seeing that she had been walking out with a fellow from Birtley who, she said, could be serious about her. He was quite aware that she hoped that this statement would elicit one from him that he too was serious about her. But it hadn't. He liked her. She was a jolly lass, good to look at . . . and to hold, but as for marrying her . . . Well now, marriage was a lifetime policy you had to take on, and like a policy you had to pay for it unto death. And from what he had seen of the lives of many a couple who had taken out such a policy he knew it wasn't for him, the bickering, the nagging, even the blows. Oh aye, the blows. Never a Saturday passed in Upper Foxglove Road but there were blows. And they didn't always start with the man; some women were like tigresses when they got going. No; marriage was a serious business and he wasn't going to gallop into it. Something would have to stir him and he doubted if he'd find that something in Nancy Parkin.

He had wanted to laugh when his aunt's face had become prim as she said, 'She's fast, is Nancy, fast.' And he retorted, 'Aye; well, I'll have to look out then, won't I, Auntie? 'Cos as me dad always said, fast women and slow horses get you nowhere.'

Carrie had sniggered, and at this her mother had turned on her. He had never before seen his aunt lose her temper. She was usually a gentle-spoken woman, but she had cried at her daughter, 'Don't be silly, girl! And you'll bide in today. At least until this afternoon when your father and I will walk you out.'

Poor Carrie. He felt sorry for her. She was sixteen now and the sap was definitely running freely in her. There was going to be a tough time ahead for Carrie.

Anyway, he had his own day planned with Nancy. First he meant them to take the train into High Shields and saunter down to the sands. He had a longing to look at the river again, especially where it opened out into the sea. There was no better sight than to watch a ship slowly making its way between the piers and into the perilous waters beyond the bar.

If he was true to himself he must admit that although he enjoyed his present quarters much better than he had done his home in Jarrow he missed the river and the chatter of his work-mates, the arguments while they had their baits sitting on timbers above the oily water and listening to the ideas that came out of some men's heads, old men, many of whom even now could neither read nor write, yet who thought and thought deeply.

There was a great difference he had found between the thinking of a townman and that of a countryman. Take his uncle for instance. Even without his religious bias he would have been a narrow-minded man. And there was Tim Yarrow. Tim was about the same age as his uncle and he rarely had anything to say, but when he did talk it was mostly about what happened in the hamlet when he was young when it had been three times the size before the fire had burned down a row of cottages. And even now he spoke of Lamesley as if it was a town instead of a village.

Ah well. He bent down and looked in the mirror and straightened his tie. There was one thing about it, his reflection told him, the country air was doing him good. His skin was clear, as were his eyes, and he had put on a little flesh. He'd have to watch that, he didn't want to become pot-bellied.

He patted his pocket. He had his money, and a clean handkerchief, and his new overcoat on. He felt smart, and he should do; the coat had cost him quite a bit.

Well, now he was ready. He had to meet Nancy on the Lamesley road, just above the fork. He looked at his watch. It was time he was making a sprint, she didn't like being kept waiting . . .

Five minutes later he approached the fork and saw Nancy Parkin standing in the shelter of some shrubs. As he neared her he laughed and called out, 'I'm not late. Now I'm not late, so put the gun down.'

But she did not laugh in return. Looking at him with a straight face, she said, 'I . . . I can't come. Our Mary Ellen says Harry's comin' over. He's . . . he's heard about you, and he's mad.'

'Oh, is he? Well, I'm sorry to hear that.'

'What are you gona do about it?'

His face was straight now as he asked quietly, 'What do you mean, Nancy? What am I going to do about it?'

'Well—' She turned her head to the side and wagged it before answering, 'Ma says I've got to find out if you're serious.'

'Oh, come on. Come on, Nancy. We've only known each other a matter of weeks.'

She turned on him now, her voice raised.

82

'Weeks! You can't count, 'twas November when we first went out.'

'Yes.' He nodded at her slowly now and, his voice cool, he said, 'But how many times have we been out since that? Not every week, not every other week. Six to eight times in all, I should say. Does that qualify for going serious? Look'—his eyes narrowed at her now and his jaw tightened—'the best thing you can do, Nancy, is to go back and tell your mother to get you married off to this Harry if she's in such a hurry to get rid of you.'

'Oh you! Rob Bradley. You just play on a girl's feelings, that's all you do. You've led me on.'

'Well, if I've led you on, apparently I'm not the only one. Harry's been doing his share an' all.'

'Oh, you think you're funny, don't you?'

'No, I don't think I'm funny.' His face was straight. 'But I look at things clearly. And I can tell you and your mother this right away, I'm not being pushed into anything, so I'll say goodbye, Nancy. You go back now, and hurry because Harry'll be waiting for you. And you can tell him you're all his.' And on this he turned on his heel and left her.

But almost immediately her voice seemed to hit him in the back of the neck as she bawled as loud as any drunken trollop on a Saturday night in Jarrow, 'You're a bloody upstart, that's what you are. Everybody says it. You should never have come to the hamlet. You don't belong among us, act as if you are somebody. And who are you anyway? . . . A bloody towny. I hate you. Do you hear? I hate you, you rotten bugger!'

He was half a mile further along the road before he stopped and, leaning over a farm gate, looked to where some lambs were leaping in play. There

83

were about a dozen of them on a low mound and they were actually playing 'King of the Castle'. Another time the sight would have warmed him and he would have laughed aloud, but now he was angry, not so much at the fact that he had lost the company of Nancy because he wouldn't commit himself, but at the things she had yelled at him as he left her, calling him an upstart, saying that he didn't belong among them.

Presently he brought his elbows off the gate and gripped the top of it as he said to himself, 'I'm no upstart. Just because you like to dress decent and don't swill your drink, you're an upstart.'

Of a sudden the anger seeped from him and he gave a short laugh. Well, well, him an upstart. What was an upstart, anyway? What was the meaning of it? Somebody who got above themselves, rose in the world and forgot their beginnings, looked down on them. So an upstart was somebody who was getting on in the world. You couldn't then put the term upstart to the penniless or to a begger. No, when he came to think of it, an upstart was a kind of compliment. Well, well, so that's what he was, an upstart. So be it, he'd be an upstart. From now on that's what he'd be, an upstart.

He turned from the gate and walked briskly down the road in the direction of the station. He was out for the day and he was going to enjoy himself. He was a bloody upstart and a rotten bugger. Aye, by! come to think of it, that wouldn't be the first time she had used that language, but up till now she had appeared so polite, so pi. Eeh! women. It just showed you, didn't it?

*     *     *

84

But he didn't enjoy himself, at least not to the extent he had imagined he would. The river was quiet, dead. He should have expected that at a holiday time. He saw no ship passing out between the piers. Mile End Road seemed to be lined with children, all making their way down to the sands. Many of them he knew would have tramped from Jarrow and Hebburn. They all looked bright-eyed and eager, but by tonight their feet would be dragging and tears would be streaking many faces as they made their way home. He had seen it so often. 'We're going to the sands the morrow, I've got *threepence*. We're going to the sands the morrow.' Some went even on a penny, and some on nothing. Other times he had been happy to see the bairns going to the sands, but today they looked like a gigantic swarm of hungry children, hungry for a little pleasure. Somehow it troubled him, pained him.

He went into a café and had an indifferent meal, telling himself he'd eaten better in Lockhart's working men's café in Jarrow.

By four o'clock in the afternoon he was in Newcastle. He liked walking round the city. The buildings were fine and you could see them on a day like this, for it was like a Sunday. But it wouldn't be so on the Town Moor. He didn't go to the moor, telling himself that you couldn't enjoy a fair on your own.

It was six o'clock when he alighted from the train at Lamesley, went up the bank and through the village, but didn't take the road that would lead to the hamlet. He wasn't going indoors yet awhile, for his uncle would likely question him as to what

85

depths of depravity he had sunk to in the big city. He skirted it by taking the field path that brought him out on the road to The Bull. He liked The Bull and Billy and Mary Taggart who ran it. When he arrived it was to find the tap room quite crowded, and after exchanging greetings with Billy Taggart and ordering his half-pint, he took his stand at the corner of the bar. There was no chance of getting a seat, not in this taproom. He had once made the mistake of sitting on a vacant seat at the end of the settle, but Billy Taggart's wink and a lift of his chin had brought him to the bar counter, to be told in a whisper that that was Dob Holler's seat and that he'd be in any minute. He was amused sometimes at the hierarchy that prevailed in this room. Hierarchy, his dictionary told him, was a division among the angels. Well, there were certainly no angels among this lot, but the division was as pronounced.

A tall thin middle-aged man came to the counter and stood beside him while saying to the barman, 'Same again, Billy.'

'Same again, it is,' said Mr Taggart.

The man put his tuppence on the counter for the half-pint and Mr Taggart picked it up, and he rattled it in his hand as he looked at his customer before saying, 'Don't look very happy the night, Arthur. What's it now?'

'What it always is, Billy. The new bugger scarpered the day.'

'Never! You mean the one that took over from Jimmy?'

'No; we've had two since him. This one said the work was too heavy. Six till six was his time and not a minute after. Of course—' The man now took a drink from his mug, then replaced it on the counter before saying slowly, 'Tell you the truth, I cannot blame them. Three of us to do the work of ten. It's impossible; takes me all me time to keep the vegetables going. Some of the greenhouses are dropping to bits. It's a disgrace. Eeh! when I think of it, we used to have bunches of grapes as big as turnips. And Greg, he's at it from morning till night; but the horses take up most of his time.'

'How many have you got now?'

'Three, but there'll soon only be two, Prince won't be able to pull his weight much longer. Well, he's past twenty. He should be put out to grass, but I'm afraid'—he pursed his lips—'knowing the master, he'll be for the market.'

'Things that tight?'

'Aye, and getting tighter I should say. It's been a strange house since the mistress died. You don't know what's going to happen next.'

'How's the young miss?'

'Oh, she's all right.' The man smiled gently now. 'Still flitting, can't keep her out of the wood. But she's all right.'

The young miss still flitting. The man must be from Foreshaw Park, and the young miss was the one who was known round about as Thorman's Moth. And, by aye! she'd looked like a moth that night all right. He'd taken a long time to get over that experience, weird it was. He had passed that way often since but had never ventured beyond the broken railings. But he must admit, he had looked for a glimpse of her. In a way, she had been beautiful, and strange. And her sister? There was no resemblance between them. One looked all softness and light and the other prim starchiness,

87

definitely the Lady of the Manor or the elder daughter as he now knew she was. Well, by the sound of it, she hadn't much to be uppish about, for apparently they were on their beam ends.

His attention was brought back to the man who was saying, 'He's been drinking like a fish, at least he does when he's at home. But sometimes he's away for days. They say he's got rooms in Newcastle, and'—his voice dropped—'from what I can gather he's never lonely there. The one I'm sorry for is Miss Agnes. She's got the lot on her shoulders. It'll be a good thing for her when she's married and she goes off. Although what's going to happen then, God alone knows. I don't know what they'll do with the young 'un, although I do know the master's all for having her put away. From what I gather from the kitchen, there's hell to pay atween Miss Agnes and him at times. Still, we'll have to wait and see.' He finished his drink, then said, 'I'll be off then, Billy. Be seeing you.'

'Aye, be seeing you, Arthur. Take care.'

Billy Taggart now wiped the counter around Robert's tankard before saying, 'Sad business, that.'

'Does he work at Foreshaw Park?'

'That's it, Foreshaw Park. If ever a place has galloped downhill that has. They used to have the smartest team of horses round about. With this one's grandfather, I mean the present owner's grandfather, money was spent like water then. But mind, he was a man who worked for it, he was a business man. He had good shares in two or three of the coal mines around, not counting a chain factory and a candle factory an' all. Oh, he had his fingers in all kinds of pies. But the trouble was, he spoiled his son, the present one's father, so the story goes. And this one's been on the downgrade since he finished school, and long afore, if all tales are true. He was saved by marrying his wife. But then her dad went bust. You can see it's a tale of bad management right through and it wouldn't surprise me to see them all out of there in a year or two. I'll tell you one thing, he's badly liked around here, very few have a good word for him. Oh'—he moved his head slowly—' 'tis amazing how the mighty can be brought down. Still, I have very little pity for them. It'll do them good to see how the other half live. Are you having another?'

'No thanks, Billy, not the night.' Then leaning forward he grinned at Billy Taggart while whispering, 'I don't want me breath to knock him over.' The barman put his head back and let out a high laugh and said, 'I'd like to see that. Aye, I'd like to see that, old holy Joe being floored. Well, good night to you.'

'And to you.'

The twilight was deepening when he left the inn, and he had decided to take the roundabout road back to the hamlet because this way he wouldn't have to pass Nancy's door.

He had just looked at the signpost which pointed the way to Tanfield when he heard a giggle coming from behind the hedge that bordered the road. It made him pause in his step. He imagined that it was Carrie he was hearing for she giggled like that. But he told himself that there must be lots of lasses who giggled like Carrie, and whoever it was behind the hedge it certainly wouldn't be Carrie, although he bet she wished it was.

He was only a hundred yards from the gateway that led into the carpenter's yard when he saw a figure running towards him, and long before it reached him he recognized his aunt.

Alice Bradley was gasping for breath as she came up to him, and her voice was a gabble as she asked, 'Have you seen anything of Carrie?'

'Carrie? No.'

'Oh, dear Lord! Dear Lord!' As she turned now and looked from side to side he caught hold of her arm, saying, 'What's happened? What's the matter?'

'It's . . . it's Carrie. She went out after dinner and hasn't been seen since. You know she wanted to go out walking with Gladys, well I let her, unknowest to Mr Bradley, but . . . but Gladys went to her aunt's in Gateshead on Saturday for the week-end. She was lying. My . . . my Carrie was lying. And Mr Bradley is beside himself. You haven't seen her?'

'No. No, Aunty.'

'Oh dear! Oh dear! He's demented. If she doesn't come back he'll go off his head.' She became still now and, looking into his face, she said, 'His life revolves around her. He thinks or cares for no one else, no one.'

There was a sound of tears in her voice and he said soothingly, 'He thinks of you, Aunty. He's very fond of you.'

'No, no. You don't know anything, Robert. You don't. You don't.' Her head was moving wildly now from shoulder to shoulder. 'He thinks the sun shines out of her. She's just got to laugh and he's happy.'

Just got to laugh. He recalled the giggling sound behind the hedge but dismissed it with a No, no! Then came back at himself with a *Yes. Why yes.* She was ripe for it, wasn't she? Had been for some time now. Good God!

'Look, Aunty'—he bent over her—'stay here. I'll be back in a few minutes, and likely with her.'

'What! You know where she is?'

'I'm not sure. But just remember this: you know and I know she's no longer a little girl. She's a young lass and growing fast. You understand?'

She said nothing but the look in her eyes told him that she understood only too well. And now he turned from her and ran back along the road he had come. But before he was within sight of the signpost he saw her coming towards him, and when he reached her he grabbed her roughly by the shoulders, saying, 'What do you think you're up to, Miss?'

'What's the matter with you?' She shrugged, trying to release his hold, and he said, 'You know what I'm up to. Who was that with you behind the hedge?'

'I . . . I haven't been behind any hedge. I've . . . I've just been for a walk.'

'Don't you lie to me. I passed this way five minutes gone, and I heard you giggling. You're a little slut, that's what you are, Carrie Bradley, a little slut. And you've upset your mam and God knows what's going to happen when you meet your dad.'

Her whole manner changing now, she said, 'Is . . . is he mad?'

'What in the name of God do you expect him to be! You know what he's like. They've been looking for you all afternoon.'

'I . . . I told them that I was going with Gladys.'

'Well, they found out that you couldn't have gone with Gladys, she's been away for the week-

91

end,' he said, and at this she put her hand across her mouth.

'Come on.' He almost dragged her along the road now, and when they met up with her mother, Alice was so overcome she could scarcely speak. But when she did, all she could mutter was, 'Girl! Girl!' Then after drawing in a number of short breaths she said, 'Where have you been?'

'Just . . . for a walk, Mam.'

'You couldn't have been walking all this time, girl. Tell me where you've been. Do you hear me?'

'Just for a walk.' Carrie's head was lowered now, her chin on her chest, and her mother, stepping wholly out of character, almost screamed at her, 'Don't lie to me, girl! You haven't been walking for nearly seven hours. And your father, he'll . . . he'll kill you if he thinks you've been up to anything. As much as he loves you, he'll . . . Oh dear me!' She now looked at Robert and appealed, 'What are we going to do? What are we going to say?'

'She can only tell him the truth: she went out for a walk, and kept on.' He glanced at Carrie. Her head was still lowered, but was moving slightly as if in defiance. 'Come on,' he said, and he took them both by an arm and led them forward and into the house.

They had entered by the back door and Alice was pushing her daughter up through the kitchen towards the far door, saying as she did so, 'Get your things off and settle down before your father comes . . .' when the door leading into the hall was thrust open and there, like the avenging angel, stood John Bradley. His gaze, fearsome, came immediately to rest on his daughter. He stared at her for some seconds before swallowing deeply and

92

saying, 'Where have you been, girl?'

The expression on his face seemed to have frozen Carrie, for she stood perfectly still staring back at him, and he bellowed, 'You heard me, girl. I say, where have you been?'

He now advanced towards her and when his hand shot out and grabbed the front of her coat, almost lifting her from her feet, she squealed, 'For a walk, Da . . . Da . . . Dad. Only for . . . a . . . a . . . walk.'

'All this time? Don't lie to me, girl. You have been with someone, haven't you?' His hand gripping more of her coat now, he shook her as he cried, 'I've never laid a hand on you in my life, but I swear to you before my God this minute that I will thrash the truth out of you.'

'Oh Dad, Da . . . ad!'

'You won't soften me, girl, with, Oh Dad, Dad!' He now turned his infuriated gaze on to his wife, saying, 'Where did you find her?'

'She . . . she was along the road. Er . . . Robert . . . Robert.' She glanced in agitation towards Robert now and she let her eyes linger on him for a moment; then eyes and mouth opening wide, she seemed to take in a great draught of air before she spluttered, 'She was with Robert. She's come to no harm, she was with Robert.'

'No, look!' It was a thin mutter but a definite protest, and he would have gone on but Alice Bradley caught hold of his hand with both of hers and squeezed it as she looked at him, deep pleading in her eyes, saying, 'Tell Mr Bradley, she . . . she was with you, and . . . and you took her into Newcastle. She's come to no harm because she was with you. Wasn't she? Wasn't she?'

Before he could speak, whether to protest, or to go along with what she had said, John Bradley had left loose of his daughter and his hands were now on Robert's shoulders, thrusting him backwards towards the wall. But only for a moment, for Robert, crossing his arms in front of his chest, snapped them wide, so breaking John Bradley's hold. Then he cried at him, 'Don't you come that with me, Uncle, or you'll end worse off.'

The older man stood panting now, his body bent forward, and like this they glared at each other until Alice put in softly, 'She came to no harm, Mr Bradley. She came to no harm. She never would with Robert.'

John Bradley turned a disdainful glance on his wife, then asked, in a voice that still trembled with anger, 'You knew what was going on?'

Alice was nonplussed for a moment; then she muttered, 'No. Well, yes. It was nothing. She's always been fond of Robert; they . . . they are cousins, remember?'

'I remember that only too well, woman.' Again John Bradley was looking at Robert, and he now demanded, 'Why didn't you ask my permission?'

Robert looked past his uncle now to where his aunt stood, the deep pleading in her eyes, her lips opening and shutting as if she were begging him audibly not to betray them, and so it was with an effort that he said, 'You weren't about.' And it was true for he remembered now that his uncle had gone in that morning to Lamesley to talk with the vicar. His uncle often paid visits to the vicarage and would talk about the big fine square house. Being a sidesman of the church he interested himself in all its doings. Robert had met and spoken with the

94

parson once, and his impression had been of a reasonable man, quite opposite to his uncle.

John Bradley now turned on his wife demanding, 'Did he ask your permission then?'

But before she could reply Robert put in, 'No, I didn't. I didn't ask anybody's permission.'

'Well, it is the first and the last time you will take her out without doing so, and not her permission but mine. Do you understand that?' The man's face trembled now, it was as if he was about to cry, and he ended, 'I'm disappointed in you, very disappointed. I . . . I trusted you. But then I should have known, like father like son. He robbed me. Yes, he did. Your father. And now you're aiming to do the same.'

'I'm doing no such thing. And I can tell you this: I can promise you here and now that never again will you have reason to ask if I've walked with Carrie. Never. Do you hear me?' And on this he pushed past the man and stalked out of the kitchen, through the hall, up the stairs, along the corridor and into the dark roof-room, and there he banged the door behind him. Then groping his way to the foot of the bed, he gripped the railing and bent his body over it, exclaiming as he did so, 'God Almighty! What next, eh? What next?' Oh, why the hell had he come here.

He let out a long slow breath, straightened his back, then made his way to the mantelpiece and lifted down the lamp. Having lit it, he began to undress, not folding his clothes as he usually did but almost tearing them off and flinging them on to the floor. He never slept in his linings.

As he lay, his hands behind his head, half propped up on the pillows, he heard the distant closing of doors, which meant they had all gone to bed. And he recalled lying in this very same position first thing this morning and looking forward to the day's holiday. Well, it had been a disaster from beginning to end. But the end had certainly been worse than the beginning. By God, aye! His uncle must be slightly unbalanced, and slightly was putting it mildly. What with his religion and the possessive love he had for his daughter, he was a danger. A little while ago, back there in the kitchen, he had looked as if he meant murder.

As for his cousin, Carrie, she had the makings of a little trollop. That had been her behind that hedge and her giggling hadn't been evoked by holding hands if he knew anything. Nor was it, if he knew anything, the first time she had become acquainted with the hedge.

He suddenly sat bolt upright in the bed. Now, when he did come to think of it, he had seen her scampering across the field as recently as one night last week. At the time he hadn't taken any notice, imagining she was returning from some errand to one of the cottages down below. Then there was that time he was down in the workshop in the evening. He had been doing a bit on his own. He liked carving and was having a go at a ship, the last one he had worked on in Palmer's; he could remember nearly every detail of her. Carrie had come in and said, 'Dad has gone over to Mr Marshall's on North Farm about the order. If Mam asks for me, tell her I've just slipped in to talk to Gladys.'

He had said to her, 'Why don't you tell her yourself?' and her reply had been, 'She might stop me, because she doesn't like me to disturb the family in the evening.' She hadn't giggled or laughed, and he remembered he couldn't find a word to put to her expression, but there was a sort of plea in it . . . Aye, yes, there would be a plea in it when she was eager to get about her capers. Who was she meeting anyway? Likely a farmer's son; it wouldn't be any of the pit lads because she was madam enough to scorn them.

Well, she wasn't going to get him involved. He lay back on his pillows; then, as if speaking to someone beside him, he turned his head and nodded, saying, 'She's done that already. Or at least her mother has.' Anyway, it began the night and it ended the night; he was having no more of it.

He settled down in the bed; but then found he couldn't sleep, and it must have been all of an hour later when he swung round on to his side as he heard his door being opened. It had a special creak and groaned like old wood often did. He pulled himself up in the bed and leaned his elbow on the pillow thinking, if he's come to have another go at me I'll lash out at him, as old as he is.

When he saw the match being struck and the candle shielded, he thought for a moment it was his aunt; and then he gave an audible gasp as, in the flickering flame, he saw Carrie's face, and she was moving towards him.

'Look!' His voice was a deep growl. 'Get out of here. Get back to your room.'

'I . . . I just wanted to say, thank you, Robert.'

'I don't need any thanks. Have you any idea what your dad would do if he found you here? He would attempt to murder us both. He's a maniac. *Now get out . . . away.*'

He had to look up at her now because she was

97

standing above him, and for the first time he became conscious he was naked to the waist. Grabbing at the quilt, he pulled it up to his neck and now he was hissing, 'Look! if you don't get away, I'll let out a yell that'll bring them. I mean it, mind. You had no right to come here at this time of night . . . at any time.'

'Don't be mad at me, Robert, please. As . . . as I said, I just wanted to say thank you for saving me.'

'Saving you! I should imagine it'll take a lot to save you now, Carrie. You've been at this game for some time, haven't you? Who is it?'

'Nobody.'

'You're a little liar. You know that?'

He saw her now hunch her shoulders, then she said, 'You used to like me.'

'Well, for your information, let me tell you, I've never liked you, not that way, just as a child, that's all, which I thought you were, for a short time anyway. Now look. I said, get goin', or I'll get out of here and I haven't a stitch on, and just imagine your father if he witnesses that, eh, just imagine it.'

She now backed from him, saying, 'He doesn't mind you, not really. I knew when he was going on he didn't mind if it was you taking me out.'

'*Get out!* Do you here? *Get out!*'

Her face receded from him, then was lost in the darkness as she snuffed out the candle.

It was a full minute after the door had creaked again that he lay back. Then speaking aloud to himself, he said, 'Dear God! If that man had come in and caught her he would have done murder.'

He'd have to get away from here. The thought came as a flat statement in his mind. If he didn't, something would happen, because that miss was

98

hot and somebody was going to burn their fingers on her. And there was one thing sure, it wasn't going to be him.

## CHAPTER TWO

He would have been gone weeks ago had not his aunt begged him to stay. His uncle, she said, was very fond of him, looked upon him as a son. Yes, he had thought, and he would like to domineer him as he might have done a son. But simply because of her pleas, he had stayed. Yet he knew that sooner or later he would have to make a move, for the atmosphere in the workshop and the house was tense.

Carrie was never allowed out of the house unless one or the other of her parents was with her. And strangely, especially over the past three weeks, she hadn't seemed to resent this. What was more, she seemed to have lost a lot of her pertness. Once or twice he had looked at her while she was sitting sewing and she had appeared pathetic and, he had fancied, even a little frightened. Well, she had a good right to be afraid of her father. Such men were fanatics and fanatics were dangerous people, whatever line they followed.

Just how dangerous his uncle could be, Robert found out on this day. It was the Wednesday in the last week in May. Work started at seven in the morning, then stopped at half-past eight for breakfast. Tim Yarrow brought his bait with him and ate it beside his bench. But John Bradley and Robert went indoors to a set breakfast, which was always preceded by a grace.

For the past two mornings, Carrie had come down late for breakfast and her father had reprimanded her. This morning she was standing behind her chair. Her father had finished the grace and her mother was placing a side dish on the table on which were a number of slices of fried bacon and four fried eggs reposing on slices of fried bread, and on the sight of them Carrie swung round and dashed to the shallow stone sink that was set below the kitchen window and vomited.

Robert did not look towards Carrie, but at his aunt. Her face was blanched, her hand was over her mouth. He had thought for some days now that Carrie hadn't been looking well and had seemed agitated, and in a way his aunt hadn't seemed herself either. Now, like a stroke of lightning, the reason sprang at him. He hadn't been married, nor as yet got any woman pregnant, as far as he knew, but he knew enough to know that at a certain time they were sick. The knowledge had a strange effect upon him. He had the desire to take to his heels and run like any scalded cat out of that door and along the road, anywhere, anywhere.

'What's wrong with her?' John Bradley's voice was deep and already it held a menace.

'She's . . . sh . . . sh . . . she's sick.'

'I can see that, woman. I can hear that. But what's caused it? Do you know?'

Alice did not answer him but looked towards her daughter who had now turned from the sink and was leaning with her back against it as she wiped her mouth.

Slowly now her father advanced towards her; but before he reached her Alice flung herself between

100

them, crying, 'Listen! Now listen! John.' It was the first time that Robert had heard her use her husband's Christian name, and again she pleaded, 'John. John, listen.'

'I'm listening.'

'It . . . it can't be helped, it's done. She . . . she made a mistake.'

'What mistake, woman?'

But Alice couldn't say it. What she did say was, 'She's . . . she's but a child, she's made a mistake.'

'Oh, she's made a mistake, has she? And who's helped her?'

There was silence in the kitchen and whether inadvertently or intentionally, Alice looked past her husband and let her eyes rest on Robert for a second; but it was sufficient to bring John Bradley swinging round. His voice no longer level but almost a scream, he cried, 'You! You Judas! You destroyer of innocence.'

'Look here!' Robert backed towards the end of the table, shouting now as loudly as his uncle, 'You've got the wrong end of the stick. I've had nothing to do with her. Ask her. Ask her.'

Again John Bradley was facing his wife and daughter. But now, their faces both alike in that each almost bore the pallor of death, they remained silent. And Robert screamed at them, 'Oh! for God's sake, tell him. He can't kill you. Whoever it was, he can't kill you.'

'No, I can't kill them, but I can kill you.' John Bradley had swung round and was now leaning over the end of the table, and it should happen that his doubled fist rested against the bread board and the handle of the large bread knife lying there. When he grabbed it and lifted it upwards Alice's

101

scream rent the room: 'No! no! Please! They . . . they could be married.' She was now hanging on to her husband's arm. 'Don't you see? Robert will stand by her. Won't you, Robert? Won't you, Robert?' She turned her head in Robert's direction, and for answer he said, 'No, by God! I won't, Auntie. You're lying and you know you're lying and I'm not taking this on for you or anybody else. I'm not going to be blamed for somebody else's dirty work.'

'You! You! Somebody else's dirty work? Dirty work's in your blood. Your father did dirty work on your mother, that's why she had to marry him. I've been robbed twice, twice from the same core. Dirty work? . . . Bastard!' The word ended on a loud cry and with it the bread knife sprang from his hand and the next second it was Robert who cried out as the blade of the knife seared his skin from the corner of his right eye over the top of his ear and through a line of his hair.

For a moment the room hung in a stillness. As if they were posed for a photographer, they all held their positions: John Bradley, leaning over the table, his hands flat on it, his head tucked into his shoulders, his eyes wide and unblinking; Alice to his side, one hand covering her face, the other raised in the air as if about to wave goodbye to someone; and Carrie half-turned towards the sink, both hands gripping its ledge, her shoulders hunched, her mouth wide open. As for Robert himself, he was so stunned that he too remained still, his hand across his cheek, his blood now flowing over it.

When they snapped back into life, Alice ran to him, crying, 'Oh my God! Oh my God!' But he pushed her off. He did not know how deep the wound was; he felt no pain only a feeling of sickness as the blood flowed into his mouth.

It was Carrie who now came rushing to him with a towel in her hands, and he grabbed it from her while saying, 'You keep away from me. Do you hear? Keep away from me.' Then turning his head, he cried, 'All of you, because I'll be out of here as quick as me legs'll carry me.'

'Oh no! No!' It was like a drawn out wail, and Alice now looked appealingly at her husband. But John Bradley uttered no word. Stumbling towards a chair, he dropped into it and, his forearms on his knees, he gazed at the floor.

'All right. All right.' Alice pleaded with Robert now. 'It's over, only . . . only let me bandage your head. Let me see to it, please. Please.' She now tugged at his arm and he allowed himself to be led from the room. But in the hallway the sickness in him increased and he dropped onto the wooden chair by the front door, then spat out the blood from his mouth on to the towel. Alice was examining the cut, all the while making moaning sounds. Finally, she said, 'It'll need stitching. You'll have to have the doctor. I'll send for him.'

'You'll do no such thing. If I want a doctor I'll go to him. Get by.' He got to his feet, and now he folded the blood-stained towel into a long strip and tied it round his head, then said, 'I'll take what things I can with me, and me tools. I'll send for the rest.'

'Oh, Robert, Robert, try to understand.'

He rounded on her now, crying, 'I understand well enough, Aunty. You would have saddled her on me with no real thought for either of us.'

'She's fond of you, Robert.'

'Aye, and of others an' all I should imagine. You did a wrong thing, Aunty, a rotten thing. She would have come clean and I would have stayed here and helped all I could to pacify him, but now all I can say is, thank God I'm going.'

'But where will you go?' Her voice was a whimper now.

'I don't know, but I'll find some place.' He turned about and walked away from her and up the stairs.

In his room he went immediately to his bed and sat down on the edge of it, for his head was swimming.

After a time he rang out a towel in the wash-basin and wiped the blood from around his face, neck, and head. He wasn't bleeding so freely now, but his hair was matted with the blood. Going to the drawers, he took out a shirt and tore strips off the tail which he used as a bandage, winding it the best way he could around his head, before once more sitting down.

It was a good half-hour later when he got to his feet and started packing. Most of his underclothes went into the bass hamper that had belonged to his mother, the rest into a tin trunk that he had bought secondhand in Jarrow before coming here. The last things he packed were his books. He had twenty-eight in all and he tied them up in four bundles with string.

Following this he went down into the workshop where Tim Yarrow was busily working and who, on the sight of him, exclaimed, 'God! What's happened to you?'

Robert answered briefly: 'He aimed to blind me,

104

or finish me off. He just missed.'

'Almighty! Why?'

'Oh, you'll know all about it soon enough. The only thing I'll say to you now, Tim, is, it's got nothing to do with me . . . Look, I want me tools. Where's me box? It used to be here.' He went to the corner of the workshop and Tim Yarrow said, 'He moved it, up on to the shelf there.'

After he had gathered his tools together, Robert turned to Tim Yarrow, who had been standing silently by looking on, and said, 'Will you help me down with my things the back way? I'll put them on the handcart . . . I'll send it back.'

'Where you goin'?'

'Along to The Bull, they take a boarder in now and again. And there's an empty barn outside; Billy Taggart will likely let me store me bits of things in there. I'll send for them later on.'

'But man, you're in no condition to push a handcart all the way to The Bull. It's a weight in itself.'

'I'll manage.'

'If I asked him he'd let me give you a hand.'

'No, no. Thanks all the same, Tim. I'll ask no favour of him. He's given me enough, don't you think?' He motioned towards his head.

'Is it a big cut?'

'I don't know how long it is, I only know it goes well behind me ear and that it just missed my eye. By God! he could have blinded me. He's a madman.'

'Well, I wouldn't go as far as to say that. But he's got some very odd ways with him, I must say, and a vile temper. It's odd'—he shook his head—'he nearly did for your father you know.'

105

Robert turned towards him, a question in his eyes.

'Oh aye. They fought in the yard there like two maniacs, and he threw him into the saw pit, and would have finished him off if it hadn't been for me and old Roger Twait. Your mother was the trouble then. Yet, when you see him in church he acts like the angel Gabriel, and is as soft spoken as the Lamb of God himself.'

'He's a fanatic.'

'Aye, that an' all. But one thing you can say for him, he's honest. If he's in the wrong he'll admit it. He apologized to me once. Aye, he did. It was over an order about the painting of a farm cart. I said Farmer Reed had told us one thing and he said he had told us another. Well, I happened to be right and he came to me and said he was sorry. He's a strange man.'

'There was never a truer word. Come on, help me down with me things, will you?'

Tim Yarrow helped him down with the things. They loaded them on to the handcart, the tin box, the bass hamper, the books and the box of tools. And no one came from the house to see what was going on.

As he pushed the cart through the gate Tim Yarrow called, 'You'll never make it all that way. You look done in already. Why not slip down and ask one of the Mortons? Harold'll be in, he's on late shift.'

That would have been a good idea, except that to get to the Mortons he would have to pass the Parkins' door and Nancy had only to see him like this to find out the cause within minutes. And he could see her head wagging as she said, 'I'm not

106

surprised, not a bit.'

He never passed the Parkins' door unless he had to for, as Carrie had informed him some time ago, the rumour was he had let Nancy down, and his laughing reply to this had been, 'That's not right 'cos I've never picked her up.' Whereupon Carrie had giggled. But Carrie was giggling no more. He doubted if she'd ever giggle again while living in that house, in an atmosphere that was thick with retribution for sin.

Up till now he had imagined it was only Catholics that went crazy about religion, with their Confession, Communion, Easter duties, and such. They could be mortalious on a Saturday night, but you'd find them at Mass on a Sunday morning. What drew them? Fear, he thought. Yet after Mass, there they would be again filling the pubs the whole length of Jarrow. Methodists were almost as bad, he thought; but there was something to be said for them for they did go in for teaching, enlightened teaching. But his uncle was Church of England and of all the denominations they were the most easygoing. But then, he should know that there were extremists in every walk of life. Look at those in the shipyard for instance. He himself had always trod the middle way . . . Aye, and look where it had got him.

God, but he felt rotten.

It was just a little under two miles from the hamlet to The Bull and the only person he met on the road was a drover driving a couple of dozen cattle. The man did not speak to him, only paused and stared for a moment, then went on, yelling to his charges, 'Oop! there. Oop! there.' The children were at school and everybody else was about his business.

He made frequent stops on the way, but even so, on reaching The Bull and lowering the handles of the cart to let the two legs rest on the cobbles, he stood gasping, his body bent; and still in this position he looked through the open door to where Mrs Taggart was sweeping the sawdust from the taproom floor. On catching sight of him, she thrust the brush aside and, coming out, she stopped for a moment and, her eyes narrowing, she said, ' 'Tis you, Robbie?'

'Yes, Mrs Taggart, 'tis me.'

'What in the name of goodness has happened to you?'

'It's a long story. Can I come in?'

'Certainly. Certainly. Goodness me! Look at your head, lad. Have you had an accident?'

'Yes, you could say that.'

He did not resist her help as she led him into the taproom, calling as she did so, 'Billy! Billy!'

When her husband emerged from the cellar, saying 'What is it?' he stooped before approaching the settle, the private settle where Robert was now sitting, and after a moment he exclaimed, 'Why! what's up? You've been shot?'

He bent above Robert, and Robert, forcing a wry grin to his face, said, 'Something like that, except there was no gunpowder, 'twas a knife.'

'A knife?'

'Aye. Do you think I could have a drop of something . . . spirit?'

'Of course. Of course.' Mary Taggart now ran behind the counter while Billy, taking a seat on the opposite settle, leant forward and said, 'Trouble?'

'Yes, trouble.'

'With your uncle?'

'Who else?'

'Here, get that down you.' Mrs Taggart handed him a good measure of whisky and he gulped at it, then coughed and spluttered—he had no taste for whisky or spirits of any kind—the violent jerking of his head dislodged the rough bandage and caused Mrs Taggart to exclaim, 'My! Look at that gash.' She now unwound the bandage, talking all the while: 'Dear God! you're lucky. It's just missed your eye, and it could have gone through your head. What was it? A dagger? Look at this, Billy. It goes right past his ear. Eeh! you'll have to have this stitched. How did it happen?'

Before answering her, he took another sip from the whisky, and then he gave them details of the incident. And when he had finished, Billy Taggart said, 'And you have no idea who the fellow was, I mean that night, you didn't get a glimpse of him or anything?'

'No, just heard her giggling. But I only know that that wasn't the first time they had met up, and so he must be local. Anyway, the main point in my coming, Billy, is to ask if I could stay a few days until I find out what I'm going to do.'

'As long as you like.' The husband and wife spoke almost together. 'There's plenty places outside to store your stuff: you've got some nice home-made furniture, I know; Tim Yarrow told me about that. He's not very forthcoming is Tim, but he did say there wasn't a better worker with wood. Well, if I were you, I'd get upstairs and have a lie down. And Andy Patterson should be along any minute. He's doing the carrying now around this district and he passes Doctor Miller's house. I'll get

109

him to ask him to call in. Doctor Miller's a good doctor and he likes coming here. Doesn't he, Mary?'

She laughed. 'Oh aye, he likes coming here. Gets his whistle wet on his visits. I used to have him a lot for our Georgie, 'cos he caught everything under the sun from measles to T.B. And although that's cured, I always say he should never be working in the Brick Works. Still, that's beside the point. Come on, let's get you settled.'

*      *      *

He got settled in. He was put into a comfortable room, in a bedroom that had, of all things, a couch at the foot of the bed; and he lay on this and dropped into an exhausted sleep almost immediately. It was almost three hours later when he awoke to find the doctor's hand on him.

Doctor Miller was an elderly man, saying little, but looking a lot. He put eight stitches into the cut and when he had finished he said, 'There. You're lucky. Do you know that? You're lucky; it could have been your brain. The man's a maniac. What are you going to do about it? Take it up?'

'What do you mean, take it up?'

'Charge him with assault.'

'No . . . No, of course not.'

'I understand you don't hold yourself responsible for deflowering his daughter. Huh! That's how he would look at it, deflowering. The man's a religious maniac . . . You've got good blood, it clots easily. You should be thankful for that. But I'd keep quiet for a couple of days. Anyway, you're in good hands; Mary'll see to you.

110

My fee on this occasion will be three and six.'

Robert put his hand into his trouser pocket and drew out the coins and the doctor, taking them, said briefly, 'Drink plenty of stout, it'll make blood. Good-day to you.'

Robert mumbled his, 'Good-day,' and lay back. His head was aching. He wondered if he would have a scar from the corner of his eye. Well, he still had his sight, that was something. Three and six he had charged, that was for stitching him he supposed. The doctor in Jarrow only asked two shillings a time.

Say this one asked three shillings and sixpence for every call he made, he'd make some money in a week. But of course there was the travelling in between calls. It was a good job being a doctor, but then you had to have education. But with all his education, he bet he couldn't make a chair or a table. What day was it? It was Tuesday. No, no, it was Wednesday; yesterday was Tuesday. He felt dizzy, sleepy. He couldn't think straight. Well, what did it matter? He sighed deeply, closed his eyes. Then to his utter amazement he found that he was sitting by the water like that night in the moonlight, and he saw her coming towards him. She was coming over the foot of the couch, smiling widely. He had a return of the weird feeling of fear; then she was looking down into his face, saying, 'Oh, I'm glad you've come back.' And on this he fell asleep.

# CHAPTER THREE

He knew that there were debates in the taproom as to who had given Carrie Bradley the child. As Mary said, they were all with him with regard to the fact that it wasn't him. But it was Georgie Taggart who came nearest to the solution.

One night after closing time when they were all seated in the back room, Billy Taggart had been saying yet once again that Robert should go up to Foreshaw Park, for they still couldn't get anybody to take on the job. Admittedly the money wasn't good, Billy said, but he had to take into account he'd get his food and housing.

Yes, he knew Billy was right, but he couldn't say to him it wasn't a matter of money that was staying him but the fact that he'd been in contact with that girl, Thorman's Moth as they called her. Not that he was afraid of her or anything like that, in fact, he had liked what he saw of her. But there was something deterring him. Perhaps it was that bit of delirium he'd had after the doctor had stitched him up, when he had seen her coming over the couch at him. 'I'm glad you've come back,' she had said. That had been a weird feeling and had been as strong with him when he woke up as when it had happened. It was at this point in his thinking that Georgie exclaimed, 'I know. I've been wondering for some time, and now I remember. Dad, do you recall Stephen Crain who worked over at Dodsworth's?'

'Yes, yes, I recall him. What about him?'

'Well, do you mind the night they were all

arguing in the bar there about religion, and John Bradley's name came up and 'twas said how he held a tight rein on his lass and wouldn't let her out of his sight?'

'I recall them argufying about religion. But they're always on about something, and I never take in details.'

'Well I do. An' you must remember young Crain spluttering into his beer and you saying, "Hi up! there. I don't want it back." He messed up the counter. You remember?'

'Aye, aye I do, now I come to think.'

'And you asked him what he was laughing at, and you remember what he said back to you? 'Cos I was standing beside you.'

'No, no, I can't recall that, 'cos it's weeks gone.'

'He said, "You'd laugh an' all if I told you".'

'Well, what does all that mean? What are you leading up to?' his father asked, and Georgie said, 'Well, he skedaddled a month ago, or a bit afore that. Asked for his money one day and went off, just like that, the way he had come. He had been on the road last year, I understand, and Farmer Dodsworth took him on to see to the pigs and muck out an' things like that. It was no job. And he was a young good-looking fellow, remember?'

'Oh aye, I remember him. And you think . . . ?'

'Well, what do you think?' Georgie looked from one to the other. Then his eyes came to rest on Robert, and after a moment Robert nodded his head slowly and said, 'Could be, could be.'

'Like to bet it was,' Georgie said, ' 'cos if I'm not mistaken Farmer Dodsworth got things done in your shop, didn't he?'

'Yes, he did, now you mention it. And I

remember the fellow an' all. Aye, yes, indeed I do. Well, I'll be damned.' Robert rose to his feet, adding now, 'Just under their noses.'

'Well, if that's the case, there's nothing can be done about it.' Mary Taggart too got up from the table. 'It's a closed chapter, except for her. She's got to live in that house and bring up the child there. God help them both, that's what I say. And she was young and gullible. Poor lass.'

Looking at Mrs Taggart, Robert said, 'You're not blaming me for not taking her on, are you, Mary?'

'Oh, no, no, lad, no. I wasn't meaning that. Only you can't help feeling sorry for the lass, bringing a bastard into the world. They're not very welcome you know, bastards. And having to live with a man like that as its grandfather. Whether it's male or female it'll be reminded of its state from the day it leaves the breast I should imagine.'

A few minutes later they parted for the night, and as Robert went to his room he couldn't help but still think that there was a slight note of condemnation of him in Mrs Taggart's attitude. She was a woman, and of course looking at it from a woman's point of view, she might be thinking that he could have stood by Carrie.

But no, he could never have stood by Carrie. Nor could he have stood by Nancy Parkin or Polly Hinton in a similar predicament. He could never see himself getting tied to someone he didn't really care for, like loving. Yet he knew that he might never experience love, because to him this must be a feeling which would, in a way, obliterate himself. His feelings had so far not centered round whom he wanted, and whether or not he could put up

114

with her every day. Could he look forward to working for her for the rest of his life? Would he want to die if he lost her? No. As yet he had never felt anything like that, and he doubted if he ever would. But what did it matter? What he needed now was a job, because the bit of money he had saved wouldn't last forever, in fact it wouldn't take him further than the next three weeks.

This thought was with him as he got into bed. It was still with him as he lay wide awake at two o'clock in the morning. He did not go to sleep until he had made up his mind that on the morrow he would go to Foreshaw Park.

# PART THREE

## Service

# CHAPTER ONE

The drive was long and winding, becoming more unkempt the nearer it approached the house. He had come in by way of the North Lodge. There was no lodge-keeper, and it looked as if the lodge had not been occupied for years.

The gates had been closed but not locked. This had surprised him, until he had tried to lift the latch and found it firmly embedded in the slot. The young lass would have had a job to lift it on her own so that was likely why they hadn't bothered to lock it.

It was evident that this was the way used by the household, for there were deep wheel tracks, and also the imprints of horses' hoofs all over it.

When the drive turned abruptly and divided into two he was confronted by a large stableyard to the left and the house to the right.

He thought the house big but unimpressive: he had seen much finer places round about. He walked steadily into the stable yard where he stood looking about him for a moment. There wasn't a soul to be seen, nor yet the sound of any animal. Didn't they keep dogs?

When a cat strolled over to him and rubbed itself against his trouser leg, he put his hand down and stroked it, saying quietly, 'Hallo, miss. Anybody about?'

As if in answer, a young woman appeared from an alley-way. She was plump of body and face and her starched cap sat crookedly on her black untidy hair. It was she who spoke first. Advancing towards him, she said, 'Yes, an' are you after somethin'?'

'I . . . I've come after the job. I understand there is a vacancy.'

'Oh aye, aye.' Her words seemed laughter-filled: her face too expressed laughter and he noted that her body shook slightly as she talked, as the body is apt to do when hearing a joke. 'Oh'—she went on—'it'll be me Uncle Dave you're wantin', an' then the master. Come away in.'

He followed her across the yard then through a door and into a small boot room that led into a kitchen, telling himself that it was a good start anyway. And the girl was cheerful, and that made up for her being as plain as a pikestaff. In fact, in a way, he could say she was an ugly young woman, God help her. He laughed inwardly, for his thought sounded almost as Irish as she did. Her voice was raised now, saying, 'Here's a fellow after the job. Where's Uncle Dave?'

Peggy Waters took her hands out of a bowl of flour, clapped them twice together before drying them on a piece of coarse towelling that lay on the table, then looking at Robert, she said, 'You've come after the job?'

'Yes, missis.' He had thought it best to add the missis, she seemed to be the cook.

'Come and sit yourself down.' She pointed to the wooden settle that was set at right angles to the fireplace. 'And you, Betty'—she turned to the girl who was at the sink washing pans but whose attention had become diverted from her work—'go on outside and tell Mr Bloom he's wanted for a minute. And you Maggie, go and see Ruthie, she'll be in the dining-room. Tell her to go upstairs and see if her father is finished with the master, not to go into the room though, but to just wait. And when he comes out, tell him he's wanted down here; there's a man come after the job.'

Left alone now with this elderly woman, Robert looked at her. She didn't look his idea of a cook, he imagined cooks having a nature corresponding to their well-fed physical condition. But this woman had a sad expression. Perhaps he had come on a bad day for her: everybody had their good days and bad days.

She made no conversation, so he sat looking around the kitchen. It was long and high and definitely a working room. The upper part of one wall was taken up entirely with racks stacked with crockery, the bottom part acting as a sideboard with cupboards below. There was an iron oven at each side of the firegrate, and a scrubbed table took up the centre of the room. The floor was made up of large slabs of stone. The only signs of comfort were a rocking chair and an old horsehair chair placed at the opposite side of the fireplace from the settle. There were a dozen or more copper pans hanging on nails above the mantelpiece. Some were burnished, but those nearer the ceiling hadn't apparently been used for some time for they were dull and dust covered.

When both the door by which he had entered and the green baized one at the far end of the kitchen opened simultaneously he looked first one way and then the other. The girl who had been addressed as Betty came running into the room, saying, 'I told Mr Bloom; he says he'll be here directly.'

Through the other door there had come the Irish girl and a woman much older than her, a settled woman in her late thirties, and she too, he told himself, wasn't much to look at. But she had a kindly expression.

The one called Maggie and the one called Ruthie now stood at the end of the table and looked at him while Ruthie said, 'I told Dad. He'll be here in a minute, but he said he'd let the master know first.'

'What's your name?' It was the woman he thought of as the cook who had turned to him and asked the question, and he said, 'Robert Bradley, missis.'

'Bradley?' she repeated, screwing up her eyes. 'You from these parts?'

'Well, no. I only came here last year. I . . . I used to work in the carpenter's shop in the hamlet.'

'Which hamlet?'

'The one near Lamesley.'

'Then you're John Bradley's nephew, I take it?'

'Yes, that's who I am, missis.'

'Oh.'

The woman now turned and glanced at the other two standing at the end of the table. She took no notice of the young girl who was back at the sink but who had her head turned towards him.

When the woman looked at him again, her voice was stiff as she said, 'You're not there any longer I understand?'

'You understand right, missis.' His voice was as stiff as hers now. 'I'm at present staying at The Bull.' He had risen to his feet.

' 'Tis true that he tried to murder you, your uncle?'

'Be quiet, Maggie.' The woman turned on her.

'Well I was only saying, Aunty. Things get about.

122

You can't keep anythin' like that quiet, can you? Can you now, I mean?'

She had addressed Robert and he, in answering her, said, 'No, no, you can't. You're right there. Especially in a gossipy little village.'

'Oh, I don't know so much. They can do their share in the towns: clackety-clack, and . . .'

'*Maggie!* I've told you. Now get about your business.'

As Maggie turned to get about her business, Dave Waters entered the kitchen and it was evident that he recognized Robert immediately for, standing in front of him, he stared at him for some minutes before saying, 'You? And you've come after the job?'

'That's it.'

'Do you know what it entails?'

'I've been given a good idea.'

'Hearsay?'

'Yes, that's all I've had to go on.'

'Well, you'll have to see the master. It's up to him.' But the tone implied to Robert that if it had been left to this man he'd be out of the gates quicker than he came in; and as he went on listening to him explaining what the job entailed, he thought, he's doing his best already. Apparently he would have to do gardening, help with the horses, muck out, do hedging, do dry-stone-walling, besides carrying out whatever jobs were necessary in the house.

Robert stopped him at this point, saying, 'If you're intending to frighten me off, mister, you're wasting your time. I could take all that in me stride. Except the garden, but I'm quick at picking things up. And would you like to tell me now what wage

123

I'm to get for my Herculean tasks?' He had the pleasure of noting that the man was slightly taken aback by his use of the word Herculean, and also that it didn't do anything to help his case, for the man now snapped, 'The wage is ten shillings a week, your food and your lodgings. That's if you suit and that's got to be seen.'

He almost laughed in the man's face. Ten shillings a week! For years now on good weeks he had picked up two pounds or more, and here he was being offered ten shillings. He had heard they paid poorly, but this was an insult. He was twenty-five years old, it was nineteen hundred and thirteen, not a century earlier. He was about to say, to hell with you and your job, and then to stalk out, when once again the green-baized door opened and there came into the room a young woman. She was dressed in grey. Her dress was made of some kind of soft material and trimmed with white on the collar and cuffs. Her hair was a dark chestnut, dressed in rolls on the back of her head. Her eyes were large and seemed to pick up the colour of the dress. She was slightly above middle height. Her step had been quick when she entered the room but now it slowed as she neared the table, and her glance ranged between him and the old fellow standing opposite him. Then she too came to a stop at the end of the table next to where the one called Ruthie was still standing, and she stared at him and her head came slightly forward and her lashes blinked a number of times and the expression on her face told him she was trying to recall something. And then she was prompted by the man who said, 'This fellow's after the job, Miss Agnes. He's . . . he's the one you may remember who

124

trespassed that night.'

Agnes's lips fell apart. She stopped blinking and, her eyes wide, she continued to stare at the man. Yes, yes, she remembered. She recalled his face as she'd seen it that night, ablaze with temper. She also recalled that Millie had talked of him for days afterwards. And here he was, wanting to come into their employ. It wouldn't do. It wouldn't do. But only that morning she had said to her father, 'We must have more help; we just can't go on like this. And Hubbard will be the next one to go if he doesn't have more assistance. There's too much expected of them.'

The man was looking at her, right at her, boldly. He wasn't like any of the others who had come and gone within the last year. She found herself addressing him. 'My father will see you; he's in the study,' she said. 'Dave will show you the way.'

After Dave had reluctantly, it would seem, preceded the visitor up the kitchen and out through the door, Peggy Waters put her hands back into the flour and as she began rubbing it between her fingers she said, 'He's not the type that'll last long here. Bit of an upstart, I would say. Trying to ape his betters in the way he talks. And look at his clothes. You know who he is?'

'Yes. He's the man that Millie was talking to that night she went down to the water.'

'Oh, besides that. He's old John Bradley's nephew. You wouldn't know, but old Bradley is a carpenter down in the hamlet just a little way from Lamesley. And if the tales are true, there's been near murder done just lately down there. He's got a daughter, and she's got her belly full, and apparently he was named, that one.' She inclined

125

her head towards the far door. 'But he denied it and the father knifed him. You can see the scar running from his eye up into his hair. Did you notice it?'

'No. Is he still living there?'

'No, from what he says he's staying at The Bull, and to my mind he's not the type you should have here.'

'Well, his morals won't have anything to do with us, it's a worker we want.'

'Oh.' Peggy Waters again dusted the flour from her hands and, casting her eyes back towards the sink where Betty Trollop was now busily scrubbing the pans, she said, 'One never knows, you can't be sure of anything with men like that.' Her voice was now merely a whisper and she added, 'And then, if I remember rightly, Miss Millie took to him an' all, didn't she? Yapped on about him all the time. Anyway, if the master knows what he's been up to in the hamlet there won't be much chance for him.'

It was on this that Agnes turned away. The man's morals shouldn't affect her father very much, as his own certainly couldn't bear scrutiny. But she would rather know that he was indulging in immorality in Newcastle than sitting drinking himself blind as he was doing most nights now . . .

Robert stood in front of the desk behind which sat Reginald Thorman, and as he listened to the man talking he felt inclined to burst out laughing. If he were being interviewed for the post of High Commissioner somewhere or other abroad he couldn't have been interrogated more. Yet another part of him wasn't laughing at all. The man was, a phoney and he'd seen enough of the result of heavy drinking to know that this gentleman was a soaker.

He gave himself away in his voice as there was a permanent tremor in it.

'Have you any uniform?'

Had he any uniform! 'No, sir. I have never been in service before.'

'Oh, well, then you'll have a lot to learn. We live a different life you know, we people in the country, to those in the town. What did you say? Oh yes, yes. You did carpentry. Well, well, there's plenty of odd jobs around here that need a carpenter. You could see to them in your spare time. You say you haven't any uniform?'

Robert did not answer, but stood looking down on the man who, if he had been thinking clearly, would have recognized the disdain in the look.

It was true, Robert thought, what that fellow had said in Newcastle. He had met up with him in a bookshop. He was a pitman, and they were both looking at the same shelf and got to talking. Afterwards they'd had a drink together and talked books. The fellow had said that education had nothing to do with intelligence and that half the so-called educated were numskulls. The man said he was a hewer in Boldon Colliery pit, and he remembered he had been amazed to hear this for the fellow had been real learned and had read God knows what books he himself had never heard of. His name was Lawson, Jack Lawson. They had promised to meet again sometime, but as yet nothing had come of it. By! that fellow would have left this one flat with his knowledge.

How was it that men like this happened to get big houses and rule other people? Here he was, servants to wait on him, not many by the look of things, but still expecting to be adhered to, playing

127

Lord of the Manor to the very end. Aye, to the very end, because there was always somebody to come along and give the likes of him a helping hand, to see he didn't sink below his class.

'Waters has explained things to you, has he?'

'Yes.'

'What?'

'I said, yes.'

'You've forgotten something, man.'

God, why was he standing here taking this? The other one hadn't stayed long so he'd heard, but he himself would be gone afore he started. Yet he heard himself saying, 'Sir.'

'That's better. As I said, we live a different life in the country. People know their place. I suppose it was different in a shipyard. Well now, you will start as from tomorrow and we will see how you shape. Give you a trial, eh, say a month. That's all.'

Robert turned away without a word, but when he was about to open the door he saw that the man was standing behind the desk now, the colour of his face an almost scarlet hue, and looking as if he was on the point of making a protest. Hoping that he was, Robert paused for a second, but his new master resumed his seat.

He went out and down the passageway towards the hall. Within the archway he stopped and looked about him and the breath he drew in sprang his top waistcoat button. He felt it going and he picked it off the thread and put it in his pocket.

He was about to walk on when there came a cry from the stairway to the left of him, and, looking up, he saw the girl; in fact he saw the two of them, the sister also, and the sister was restraining the girl, holding her by the arms. But the girl called to

128

him in a high excited voice: 'Hello. Oh, I'm glad you've come back.'

The sensation he had experienced when he first saw her again ran through his body, not so much at the sight of her now, but at what she had said. They were the same words as when he had imagined she had come over the bottom of the couch at him: 'Oh, I'm glad you've come back.'

Why had he come here? God knew . . . he wished he did.

As he went past the foot of the stairs the older one was almost dragging her sister back up to the landing and the girl was protesting loudly, 'I just want to talk to him. He's nice.'

\*     \*     \*

Two days later he was installed in a room above the stables. His orders with regard to the garden he took from Arthur Bloom; those with regard to mucking out the horses and grooming from Greg Hubbard. But they both seemed to take their orders from Dave Waters, for it was this man, Robert realized, who ran the place and apparently had done so for years.

The boss, Hubbard said, rarely troubled them; and when the sons were home, it was young Master Stanley who apparently took over and did what bossing there had to be done. But even so he, too, seemed to defer to Waters. And Greg Hubbard warned him, keep away from Miss Millie, and that if she were to come trotting after him he should get into the open, for if Waters found her in any enclosed place with a fellow he seemed to go berserk. Sometimes, Hubbard said, you would think he was her father. As for Miss Agnes, Hubbard's opinion was that she was all right, a bit stiff but all right at bottom, and nobody envied her her job because if anyone saw to the running of the place, that was, anyone above Waters, it was her. She was almost a skivvy, the things she had to do, and worse off than the staff, so Maggie said, as she wasn't paid. What they would do when she left to get married, the Lord only knew.

The room above the stables was cramped. It had no heating except what came up through the floor from the horses. It had one small window and the whole place stank. Whoever had lived up here before had evidently forgotten what soap and water were for.

In his routine he rose at six and helped Hubbard to water and feed the horses, then helped with the strapping of them. All this was new to him. He had never imagined that a horse needed so much care and attention, nor that it needed so many bits and pieces of harness before it was ready for the road, nor that the gear, as Hubbard referred to it, required so much spit and polish. And of course, there was the mucking out. Following this he saw to the boiler for the pig swill and the hen crowdy. There were six pigs, one in litter, and four dozen hens.

At seven o'clock he went over to the kitchen with Hubbard and there, together with Arthur Bloom, they were each given a mug of tea. Following this the pigs were seen to, the hens let out and eggs gathered, the yard swept, and, what he hadn't bargained for and which Dave Waters hadn't mentioned in his list of duties, was the emptying of a row of slop buckets that Maggie and

Ruthie placed outside the side door. These had to be carried down the back garden to the cesspit. The first time he did this it turned his stomach and left him in no fit state to enjoy the communal breakfast.

Following the breakfast he was detailed, weather permitting, to turn and weed different plots in the garden. Should it be raining he was told he would work in the greenhouses.

Before the end of the first week he was repairing doors around the courtyard and renewing floor boards here and there. By six o'clock at night when he went into the kitchen for the last meal of the day he was so tired that afterwards he could not bother to get dressed and take a ramble, although he knew he should sometime go to The Bull, if only to tell the Taggarts how he was faring and to thank them once again for their kindness to him.

During the first week he had come across the mistress of the house only once, when she had come to the stables to tell Hubbard to get the trap ready as her father wished to go into town.

On that occasion she had paused for a moment before him, saying with some diffidence, 'How are you getting on?' To which he answered, 'Slowly, I think, miss.'

He noticed that she had a habit of blinking her eyelids which to him indicated some inner confusion, and when she said, 'It's not work you have been used to,' he replied, 'No; quite different, miss.'

'Yes, yes, of course.' She had turned away without further words, and he watched her walk out of the stable, thinking she was stiff-necked, definitely the county lady and not letting you forget

131

it. Yet there were all types of county ladies. There was that one who came into The Bull. The Taggarts thought the world of her. She sat in the back kitchen and drank with them. An earl's daughter, they said she was, who had married a farmer. But he was a gentleman farmer. Oh aye, he smiled to himself as he remembered the Taggarts emphasizing this, he was a *gentleman* farmer, with near two thousand acres.

There was one thing he had been made definitely aware of from the beginning, he wasn't accepted in the kitchen, at least not by Mr and Mrs Waters. Their daughter Ruthie was civil enough, and Betty Trollop an' all, she was a canny bairn. As for Maggie. Oh, Maggie would be civil to the devil. She was a lass, was Maggie. He had never known anyone with such a happy nature. Even the atmosphere in the kitchen couldn't quell it. She came out with things at the table that made the others splutter, all except her uncle, and she treated everybody alike. Last night he had wanted to hoot when her aunt pulled her up for her way of speaking without deference to Miss Agnes, and she had replied to the effect that of course she had respect for Miss Agnes, she respected her as she did all human beings, but she had no respect for animals because they hadn't souls. He hadn't been able to cover up his laughter and she'd put her hand towards him as she had cried, 'There. There, he understands what I mean, he knows I can't stand horses. I told you, didn't I? Things without souls can kick the daylights out of you.'

He could listen to Maggie for hours. She was a natural-born comic, but she didn't know it. That was her gift, she didn't know it.

It was in the early July when he had been at Foreshaw a few weeks that he was ordered to see to some sash-cords in the library windows, and he was busy on the job when he heard raised voices coming from behind a door that led into the drawing-room and he recognized them as those of the master and Miss Agnes, and although he knew it was her speaking he could hardly believe his ears for her voice was almost a bellow. Except that her tone was cultured it could have been that of any woman in Foxglove Road having a go at her man, or a neighbour, for she was yelling, 'You've got to listen to me. Soon the tradesmen won't be delivering at all. There's a stack of bills that you haven't looked at for months. The only one you have thought fit to see to is the wine merchant. And then there is the insurance on the furniture. It's lapsed . . .'

'Shut up! woman.'

'I won't shut up, Papa; this is serious. You've got to face facts, and the fact is we soon won't be able to eat unless we kill off the pigs and hens. And what is more, Dave and Peggy have never been paid for almost six months now. They put up with it, but the others won't. And what when the boys come home? Arnold would be here now if it wasn't for exams. And Roland and Stanley have had the good fortune to be invited to friends, but it's only for the next two weeks. What when they are all here for weeks on end during the vacation?'

'In the next two weeks, madam, things will be different, because I've got news for you, and listen

133

carefully to it: I intend to marry again.'

There was a dead silence. Robert looked towards the far door and in his mind's eye he saw the look on her face, lids fluttering and her mouth partly open.

And that's exactly how she did look, for as Agnes stared at her father and saw his bloated face, his nose already showing signs of his indulgence, she thought to herself who . . . who would marry him? And when his voice came at her yelling, 'That's surprised you, hasn't it? Taken the wind out of your sails,' she made no answer for a moment. When she did reply it was in a moderate tone, each word bearing weight: 'I am glad to hear it,' she said, 'and I wish your future wife luck in her position, for now I can be free to leave and lead my own life, free to marry. I only hope she brings with her enough money to engage a nurse for Millie.'

'*A nurse for Millie?*' He was screaming now. 'That's something else you've got to learn, miss. That one is going to be put away; I've already set the wheels in motion. I'm bringing no woman into this house to have to suffer that, by God! no.'

'You can't.' Agnes clasped her hands tightly together in front of her waist, her nails digging into the flesh. It was the only way to stop them thrusting out and tearing at this man's face, for in this moment she was consumed with hate of him. The feeling had been pressed down under a cover of dislike for years, but now, for a moment, she too felt insane with the intensity of it. That he meant what he said she knew only too well. And she also knew only too well that it could be brought about, especially if doctors were brought here to see Millie as she was at the present moment, for she was in one of her turns. As a rule these lasted only a couple of days, but for the past three nights she'd had to sleep in her room to prevent her wandering, and to try to still her constant talking.

'You can't do it! You won't do it!'

'*I can't?* Oh, but I can and I will, and I am going to. But there's one alternative, miss. You're always yapping on about getting married, aren't you? Well, go to your James and ask him if he'll accept another partner into the marriage. I'm sure his mother will welcome her with open arms.'

She glared at him, unable to speak now, but his jest had brought an idea flashing into her mind. The estate of Haughton Manor where the Crockfords lived was small, but there was a hunting lodge at the far end of the grounds. It had been unoccupied for years. Millie could live there with a nurse in attendance. But would James allow it? Yes, yes, she could persuade him. And she would talk to Grace and Marie; they were very amiable girls and they had liked Millie . . . His mother? . . . Oh, James would persuade her. He must. He would. She had never asked anything of him before.

She drew in a long breath. She would best him. She would best this man who had never in his life shown her any love and affection, and very little too for her mother. She said now, 'I hope your wife will be able to supply you with enough money to support your mistress.'

His lips moved upwards and away from his teeth, the upper one quivering in a sneer as he said, 'There won't be any need. In fact, there never has been any need; she's not that kind of a mistress. It may surprise you to know that at one time she was a close friend of your mother's . . . Ah, yes, that does surprise you, doesn't it, madam? She was widowed young and left very warmly off, so once she is established here as my wife, there'll be no worry about us not eating'—he stressed the word—'the only reason why she hasn't been here before now is the vital sore point in my life, which whether you know this or not is none of my flesh, for I never fathered an idiot.'

'I hate you. Do you know that? I hate you. And this moment I too wish I wasn't of your flesh, which to my mind is rotten . . .'

When his hand came out and caught her across the side of the face, she cried out as she staggered back and, grasping at the arm of a chair, she fell sideways on to it; and his voice came at her, yelling, 'For the rest of the time you are under my roof I shall certainly give you plenty of cause to hate me. You'll see that, madam.' And with this he stalked out of the room, banging the door behind him . . .

When Robert heard the sound of the slap and the cry that followed it, he left the window and moved towards the communicating door. But there he stopped, telling himself that if he went in there, it would likely mean the end of his job here. However, when he heard a further door clash closed and the sound of a low moan, his hand went out to the knob and, turning it quietly, he pushed the door ajar. And there he saw her huddled in an armchair, her body shaking with her weeping. Slowly now he advanced into the room and when he stood opposite her he said quietly, 'Can I help, miss?'

Agnes took her hands from her face before turning swiftly from him, saying, 'Go away. Please

136

go away.'

He went away, not by the same door, but through into the hall and then on to the kitchen. Going straight to Peggy, where she was lifting a shelf of loaf tins from the oven, he said, 'I . . . I think you should go and see to Miss Agnes. There's been a do in the drawing-room. He hit her.'

The loaf tins were slipping from the shelf before it reached the table and, her hands still on it, she turned to him and said, 'What? What did you say?'

'The master and Miss Agnes, I heard them from the library where I was working, they were having an argument. He hit her, and she's crying her eyes out.'

Without a word, she sped up the kitchen, leaving him looking at Maggie who was now turning the bread out of the loaf tins and tapping the bottom of the loaves with her knuckles, and as she did so she talked as if she were addressing the loaves, saying, 'I'm not agenst a man drinkin', I even like a drop of port meself, but he's been washin' himself in it these last few weeks I would say. Begod! the money he swilled down his neck just last night would have pacified the coal man the day.' She now looked up at Robert, adding, 'Did you hear the rumpus in the yard? Wasn't going to leave the load, he wasn't. If it hadn't been for Uncle saying he would see to the bill if it wasn't settled within the week, just for this load like, not for the rest, he would have turned his backside and that of the horse on us and yanked it all back, and then where would we have been? Burnin' wood I expect. There's plenty of it, but it's a shame it is to cut down trees. What did he hit her with? His fist or did he throw somethin'?'

'I think he slapped her face.'

137

'Oh—' She turned from him and went to the oven, saying now, 'I wish I was a man. Oh, the times I've wished that. I sometimes think they only left one part off me when I was born, because in spite of all me good humour I have urges to hit out meself.' She turned and looked at him over her shoulder. 'Would you believe that now?'

He had to smile, and he said, 'I'd believe anything you say, Maggie, anything.'

'You're a nice man. I said it from the beginning. No matter what t'others think, you have me opinion, you're a nice man.'

There was no smile on his face now, but his voice was gentle as he said, 'Thank you, Maggie,' then added, 'I'd better get back to me work.'

'I would if I were you, but go t'other way, not the way you come.'

'Of course. Of course. I never ask for trouble.'

'I don't meself, but with me it never waits for the askin', it nearly always gallops half-way to meet me.'

He went out to the sound of her laughter. Nothing seemed to down Maggie. She was a great spirit. She seemed the only bit of lightness in this tormented house, except for the poor creature that was the centre of the trouble.

He had seen Millie at close quarters only twice since he came, but both times she had been accompanied, once by Miss Agnes, the other time by Mr Waters. It was strange the affection that old fellow had for her. His whole manner changed when he looked at her: it was as if he were indeed her father, and a loving, caring one at that. In a way, he was another like his uncle, but not so obsessed he hoped . . .

138

The window sash was back in place and he was gathering up his tools to move further along the room when the far door of the library opened and who should come in but the young creature herself. She was dressed in a blue print dress; her hair hung slack down her back, tied loosely with a blue ribbon that finished in a bow on the crown of her head. For a moment she seemed surprised to see him; then coming towards him, she said, 'Are you working?'

'Yes, miss. I'm putting in window sashes.'

'You call them sashes?'

'Yes, miss.'

'I thought only dresses had sashes.'

'Well, these are a different kind of sash, miss.'

'It's a very nice day, isn't it, Bradley?'

'Yes, miss.'

'They say I've got to call you Bradley, but I like Robert. Still that is your name, isn't it . . . Bradley?'

'Yes, miss. That is my name.'

'Do you mind if I sit and watch you work?'

He paused before he said, 'No, not at all, miss.' And as he eased off the old frame of another window he wondered whether any doctor would dare to certify a lass that was talking as calmly as this one was. The only odd thing about her so far was that she wanted to sit and watch him work.

'It's a very nice day, isn't it?'

'Yes, it is, miss.'

'Strange, isn't it, Bradley? But I have no desire to take walks in the daytime. I do go for walks but then it's mostly with Aggie or Maggie or one or other of them. But I like to walk at night-time, because the world is quiet at night-time. The birds are asleep, except the owl and the bat; they too like

139

to come out at night-time. I know a story about why the owl and the bat come out at night-time. Do you like stories, Bradley?'

'Some, miss.' He took part of the framework down and laid it along the bare boards that edged the carpet all round the room.

'I can't read or write, Bradley. Do you think that is strange? I am seventeen years old. No, Aggie says . . . eighteen . . . now, yet I can't read or write. Aggie reads beautifully. Do you read, Bradley?'

'Yes, I read a lot, whenever I can.'

'Oh, that is strange.'

'Why is it strange, miss?'

'Because Dave says I hadn't to worry about not reading or writing because most people can't read or write, like servants. And you are a servant, aren't you, Bradley?'

He raised his eyebrows, pursed his lips, picked up a chisel and went to the window before he said, 'Aye, miss, yes, that's what you could say, I'm a servant.'

'And you can read and write?'

'I can read and write, miss. And it isn't true that most people can't read or write.' Immediately he had spoken he knew he had said the wrong thing. Then he added quickly, 'What I mean is, it isn't necessary that everybody should read or write.'

'Bradley.'

'Yes, miss?'

'I'm not very happy.'

'You're not, miss?' He stopped, turned and looked towards her.

'No, I am not, Bradley. But most times I feel happy. I used to sing inside especially on moonlight nights, but now I don't want to sing. I feel very odd

140

at times and, and I'm afraid.'

'Oh'—he took a step towards her—'don't be afraid, miss. There's nothing to be afraid of.' Little did she know, poor creature, that she had everything to be afraid of. In her odd way she was alive to the atmosphere in the house, and she could probe it.

'I . . . I would die if Aggie went away. I couldn't live without Aggie.'

He said nothing to this but stood looking down at her. Then he started as there came a sharp rap on the window, and there standing glaring at him was Dave Waters. Taking a piece of wood from the floor, he quickly pushed it under the frame of the upper part of the window and, grasping the hooks attached to the bottom of the window, he hauled it upwards, to be met with the harsh whisper of, 'What do you think you're up to now?'

And as quickly and as harshly he answered back, 'Look here, Mr Waters, I'm doing me job. The miss came in and sat down and talked. She's distressed. Now don't make matters worse.'

The man stared at him; the muscles of his face worked, and then he said, 'Aye, well.' And he made an attempt to step over the sill; but Robert's hand checked him for a moment and under his breath he said, 'I don't know whether you know it or not, but there's been trouble indoors between the master and Miss Agnes. She . . . the lass senses it.'

Their faces were close and they stared into each other's eyes for a moment and Robert thought he detected a glimmer of understanding in the older man's face. Stepping aside, he made way for him to enter the room, then listened with interest as he spoke to the girl, addressing her in fatherly tones, saying, 'There you are, me dear. I've been looking for you.'

'Have you, Dave? Well, I've just been sitting here talking to Bradley. He's a great reader, is Bradley. Did you know that, Dave? And I think we should ask Aggie if he can read the books in here'—she spread her arm outwards—'because nobody ever reads these books, do they?'

'They are not the kind of books people want to read, me dear. They're all about coal mines and engines and shippin' and the like. But come along, come along to the kitchen, I think Peggy's been bakin'.'

'Oh, has she?'

'Yes, and you'd like a hot currant bun, wouldn't you?'

'Oh, yes, I would, Dave.'

As she rose Dave Waters turned to Robert, saying, 'I was looking for you. I want you to take the cart into Birtley to the chandlers to get some feed. Ask for a fellow called Eddie Palmer, he'll give it to you without any trouble. Try to avoid Mr Taylor . . . he's the boss. Go in the side door; you'll likely see Eddie there. He'll know what to give you. Just leave that'—he pointed—'you can finish it the morrow.' Lowering his voice, he added, 'But don't go until the master leaves; he's taking the trap now. In the meantime you can harness the horse.'

Robert began to gather up his tools while Dave Waters took Millie by the arm, and as he went to lead her from the room, she turned in Robert's direction, saying, 'Thank you, Bradley. It was nice talking to you.'

In the drawing-room she said to Dave Waters, 'He's a nice man, isn't he, Bradley? He's kind and

142

he reads. I think he's very clever to bc able to read, don't you, Dave?'

Dave Waters muttered something under his breath, then opened the far drawing-room door and she went before him at a tripping run now across the hall and into the kitchen. But on seeing Agnes by the fire with Peggy bending over her, she paused, seeming to sense there was something wrong and to shy away from it. But Dave gently pressed her forward and as he seated her in the rocking-chair Peggy addressed him without looking at him, 'It's coming to something when he starts using his hands. He's hit her.'

'Why?' Dave too was bending towards Agnes now, but before she could make any reply Peggy, straightening her back, turned to where Maggie was coming into the kitchen with a bowl full of eggs and she said to her, 'I'm wantin' some fruit for the pudding the night. Take Miss Millie here with you and she'll help you to pick some. Blackcurrants I think we'll have.'

After one glance at Agnes's lowered head Maggie took in the situation and, going to Millie, she held out her hand, saying, 'Come away with you, miss. We'll go and raid the garden. What do you say?'

'Well, if you would like that, Maggie.' There was a note of reluctance in Millie's voice, but nevertheless she rose from the chair as Maggie said, 'I would like that dearly, because there's nothin' I like better than a bit of company, good company like yourself.'

At this, Millie gave a tinkle of a laugh and she looked towards the others as she said, 'Maggie's funny.'

143

'I am that. I am that. And nobody knows better than meself how funny. When the good Lord thought me up He said, "I'll make her nothin' to look at but she'll be good to listen to." Come away with you now an' listen some more.'

As the door closed on them Agnes raised her head. One side of her face was scarlet, the other very pale. And looking up at Dave, she said, 'He's going to be married . . . Father, and he's already making arrangements to put her away.'

'*No! No!*' Dave backed from her. 'He wouldn't.'

'He would. Oh yes, he would, and he can. He can ignore Doctor Miller and in fact I'm sure he will because he doesn't like him. And he can get two other opinions. Doctors are not above bribes.'

'In the name of God!' Dave put his hand to his brow and turned away; then as quickly turned back to her again as he asked, 'Who is it? Who's he bringing here?'

Agnes turned her head to the side and as she was about to answer Peggy put in angrily, 'His harlot, who else? But meself, I thought there was something had gone wrong atween them and that's why he had taken to the bottle; and, too, he's been in the house for days at a time these past weeks, and that never used to happen. He was never away from her.'

'Was she a friend of Mother's? Did you know her?' Agnes's softly spoken question brought a big 'Huh!' from Peggy before she said, 'Know her! Yes, I knew her. She was never out of this house at one time years ago when your mother and father were first married. Your mother's best friend she was supposed to be. Best friend indeed! Even in those days two wasn't enough for her because her man

144

was alive then. I don't know how the master's kept her all these years? Oh, but I do, money. According to Greg, who's seen her lately, she's laden down with expensive jewellery. She always was an expensive hobby.'

'Do . . . do you think the boys know?'

She addressed this question to Dave Waters, and his answer was brief: 'They are men, they'd be blind if they didn't,' he said.

Agnes now sat looking down into the cup of tea that Peggy had handed to her and, shaking her head slowly, she said, 'What's going to be done?'

No one answered, and in the short silence there emerged from the long scullery Betty Trollop. She had likely heard every word that had been said. But that didn't seem to matter; they took no notice because Betty too was like one of the family. She had been working in the kitchen since she was eight years old. As she laid a loin of chops on the table Peggy, looking towards her, said, 'Get them cut up and put in the oven.' And Betty, taking a chopper from a drawer, put the loin on the chopping board and began hacking at it.

Each blow of the chopper as it struck the bone seemed to vibrate through Agnes's head. Her nerves were on edge; her mind in a whirl, yet all the time asking the same question, What was to be done? What could she do? Well, there was only that one avenue left open for her, James, and the hunting lodge. She would put it to him when he came tonight . . . She checked her thinking for a moment: the question was, if he came tonight. She hadn't seen him for nearly a fortnight. The last time they had talked, he had told her how very busy he was. He had been doing a round of the shops,

145

checking up on the managers; there had been some pilfering at one place, and things like that could spread. It was very worrying. Well, if he didn't come tonight, tomorrow might be too late. Her father could do as he had threatened and bring doctors here and that could be the end of Millie, and of them all, for, as strange as it might appear, it was Millie who seemed to hold them together.

She rose so quickly to her feet that she startled Peggy, and when she said, 'I'll go. I'll go now,' Dave Waters peered at her as he asked, 'Go where?'

'To Haughton. I'll . . . I'll see James.'

'But . . . but what could he do, my dear?'

She turned now and looked at Peggy and only stopped herself from saying, 'He could marry me right away.' But what she said was, 'He'll . . . he'll think of something. There's the hunting lodge, you know. If . . . if he let me take Millie there. Would you come? I mean . . .'

'Oh, lass, yes, yes.' Dave held his hands out towards her, then asked, 'But how are you goin' to get there? The master's taken the trap, and Prince is not fit to ride. An' Bradley's goin' in with the cart to Birtley for feed.'

'Has he gone?'

'Who?'

'Bradley.'

'No, I don't think so.' He turned quickly to the window and looked from side to side before saying, 'He's just on his way. But you wouldn't ride on the cart along of him, would you?'

'What does it matter how I get there, as long as I get there and quickly.' Agnes now turned from them and hurried out of the kitchen. And as Dave made for the door leading into the yard, Peggy called to him, 'What do you think? He's not that kind of man.'

'We'll see. We'll see,' he replied. 'If he wants her he'll do as she asks.'

Robert was leading the horse towards the gate when Dave Waters called to him, 'Hey there! wait a minute.' And when he reached the cart he looked up at Robert and said, 'Miss Agnes is comin' along. She wants to get to Haughton. It's a mile or so out of your way. She'll direct you.' Then after a pause he added, 'And mind your p's and q's.'

Robert's face was tight as he looked down on the older man, saying, 'I know my p's and q's, and the whole alphabet for that matter. You've got no need to tell me how to act, mister.'

Once again Dave Waters was taken aback by the nerve of this fellow, and he stared at him in hostility. It more than vexed him that the man wouldn't defer to him or to anybody else for that matter. But wait, his boldness would get him into trouble sooner or later. Let him take that tack when the young masters were about and he would soon see where he stood. But then he was of such a temperament that he would likely walk out: his kind didn't think of the morrow and where their next bite was coming from; they were of a new generation who didn't like bending the knee.

He stepped back from the cart as Agnes came hurrying across the yard, the while fastening the buttons of her dust coat.

On the sight of her Robert moved along the seat and, when Dave Waters helped her up into the cart, he was about to put out his hand and take her arm, but thought better of it. His hands on the reins now, he jerked them, at the same time saying, 'Get

147

up there!' And the cart moved forward out of the cobbled yard on to the gravel drive.

They were through the gates and on to the main road before she spoke. Her voice low, she said, 'Will you please turn off right at the crossroads, Bradley, I . . . I want to go to Haughton. Do you know where that is?'

'No, miss. I've never been that way.'

'It's . . . it's about two miles from the crossroads. The gates are on the main road. I'—she paused—'I don't know whether I shall need you for the return journey. If Mr Crockford is at home he'll undoubtedly bring me back, but if he shouldn't be there, I . . . I'd be obliged if you would make your way back to pick me up. How long will the business take you in Birtley?'

'I'm not sure, miss. I've been once before but that was with Hubbard. I think it took a couple of hours there and back, that was right to the house. But if I put a spurt on I might be able to be back in just over the hour or so. Anyway, I could bring the cart up to the house and wait.'

'No, no!' The words were brusque and she had no need to add, not the cart.

Of course not the cart; he should have known that a cart like this was no vehicle on which to take a lady visiting. Mr Waters had been right, he didn't know all his p's and q's.

She turned her head and looked at him now as she said, 'I'd be obliged if you would wait outside the gates.'

'I'll do that, miss. And I'll be as quick as I can.'

'Oh, you needn't rush. If Mr Crockford is to bring me home I shall leave word for you at the gate and you needn't wait.'

148

'Very good, miss.'

They sat in silence now. The horse plodded on and the clip-clop of its hooves became loud in his ears. He would like to remark on the countryside; he would like to talk to her, but it was evident she was in a state and that she was going to this fellow of hers for help. Why hadn't he married her before now? He had been courting her for years, so he understood. But then courtships did go on a long time, at least in the working class they did, because as a rule they had to get together their bits and pieces with which to set up house. But it should be different in the class. They weren't short of a bed or furniture. No—he shook his head at himself—that was true, they weren't short of a bed or furniture, but they were short of some place to put it. Perhaps they had no more taste for living with in-laws than their inferiors had.

If he knew anything there was going to be changes up at the house, and very soon. A break-up all round. Well, it wouldn't matter to him. He would get a job somewhere and this time he'd sell his own bits and pieces, for they were hanging like millstones around his neck. He had been toying with the idea for some nights past now of trying Australia or Canada. America he thought was overrun, all Ireland seemed to have gone there. But anyway, he wouldn't be sorry to leave this job, for none of them had taken to him, except perhaps Maggie. But then she'd take to a clothes prop with trousers on, she was so kindly.

There was an oppressive feeling about the place, and he had been looking forward to tonight to get along to The Bull and exchange news with the Taggarts. From what he had gathered from Tim

Yarrow's last visit to the inn his uncle had practically tied Carrie up, and Tim thought the old boy was going off his rocker. But it was Mrs Bradley Tim said he was sorry for.

He, too, was sorry for his aunt. But in a way she was to blame, at least in part, for what had happened. He'd have likely been still living there if she hadn't tried to shoulder him with Carrie's misdeed. Poor Carrie. He couldn't help but feel sorry for the lass. But they weren't the only ones who had trouble; there was trouble in high places too.

'We are here. Will you stop please?'

He hadn't noticed the gates, they were set well back in a half-moon from the road and there was no wall or fence leading up to them, not on this side anyway. The border consisted of an avenue of trees that you could walk into from the road. There was likely a fence someway behind them, because he couldn't see any of the land-owners leaving their parks open to the casual passer-by.

He had jumped down from the cart and was now helping Agnes to the ground. When his hand gripped her elbow, he felt the thinness of it and was in a way reminded of Miss Millie. Somehow there seemed to be the same quality about them both, only where Miss Millie was open and embraced the world in her naivety, this one lived as it were behind tight shutters, rarely allowing her natural self to peep through.

'Thank you, Bradley.'

'Goodbye, miss.' He didn't know why he had said that, but she turned as she went round the back of the cart and paused for a moment before answering, 'Goodbye, Bradley.'

150

She walked through the gates and up the well-kept drive towards the house. But before she reached the end of the drive she paused on the sound of laughing voices coming from the left of her. That was where the lawn tennis court was. She had been on the court only twice. She was no hand with a racquet, and on both occasions she knew James had become irritated with her, although he had laughed at her efforts.

The tennis court was on the west side of the house and steps from a terrace led down to a large lawn facing it. Sometimes the family had tea there, but it was past tea-time now. Likely it was the girls playing with some visitors. James wouldn't be playing, for he was rarely at home before five o'clock, and it had only just turned five. She paused and looked towards the house, low spread and spruce. It wasn't nearly as big as their own house, but it was so well kept that it made her feel at this moment that she had come from some slum habitation; and that was likely how James viewed her home.

Mrs Crockford, she guessed, would be ensconced in the drawing-room working at her endless tapestry. It wasn't likely she would be out in the sun: she didn't like the sun; it wasn't good for the skin, she had said. In her late forties she remained a vain woman, but she was still very good-looking. James took after her in this way.

She told herself that she would rather talk to the girls and find out if James was in or when he was expected, so she took the narrow path that led from the drive towards the tennis court, and at the end of it she stopped abruptly, for there in white flannel trousers and a cream silk shirt stood James poised to serve to his sister. The two girls were on the far side of the court, and James's partner, she saw, was a tall fair girl whose face was bright with laughter.

It was Marie Crockford who caught sight of her first and she cried to her brother, 'James! James! Look! Look behind you. Here's Agnes.'

James stopped in the act of picking up a ball, then turned abruptly towards her, and she sensed immediately that he wasn't pleased to see her. His step was slow as he came across the grass. She had not moved from the end of the path and when he stood in front of her he said, 'Well, this is a surprise.'

'Yes, I suppose it is.' She could not keep the tartness from her tongue, and she went on, 'I didn't really expect you to be at home as I knew you had been so busy of late.'

She watched his jaw move from side to side before he said, 'Yes, I've been busy of late, Agnes. But I took a little break this afternoon as we have a friend staying, Grace's friend Eileen, Eileen Chambers. I . . . I don't think you have met.'

'No, we haven't met.'

'Well, come and be introduced.'

'I . . . I would rather not, if you don't mind James, but I would like to speak to you privately.'

'Well . . . well I was just in the game. Is it important?'

'It's very important.'

'Oh.' He turned now to where his sisters and Miss Chambers were standing and he called to them, 'I'll see you in the house later.' And at this Marie called, 'Wouldn't you like a game, Agnes?' And Agnes replied, ' No thank you, not now.'

152

'We'll see you then,' said Marie. And to this Agnes inclined her head before turning away and walking back up the path on to the drive.

They had walked a few steps side by side before James Crockford said, 'Would you like to see Mother?'

'No, no. I'd rather not. I . . . I just want to talk to you.' She turned and looked at him, her face now soft, the appeal in her eyes deep, and he sighed and said, 'Trouble?'

'Yes, you can say that, trouble.'

Inside the house the impression was the same as outside, everything was spruce. The furniture somewhat modern but good, the carpet covering the entire floors was of a deep red and seemed to spread its glow everywhere. The first time she stepped inside this house, she had thought, how wonderful. I'll likely be mistress of it some day. Now she wasn't so sure, she wasn't sure at all.

He had led her into his study and although he didn't actually take his seat behind the desk he did, after he had seen her seated, sit against the edge of it. Then, his head poked forward, he said, 'Well, what is it? What has happened?' And without any preamble she answered, 'Father is going to marry again. The woman is . . . is she who has been his mistress for years. And he is determined to put Millie away. I can't stand it, James. I just can't stand it. I couldn't stand living in the same house with that woman, much less could I stand Millie being put away. Oh'—she put her hand up—'I know what you think should happen to Millie and I know you will say, as you have said so often, it would be the best thing for her, but it would be like caging a lark. Can't you see?'

153

She watched him get to his feet and pass her and go towards the empty fireplace, and there, turning sideways to it, he leant his elbow on the mantelshelf before he said, 'Yes, I can see, and I can see it's the best and only thing for Millie. It'll come in the long run. You've got to face that, Agnes. If anything should happen to you tomorrow, she would be put away. As it is, you are prepared to make a number of people embarrassed, even miserable, because you won't face up to the fact that Millie isn't normal. And I'm telling you, something will happen some day to her and the matter will be taken out of your hands.'

'Well, until that something happens, James, I can't let her be put away. Doctor Miller says she is not mad or insane, not in the accepted sense.'

'Doctor Miller is an old fool. He's drunk half his time and will say anything to please anyone as long as it means he will not have to bother himself. And I am going to say this straight to you, Agnes. I understand your father's attitude in this. I may not condone his marriage to this particular woman, but that is his own business. And think, Agnes, you couldn't possibly expect him to bring his wife into that house with a crea . . . with a person like Millie there.'

'You were going to say creature, weren't you?'

'Yes, I was.'

'I can't understand you. I . . . I can't, James. And now you will never understand me or the reason for my visit, but I'm appealing to your compassion, I . . . I want to ask you if you will let us, if you'll allow me to bring Millie here. I mean to the hunting lodge. I could bring Dave and Peggy with me. You would not see her, I can promise you. You would

154

not be troubled with her.'

He had stepped from the fireplace and he was standing stiffly now, his arms held out some little distance from his sides, his whole attitude one of utter incredibility. His face was so screwed up that his eyes had become slits and through them he peered at her, saying, 'You too must be out of your mind. You propose to bring your sister here knowing what I think about the whole situation? Huh!' His arms now sprang outwards and they remained so as he swung round, and now, with his index finger, he pointed towards the door, saying, 'Across that hall in the drawing-room sits my mother. You know my mother, don't you, Agnes?'

She made no reply, she just continued to stare at him.

'Well, apart from your preposterous suggestion, which not even I would dare put to her, she's not in favour of our marrying. I might as well tell you the truth. And what is more, Agnes, I at this point can't see any use in furthering our friendship, because there is no way you are going to alter your mind about your sister. Now is there?'

She continued to stare at him and as she did so a strange thing happened: she saw his clothes drop from him. He stood before her mind's eye stark naked. Then his skin seemed to melt and she saw his skeleton. Then that too disappeared, at least up to his neck, and the only thing that was left was his head and his heart, and she saw that the heart was encased in a box. But behind his skull his brain was working. Like thousands of worms crawling over each other, she saw it working. Then the whole of him disappeared, and in his place stood the tall fair girl with the blonde hair, and immediately she

155

recognized her. He had said they had never met and he was right, they had never met. But she had heard her mother speak of the Chamberses. They were wealthy, millionaires in fact, with steel works and rolling mills.

She put her hand up to her head and as she did so she pushed her hat to one side, then made an effort to straighten it. She was still staring at him but asking herself now, was she going mad? Had the thing that had touched Millie also touched her?

Well, it was over. What had possessed her to come? Why had she thought that anything she could say to him would have any effect? Because he didn't love her. Had he ever loved her? Why had he asked her to marry him in the first place? Had he seen her as someone he could dominate? No, no, that wasn't the reason, because she had never been pliable. Then why? Why? Then she had the answer. He had asked her to marry him because he loved to wallow in adoration and she had openly adored everything about him from the first moment they had met. But as her adoration had worn thin so his need for her had evaporated.

Well, it was over and God knew what she was going to do. But there was one thing she could do, and with dignity.

Slowly she drew off her engagement ring and handed it towards him. Her eyes were steady on his face, which was now suffused with colour. And when he said, 'No, no, Agnes, you can keep it. And . . . and there's no reason why we shouldn't still be friends,' his use of the word friend for the second time to explain their association that was meant to culminate in marriage was like a knife cutting the thread of her self control. Away went all thoughts

156

of dignity: her voice now almost a yell, she cried at him, 'You previously alluded to our years of engagement as our friendship. Friendship indeed! It was a promise of marriage, remember? You asked me to marry you, and you have the gall to term the years that I've wasted my love on you as a time of friendship. Well, the friendship is ended finally. Take it!' She flung the ring into his face, and when the row of five diamonds hit his lower lip the end stone pierced the skin causing a trickle of blood to run down his chin.

His handkerchief held to his mouth, he stared at her in amazement, and what he said now was, 'It is just as well it is ending now because you are showing evidence that it is not only your sister who is tainted.'

She looked quickly to the right and then to left of her; she had the desire to pick up something and break it over his head. Only the fact that she would be acting like any common slut prevented her from seizing the heavy glass inkwell from the table and hurling it at him. However, fearing that if she stayed one minute longer she might be driven to do just this, she flung round and rushed from the room.

As she entered the hall his mother was crossing it obviously to come to the study, likely to see what all the narration was about, and before she could speak Agnes cried at her, 'Go and attend to your little boy, his lip's cut.' And then she even horrified herself when she added, 'You didn't breed a man, only something that dresses like one. He's gutless.' And she had the satisfaction of seeing Mrs Crockford lean back against the panelling of the passage with her hand across her mouth. Then she made for the front door. Once outside and down the steps, she ran. She ran the length of the drive, through the gates and into the road. There was no sign of the cart. But then there wouldn't be, she hadn't been in there more than half an hour.

She now put her hand up to her brow and held the weight of her head for a moment as she said to herself, 'Oh my God! Oh my God!' Something had happened to her. Perhaps she was like Millie. Perhaps what had just happened was a kind of turn like Millie had. But Millie never cried and she now wanted to cry. Oh dear God, how she wanted to cry. She walked a few yards down the road; then crossed the shallow ditch and stepped in among the trees. It was cool here. She leant her back against an oak and looked up into the branches, and she asked aloud, 'What came over me?'

She was given no immediate answer, she only knew that somewhere a door had opened inside her and that it would be impossible to close it from now on.

But what was going to happen to them? What was going to happen to Millie? What was going to happen to herself? Because if they did manage to put Millie away, she herself couldn't live in that house with her father and that woman. She felt she was standing on the brink of a new existence: Millie gone, or Millie with her, things would never be the same again. And she would never be married. No, she would never be married. The thought brought a pain between her ribs as if a knife had pierced them, and she turned now and pressed her chest to the trunk of the oak and spread her arms around it and her lips against the rough ridges of the bark in an effort to quell the great wave of emotion that

158

was about to overwhelm her.

When the storm burst within her she gasped and felt for a moment that she was choking with the constriction in her throat. Then the tears, forcing their way out, sped from her eyes, her nose and her mouth, and unheeding that she was out in the open air and could be seen by a passer-by on the road, she moaned her anguish until, exhausted, she slid down the tree and sat in a huddled heap among its roots.

Never had she cried like this in her life before. Never had she given way. People of her class, she understood, didn't give vent to their feelings in public. Nor when rejected did they throw things. What had come over her? What had she sunk to? It didn't matter. Nothing mattered. There seemed to be no life left in her: there was a wish in her to sit huddled like this forever; never to think again, to worry, to feel the ache of the heart and the torments of the body; but once she rose from this ground she knew that the latter two would be with her for a long time to come.

When the hand came on her shoulder she swung round while at the same time crouching nearer to the gole of the tree and, speechless now, she stared up into Robert's face and, recognizing the mixture of bewilderment, concern and compassion in his eyes, she almost broke down again.

As her head fell forward on to her chest, he said softly, 'Come, miss, come.' And now, his hands going under her oxters, he lifted her gently to her feet, where she remained standing with her head bowed.

When she swayed slightly he put his hand on her elbow, and when again he said, 'Come,' she shook

159

her head before wiping her face with the wet ball of her handkerchief.

He groped in his coat pocket for a handkerchief he knew he had there. It wasn't still folded but he hadn't used it. He offered it to her, and she took it from him and passed it over her face; then she brought her hat from the back of her head where it had been saved from falling off by a solitary hat pin. Having straightened it, she looked down at her coat; there were some dry leaves adhering to the skirt, and slowly her hand flicked them off. Then, looking at Robert, she spoke for the first time: her voice a croaking whisper, she said, 'I'm sorry, Bradley.'

'No need to be sorry, miss. There's nothing like a good cry for getting trouble out of your system.' He was now quoting his mother, who had once said to him, if men cried more, they would be less aggressive. But he couldn't think of men crying; in a way it embarrassed him, besides showing a form of weakness. But never in his lifetime would he have expected anyone of Miss Agnes's class to cry like she must have done, and out in the open an' all. Something pretty bad had happened back there in the house.

He went before her now towards the road, but on reaching it, he turned to her and said, 'There's a brook further along. Would you like to stop and perhaps'—he paused—'well, I mean wash your face?'

She looked at him as if considering for a moment; then, shaking her head slowly, she said, 'No, thank you, Bradley. The water in the brook can't make much difference to how I feel. I . . . I may as well tell you: as things stand now, Millie—'

160

she swallowed so deeply that her chin jerked to the side before she went on—'Millie may have to be put away. My . . . my father is adamant. I had hoped . . . my last hope was that I might be able to take her away and live in'—she turned and looked back towards the gates—'the hunting lodge, but now that too is impossible.'

'I'm sorry, miss, very sorry. I've got some idea how you must be feeling for I too feel dreadful that Miss Millie should be put away. There are those that I know of ten times worse than her who are married and bearing children.' He stopped.

It was a little while before she said, 'I'm glad you think that way too, Bradley. I have never considered Millie insane, nor of being in such a state of mind that warranted her being locked up.' She now put her hand to her throat and, the tears once more coming into her eyes, she whispered, 'I mustn't. I mustn't.'

'Is there nothing can be done, miss? No one you can turn to?'

'No.' She pressed her eyes tightly closed for a moment, then opened them and blinked a number of times before she said, 'My brothers are of the same opinion, and Mr Crockford.' She now looked past Robert and across to where the horse and cart was standing before she said, 'Mr Crockford is of like mind with my father.' Then her head jerking, she looked at him again before saying in a tone which although not loud was high, 'I . . . I was to be married you know, Bradley. But . . . but no longer. It . . . it is finished, broken off. I . . . I can tell you this now because once you get back to the house you will soon hear it.'

He said nothing but just looked at her and she at

him as, her voice dropping once again, she said more in the form of a statement, 'I was engaged for four years. It is a long time.' And on this she turned from him and walked to the cart.

He followed her, and after helping her up he took his seat beside her, saying, 'Gee up!' to the horse. And so they began their journey back to the house.

As they went his thoughts ranged from deep pity for the young lady sitting by his side whom he thought of now as 'Poor lass', on to Millie who was to be put in an asylum, for that's what they meant by being put away. And now he swore to himself: 'Tis a blasted shame, a crying out shame. As to Mr James Crockford, his mind told him she was, in a way, damned lucky to be rid of him; for he had come across replicas of the same type in his own class, men who lorded it over the household, egotistical, small-minded buggers who treated their women like servants or slaves but never as partners. From what he had gathered from the talk in his shop alone in Palmer's ninety per cent of the wives never saw their husband's pay packet: they were doled out their small allowance and with that they had to be satisfied. Even when bairns were added yearly to the family, the allowance in many cases still remained the same, because a man must have his beer and his tabs, not forgetting a few bob on the horses. So, in a way, he saw Mr James Crockford as being of the same calibre.

The Taggarts knew quite a bit about the Crockford family and how they started their shops. The grandfather had had a little huckster shop in Jarrow, now there was hardly a town on the Tyne that hadn't one or two of their shops in it. As for

162

the mother, although presumably she was of better stock, she let everyone know it, which was why she couldn't keep her servants.

He heard himself ask now, 'Haven't you any relatives, miss, that would take you and Miss Millie in?'

'No, none. When Miss Millie goes I too will be leaving—' She turned now and looked at him before ending, 'Because I too will have to find employment. Life's strange. Don't you think so, Bradley?'

'Yes, miss, I do. And it isn't the day or yesterday I've thought so. I've often wondered why one is born white, or black, or yellow. And then why one person can be born rich and another poor. And why some people are given dominion over others when, to my mind, they haven't the qualities to hold such power, so to speak.'

He was on touchy ground; he shouldn't have said that.

She was looking ahead as she said, 'I understand you like reading?'

'Aye, miss, I like reading. But the more I read, the more I realize how ignorant I am. And more so lately 'cos I've become bitter at times when I think not only of meself but of all those who are deprived of proper education. Given the chance, lots of folk could make something of themselves.'

She made no answer to this and they continued the journey in silence again until, coming in sight of the gates, she turned her head towards him as she said, 'May I ask you something, Bradley, a favour?'

'Anything, miss.' He too turned his head, and now they were looking at each other and again he repeated, 'Anything, miss.'

After a moment she lowered her gaze and looked down towards her joined hands as she said, 'Would you please not mention to anyone how you found me today?'

'You needn't have asked that, miss.'

Once more she was looking at him. 'You are very kind, very understanding.'

He pulled on the horse's reins and turned the animal through the gates and up the drive, and when he went to stop opposite the front door she said simply, 'I'll get out in the yard.'

In the yard, he jumped down and helped her from her seat. She thanked him not in words but with a look, and on this he turned away and led the horse towards the stable.

After taking him from the shafts, he unharnessed him, then rubbed him down before giving him his feed, during which time he saw nothing of either Hubbard or Arthur Bloom.

In the ordinary way he would have gone across the yard and into the kitchen for his tea, but it was well past tea-time. Still, he knew there would be something kept for him, but he wasn't hungry. He went out into the yard, passed the tack-room door, and up the steep stairs that led into his room above the stables.

He sat down on the chair near the bare table and, putting one forearm on it, he leant his body to the side and stared through the small dusty window that gave him a view of the yard and the upper part of the north side of the house, and he seemed to see through the walls and into a room where she stood with Miss Millie by her side. And a number of strange disturbing thoughts ranged through his mind. Yet they had no real substance: they were

164

formless and as abstract as thoughts could be. There was nothing for him to grasp at and hold and reason with, yet his thinking brought him up from the table to stand stiffly looking down towards the floor as he muttered, 'God Almighty!'

## CHAPTER TWO

There was a feeling of expectancy in the house. Something was going to happen; something must happen; things couldn't go on like this, and Stanley voiced his opinion in those very words. Looking across the table at Agnes in the breakfast-room, he said, 'Things can't go on like this. I don't know where I am. I don't know what I'm going to do . . . what I'm expected to do. I can't get any sense out of him except the fact that he hasn't any money.'

'Well, you've known that for a long time, surely.' Agnes slowly bit into a piece of toast.

'Yes.' His voice came impatiently back at her. 'But there's a difference between not having any money in that sense and poverty, being on rock bottom. There was always the marine chandlers and the chain works.'

'Like in most things now, he has only a share in the chain works. As far as I know the marine chandlers is still his, that is if he hasn't either gambled it away or passed it over as a gift to his—' she swallowed on another mouthful of toast before ending—'woman.'

'Don't talk silly, Agnes. You don't make gifts of places like marine chandlers to mistresses.'

'Well—' her voice rose slightly and she leant

across the table towards him as she demanded—
'tell me where the rest of the businesses have gone?
He held the biggest shares in the foundry, then he
had some say in the Beulah Mine and the brick
works.'

Stanley closed his eyes for a moment before
replying, 'That was a long time ago, and as far as I
can gather his interests were reduced through
slumps and labour troubles and so on.'

'Yes, and so on, and so on. You, like the other
two, have been out of it for years and when you've
been at home, what have you done? Nothing. All
you think about is your own pleasures and whether
you will be able to return to Oxford. Do you know
things have got so bad of late with tradesmen that
they wouldn't even leave a load of coal recently and
Dave had to pay for it? Do you know that? Dave
had to pay for our coal.'

He bowed his head now against her onslaught,
muttering, 'Well, what can we do? I've . . . I've tried
to talk to him. I have. I have. But he's so sozzled I
can't get a reasonable word out of him. Something
must have upset him more than somewhat in
Newcastle the other day.'

'Yes, and I can guess what that something was.
His plans for bringing his mistress here as a wife
must have gone awry.'

Stanley lifted his head sharply now, saying
scornfully, 'He would never have gone through
with that, that was just a threat to get at you.'

'It was no threat, let me tell you.'

'You think not?'

'I'm positive of it, absolutely.'

He was silent for a moment while wiping his
mouth on a napkin; then he rose from the table,

saying, 'I couldn't see her in this place.'

'Have you seen her?'

'Well, no'—he turned towards her—'but Arnold has, and he says she's a stunner, dressed up to the eyes, terrifically smart, and quite a bit younger than him.'

Agnes too rose from the table now and as she pushed her chair back with some force under it she muttered to herself, 'A stunner!' before turning towards the door, where she was halted by Stanley's voice saying, 'Wait a minute, Agnes. Look, what am I going to do? Term will be starting soon and I've got to know.'

'Why ask me? If you can't get any sense out of Father then it should be Arnold you want to talk to.'

'Oh, Arnold! What does he care about? Or Roland either for that matter. They've both now got this Australian bug and they are going, that's definite. I'm surprised though that Roland's tagging along.'

'Then why don't you go with them? You would be well out of it then, wouldn't you? And your future would be settled.'

'I don't want to go to Australia. And anyway they wouldn't consider me going with them. They never have asked me to join them in anything.'

That was true. Neither of his older brothers had had much time for Stanley. Perhaps they saw their father in him, and weren't taken with the picture.

As she stared back at him she thought, I wonder if they ever have considered what is going to happen to me, and she was surprised to hear herself saying her thoughts aloud: 'Have any of you ever thought what's going to happen to me . . . or

Millie for that matter?'

Stanley had the grace to flush slightly, and after a moment's pause he said, 'Well . . . well, we thought you'd marry Crockford. And'—he put in hopefully now with a smile—'perhaps you could still patch it up. One has tiffs and . . . and come together again.'

'There'll be no coming together again in this case. That still leaves Millie. Have any of you given her a thought?'

She watched him bow his head, then look at her from under his lowered lids as he replied briefly, 'Yes.'

She did not now say, 'Well?' and wait for him going on; instead, after one hard look, she turned from him and went out. His yes had told her exactly what her brothers thought should be done with Millie.

As she went across the hall two things happened. She heard a door open and bang shut upstairs which meant that her father was on his way down, and this caused her to scurry towards the kitchen. But before she reached the door leading into the passage she became riveted to the spot for a second as she saw through the hall window Millie running across the gravel drive towards the entrance to the courtyard. Her mind raced: Maggie was with Millie, at least she had left her with Millie.

For the last few days they had kept an almost prison-warden-like state over Millie, even locking her in her room, because although she hadn't had one of her wandering turns for some time now it was imperative that she didn't meet up with her father while trailing from one room to the other as she was apt to do at times, for in his present state the sight of her would inflame him further. But how had she got out? Oh! Maggie. She had thought she could trust Maggie.

'Agnes.' The name came thick and fuddled like a blow on the back of her neck, and she swung round to see her father slowly descending the last few stairs. 'I want a word with you.' He didn't look at her but turned towards his study which was at the end of a short passage leading off the hall. He stopped, however, when her voice in a gabble came at him, saying, 'I . . . I'll be with you in a few minutes, Father, I've just got to . . .'

'*Now! Do* you hear? *Now!*'

He looked menacing, menacing enough to come and take her by force and this she knew he would do if she opposed him further. At this moment she weighed up which was the lesser of the two evils, that Millie should go off on one of her flitting escapades, and at this early time of the day too, which presented a change in her pattern of behaviour, with regard to her flights, or be handled by this man whom she had come to detest and fear more every day.

She found herself walking across the hall, past him and into his study and after he had entered and closed the door behind him, not too gently, he lumbered towards the chair behind his desk which was piled with papers that looked as if they had just been emptied out of a sack. Now taking up a pen he began to tap the end of it on the table and his eyes were fixed on it as he spoke rapidly, saying, 'We're in a predicament, do you know that? They could foreclose, there's the interest on the mortgage.' He glanced up at her now, saying, 'I'm . . . I'm selling some pictures. There's a man

169

coming from London the day after tomorrow. In the meantime I need some money, ready money. That . . . that'—he looked down again at the pen he was still tapping against the table—'ring your mother left you . . .' Now at the sight of the change on her face he yelled, 'What was your mother's is legally mine. She had no right to give it to you.'

'That ring is mine, Father, and it remains mine.'

'By God!' He pulled himself to his feet. 'Don't you cross me, girl. I'm in no fit state to be crossed. All right'—he drew in a deep breath—'I'll give you what it's worth back when I sell the pictures. They'll bring a good deal.'

'You said that about the miniatures, and they didn't.'

'That was different, they were sold locally, Newcastle. They rook you. These fellows from London, they're the genuine thing, so . . . so come on, let me have it.'

'No; you took all Mother's jewellery. Why don't you get it back from the person whom you gave it to? That should be easy.'

She staggered back, her forearm across her face as she saw his hand grip a heavy paperweight, and not until his fingers relaxed on it did her own come down and, with the back of her hand across her lips, she bit on the knuckle.

'All right. All right.' He was growling now. 'You keep your ring, and, madam, the first thing I do with the money I get from those pictures will be to see that your charge is put where she should have been this long, long while . . . I'll wait here for the next fifteen minutes; it's up to you.'

She actually staggered from the room and when she reached the hall, her first instinct was to rush into the kitchen and to tell them to go looking for Millie and also to throw herself into Pèggy's arms and say, 'What must I do?' The ring was her only possession, her only security; that it was a good one she was well aware, though she had no idea of its real value.

She ran up the stairs now, and on the landing she met a distracted Maggie who cried immediately, 'Miss! Miss! Have you seen her? I only left her for a minute. She was asleep as sound as a baby, an' I had me stomach trouble, I've had it all night, it's the fruit, I had to run. Never for a moment did I dream she would up and off in those few minutes. I tell you she was sleepin' like a . . .'

'Go and look for her. I'll be there in a few minutes. Tell Dave and Peggy. Go straight down to the lake.'

She now ran to her room and, going to the bottom drawer of a small chest, she rummaged under some underwear and took out the box that had held the letters and in which the ring now reposed on a piece of crumpled velvet. She had purposely hidden the box, knowing that her father wouldn't be above searching her room if just such a situation as now should come about.

Taking up the ring, she stared at it where it lay, its stones gleaming in her cupped palm. If only she could defy him. But she knew that whatever he might do with the money he got from the pictures he would keep his word about Millie, and delight in it.

A minute later she was again standing before the desk. And there she did a silly thing, a thing for which she was to blame herself for many a long day following: it was to set off a train of events, one

171

which could have resulted in someone she held dear ending in the hangman's noose.

Bending towards her father, her face not a foot from his, she hissed at him, 'Look at it well before you sell it, and know it is a symbol of love, the love my mother had for a man who loved her. You've had your mistresses, cheap sluts, one after the other, but she had one lover, one real man.'

Now, for the first and only time in her life, she saw murder in a man's eyes, and she turned and ran from it. She ran out, along the corridor, across the hall, into the passage, then into the kitchen; and here she stood leaning on the table as she looked about the empty room. They had all gone looking for Millie, because they knew that, it being so early, she would make for the road, as she had done the last time she had taken to wandering at this time of the day. Then, the driver of Parkers, the Newcastle carrier, had picked her up when she was well past Lamesley. And too, it was the first time she'd heard the term 'Thorman's Moth' applied to Millie: the carrier, a kindly man, had said, 'I'd heard tell of Thorman's Moth. It was funny, miss, as soon as I set eyes on her I knew it was her. She's a bonny wee lass.'

The bonny wee lass was then sixteen.

Where was Stanley? It wasn't likely he was out looking because he would first come to her with a wail that generally began, 'Oh! not again.' No, Stanley would likely be up in his room looking at his face and trimming his moustache. He was very vain about his complexion and his moustache . . .

Which way should she go? She paused in the yard, then made towards the end of the courtyard to the gate that led into the paddocks. But before

172

reaching it she was brought to a standstill by the sound of a light laugh; it was as if someone had laid a gentle finger in succession on the high notes of an organ. She swung round and looked towards the tack-room. The next minute she had pulled the door open, there to see Millie sitting on a wooden block, her face bright, her hands joined at her waist as if her body had been rocking with laughter, and opposite to her, near the stove, sat Bradley. He was mixing some thick dark stuff in a bowl, and he looked up at her without any surprise as she stood gripping the handle of the door, her body actually swaying with mixed emotions of relief and anger. But before she could give vent to either, Millie said, 'Oh there you are, Aggie. Bradley has been telling me about how they make a ship and what they do to make sure that the iron bottom doesn't sink when it's put in the water, because iron is heavy you know, Aggie. And Bradley makes you laugh. Don't you Bradley? He's making polish now for the harness.'

Bradley looked down at his hand that was still stirring the mixture of yellow wax, litharge, ivory black, and turps, and what he said now was, 'One doesn't know when one's being funny, miss. When you try to be funny you never are.'

Oh! that man. Agnes actually ground her teeth. He was the most disturbing creature. He had been so kind to her the other night she had changed her opinion of him, but here he was, knowing that everybody would be scouring the place for Millie yet making no move to alleviate their worry, just sitting here telling her stories.

Her condemnation was interrupted when he rose and, passing near her, he muttered, 'I brought

173

her over to the house, but there was no one about, and I heard'—he paused—'the master, and he didn't sound pleased, so I thought the best thing to do was to bring her back here.' He looked her in the face now. 'That was right, wasn't it, miss?'

Once again she thought, Oh! that man. He had the habit of putting himself in the right as he had done about his cousin. Well, perhaps he had been in the right there, as he certainly had been in this case, because if her father in his present state had come across Millie this morning, she dared not think what his reactions might have been. Perhaps he would not then have hesitated to lift the paperweight, or something similar.

Holding out her hand to Millie, she said, 'Come.' Then looking at Robert, she added, 'Would you go and tell the rest that she is all right?'

'Of course I'm all right; I'm always all right when I'm with Bradley.'

Agnes slowly turned her head and looked at Robert and, as if she had just spoken her thoughts aloud and upbraided him, she said softly, 'I'm sorry,' and he answered, 'That's all right, miss. Nothing to be sorry about. I'll go now and tell them.'

*       *       *

Around ten o'clock Reginald Thorman took the trap into Newcastle. He returned at four. That he had been drinking but wasn't entirely drunk was Greg Hubbard's opinion, as he said to Robert when he came in from the fields where he had been helping Arthur Bloom. 'If he gets through just a quarter of the box of spirits he's brought back with

174

him, there'll be nobody get to sleep the night in there. He's been high on drink afore but I've never seen him as bad as this, not this early in the day anyhow. There's something radically wrong.'

Yes, there was something radically wrong with this house altogether, Robert thought; and he was going to make a move because he had the strange feeling that he was being drawn into something that wasn't going to do him any good. Oh no, far from doing him any good, it was going to wreck him and he wasn't going to stay and be wrecked.

Having a sensible head on his shoulders, he told himself he regretted deeply now that he had ever left Jarrow and Palmers, because, looking back on life there, it may not have been easy, but it was like the calm waters of a lagoon compared to the turbulent seas he had found himself navigating since coming to this part of the world. Oh yes, he was getting out as quickly as possible, and away from the whole district.

Tonight was his night off and he was going to The Bull to talk things over with Billy and Mary. They seemed to be the only sane and level-headed people around here, anyway of those that he knew.

He was dressed ready for the road. However, before leaving the premises it was the custom, Dave Waters-made custom, to call in at the kitchen and say you were leaving and at about what time you would return.

They were all seated around the table having a meal, Dave, Peggy and Ruthie Waters, Maggie and Betty Trollop, also Greg Hubbard.

It was Peggy who said, 'You won't have a bite then?' She nearly always said the same thing to him on his evenings off and as usual he answered, 'No,

175

thanks, Mrs Waters.'

Her mouth wide, Maggie now said, 'You're a fine set-up fellow. If it wasn't that I was married with nine bairns, and me husband who's clean barmy about me and as jealous as sin, I would set me cap at you.'

Dave, his face stiff, turned to check her, but the others at the table burst out laughing and his words were drowned until the laughter subsided, when they heard him say, 'Handsome is as handsome does.'

And now Robert, looking at Old Stiff-Neck, as he thought of Waters, grinned as he said, 'Well, that's the first time that appellation's been tagged on to me.'

The laughter slid from their faces now, even from Maggie's as she thought that was what had made this one different from the other numskulls who had come and gone over the last year or so: he sounded a bit above himself at times with the words he used, all because he read so much. Only last night here in the kitchen they had said most people in service could read and write, and as good as him, but that they didn't push it like he did. Aping his betters with his twang. But she didn't agree there about his twang, because his voice was too deep and rough for him ever to be taken for anybody in the class.

'I'll be off then. I should be back afore dark.'

When Dave Water's voice came to him muttering, 'See you do,' he was for turning about and saying, 'Well, I'll please meself about that an' all.' But he let it go and went out, across the paddock and through the tangled garden to where the trees thinned out leading to the lake, as the

176

quarry pool was known. Tonight he did not even pause to look at it; he wanted to get away from this place and all in it ...

Bill and Mary Taggart greeted him warmly and each of them in turn between serving customers stood at the bar counter and chatted to him. The news that they gave him of his uncle and aunt and Carrie was much the same as before: the girl's stomach was rising, but the old fellow made her go to church on a Sunday where the poor lass would sit with her head hanging nearly to her knees, they said. But so far the parson had been kind and hadn't come out with any sermons about the sins of the flesh, which perhaps, as Billy said, must have disappointed his uncle.

Both Bill and Mary understood his feelings of wanting to get away from Foreshaw Park. Nobody seemed to stay up there long except the few old diehards who had nowhere else to go. But, as they said, jobs were few and far between around here. There was Birtley, though. Lots of things were going on there; he might get set on anywhere. There was the Birtley Iron Works and coal pits. Of course, they said, the whole place was practically owned by Lord Ravensworth and the Birtley Iron Company between them, and like all such bosses you'd got to fight them for wages. But as a sort of compensation there was a billiard room and a reading room with piles of books in it. Now that should suit him down to the ground. And of course, talking of work, he hadn't to forget the brick works. Yes, that's where he should go, Birtley.

Yes, as they said, Birtley was his best bet, and tomorrow morning first thing he'd tell them up there just where to put the job: Jack of all trades and master of none. Twelve to fourteen hours a day and for what? Eeh! he must have been mad to take it in the first place. Ten bob a week! . . .

It was getting dusk when he said goodbye to his friends and waved a cheerio to the regulars in the taproom.

The long twilight was still sending a warm glow over the land but tonight he could see no beauty in it. He loved sunsets better than dawns: he loved that period during which the light slowly fades and the night takes over, especially when it was lit by the moon. There was a quietude in that period that you didn't get with wonderful dawns. Dawns heralded a day: bring what it might, it caused the body and mind to work, whereas the night brought rest to both.

The side road had become a familiar passage to him. He always jumped the ditch where the railings were flat; he hadn't got down to repairing them yet. For the past fortnight he had been working on the drystone wall bordering the main carriage road on the south side, but as he trod on the railings now he thought, Well, you won't be put up by me; that's a certainty.

It was when he stepped from them that he heard the cry and he knew immediately from where it came and from which throat it came. There was no one who laughed or cried or talked like The Moth. And that was how he thought of her now in his own mind, because it was a good description of her.

The cry had been short and it faded almost before he had registered it, yet it caused him to run through the trees in the direction he had taken that first night and not to the left to take the path he had made for himself over the past weeks towards

178

the house.

When he reached the clearing where the grass sloped towards the pool, he was brought momentarily to a halt, for there, through the fast fading light, he could see two figures struggling. There was no sound coming from them, at least none reached him. And he saw lying to the side of them the prone figure of no other than Miss Millie. He was on the point of springing forward when there came another cry which started on a high key, then dropped away to a muffled moan. And now there was only one man standing on the edge of the quarry, and he stood stock still.

When he reached the man and turned him about he was staring into the face of Dave Waters, mouth wide, and eyes wide and filled with terror. He watched the man's mouth opening and shutting before managing to splutter, 'Mur . . . murder her. He was gona mur . . . murder her.'

Robert left loose of the man, then turned to where Millie was lying, her feet dangling over the edge of the quarry. He could see instantly that she was quite unconscious, and as he put his arms under her oxters and pulled her back he shouted to Dave Waters, 'Who was it? Who was he?' even while at the same time he seemed to know the answer. But it didn't come until he was again standing by Dave Waters and shaking him by the shoulders, for the man was still gaping but looking down now towards where the still form lay like a crumpled sack on the boulders below.

Turning and looking at Robert and in a pathetic, almost childish tone, he muttered, 'The master, he . . . he was trying to push her over. He . . . he meant to do her in . . . he did, he did.'

179

'All right. All right. Look, come back, come back here.' Robert pulled him from the edge and towards where Millie was lying, and he said, 'Sit by her. Sit by her. Go on.' He pressed him down on the grass. 'Sit there in case she comes round. Now don't move; I'll be back in a minute.'

Turning about, he ran down the slope and on to the beach bordering the water, then along it to where the boulders lay. But before reaching the figure he stopped. The man's head was lying against a jutting stone. His face was covered with blood; one arm was across his chest, the other flung out, but both hands were hanging limp.

He was trembling himself as he neared the form. He did not at first touch the body, but, taking up the wrist, he felt for the pulse. There was none. Yet, he told himself, what did he know about pulses? The man could just be unconscious. He should try his heart. Gingerly now, he put his hand out and pushed it in between the coat and the shirt beneath. His fingers now feeling for the shirt buttons, he found them and, probing a gap between them, his fingers were now touching a silk vest. He moved them slightly to the left, and with the flat of his hand across the man's ribs, he left it there for a number of seconds but could feel no response.

When he straightened up he looked down on the man and muttered aloud, 'God in heaven! What's to come of this?'

He did not run back along the beach, nor to where Dave was sitting by his beloved dear unbalanced little mistress, he returned slowly, yet his mind was moving quicker than it had ever done in his life before.

The man was dead and good riddance. It would

be a relief to many people, one in particular, and he named no names in his mind.

By the time he reached Dave Waters he had sketched a rough outline in his mind of what he meant to do, for he thought it damned unfair for anybody to do jail, or even to hang for that fellow. He hadn't much use for old Waters but he wouldn't like to see any harm come to him; and whatever happened to him would affect all those connected with him.

Waters was sitting crouched now but holding Millie's hand, and speaking briskly to him, Robert said, 'Get up. Come on, get up, Mr Waters.'

As if obeying a master, the man rose to his feet; then again he began to mutter, 'He meant to . . . he meant to.'

'Yes, yes, I know.'

'Is . . . is he hurt?'

Robert looked him straight in the eyes and said, 'As far as I can gather, he's dead.'

*'Oh my God!'* Waters now leant forward as if he were about to retch and Robert said harshly, 'Look, pull yourself together. You are not to know anything about it. Look, let's get her back.'

'But . . . but he'll be found.'

'I know all about that.' Robert's voice was rough and demanding. 'Come on, help me up with her.' He himself also knelt down by Millie's side and, taking her face in his hands, he slapped it sharply, saying, 'Come on, Miss Millie! Come on! Up! Up!'

Slowly Millie opened her eyes and stared at him. But when she made the effort to rise she seemed to lack the strength, and once again he put his arms underneath her and pulled her to her feet, then said sharply to Waters, 'Take her other arm.' But

181

when Dave Waters made no response he almost bawled at him, 'Man! what's the matter with you? Don't you realize the seriousness of the situation? You've got to get out of this. Come on!' And saying so he put one arm right around Millie's waist and his other arm around Dave Water's shoulders, and like this he moved them as quickly as he could towards the trees, then through them.

It was almost dark when they stumbled into the yard, then through the boot room. His kicking open of the kitchen door caused Peggy Waters and Ruthie to scream, but when he barked at them, 'Shut up! and take her,' they each caught hold of Millie and lowered her down on to the settle while he himself led Dave Waters to the chair by the side of the fireplace.

Once the man was seated, he dropped on to his hunkers before him and in a rapid voice, he said, 'Now listen to me. Just listen and take it in. You have to stay put; you know nothing about it. He was drunk, as he surely was, because he smelt to high heaven down there. He was takin' a walk and he has fallen over the edge. Do you get that?'

'But I . . .'

'We know all about that. What you did you did in defence of her.' He jerked his head backwards. 'But will they believe that?'

'*Will they believe what?*' Peggy Waters was standing over him now, and he looked up at her as he said briefly, 'The master was trying to finish the lass off and your husband here came across them. There was a sort of struggle and . . . well, the master slipped over the edge of the quarry. He's . . . he's dead.'

'Oh my . . .God! . . . Oh no!'

'Oh yes. Now stop it; don't go into hysterics. Listen to what I'm saying, all of you.' He turned his head now and looked towards Maggie who had joined them, and it was she who spoke.

'What you sayin'?' she said. 'Did I hear aright? He's fought the master and the master's dead?'

'He didn't fight the master. Get that into your head, do you hear? Get it into your heads, he's never been out of the kitchen the night.' He stood up. 'Do you hear that? He's never been out of the house the night. And stick to that if you don't want to see him at the end of a rope, because although I was a witness to what happened, do you think they'll take a working man's word that he was fighting to save a deranged lass? Because that's what they'll call her, a deranged lass, and they wouldn't consider any servant going to that length . . . Where's Miss Agnes?'

It was Maggie who spoke again, saying, 'She's in bed. She's got the same trouble as us all. 'Tis the fruit, we've had too much of it.'

'Well you had better get her out of her bed and get her down here.'

'I will. I will.' Maggie turned and ran from the room. And in less than three minutes later she was back, Agnes with her.

Agnes stood in the middle of the kitchen staring at this man who at times she liked but at other times she disliked intensely, as would any mistress of a servant who didn't know his place. And when the situation had been related to her she muttered, *'Dead? Father dead?'* Looking at her, Robert repeated quietly, 'Yes, dead. And it can all be got over quite simply if . . . if he's not found till later. We . . . well . . . you could become worried for him

183

like. Is . . . is Mr Stanley in?'

She paused a moment, thinking, then said, 'No, no. He rode over to the Davidsons' earlier, but . . . but he should be back at any time.'

'Well, if I may suggest, miss, you get dressed and meet him and tell him . . . Well'—he looked from one to the other—'tell him that you're worried about your father, because he was in his cups, heavily so to speak, and then you could begin searchin'. It would be best if he found him. In that case everything would go smoothly. What I mean is, there would be no need for any sort of explanation of what really happened.'

Now Agnes turned and looked at Dave and Peggy who was standing near him, and she went to them and, taking his hand, she said, 'Oh, Dave. Dave.'

'I'm . . . I'm sorry, Miss Agnes.' The voice that for years had adopted a tone of authority was now a mere whisper. He said he was sorry. Oh he needn't be sorry. There was a part of her that was being flooded with relief although at the same time she was attacking it with guilt.

'Papa took me for a walk.'

They all swung round to where Millie was looking at them. There was a dazed blankness in her eyes and she repeated, 'Papa took me for a walk.'

Turning to Maggie, Agnes said, 'You . . . you let her go?'

'It was like this, miss. We were playin' cards in her room and the master came in. He was . . . well, he was tight. But he was nice, and . . . and he talked to her and she seemed so happy that he was nice to her. And he took her out, so what could I do? I did

184

think it was funny 'cos he'd never sought her company afore, so I went in to you but you had dozed off, and you'd had such a bad do afore that I . . . well, I thought I would just let it bide. But I did come downstairs and I . . . I told you, Aunty, didn't I? And you said, better tell Uncle. He was down in the greenhouse, and so I told him. Then I went back and . . . and you were still asleep, miss. So . . . well, what could I do?' She spread her hands wide.

'Papa took me for a walk.'

'Take her up, Maggie, will you? And stay with her'—she stressed the stay—'until I come up.'

When Millie seemed either reluctant or unable to move, Ruthie went to Maggie's assistance and between them they led the limp figure from the room, and now Agnes looking at Robert said, 'I . . . I think your suggestion is very good, Bradley. If only we can all remember to act up to it.'

'I see no reason why not, miss.' Then, lowering his tone, he added, 'If we don't the consequences could be . . . well, rather—' He stopped and glanced towards where Dave Waters was sitting with his head bowed, and she followed his gaze but spoke not to him but to Peggy, saying quickly, 'Where is . . . where is Betty?'

'I sent her to bed, she's got toothache.'

'Does she know anything of this?' She was looking at Robert again and he answered, 'It would be better not, she's very young and although she's a sensible lass, you never know. She could get talkin', and she goes to that aunt of hers. And I think the same goes for Mr Bloom and Hubbard.' He had no need to add that Bloom had gone home and Greg was in bed with the same affliction that had attacked most of them through the fruit.

185

He now drew the lever watch from his pocket and, glancing at it, he said, 'Time's gettin' on.' It was as if he had said, 'Hadn't you better go and get your clothes on?' for, turning from him, Agnes glanced at Peggy saying, 'I won't be long,' then she hurried out of the kitchen.

After she had gone, Robert, looking at Peggy Waters, said quietly, 'I'll go across to me room. When Mr Stanley comes in send for me, in a hurry like. You understand?'

Peggy nodded at him, her eyes wide; it was as if she was seeing him in the position of a master and she couldn't understand it.

As he made for the door she muttered, 'Thanks. Thanks.' And he turned and inclined his head towards her before going out.

Whatever size his stature might have risen to in the kitchen it was back to normal when he reached his room, for he found that he was trembling. There was a quartern bottle of whisky in his cupboard, it was still more than half full. On nights when he was tired and life appeared monotonous and dull he would heat a can of water on the tack-room boiler and take it upstairs and top it with a measure of whisky and a spoonful of brown sugar. This he found enabled him to get off to sleep without thinking. Of late he had been finding that his thinking, especially at night, was disturbing, for at times he didn't like the road along which his mind was leading him.

Tonight he took the whisky raw, but it did nothing to steady his nerves nor did it warm him. The night had turned chilly and the room was without heat, and looking at it in the lantern light he saw, and not for the first time, its utter

186

cheerlessness: the cobwebbed beams above him; the rough uneven floor that he imagined had never seen water since it was first laid; the little window with its drab curtains. Well, he wouldn't have to put up with this much longer, he was going in any case, but after tonight's business he would show the place such a clean pair of heels they'd gather no dust.

'Bradley.'

He went to the stairhead door and, looking down, he saw Maggie standing at the foot. She held the outer door open in one hand while holding a lantern upwards with the other, and she called in a loud voice, 'Will you come down? You're wanted. Master Stanley's here and needs you.'

'Yes; I'll be there in a minute.'

He took two or three minutes before leaving the room, then went down the stairs, pulling his coat on as he did so, and in the yard asked, 'What's up?'

It was Stanley who answered him, saying, 'My father went out for a walk, presumably some time ago and he hasn't returned. I want you to help look around the grounds.'

He did not say, 'Yes, Mr Stanley,' but, looking to where Dave Waters was standing outside the kitchen door, he walked towards him, muttering, but loud enough for his voice to carry, saying, 'But it's only on ten o'clock; the master knows his own grounds surely?'

*'Do what you're told, man.'*

Robert turned and looked towards the young fellow who had never given him a civil word since he had come into the place, and he thought, My God! I'd like to meet you in a dark lane some night, young sir. I would that. I would teach you that civility costs nothing. It wasn't that he was unused to men bawling orders at him. He had been bawled at from the day he had entered the yard to serve his time, but it was a different kind of bawling, it didn't indicate from its tone that you were scum or another species of human being that had been created for servitude.

For his part, Stanley's thoughts were moving along similar channels except from the opposite standpoint: that fellow wanted taking in hand, he was too free by half with his tongue. Yet as he had said, his father should know his own grounds. Assuming he was capable. But Agnes had just told him that his father had gone out about seven o'clock and that he was rolling drunk, and, knowing him and his ways, he would never have thought of walking outside the grounds, he would have left either in the trap or on horseback. Now he could be lying anywhere in the paddocks or in the woods or down by the lake, anywhere. Thirty acres didn't mean much of an estate, but when it was dark every foot turned into a yard. He called now to Dave, saying, 'Waters, take the paddocks. And you Bradley, go towards the North Lodge. Hubbard, you come with me.' Then as he turned to move away he stopped and called, 'Whistle if'—he paused—'you come across my father.'

As Robert went to move away he heard Agnes call, 'Shall I come with you?' and he thought, Well, she's certainly playing her part. And then her brother's voice came back, saying, 'No, but I'd have another look through the house, just in case. You never know.'

No, you didn't know, Robert thought: his ghost might already be walking. By! there would be high

188

jinks here the night, and the morrow. What would happen in a case like this? Would there be an inquest, a police court? Or would the doctor just say, natural causes, and omit the words, brought about by a fall through intoxication?

*      *      *

It was just a half hour later when they brought the body back on a door.

And it was near midnight when Doctor Miller arrived and the questions Robert had asked in his mind were answered. Yes, the police must be called; and yes, there would be an inquest. This news came through the kitchen via Peggy. Then she added, 'Now he's got to be laid out and I can't bear to touch him.' And turning to Ruthie she said, 'You'll have to help me.'

'Not me, Mam,' Ruthie said. 'I couldn't lay anybody out, I would throw up.'

Then Robert was made to wonder yet again at the resilience and the accommodation of young Maggie who quietly now, and no laughter in her voice, said, 'Don't worry yourselves, I'll do it on me own, once he's on the bed. I've helped with such like afore a number of times over there.' She inclined her head slightly to the right as if Ireland just lay beyond the courtyard.

Maggie was a good lass, one in a thousand. It was a shame unto God that He had given her such a face. But then when you got to know her you forgot what she looked like . . . Many a man would do worse than take on Maggie.

As she walked up the kitchen he said, 'Well, here's one off to bed because it's going to be a busy

189

day the morrow if I know anything, comings and goings. Good-night to you.' He nodded first to Peggy, then to Ruthie, and lastly to Dave. And the two women answered him, saying, 'Good-night. Good-night, Bradley,' and there was a softness in their tone, even a touch of deference.

Waters said nothing, but as Robert made towards the door he went with him, then through the boot room and to the yard door to where the lantern was still alight and swinging from the iron bracket extending from the wall; and there he stood looking at Robert but still in silence, and Robert, putting his hand on his shoulder, said, 'Look, it'll be all right, the worst's over. Don't worry about the morrow or the day.' He turned and looked up into the sky. 'What you said to the doctor, you'll say again: the last you saw of the master was when he was in the dining-room after the meal. And yes, he had been drinkin' heavily. That's all. Good-night now, and get some sleep.' He was about to turn away when he looked back at the old man, saying, 'I've got an idea that things will be easier around here for everybody from now on.'

Dave Waters had not uttered a word but he remained looking after the figure of the man crossing the yard, the man he had never liked from the time he first started here: in his own mind he had classed him as being too much of a townie, one who would never fit in with the running of an establishment such as this, even as it was now, and one who wouldn't have lasted two minutes in the establishment as it once was. It had been evident from the beginning that he was lacking in real respect for his masters. He was civil enough, oh yes, but underneath the civility there was an arrogance, and everybody in their positions knew that arrogance was the prerogative of the class, it got you nowhere when your life was spent working for them. And anyway if, like that fellow, you dared to show it, it was given another name, bumptiousness. Yet you couldn't say he was bumptious in his talk because he had never given himself airs. Still there was that about him that demanded something that he wasn't entitled to, not in this kind of life anyway.

But, now here tonight he had taken over. Yes, true he had saved his neck, for as he himself knew and Bradley knew, the master hadn't fallen by accident. When they had let go of each other and the master had swayed towards the edge he could have thrust out his arms and pulled him back; and he had thrust out his arms but pushed him forward, and he knew now that the action had not been solely in defence of his beloved miss but was coupled with retaliation for a lifetime of thankless service, for the master had never once given him a word of appreciation, and because of it he had now put himself for the rest of his life under the dominance of that fellow, fearful of what he might say if he got a drink on him. And he did like a drink, apparently, if you took in the number of times he made for The Bull when he was off duty. It was one thing to have to be subservient and bow your knee to the class, because that was their due, but to have to do the same to a fellow who was less than yourself, if you went by status of service, was something he was going to find very hard to stomach. In fact, he didn't know how he was going to face life under these conditions from now on.

191

And what if the fellow started demanding money? The thought brought his hands up to his hair and he gripped the thinning strands as he turned away and closed the door behind him.

# CHAPTER THREE

The police had come; a post-mortem had followed, and the coroner's verdict was accidental death. That's what was reported in the papers, but many said there should have been added: through being blind drunk. The landlord at the inn at Lamesley had said that Mr Thorman was already three sheets in the wind when he called in the saloon on the day he died, and that he would have liked to refuse him but what could you do, he was a gentleman!

The funeral was well attended by those who mattered. The cortège itself was imposing, not as elaborate as some, but nevertheless eight black cabs followed the hearse, and these in turn were followed by a number of private vehicles most of whose occupants returned to the house after the burial service to be regaled with a sit-down meal.

But now at five o'clock in the afternoon only one carriage remained on the drive. It belonged to Lady Emily Clinton-Smyth and her husband Gregory. No one was ever known to address the couple as Sir Gregory and Lady Emily, Lady Emily came first in all ways as she was demonstrating now in the drawing-room. She sat looking at the three young men and the young woman sitting opposite to her as they had done for the past half-hour while she talked non-stop.

Agnes, looking at the woman whom she used to call Aunty, but which title was a mere courtesy one as she was no relation whatever to the family, thought that her brothers were sitting as quiet as they were because they were fascinated by the face that was so plastered with make-up that the muscles seemed to have become glued, only the eyeballs and the lips moved, the upper showing a myriad of lines darting away towards the nose and those on the lower lip radiating towards the chin.

How old was she? In her late seventies or perhaps early eighties. Agnes recalled her mother saying that no one knew when Aunty Clinton had been born, and no one dared to ask. She was an intimidating woman, not likeable yet one couldn't actively dislike her. She was a gossip-monger and could make or mar a reputation. That seemed to have been her occupation in life, making and marring reputations. She had marred a few, too, in the last half-hour but in a way that could have evoked laughter had one dared to laugh on such an occasion, because she punctuated all her remarks by appealing to her husband who was stone deaf. She was doing so now, crying, ' 'Twas so, Gregory, wasn't it? He bet on everything in the house—didn't he?—Paddy Shamon, and when he had nothing more to gamble he put up the parlourmaid. You remember, Gregory? He put up the parlourmaid, didn't he? At least for the time she was bonded to his service. We were just engaged at the time, remember, and the girl was willing. My God! the things that happened.'

Agnes heard a faint splutter from the chair beyond that on which Stanley was sitting. That was Arnold. She, too, would like to laugh: it was

193

wonderful having light relief like this after the last five days, which had been like a nightmare in which she had to play a part, in which they'd all had to play a part, the only one not seeming to feel any concern being the one who was at the centre of the tragedy, Millie, because since those telling words in the kitchen Millie hadn't opened her mouth. It was as if her mind had closed down, not only on the incident but on life itself. She ate, she slept, she did what she was told without murmur, but she didn't speak.

Agnes hadn't asked Doctor Miller to see her, for he was sharp was old Doctor Miller and he might have put two and two together. Later, if she continued in this way, she'd have to call him in.

Something Lady Emily was saying caught her attention and caused her eyes to widen.

'Damned nerve I'd say. Brazen as brass. The first time I saw her was in this very room with Kate, your mother you know.' She nodded towards the four figures who were staring at her. 'It was here she met Gerry Bendicker and she made a dead set for him, she smelt his money. Mercenary bitch she was, right from the first. She and your mother were friends, different as chalk and cheese. You were a toddler then.' She pointed at Roland, then said, 'No, you're the wrong one. It was you, wasn't it, Arnold? Yes, it was you. But she hadn't hooked Bendicker five minutes until she started on her games with Reggie. Didn't she, Gregory? I say, didn't she?' Her voice was a bawl now and the old man, leaning towards her, said, 'What's that, my dear?'

She turned now and looked at Agnes, saying, 'Deaf as a post. Deaf as a post. Senile an' all. But

194

we've all got to come to it. And that's what I said to her today: we've all got to come to it, I said. But she didn't like it because she still thinks she's good-looking. But her skin's going; her nerve isn't, though. My God, I couldn't believe it when I saw her on the drive there getting out of her carriage. The nerve to come back to this house to his funeral. When she was giving him up, serve him right, I said, him being hoodwinked over the past year or more. I got the whole story from Christine Mayburn because it's her man's cousin she's hooked now. They were all laughing up their sleeves at Reggie, saying it served him damn well right for the way he'd treated Kate all these years. But then, for that whore to come and show her face here today, that was the limit. And she talked to you, didn't she?'

Agnes stared at the painted mask topped by the high velvet hat with a veil hanging down each side of it, and she opened her mouth but found she couldn't answer because she hadn't known that woman in the plum taffeta with a black band round her arm and the black chiffon headwear had been *the* woman, her father's mistress. What would she have done if she had known? Ordered her out? She remembered now that it was she who spoke to the woman, not the woman to her, because she was standing alone as if she was a stranger. People must have been avoiding her, they had all known who she was. But what did it matter? She would never come here again. And her father was gone and she was safe. At least she had a home. And Millie was safe. Oh yes . . . Her thoughts had been about to add, Oh yes, Millie was safe, but they were checked as she glanced towards her brothers. No one of them would take responsibility for Millie and they would, she knew, put her away as quickly as their father would have done except for the obstacle standing in their way. And she was the obstacle: as long as they needed her to run the place they would put up with Millie. But for how long would that be?

She had no time to worry over this point because Lady Emily had now dragged herself to her feet and, looking towards her husband who was nodding in his chair, she bellowed, 'Up! Gregory, and at 'em.'

As Arnold Thorman moved to the old man's side to assist him to his feet, Roland went hastily to open the door while Stanley offered Lady Emily his arm. But before taking it she turned to Agnes, saying, 'Got your hands full, girl. Want any advice at any time come across to me. Don't suppose I'll come to this place again.' She moved her scraggy neck stiffly and looked about her. Then on a somewhat sad note she ended, 'Spent some very happy times in this room. Your grandfather was a fine dancer. Yes, had some good times in this house. But that was a long, long time ago. 'Tis dying now, if not dead.' Her voice sank on the last words and with them she turned from Agnes and, taking Stanley's proffered arm, walked stiffly down the room and across the hall.

From the top of the steps Agnes watched her brothers helping the couple into their coach. She saw them put the rugs around their knees, then give a signal to the coachman. And so the last visitors of the day departed.

When they were all in the drawing-room again there was silence among them for a few minutes. It was Stanley who spoke, saying, 'What an old horror! She's like an animated corpse. People shouldn't be allowed to live that long. You wouldn't keep an animal in that condition.'

'Oh, shut up!' Arnold pressed his hand towards his brother, saying now, 'Wait until you're fifty or so.'

'But she must be nearly twice fifty.'

'Her tongue's still young.'

Stanley now turned to Arnold and he nodded at him, saying, 'You're right there, she's as sharp as a needle where scandal's concerned.'

'I could do with a drink.'

'You're not the only one.' Arnold went to the small table on which stood a tray and a decanter and glasses. Before pouring out any of the spirit he looked towards Agnes, saying, 'Would you like a drop?'

She nodded her head in assent, then said, 'Did you know who the woman was that Lady Emily was talking about?'

'You mean Father's mistress?'

The bold statement put Agnes's teeth on edge for a moment. 'Yes, that's who I mean,' she said. And for answer Arnold lifted up the decanter, poured out a measure of whisky, brought it to her, before saying, 'Yes, I knew, and there's no need to look so shocked.'

'I'm not shocked.'

'I'm glad to hear it, because he was no better or no worse than any other man.'

'Yes, he was.'

She was immediately confronted by her three brothers now, their faces straight as they stared at her, slightly surprised by her attitude. 'You knew nothing about him. You don't know the life we've had to lead in this house. You got what you wanted, the three of you, and that was to get away, while we, the house and everybody in it, had to suffer because of it. In other circumstances you would have had to work, and if you had we wouldn't have been in the pickle we are today. If even only you, Arnold, had stayed at home and gone into the businesses, seen to one of them, we might have been able to survive. But no, you're all your father's sons, self first. As I've already pointed out to Stanley here, how do you think I felt when I had to witness a servant paying for our coal? No money, no coal. And it's the same now with the tradesmen. That man is returning tomorrow to see about the pictures. You hadn't arrived when he first came, and whatever you get . . . I suppose now it is you who are responsible, Arnold, so I say, whatever you get, before it is swallowed up supplying all your needs, the tradesmen must be seen to.'

'The tradesmen will be seen to.' Arnold's voice was stiff. 'I hope when Rawley calls tomorrow and things are straightened up there will be enough to clear all the debts.'

The sound that escaped from Agnes caused the three of them to look at each other for she laughed, a high derisive laugh. Her head back, her eyes cast towards the ceiling, she reverted not only to Peggy's saying but to one of Maggie's when she said, 'I hope in God's name it keeps fine for you.' Unconsciously the words came out on Maggie's Irish inflexion, and on this she spread over them one look that now had no laughter in it before walking out of the room.

*       *       *

198

It was three o'clock the next afternoon; the sun was shining brightly through the long windows of the library. Agnes sat with the men, looking at Mr Rawley the solicitor. He had finished reading the will that her father had had drawn up ten years ago. In it he left everything to his eldest son. When he mentioned his wife it was merely to say she could live in the house until his eldest son married, when it would be at his discretion whether or not she remained. There was mention of the four different factories in which he then had shares, and from the income of which money should be provided to put his two younger sons through university.

Like her brothers, Agnes sat silent, listening to Mr Rawley as he said, 'Of course things have changed vastly since that time. Your father sold his shares in three of the factories; there is only the marine chandlers left. If this were sold his personal debts could be met and also provision made for the interest on the mortgage'—apparently her father had taken a second mortgage on the house five years ago—and Mr Rawley ended, 'and leave sufficient to clear off local debts, which in many instances are rather heavy.'

Although the contents of the will came as no surprise to Agnes, she felt that the three men had been stunned. Perhaps for the first time they were realizing she was right and that they had known nothing about their father or of his ways over the past years. One thing hurt her: not that her father had made no mention of her in the will but that he made no provision, even at that time, for Dave and Peggy. Already, they had given him a lifetime of service, and for all he cared they could end up in

199

the workhouse. She looked at her brothers. She wondered if it had struck them that there had been no mention of Dave and Peggy in the will. But no, she could almost read each of their minds. Each one of them was concerned about himself and his future. The men in this family are a poor lot, she thought, selfish, thinking only of what was going to happen to them. But then, they hadn't the monopoly of selfishness. What about James? It seemed that all the men she knew were made in the same mould, everyone was out for himself. Well, that being the case, it would pay her to be out for herself, and for Millie too; and for Dave and Peggy and Ruthie; yes, and Maggie and Betty. As for the men, Arthur Bloom and Hubbard and Bradley, well they were men and they could fend for themselves, especially Bradley. In any case, he had been here such a short time. Her mind dwelt on Bradley as it had been doing a lot over the past week. He was a strange man, disturbing. He seemed to have taken over the kitchen side of the house, like a steward might do. She felt it. There was a change in Peggy's attitude towards him and in Ruthie's too. Of course, she had always considered Maggie to be for him. But Dave, how did he view him? In a way, he owed his life to Bradley. Dave was a changed man: he had become very quiet, old all of a sudden. Peggy said he sat about staring into the fire at night, whereas before he had always found something to be busy with.

It was odd the things that had happened since the man Bradley had come into their employ. She had lost James, and Bradley had found her crying. He had picked her up from the ground and talked to her and soothed her. And there was that business concerning him before he came here, the business with his cousin and her having a child. Then for him to witness how her father had died; and then to direct them all as to what they must do. And apparently he had told Hubbard, and Hubbard had told Peggy, that he was thinking of leaving.

Of a sudden she again felt disturbed. What if, when he left, he should talk? He wouldn't feel so constrained to keep silent if he was away from here . . . But he wouldn't talk, he wasn't that kind of a man. How did she know? Oh, why was she bothering about Bradley when Mr Rawley was talking. He was saying:

'I'd be careful about letting the pictures go to London, unless you investigate the firm. Anyway I wouldn't advise selling them privately; the best thing would be to auction them. They are very good auctioneers up there and they attract foreign bidders. I would think twice before you decide how you're going to dispose of them. Well, that is all, gentlemen. If you should need me for anything more you only have to call, but in the meantime I'll look into what the business might bring and let you know as soon as possible.'

Arnold had got to his feet now and he said, 'I should be obliged if you would do just that, because I intend to leave for Australia as soon as possible. I have a post awaiting me there, and my brother'— he indicated Roland—'is coming with me.'

'Oh . . . Oh, who is to look after the estate then?' Mr Rawley glanced from one to the other and Arnold said, 'Stanley will be in charge, but we hope that he will be able to finish his time at Oxford. In the meantime, Agnes here will be seeing to things.'

Will she? Will she? The words were loud in her head. No asking Agnes. No, what are you going to do with your life, Agnes? No, you're here to the end of your days, or until Stanley marries, and then you can be nursemaid to his children. Damned if I will. I'll do something: I won't put up with it. Who do they think they are, anyway? ...

*Be quiet.* Be quiet. This was no way to go on. Well, they were acting as if she were of no account. Oh, if only there wasn't Millie she'd let blaze at them. If only she had a friend, someone she could turn to, run to, to get away from here. But then she couldn't run to them alone, she'd have to take Millie by the hand. And would any friend accept Millie? Oh! to think that she'd have to take orders from Stanley. It wasn't to be tolerated. Stanley hadn't the brains he was born with, he was empty headed, vain. She liked Stanley least of the three.

*Will you be quiet!* The controlled self that had been brought into being under the training of Miss Burrow's private school, then under the ice-like exterior of her mother, stood up stiffly against her other disturbing self.

'I could give piano lessons.'

They were all staring at her, and she was staring at herself, inwardly. Why in the name of heavens had she said that aloud? Her mind had been looking for a way of escape and the idea presented itself to her. But to give piano lessons you must have a piano and a house to put it in.

'What did you say?' Arnold's brows were meeting above the top of his sharp nose and she gave a slight laugh as she said, 'What I meant to say was, I suppose I could give piano lessons to provide me with pin money as nobody seems to have

202

considered my needs.'

Annoyance, embarrassment, and amazement showed on the faces of her brothers, but it was Mr Rawley who, smiling at her, said, 'I don't think you'll be brought down to that, Miss Agnes; I'm sure your brothers'—he nodded to them now—'will see that you are amply provided for within the means at their disposal.'

Agnes watched Mr Rawley look inquiringly at her brothers, and it was when Arnold said, 'We shall do what we think necessary,' that she became infuriated inside, but she said nothing, at least until the goodbyes had been said to Mr Rawley. However, alone with them, she picked up the conversation as if only a second before Arnold had made the statement: 'We shall do what we think necessary,' for now, looking at him, she said, 'And what do you think necessary, Arnold, for my comfort?'

'What on earth are you talking about! What's come over you, Agnes? I've never known you be like this. Of course'—he inclined his head now slowly towards her and his voice dropped to a lower tone as he went on—'I can understand your disappointment over Crockford and I do think it was a dirty deal, but that is no reason why you should adopt this manner towards us.'

'I adopt this manner towards you all, Arnold, because of the lack of consideration you have adopted towards me. Have any of you given a thought to my welfare? You, Arnold, and Roland, are to go to Australia. Australia is a long way off. And the business of the house supposedly to be left to Stanley. And what does Stanley do? He goes to Oxford, and who has to see to the running of the place? Oh, someone who doesn't count, it's her duty . . . Agnes! Anyway, if she didn't do that, what else could she do? As I just said, I could give piano lessons; I'm quite free. Oh! Oh!' She now wagged her finger from one to the other. 'Don't hold up Millie as an obstacle to my departure. Millie is not my responsibility, she is the responsibility of the head of this house and that is you, Arnold. And if you delegate that responsibility to Stanley, then she is Stanley's. And if between you you decide to put her away, you can't put her into the workhouse, and private homes cost a lot of money, as father found out when he made inquiries along that same road. I repeat, Millie isn't my responsibility, so now, dear brothers'—she looked from one to the other—'get your heads together and tell me, that is when matters are straightened out, exactly what I am to be allowed for the running of the establishment and also what is to be my private allowance? Call it a dress allowance, but an allowance of some kind I must have.'

She now inclined her head to each brother in turn, then swung around with what could only be described as a flounce, and left the room; but not quickly enough to close her ears to Roland saying, 'Well, I'll be damned! What's come over her?'

Up in her room she sat down by the corner window, one part of which looked down on to the front of the house and the other on to the side of the courtyard. All fight had now gone from her. She slumped forward and rested her elbow on the broad sill and laid her cheek on her hand and a voice inside of her was a whisper as she said, 'What's the end going to be? Where am I going? Surely this is not all that life has to offer?'

As she stared down into the yard she saw Bradley leading Nippy from out of the stable; he was patting its head. She drew to one side and stared down at him. There was a man who was free, independent, no ties, no nothing. And he was attractive to women. What was it about him that made him attractive? He was pleasant looking but not all that good-looking; he was tallish but his body was bulky with it, thickset. Perhaps it was the strength he gave off that women admired.

She now watched him pull the horse to a stop as if someone had called him. Then Maggie came into view. She ran up to him and said something that made him laugh, and he put out his hand and touched her cheek. And at this she knew a feeling of indignation. Surely he wasn't out to captivate a girl like Maggie because Maggie was really coarse looking, even ugly. She had a sweet nature, admitted, and she could be very amusing at times, but surely that wouldn't attract a man like him unless he was the kind of man who was out to pay court to every woman who smiled at him.

She rose from the window-seat. Her hands, now joined at her waist, were tightly gripped together, and realizing this, she flung them apart as if she were separating combatants.

She would go and see Millie, read to her.

*Oh Millie! Millie!* At this moment she could hate Millie.

No. No. Going to the bed now, she flung herself across it and, gripping the pillow, she buried her face into it and the tears came spilling from her eyes and nose. 'What is it?' she cried at herself. 'What is the matter with me? Am I too becoming odd? Is this what spinsterhood does to one?' She

205

eased her face from the pillow. *Spinsterhood.* She hadn't thought of it like that before, but she was twenty-six, and there was no hope of her marrying now, because who would visit this place. Certainly no eligible young men, not even eligible middle-aged ones. She was a spinster.

The realization seemed to sadden and sober her at the same time and she rose from the bed, went to the wash-hand stand and sluiced her face; then going to the mirror, she combed her hair back from her forehead and as she peered at her reflection in the glass she thought, I'm not even like the parson's daughters who at least have the satisfaction of doing good works. Suddenly she found herself envying them, and likewise those ladies who went in for nursing and teaching; at this moment she even envied the women of the lower classes who served in shops. Straightening up, she smoothed down her dress; then as she made for the door her mind seemed to accept the fact that she was entering a new kind of world, the world of spinsterhood, and she saw it as something that had to be faced, lived with, endured. But with the handle of the door gripped in her hand, she looked down at it as she thought bitterly, What a waste of life!

# CHAPTER FOUR

It was the first week in October. Yesterday, Stanley had left for Oxford to begin the first of his final three terms there; Arnold and Roland were to leave tomorrow; and she couldn't wait for them to be gone. She was on her way downstairs now to see to the last dinner they were likely to have in the house for a long time. She was walking along the gallery that faced the north side of the house and the courtyard, and through the tall windows she could see in the fading light the line of horse boxes where once bobbing heads hung over the half-doors. But now, all were closed, except two at the end.

As she was passing the last window before opening the door to descend the back stairs into the kitchen passage, she was brought to a halt by the sight of Maggie running through the archway that divided the barn from the storerooms. She had her head down and her hand to her face; she watched her hesitate before running across the yard to the grain store.

Why was she running like that, and holding her head?

Before she could answer the question in her mind, she saw Bradley. He came into view as if he had come out of the house through the boot-room door. He had a lantern in his hand and he stood for a moment looking towards the door of the grain room; then he made towards it and he too went in.

She didn't move from her position but kept staring down across the yard waiting for the door to open and for them, or one of them, to emerge. But when it remained closed there arose in her a feeling that wasn't new but now had something added to it, annoyance touching on anger.

When Ruthie passed her, saying, 'Nights are drawing in now, aren't they, miss?' she muttered, 'What?' glanced over her shoulder for a moment, then said, 'Oh yes. Yes, yes, they are, Ruthie;' then brought her gaze back on to the yard. And now the anger in her consuming all her other feelings, she cried within herself, Oh, I'd like to tell that man something. Who does he think he is, anyway? He imagines he has just got to lift his little finger and women come running. And since that business of Dave and Father he seems to have taken over. And Dave doesn't like being beholden to him, I know he doesn't . . . But taking liberties with Maggie . . . Oh! I would like to tell him what I think of him . . .

Across in the grain room Robert was actually repeating her very words. A few minutes earlier he had picked up the lantern from the boot room, lit it and walked into the yard, intending to hang it on a nail outside the kitchen door, when he saw Maggie running across the bottom of the yard, her head down and her hand up to her face. When he called softly to her and she didn't answer but dashed into the grain room, he followed her, there to see her standing against the post that supported one of the bins, her face buried in the crook of her arm. The sight brought him to a standstill just within the door: Maggie the joker, Maggie the laughter maker, Maggie who had a kind word for the devil, Maggie the plainest woman he had ever come across, but also the best-hearted, was crying. It was so out of character that for a moment he was at a

208

loss. Then with a swift movement he put the lantern on a hook and went to her and, taking her by the shoulders, he pulled her round, saying, 'What is it? What is it, Maggie?'

She gulped in her throat, coughed as if she was going to choke, then muttered, ' 'Tis nothing, 'tis nothing.'

' 'Tis something. Now come on, what's happened? Somebody done something to you, said something?'

She gulped again and, taking her hand, she passed it over her face, muttering now, 'I'm silly. 'Tis soft I am to take notice. Just talk. Just talk.'

'What talk? Whose talk? Come on, come on.' He shook her gently. 'It would have to be some great talk to make you upset like this.'

' 'Tis nothing, Robert.' She had called him Robert as had Peggy and Ruthie and Betty since the night when he had straightened things out for them all.

'Look, has somebody been at you? Greg?'

'Oh, Greg.' There was a small smile came through her tears and she said, 'Greg? Never! Never!'

'Then who?'

' 'Tis nothing.'

'Tell me, somebody from outside, somebody got in?'

' No, no.'

'Well who then? I'm not budging from here until I know, and if you don't tell me I'll go across and get your uncle and aunt and they'll get it out of you. So you may as well tell me; it might be better in the long run. What's it all about?'

She hung her head for a moment, then said, 'I'd

been down the garden to Mr Bloom to tell him what we wanted for the morrow in the way of vegetables like and . . . and I was comin' back by the big hedge and . . . and the young gentlemen were on the other side. They . . . they had been to Newcastle. They had gone by train as you know and likely not knowin' what time they would be back, they hadn't ordered the trap for you or Greg to meet it, so they must have come across the fields as a short cut. Anyway, there they were, walkin' up on yon side of the hedge, and me meself on this side, and they were talkin'—' her head moved from one side to the other now before she muttered, 'about their . . . their exploits with . . . with the women in Newcastle. I . . . I didn't take much notice, tried to shut me ears, yet you know how it is. An' then Master Arnold said at one time they wouldn't have had to make the journey, they . . . they could have been—' again her head moved before she muttered, 'could have been served in the house, but now there was only Betty . . . and me.'

Her head now sank lower and once again the tears began to stream down her face, and when Robert said, 'Yes?' she muttered, 'Master Roland then said anybody would be hard pushed to take me, even—' now she had to gulp deep in her throat before she could end, and then on a stammer, 'w . . . w . . . with their eyes blindfolded.'

Her mouth wide open now and the tears running from her cheeks on to her lower lips, she looked at him. ' 'Tis hurtful, 'tis hurtful, Robert,' she said. 'I know I'm no beauty, not even plain, I know all about myself, so I laugh and joke, but I've got feelin's, I've got feelin's like any other lass . . .

210

woman 'cos, 'cos I'm no lass. I thought I'd got over being hurt, cryin' like, but you never do.'

'Blast them to hell.' He put out his arms and pulled her close to him, and she sank her head into his shoulder. Pushing her cap away, he stroked her hair, saying, 'Don't cheapen yourself like that, lass. Let me tell you, you're better than any woman I've met, it's the heart that matters, and . . . and many a man would be glad of you. Come, come on now. Quiet, quiet.'

As he spoke the last word the door was thrust open and there, like the avenging angel, stood his mistress. And what she said was, 'What may I ask are you up to, Mr Bradley?'

As he felt Maggie go to pull herself from his embrace he held her tightly while, looking over her shoulder, he stared through the lantern light at Agnes and replied, 'I'm up to comfortin' somebody who needs it, Miss Thorman.'

'You're philandering, Bradley, and I won't have it. I won't have Maggie annoyed, upset . . . Get back into the house, Maggie.'

Maggie now tore herself from Robert's embrace and, looking at Agnes, she said, 'He . . . he was only tryin' to help me, he was . . .'

'*Go into the house.* Do as you're bid.'

Maggie did as she was bid and at a run.

Now with one deadly look in Robert's direction, Agnes was about to follow Maggie when Robert sprang forward and with outstretched arm clashed the door shut.

Agnes startled, pressed her back tight against the door, and Robert's wrist almost touched her cheekbone as they stood glaring at each other, only, in Agnes's eyes, there was now a slight touch

211

of fear, which came over in her voice as she demanded, 'Open the door, Bradley, this minute.'

'I'll open it when I'm ready.' He omitted to add 'miss,' but went on, 'It isn't so long ago, is it, since a man played the dirty on you, and you knew what it was then to cry your eyes out, didn't you? And you weren't above accepting a little sympathy . . . from an inferior. Well, I was handing out another little bit of sympathy, but to an equal. Maggie is no child, she's a woman, and if I want to hold her, I'll hold her.'

'You . . . you are a philanderer, Bradley. You don't mean any good by Maggie. She is not your type of . . . of . . . of woman.'

'How the hell do you know what my type is, miss?'

'You forget to whom you are speaking.'

'No, I don't forget to who I'm speaking, and I repeat, how do you know what my type is? There's more worth in Maggie than in you or any of your kind.'

'Well, I'm . . . I'm glad you recognize it. So now will you please allow me to leave?'

'I'll let you leave when I'm ready and when you've heard me out and when you hear why Maggie needed comfort.'

Their faces were not more than a foot from each other, their clothes were almost touching, their breaths were mingling as were their angers, and Agnes found difficulty in speaking as she said, 'For whatever reason you were comforting her, the point is, do you mean well by her? What are your intentions? Do you mean to marry her?'

'Huh!' He laughed aloud and it wasn't without mirth, and the answer he gave her was, 'You lot

212

amaze me. You know that? You with your codes, your codes for other people, for the underlings, you simply amaze me. You can have your mistresses, your lovers, you can do any damn thing you like in that way, but when it comes to one of what you term the lower class, you begin to moralize. Well, let me answer your question, miss, whether I intend to marry her or not is my business and nobody else's. But just on the side, let me tell you, if I had to marry every lass I've held in me arms I'd have a harem by now. But that's light talk, what I aim to tell you is why Maggie was crying. Maggie, whose one aim in life is to laugh and make other people laugh, she was crying because she was hurt, and who had hurt her? Well, listen, miss, listen. 'Twas your brothers.'

He watched her whole face stretch, her eyes widen, her lips fall apart, even the tip of her nose seemed to droop, then all the muscles of her face contracted and were screwed up before she repeated, *'My brothers?'*

'Yes, your brothers.' He put his head on one side now and shifted the position of his hand against the door, moving it upwards, and like this his thumb was almost buried in her hair, and then he went on, 'They had been in Newcastle this afternoon for a purpose I will leave to your imagination. They happened to be walking along one side of the beech hedge while Maggie was walking along the other. They were discussing the disadvantages of having to go into Newcastle for their pleasures because apparently at one time these had been available in the house, among the lower orders of course.' He nodded his head at her now. 'But times have changed, they said, and now there was only

213

Betty and Maggie herself. And at this Maggie naturally pricked up her ears, only to hear your brother Roland saying that he would be hard pushed if he had to take Maggie to supply his needs even, he added, if he were blindfolded.'

The muscles of her face had again stretched, once more her mouth was hanging open, but she snapped it closed and gulped as he asked, 'How would you have reacted if you had heard that somebody would have to be blindfolded before they could touch your body?'

He watched her blink rapidly, he watched the colour flood up over what had been her deadly pale skin; then he took his hand from the door and stood back from her, and his voice was quiet but deep as he said, 'What I'd like to do now is to go in there and bust their mouths for them, and I could do it, but I know where I'd land, and they're not worth it. So, I'll just say to you, miss, the quicker I get out of this place the better; I've put it off long enough. I'm engaged by the week, so as you seem to be running the show, I give you a week's notice.'

She was staring at him speechless. Then her body jerked to the side as his hand again thrust forward; but it was to open the door, and she slid round the door and out. When she was gone he closed it again and now stood with his back to it and his eyes tightly shut and, his hands turned into fists by his side, he muttered, 'God! that woman.' Then bringing himself from the door, he drew in a long breath as he muttered to himself, 'Well, it'll soon be over.'

\*　　　\*　　　\*

'You must apologize to her.'

'What?' Arnold Thorman looked at his sister as if she too, like Millie, had become abnormal; then he added, 'Don't be stupid. *Apologize to Maggie?*'

'Yes, apologize to Maggie. You should be ashamed of yourself. And you too.' She now looked at Roland and he, staring at her coolly, said, 'You are being ridiculous. How old are you now? Twenty-five. No, twenty-six, and you're talking as if you had just come out of school, a convent school. In fact, that type is more aware of life than, let me tell you, you seem to be. Why, our grandfather used to . . .'

'I don't want to hear what our grandfather used to do; I only know that Maggie has been hurt, more than hurt, insulted.'

'You don't insult that kind of person, Agnes.'

She stared at her eldest brother now and again there came into her mind, how different she was from them all on this side of the house: she was, as she had felt before, more akin to those on the staff, except of course that Bradley individual. Oh, that man!

Looking back at her brother she said quietly, 'Arnold, you are acting like Lord of the Manor, and you are not a lord, and this is not a manor, it isn't even a decently run establishment. And let me tell you something. I don't know how much reading you've done about Australia but, from what I've read, it's a raw country, and I'm afraid your gentlemanly and, I might add, archaic ideas of what rights gentlemen are entitled to are going to be shattered somewhat, and I only wish it were possible for me to be there to see the process.'

She turned from them and as she walked down

the room Roland called after her, 'This is a nice send-off, I must say. Our last night here too.'

At the door she stopped and, looking back at them, she cried, 'Then why not return to Newcastle and continue your entertainment.'

As she entered the hall and made for the stairs she saw Ruthie coming through the door from the kitchen, leading Millie by the hand, and, drawing her quickly across the hall, she said, 'She's upset, miss. She's just heard that Robert . . . Bradley's leaving. He's in a paddy: he's had an upset of some kind; must have been with Bloom. And there's our Maggie been crying her eyes out; she's got a spasm of toothache. My mother says she'll have to go into the dentist the morrow. Will it be all right if I take her in, miss?'

Tempers, toothaches, brothers and their prostitutes, and Bradley.

'Yes, yes; we'll see about it tomorrow. Come along, Millie.' She almost grabbed Millie's hand and pulled her up the stairs, and when Millie showed some reluctance to go into her room, she stopped and, wagging her finger in her face, she said, 'Now Millie, don't you start, because I'm in no mood tonight to put up with any tantrums. You understand?'

'Bradley. I like Bradley.'

'Too many people like Bradley. Come on.'

In the bedroom she ordered, 'Get your things off and get to bed.' She wasn't, however, immediately obeyed, for Millie, standing firmly in the middle of the room, said quietly, 'But Aggie, I don't want to go to bed yet.'

Agnes was at the wardrobe taking down Millie's dressing-gown and her hand became still on the

216

rail. Millie was talking. She had not talked coherently like this for some time. She turned and went towards her, saying quietly now, 'Bradley wants to go away, Millie, and if he wants to go, he'll go; nothing we can say will stop him.'

'He's nice.'

Agnes walked to the bed and laid the dressing gown across the foot of it; then picking up a nightdress case, she pulled out Millie's nightdress and shook it gently as she said, 'What makes you think he's nice?'

The lucidity of the reply she got brought her slowly round to survey her sister, for Millie, speaking quietly, said, 'He talks to me as if I was like anyone else. He is not fearful of me, and he laughs with me and understands what I say. When I told him yesterday I would like to fly, he said, he, too, had always wanted to fly and he wondered why birds could not only fly but walk, not hopping but putting one foot in front of the other like we do. And then some of them could also swim. He said it was very unfair that we could only walk. Nobody has ever talked to me like that. You haven't, have you, Aggie?'

Slowly Agnes sat down on the side of the bed and stared at this beloved creature. She was right. No, she hadn't talked to her like that, and if she had said that she wanted to fly she would have replied, 'Don't be silly! You are not a bird, humans can't fly.' But Bradley had apparently voiced what many men dreamed of doing, and that was flying. Only recently there had been something in the paper about a man making silk wings and jumping off a bridge, only he fell into the water and sank. But they were now making great machines, she

217

understood, that flew in the air. Zeppelins they called them. But above all, what Bradley had done was to get her talking again, and this had likely obliterated the events of that particular evening, which must have been terrifying for her, so much so that it had made her dumb for weeks.

'Nothing stays nice for long, does it, Aggie?'

Agnes rose from the bed and, going towards the slim form, she enfolded it in her arms, saying gently, 'No, that's true, dear. But from now on things will be different. We'll . . . we'll go for walks and I'll read to you, and during the winter months we'll play the piano together, because you can play some little pieces, can't you? Then in the summer we will take a part of the garden, all to ourselves, and make it new again. There now.' She pressed her sister gently from her and looked into her face, smiling as she said, 'Isn't that something to look forward to?'

Millie now smiled back at her, saying, 'Yes, yes, it is, Aggie, something to look forward to; but'— her head drooped—'I do wish you would ask Bradley to stay. Could you ask Bradley to stay? I . . . I think he would stay for you.'

Agnes felt the colour rising once more over her face as she asked, 'What makes you think that?'

'Because . . . because I think he likes you, because when I talk about you he talks about you.'

'He does? When has he talked about me?'

'Oh, when he was doing the windows and the floor in the library where the dry rot is. That was funny, wasn't it? We laughed about that. Why do they call it dry rot, he said, when it's caused by wet?'

'And what did he say about me?' Agnes brought

her back to the question.

'Oh'—Millie turned her head to the side as if trying to recall something—'he . . . he said you had lovely eyes, and . . . and I said you had lonely eyes. And then he said, yes, yes I was right, you had lonely eyes.'

'Here!' Agnes's voice was sharp now. 'Get your things off. And Millie . . . Millie, look at me. You are not to discuss me with Bradley. You understand? For the time he is here, you are not to talk about me to Bradley.'

'Yes, Aggie. All right.'

As Agnes busied herself about the room, Millie slowly took off her clothes, muttering the while to herself; then when she was in bed and Agnes was seated ready to read to her, she suddenly sat up straight, saying, 'Oh, Bradley promised to bring me a puppy. He was going to ask you if I could have a puppy. He knew of a lovely puppy. Oh, I do want a puppy. Can I have a puppy? Will you let me have a puppy, Aggie?'

'Yes, yes. Lie down. All right, you may have a puppy, but . . . but he must be kept outside.'

'Outside?'

'Yes. We'll have a special place made for him outside.'

'But . . . but I want him in the house, in here'— she pointed down to the counterpane—'in bed with me.'

'You can't have a puppy in bed, Millie.'

'But . . . but Bradley said he had a puppy and it used to lie beside him in bed.'

'Lie down!' Her voice was almost a scream and Millie lay down, and Agnes, closing the book with a bang, put it on the side table; then looking down again on the thin pale face, she said, 'I'll be back shortly. Lie still now, I'll be back shortly.'

A few minutes later she was standing in her own room and with her hands joined tightly in the curve of her breasts; her lips were pulled into a thin line and her eyes were screwed tight and her mind was crying, Bradley! Bradley! Bradley! If I hear his name once more tonight, I too will become demented.


# CHAPTER FIVE

Greg Hubbard took the horse out of the shafts of the trap and passed them over to Robert, saying, 'Not a copper.'

'What do you mean, not a copper?'

'Well, I expected at least half a sovereign, 'cos yesterday he said to me, "Keep things going as well as possible, Hubbard, won't you?" And I said, "Yes, sir, I'll do me best." So I thought, well, this mornin' . . . just a little appreciation. But no, not even a damned penny, only, "You sure everything's in the van, Hubbard?" ' He was imitating Arnold's voice now. ' "Good. Do as you said now and see to things. Goodbye." '

He now followed Robert into the stables, saying, 'Anyway, I'm glad they've gone. And the other young snot too, up there learning how to be snottier. We might have a bit of peace for a time now. But then I don't know because Miss has been going round this morning like a bear with a sore skull. And things are not right in the kitchen either. That business last night about Maggie having the toothache, she's got no toothache. But she was upset over something, and I can tell you I was upset to see her in such a state. She's a good lass, is Maggie, and she wouldn't have been crying like that for nothing. I couldn't get to sleep last night for thinking about it. Do you know owt? And then about you leaving; man, that surprised me.'

For answer, Robert turned to him and said, 'You like Maggie, don't you?'

'Aye, I do. She's good company, she's a real good lass.'

'Have you ever thought of marrying her?'

'What!' Greg Hubbard peered at Robert through narrowed lids and Robert came back at him sharply saying, 'You could do a lot worse; many a man could do a lot worse.'

'Shut up! Don't go on. You're tellin' me. I know I could do a lot worse, but look at me, forty-one come the first of November and her just on twenty. I'm old enough to be her father, an' a bit.'

'What's age got to do with it? You're a well set-up fellow.' He turned his head and looked Hubbard up and down, a half smile on his face; then after a moment he confronted him fully, saying, 'No, she hadn't the toothache last night, as you surmised, and I'll tell you what she was crying about if you'll keep it to yourself, and then she won't think whatever action you take in the future is out of pity.'

And so he told him the reason for Maggie being upset, and when he had finished Greg Hubbard remained silent for quite some seconds before he said, 'Well, Robbie, it's a damn good job I didn't know this afore those two left, as there's one thing sure, I'd be going along with you, and not next

221

week, but the day, for I'd have busted their gobs. By God! I would that.'

Robert went on with the rubbing down of the horse, but as he did so he said, 'You're to go to the Durhan Cattle Fair on Monday, so I heard Mr Waters tellin' you?'

'Aye, I'm takin' a crop of hens in.'

'Well, take Maggie along. She never gets anywhere; she'll jump at the chance.'

When there was no response to this Robert turned and looked at Greg, saying, 'Well?'

'It's a thought.' Greg gave a twisted smile, then he added, 'But what if she laughs in me face. She mightn't be any oil paintin' but she's young and healthy and . . .'

'Maggie'll not laugh in your face; she'll laugh with you but not at you. Anyway, I should think it's worth a try. What have you got to lose? On the other hand, what have you got to look forward to? Old age on your own.'

'Aye, there's that in it.' Greg walked slowly out and Robert resumed his work again with the feeling that Maggie's future was settled. That would be something good coming out of this house of turmoil. He had six more days to go and then he would be free and by God! wouldn't he be glad to see the last of this place and everybody in it. Aye, definitely, *everybody in it.*

\*         \*         \*

The meal in the kitchen was constrained: there was no small talk or laughter, and every time Robert looked up from his plate he felt Dave Waters's eyes on him and he wanted to say, 'It's all right, don't worry, I won't talk, I'm not a blabber.' And he would say this to him before he left and so try to put the man's mind at ease.

What was troubling him not a little was that Maggie didn't look at him at all, she kept her eyes averted. But Ruthie looked at him, as did Betty Trollop. They smiled covertly at him, and this made him think ironically to himself they considered Maggie as another notch on his life tree. By! was there any man so misjudged as he where this particular thing was concerned? One of the main reasons for his leaving Jarrow was for him to escape marriage, and since then he had been accused of coming between a lass and her intended, giving another one a bairn, and now he shouldn't be surprised if they thought he had been making advances to Maggie; and, of course, they weren't taking into account Miss Millie's preference for his company.

Well now, he promised himself, the very next time any such label was stuck on him there'd be some truth behind it, and that without a wedding ring on the finger. He might have to make a run for it afterwards but he was getting used to change.

Later that night in bed he had the same trouble getting off to sleep as he'd had the night before, because the picture in his mind was of himself standing with his arm outstretched, his hand against her hair, his face close to hers, and the peculiar scent of her body wafting up his nostrils.

\*       \*       \*

It was ten o'clock the next morning and they were facing each other once again, across a desk this

223

time. Last night she had received what amounted to a deputation headed by Dave. At any other time, had he spoken to her in like fashion, she would have said, What has come over you Dave? But since the accident with her father she had realized that Dave was a changed man and was probably still suffering from shock, and so when he said, 'You can't let him go, you've got to ask him to stay; he could open his mouth and then where would we be?' she could have answered, 'You mean, where would you be?' But she didn't for wasn't there some law whereby one could be implicated for hiding the truth and for harbouring what was in plain and terrifying language, incredible as it sounded when applied to Dave, a murderer?

He had gone on to say, 'What's more, you'll not get another like him, I mean, as handy with wood'n that. You'd have to pay a carpenter's firm a mint for the work he's done on the windows and the floor and skirting in the library. Then he helps Bloom. He's as strong as a bull, sort of tireless. You'll not get another like him. And the women . . . they're upset.'

And the women *were* upset, Peggy had come up to her room last night and, sitting on the foot of her bed, she had said, 'I don't know what's happened rightly to upset him, but if you let him go he's going to be a loss. You know the ones we've had afore him, they would neither work nor want. Dave spent more time on their tails than it would have taken him to do the jobs himself.' She had then ended, 'If it wouldn't upset you too much, don't you think you could ask him to stay on, lass?'

She had looked at Peggy. Peggy had said she didn't know the reason for Bradley's leaving, but

224

she knew all right: Maggie had likely filled her in, at least given a description of the compromising situation . . . Why did she use such words? Compromising. What was compromising about a man holding a woman? And her, as he had pointed out so strongly, of his own class.

Then this morning, when Maggie had brought her an early cup of tea she had stood looking down at her, her eyes lowered as she said, 'I was daft, Miss Agnes, to make all that fuss. An' look where it's landed him, out of a job. An' him just being kind. There was nothin' more in it, miss, he was just comforting me.'

That word again, comforting. Oh, as she had said, Bradley was the exponent of comfort all right where women were concerned. She wanted to be rid of him, she wanted to see him go, for then, knowing that she would never set eyes on him again, her mind would fall into familiar channels of thinking and her imagination would not run rife.

She had pulled herself up in the bed and demanded of Maggie, 'Why should I ask him to stay? It isn't seemly. You know that yourself, Maggie, it isn't seemly. He should be the one to come and ask to be reinstated.'

'Oh.' Maggie had half turned away as if about to make for the door, then had paused and, looking downwards, had shaken her head as she said, 'He wouldn't do that. He's not made that way.'

'Not made that way?' The words had seemed to tumble from a platform high in her head, and they verged almost on a shout. Then lifting the cup and saucer from the tray, she had gulped on the tea before saying in a voice that her mother might have used, 'That's all, Maggie, thank you. We . . . we'll look into the matter.'

When Maggie left the room, she had lain back on her pillows, repeating, He's not made that way. Did you ever hear anything like it? He's not made that way. And as she lay staring fixedly ahead it came to her that she was reacting exactly as her mother would, or anyone else in a like position, on being told that a servant would not bring himself to apologize, apparently under any circumstances whatever.

Her fingers tapping on the eiderdown, she had sat inwardly fuming at the prospect that, she knew, lay before her. And there had come into her mind the picture of herself confronting her brothers only two days before and Arnold saying, 'You are being ridiculous. You don't insult that kind of person.' So what was the difference? Really what was the difference, her brother refusing to apologize to a servant or a servant refusing to apologize to his mistress? They were both men; the only difference between them was their position, one had been fortunate enough to be educated. But as men, which one was the better, Arnold or Bradley?

When the answer came she had flung back the bedclothes and after going across the room to the wash-hand stand she had poured the cold water from the jug almost filling the basin to the rim; then dropping her nightdress to her waist, she had knotted the sleeves and with a jerk pulled them tight, then proceeded to wash her face, arms and upper body while she shivered both inside and out.

\*      \*      \*

And now she was looking at the bone of

contention. She did not look into his face but at his clothes. He was wearing breeches and leggings and under an old tweed coat his blue striped shirt was buttoned to the neck. He had nothing on his head and he wasn't holding a cap in his hand.

'You wanted to see me, miss?'

'Yes, Bradley. Will you please be seated?'

He turned round and pulled the leather chair straight and in line with the desk before sitting down.

When she picked up a pen he recalled that her father had done something similar as he sat in that chair and rolled off the work he wanted done for ten shillings a week.

'I . . . I suppose I owe you an apology.' She raised her eyes to his face and waited for his response; and when none came she looked away from him down to her hand now that was tapping the pen on the blotter. What did he expect her to say! She had apologized. He was an impossible man, he didn't know his place . . . Oh! be quiet. What place? What place? There it was again that section of her mind at war with her upbringing. Now she heard her voice saying, even contritely, 'I . . . I was only thinking of Maggie. I . . . I had her welfare at heart.'

'Which would seem to prove the low opinion you have of me, miss.'

'Oh, no, no.'

'No?'

'No, no; only . . . Well—' Oh, what could she say? How did one deal with a man like this? Better to come to the point straightaway and get it over.

'What . . . what I wanted to see you about was . . . well, would . . . would you reconsider . . . I mean

227

stay on? I . . . I mean . . .' She couldn't go on. Her head drooped, the pen stopped tapping. And he put in quietly, 'It's all right, miss, don't worry. You've been put under pressure, I can gather that. Mr Waters imagines that once I leave here I'll open me mouth. He doesn't know me. It appears that nobody here does. I'm not a blab, and what I don't thank them for is putting you on the spot because I know you don't want me here. You haven't done so from the start. An' so I would sooner go.'

'Oh. Oh, you're wrong, Bradley, quite wrong. There is nothing personal. I mean you have done so much good work, the . . . the library and the windows and things. Oh, there's nothing personal, it is only that you're . . .'

A silence fell between them before he said, 'That I'm what, miss?'

She smiled faintly now as she looked at him, saying, 'Well, you must admit that you're not the usual type of servant. It is because you haven't been brought up to this kind of life. Being bred in the town, it . . . it makes a difference.'

'What you mean is, I'm not subservient enough, miss?'

The smile slid from her face. Subservient? Yes, that's what she meant. But she also meant something else, and it was still connected with the word he had just used, subservient. He used words. Given the chance, the same chance as her brothers, he would have been someone, he had that kind of drive. As it was he had trained to be a carpenter, and he was an excellent carpenter. But had he trained in law or business he would have done an equally excellent job.

She did not at this point question her radical

228

thinking but her face once again slid into a smile, wider this time, and she nodded at him as she said, 'Yes, I suppose that's what I mean, subservient. And I think that would come very hard to you, Bradley, wouldn't it?'

'It would all depend upon the circumstances, miss. For instance, I'd bend me knee to anybody who could teach me anything, say an intelligent or wise man.'

'Yes, Yes, I can understand one adhering to the sayings or precepts of an educated man . . .'

'Not necessarily educated, miss.'

'No?' There was both question and surprise in the word.

And he repeated, 'No; from what I've seen of some educated men, their intelligence is nil. There's a big difference atween intelligence and education, miss. At least that's how I see it.'

Yes, yes; of course he was right. Strange, but she had always linked the two together, feeling that without education you couldn't be intelligent. But how on earth had they got on to this subject?

As if he had picked up her thoughts he now said, 'But intelligence or education doesn't come into this matter, does it, miss? The question of the moment is, do I stay or go?'

'Yes, Bradley, the question of the moment is, do you stay or go?'

He stared at her. The width of the desk was between them but her face seemed to swell before his eyes until it covered the whole room. He stood up abruptly, saying, 'I stay as long as I'm needed.'

'Thank you, Bradley.' She too had risen to her feet.

'Thank you, miss.' His voice was low and his face

was straight.

As he went towards the door she brought him to a halt by saying, 'Bradley.'

'Yes . . . miss?' He was looking towards her, but it was some seconds before she spoke and then she said, 'If . . . if you should like to further your reading, you may help yourself to books from the library. There . . . there are all kinds of reading there, some very dry, but no doubt you would find something of interest.'

'I . . . I surely will. Thank you, miss.' His expression still didn't alter.

When the door closed on him she turned to the desk and, putting her hands flat on it, she leant over it for a moment; then her body snapped upwards as she heard a high excited cry coming from the direction of the hall. That was Millie. That cry always heralded the turn or some change in her demeanour that didn't augur good.

She pulled open the door, then ran along the passage, only at the end of it to come to an abrupt halt, for as she looked into the hall, there stood Bradley. He was facing her, his hands hanging by his sides, while in front of him was Millie and she was leaning against him, her hands around his shoulders.

Slowly, she walked towards them and when she was an arm's length from them, Robert, looking at her with a twisted smile on his face now said, 'She says she is pleased to know I am staying, miss, but I beg you to witness that I am giving her no comfort.'

Agnes drooped her head, and she bit tight down on her lip and only just stopped herself from laughing aloud. But when she put her hands out to draw Millie away, her eyes were bright with

230

suppressed laughter that was mirrored in his, and as their gaze held, the barrier that both of them had contributed to building up one against the other fell. Yet in the falling it revealed more clearly the immeasurable gulf that lay between them, and they both recognized this.

# PART FOUR

## The Inheritance

# CHAPTER ONE

It was Wednesday the twenty-fourth of December, nineteen hundred and thirteen. He had spent the afternoon going round the markets in Newcastle. And now he had something for everybody, nothing very big, but all new with the exception of one thing, and to him it was a find. It was a first edition of Cobbett's *Rural Rides.* It wasn't even soiled, and he had paid half a crown for it. He had read it some time ago, having got it out of the Institute in Jarrow. But he hadn't bought it for himself. Now he was asking himself if it wasn't like taking coals to Newcastle. And another thing, was he overstepping the mark by offering her a present? Anyway, he would see how things went. They had been going pretty smoothly of late; it was as if since that morning in the hall when they had laughed together over Miss Millie they had decided to call a truce.

She had looked happier over the past weeks than he had ever seen her before. She had been freer, less tense. At least she had been until some days ago when the young one returned. He would never be able to get on with him. If after finishing at the university he should plump to stay at home and not to follow his brothers or to take up some occupation that would take him away, he doubted if he'd be able to stick him.

He had been blowing his mouth off about Miss Millie, so Ruthie said. Didn't want her to have her meals in the dining-room when he was there, said they should be served upstairs.

It was odd but over the past weeks Millie had talked and acted so normal that it was hard at times to believe there was anything mentally wrong with her. Yet since her brother had come home she had reverted somewhat, talking a bit wild, like the other day. She had said, 'I don't care if Stanley locks me in my room because I can get out. I can fly. I can, Bradley, I can fly. With the aid of the wisteria I can fly.'

Later when he was going round the west side of the house he had looked at the wisteria. The branches spread all over the wall right up to the roof, and some of them were thicker than his forearm. Yes, of course she could fly with the aid of the wisteria, she could climb down it. She hadn't been talking so silly after all. Nor had she been talking silly when she said, 'If Stanley wants to take me for a walk like Father did, I shan't go.'

That remark had startled him, and he had asked himself if she perhaps remembered all that happened that night and had been clever enough to keep quiet. He was of the opinion that Miss Millie was underrated, and that she wasn't half as unbalanced as was supposed.

He had got a lift from the station on the carrier cart that dropped him at The Bull. The taproom was packed tonight, he could hardly see through the steam of breaths, and Bill and Mary Taggart were kept busy serving. He was standing in his usual place at the end of the bar and every now and again one or the other of them would stop and have a word with him. And now it was Mary's turn. She wiped the sweat off her plump neck as she smiled widely at him, saying, 'It's a good job the snow didn't lie, else many of these here wouldn't be able to find their feet the night.'

'Well, it's Christmas Eve.'

'Aye, it's Christmas Eve. What's happening up there?'

'Oh, as far as I can gather, there'll be a big spread the morrow, but like all us mad northerners they're saving the best for the New Year. By the way—' he leant towards her—'have you heard if young Carrie's got her trouble over yet?'

'No.' She had to raise her voice above the babble in the room, and she repeated, 'No; from what I hear she's still hanging on. Bill Parkin, you know him who lives down below your uncle, he was in here last night and he said, "God help that bairn when it's born. It'll likely be put in a straitjacket." He thinks your uncle's going round the bend: twice to church on a Sunday and dragging that poor lass with him, and the sight she is. She can hardly put one foot in front of the other, he says. And a week gone Sunday when we had that first fall of snow he saw them passing the window, walking mind because they couldn't risk the horse and trap. He said he felt like going out and saying, "You silly old bugger, do you want to kill her? Kill them both?" Anyway, last Sunday he said your uncle made the journey alone, so he thought the lass's time must be very near.' She paused, then added, 'Oh, by the way, don't go without the puppy.'

'Never fear. That's what I've come for, not the beer, just the puppy.' They laughed together, and then he drained his glass.

Half an hour later when he left the inn, his bag of Christmas presents in one hand, the puppy in a basket in the other, he looked up into the sky that was alight with stars and, his mind going back to

237

Carrie, he thought, Poor lass; it won't be much comfort to her if her child, like Christ, is born on Christmas morning. Yet the old fellow might take it as a sign, likely that God had forgiven her. Poor lass. Poor lass.

## CHAPTER TWO

John Bradley *was* taking it as a sign, not that God was forgiving his daughter, but that He was heaping more humiliation on his head, for he'd surely be the laughing stock if his daughter was to give birth to a bastard on Christmas Day. Those who scoffed at his high morality would be roaring with mirth; they would even say, as that heathen midwife had dared to say, that were the child born tomorrow then it would be in good company, for was not Christ himself, if the truth were known, nothing but a bastard, for there weren't so many numskulls now who believed that the seed had been pushed into Mary's womb by the hand of God.

He had overheard her speaking to Alice in the kitchen and he had stormed in, his hand raised, crying, 'Get out, woman! Get out of my house,' only to be confronted by his wife, his wife who had changed character so much in the last months that he sometimes wondered if she too had been impregnated with the devil himself, for she defied him in all ways. But in one thing had she not succeeded and that was she had not prevented him from taking his daughter to church on a Sunday. When her protestations had become physical and she had dared to lay hands on him, he had thrust her from him and on to the floor, and his daughter had decided between them. Wisely, she had said she would accompany him, and she had suffered the scorn of most of the congregation as was only right.

One thing he couldn't understand, why the parson whom he had assisted and worked with for years should turn against him and tell him that his behaviour was unpleasing to the Almighty and that he himself would be condemned for his uncharitableness.

But he knew what the Almighty wanted him to do. In his heart he was close to the Almighty and the Almighty said there must be retribution for sin and unclean living. And his daughter was unclean.

The only thing he'd had to cherish in his life was now a wanton, a slut, a hedge fornicator, a haystack biddy. She was all of these things; she was no better than the women at the fairs. But there was one saving grace: she had a lifetime before her in which to repent, and he would see that her tainted child, whatever it was, male or female, would be brought up in the fear of God. Oh yes, in the fear of God.

He sat in the chair to the side of the fire and watched his wife filling the copper water can from the kettle. She had been running up and down the stairs for the past hour, so that meant the time was near. He looked at the clock. It said a quarter to twelve.

When the kitchen door closed behind his wife he joined his hands together and looked up towards the low beamed ceiling and murmured, 'Lord God, let it come before the hour. Don't heap this humiliation on me. Enough that a sin is coming

239

into the world, don't let it contaminate the birthday of Your Son. Lord, hear me.'

The minutes ticked by and when the workings of the old clock ground out twelve strokes, he bent his head deep on his chest and his body sank deeper into the leather chair.

After a time he pulled himself upwards and, his chin thrust out, his head back on to his shoulders and to the side, he sat listening, waiting for the first cry of the child. He sat in the same position for so long that his neck began to ache. There was no sound from up above. Nobody had been downstairs for more water. He looked at the clock which said twenty-five minutes past twelve.

At ten minutes to one he rose to his feet and stood with his back to the fire, his eyes cast towards the door, and at five minutes past one the door opened and Bella Pope appeared and without ceremony she said, 'You'd better get yourself away for the doctor.'

'What do you mean, woman?' His voice was a growl.

'Just what I say, she's in a bad way. I've done me best. I can't stop the bleeding. The youngster's gone, you'll be pleased to hear that.'

'Woman! one day you'll . . .' He paused. 'What did you say about the . . . ?'

'You heard what I said, the bairn was born dead, and it looks to me as if his mother's gona follow it soon. Perhaps you'll be pleased to hear that an' all.'

He almost knocked her on her back as he made for the door. Within seconds he was in the bedroom; but just within the doorway he halted. The room looked a shambles and the stifling heat hit him, as did the stench of blood. His eyes became riveted on the bed where lay his daughter, her limbs exposed amid a tangle of bedclothes.

He now had consciously to lift one foot and place it before the other to approach the foot of the bed where his wife was trying to stem the flow of blood running from his daughter's womb. He moved around her and up the side of the bed to stand and stare down on what was once his beloved child. Her face was running with sweat. It wasn't deadly white as one might have expected, but a rosy pink. Her eyes were wide, her mouth agape, her breathing seemed shallow except that every now and again her chest heaved as she drew in a deep intake of breath. Her eyes, he saw immediately, held fear, and something besides, something he had seen in them for months past now, which had been veiled but was now naked and it was hate, stark hate. And if he'd had any doubts about it they were utterly dispelled when she spoke. Her words came out dull-edged, rasping, as she said, 'It's dead. Are you happy? It's dead, and I'm goin' to join it. I know I am . . . I want to. I'd . . . I'd rather be dead than live with you. And . . . and I'm glad it died before me. So now, you . . . you have nothing to torture. And . . . and I want to tell you something, something that's . . .' She closed her eyes tightly and gripped the sides of the bed and gasped, and her mother whispered, 'There, there. There, there, my love; the doctor's coming.'

After some seconds she opened her eyes again; and her voice now was smoother and quieter as she went on, 'You . . . you were very fond of Robert, more than fond, yet not fond enough to forgive him for making me sin, or so you imagined. So . . . so let me tell you something, Father. 'Twas not Robert

241

who gave me the child, it was Stephen Crain. You remember Stephen Crain? He was Dodsworth's farm labourer; he used to call here on errands. We hoodwinked you. I'm happy about that, we hoodwinked you, because you are a tyrant, a miserable unhappy tyrant.'

'Sh! dear. Lie still.' Alice now drew a sheet over her daughter's legs. Then without looking at her husband, she said, 'Don't stand there, get the doctor.'

He stood for a moment longer staring down at this flesh of his that he couldn't recognize, this girl that had turned into a woman, who was saying things to him that no one had ever dared to say, not even his wife, and he was about to turn away when he was checked once more by her voice, 'Father.'

He looked at her again, and she returned his look for almost a minute before she said, 'Everybody hates you. Do you know that? But no one hates you as much as I do. Remember that, because I won't be seeing you again. I know where I'm goin'.'

'Child. Child.' Alice was holding her, but she turned her face to her husband, muttering bitterly, 'Go on, fetch him. Quick! Go on.' And he went from the room, staggering like a drunken man.

\*    \*    \*

Carrie did not die before the doctor came, and Doctor Miller knew it was hopeless from the first sight of her but he stayed with her until the end, which came at five o'clock on the Christmas morning. She went calmly, even peacefully, but some time before she died she said to her mother,

'Don't let me be buried here. I hate that churchyard and the church. Parson Croft will understand. And lay the baby with me.' And Alice said, 'Yes, dear; it shall be done. Yes, yes, it shall be done.'

\*     \*     \*

With the help of Bella Pope, Alice Bradley laid out her daughter and her child beside her. Carrie's round face was now pale and smooth and looked like that of a child, a child peacefully at sleep, and her baby, which had been placed in the crook of her arm, looked strangely like her. The wrinkles of birth were no longer to be seen, its face was like that of a china doll.

The room tidied up, Alice went downstairs in search of her husband. How was she going to approach him? She didn't know.

When she found that he wasn't in the house, she went across the yard to the workshop. But she didn't enter, she merely looked through the window and there in the cold morning light she saw him sitting at his bench. His hands were on the wood in front of him, not joined but palms down, pressed close to the grain. His head was bent on his chest, his back was curved, and he gave the appearance of utter dejection. She did not open the door and go into him and give him a word of comfort as she might have done but for one thing, and that one thing was etched in her mind, the torture he had put her daughter through in dragging her to church twice every Sunday.

Yet she was surprised later when he did not come into the house and get ready for the morning service.

For the first time since she had known him he missed the Christmas Day Service . . .

And the Christmas Day congregation were aware of his absence, as they were also aware that his daughter had died giving birth to her child of sin. And any who might have said it was God's justice were made to think again when the Reverend Croft ended his sermon with: 'A young girl, on the verge of life, died this morning, her child with her. In the sight of others she bore her burden with fortitude, although her sin, as it were, was printed in large letters on her. And who among us has not condemned, except one, and He said, *"He that is without sin among you, let him first cast a stone at her."* '

# CHAPTER THREE

Robert was saddened by the news of Carrie's death and that of her child, and a strong thread of guilt ran through his feelings. Would it have happened, he asked himself, if he had taken her on? She must have been exposed to so much worry that it had affected the birth. Yet what would life have been like for all of them in that house? It wasn't likely that his uncle would have condoned the act and treated them normally. No, his own presence there would have given the man scope to practise his retribution for sin.

He had pondered whether he should go to the funeral; he understood she wasn't being buried in Lamesley churchyard. He did put in an order

244

though at a Birtley florist's for a wreath to be sent, but he did not have his name attached to it . . .

He had been in The Bull only once since Christmas and on that occasion he had met Tim Yarrow who had said that the old man was taking it badly and spent most of his time down in the workshop, working sometimes ten hours without a break. And Tim went on to say, although the old fellow had led the lass a hell of a life one couldn't help but feel a bit sorry for him, the way he was taking her going. Yet, as he said, he had to admit that he felt the lass and her bairn were well out of it because nobody could look forward to a lifetime of what he undoubtedly had in store for them.

Robert thought that he would like to have a word with his aunt; write her a letter perhaps. But then if he did there was the chance it would be opened by his uncle.

He knew that he himself was coming in for some condemnation. Hadn't the lass named him? Why hadn't he stood by her? She wouldn't have had to lead the life she had if he had married her. On and on, he knew the gossip was flowing; even in the kitchen here he had been under discussion.

Anyway, it was over. It was no good looking back, and today was New Year's Eve and by the signs of things they were going to have a nice bit of jollification tonight. It had been a nice week altogether. Truthfully, he had never experienced a better. His Christmas presents had been accepted with gratitude, if with some surprise from one quarter and a question from another. The latter had been from Dave Waters as he looked at the cherry-wood pipe: 'How do you manage to buy a thing like this besides all the rest?' he had asked.

245

And to this Robert had jokingly answered, 'I robbed a bank. But before I did I sold a miniature chest I'd made for a man in The Bull. It took me weeks of odd hours but I got twenty-five shillings for it. Does that answer your question?'

The surprise had come from Agnes, and he had sensed it was accompanied by not a little embarrassment. Yet she had received the book graciously, saying she had never read it; she had heard of it of course, and this was such a lovely edition, being bound in fine leather.

His Christmas box from her had been the same as both Greg's and Arthur Bloom's, which was two pocket handkerchiefs, one white and one red, and a pair of socks. All very acceptable.

On Christmas Day she and Miss Millie had dined alone.

While sitting at the laden board in the kitchen, his thoughts had swept through the green-baized door to the dining-room, thinking, why couldn't her brother have stayed home to spend Christmas with her? They were selfish pigs, the three of them. But later on Christmas Day he knew that had Master Stanley been present there would have been no invitation for the staff to come into the drawing-room to hear her play and to join in singing carols. It had been a good evening, different from anything else he had ever experienced because for a couple of hours there was no class barrier.

He had stood by her side and turned the pages of her music, often at the wrong time; while he marvelled at the dexterity of her fingers, she played beautifully. He could have sat and listened to her all night long. But at nine o'clock, answering the signal from Mr Waters, they all returned to the kitchen, there to have a late meal and a sing-song on their own, which, after the drawing-room episode, rather jarred on him, and this, later on as he lay in bed going over the proceedings of the day, caused him to chastise himself, saying, 'Come on, lad. Come on. Know your place. Don't get ideas, at least about tastes in music. Remember that you've always enjoyed a barrack-room ballad, and not in such a refined style as Robert Service's either.'

But tonight was to be a very special do. They had cleaned up the servants' hall, which wasn't used as such these days. A long table had been set against the wall. Arthur Bloom was to bring his accordion, and Greg was no mean hand on the mouth-organ. So it promised that, nineteen-fourteen would be ushered in to music and a singsong.

It was Ruthie who put the suggestion, what about asking Miss Agnes to join them to see in the New Year, and of course Miss Millie along of her.

They were sitting round the kitchen table having a cup of tea around five o'clock. The only one of the staff missing was Arthur Bloom: he had gone home but would return later with his wife. Robert watched both Dave and Peggy Waters look at each other before turning their gaze on their daughter, and he was expecting her father to say, 'We'll go and wish her a happy New Year, but don't let us forget our place.' However it was her mother who answered, saying, 'Well, it's the first time they've been on their own for as long as I can remember.' And then she looked down the kitchen towards the far door that led into the passage and she added slowly, 'There used to be great do's at one time on a New Year's Eve, dancing in the hall, and sometimes a piper. That was when the MacNeils were in the Manor House. But even last year, the boys were home and they saw it in. She's bound to feel it being on her own.' She looked back at her daughter as she ended, 'I don't see why not, Ruthie. There'll be no harm in asking.'

'Will you ask her, Ma?'

'Aye, I can do.'

'I wonder if she'll give me the first dance?'

They all looked at Greg Hubbard before bursting out laughing, and Maggie, pushing him in the arm, now said, 'You'll have to put your name down on her card. That's what they have at the big dances, young ladies, cards. Don't they, Aunty?'

'Yes, that's what they have.' Peggy nodded across the table at Maggie. 'And Miss Agnes has got a lot of her mother's cards, one special one that she had at her coming out ball in London when she was presented to the Queen.'

'Eeh! fancy that—' Maggie shook her head— 'being presented to the Queen herself. I would have dropped down dead.'

'And they would have given you a military funeral with the Durham Light Infantry, The Horse Guards, and the Royal Salute from The Tower.'

They were all laughing and looking at Greg Hubbard. By! there, Robert thought, goes a changed man if ever I saw one. And all because he's in love. Well, they say that particular emotion either makes or breaks you. And Maggie was willing. He was glad of that. He wondered if Dave and Peggy Waters knew, or if Ruthie had twigged anything. Perhaps when it did come into the open Ruthie would be a little jealous for she was nearer Greg's age, but although she wasn't as plain as

Maggie, she hadn't the advantage of Maggie's disposition.

As the laughter died away the green-baized door at the far end of the room opened and Agnes entered, only to come to a stop, saying, 'Oh, I'm sorry. I didn't realize you were at a meal.'

Dave Waters was the first to rise from the table, saying as he did so, 'We are not at a meal, Miss Agnes. Were you wanting something?'

Robert too had risen and he watched her move again slowly down the room, and as she neared the table Peggy said, 'We are just having a cup, we're keeping our appetites for later on.'

'Oh, yes, yes.' Agnes now looked from one to the other, and she seemed to embrace them all as she said, 'I . . . I wondered if you would care to come to the drawing-room later to see the New Year in?'

'Well, well.' Peggy smiled broadly now and stepping near to Agnes, she went to put her hand lightly on her arm but stopped, then said, 'We were just planning to come and ask you to join us. We're having a little do in the hall, a bit of jollification like. We'd be very happy if you and Miss Millie would come and share it with us.' It was one thing for Peggy to speak to her mistress on an equal footing when they were alone, but she always gave her her place when in the presence of the others. And now she added words that she might have used to Agnes's mother long ago when to be mistress of this establishment meant something: 'We'd be honoured if you would, miss,' she ended.

Agnes looked from one to the other and she was smiling as she answered, 'I'd be very pleased. Yes, indeed I'd be very pleased to join you. And I'm sure Millie will be delighted. But—' her smile

249

widened and her eyes seemed to rest on Robert for a moment as she said, 'you won't have to be surprised if she wants to dance.'

'I'll show her how to do the Irish jig, miss.'

'Maggie!' Her uncle almost barked at her, but refrained from adding, 'Your manners, girl!' which he might as well have done. But apart from lowering her eyelids, Maggie seemed unmoved by the rebuff, and Agnes relieved any further tension by saying, 'What time will you? I mean what time should we . . . ?'

'Oh, any time after ten,' said Peggy. 'We're going to have the meal around eleven, if that would suit you.'

'Of course, of course.' Agnes nodded, 'I'll look forward to it.' Then she took a step backwards before turning and going hastily out of the room.

In the drawing-room she sat down before the fire and looked at Millie who was sitting curled up in a deep chair to the side of the fireplace with the puppy lying asleep on her lap; she had one hand on its head while the other supported a picture book resting on the arm of the chair. Agnes was beginning to bless that puppy: wherever the puppy was there she would find Millie. It was wonderful to be able to leave her for five minutes, knowing when she returned she would find her in the same place.

In a way the puppy seemed to have taken Bradley's place in her mind. And yet, not altogether for whenever she saw Bradley she made for him, and he would talk to her, they would talk to each other. There was no getting away from the fact that Millie wasn't normal, so how was it that Bradley should make her appear as if she were? He was a perplexing man; she could not really understand him. No she couldn't. And she had already ceased to ask herself if there was any need to do so.

Tonight she was going to a party, a New Year's party, at which it had been decided that he was to be first-foot. But this business of first-footing had never been kept up in the house proper, only in the kitchen quarters, and she knew that on New Year's Eves Dave had always gone outside with a lump of coal and a flask of whisky to wait for the hooters to herald in a New Year, but she herself had never witnessed it. But she remembered the piper playing it in, and all the family and friends joining hands in the drawing-room.

It was Maggie as usual pushing in where angels feared to tread who had apparently suggested that Bradley be first-foot this year because he was darker by far than Dave. Peggy had reported that the suggestion had at first upset Dave, and that Bradley had noticed this and had refused the honour. However, afterwards Dave had gone to him and said, he must do it, as younger blood might bring a little luck to the house for it was badly needed.

The hall was decorated with holly—another thing that hadn't happened for some years—and there were sprigs of it above some of the pictures in the drawing-room. She'd had a number of Christmas cards and these were arrayed on various tables in the room. The whole house seemed to have taken on a festive warm feeling, but this had found no answering note within her, for she was lonely. At times she even longed for the company of James, just his company would have done, without passionless kisses or embraces, just to sit and have her hand held. She had hoped all day that Stanley would return, yet at the same time knowing if he had she would not have been able to join the party in the servants' hall. No doubt he would have acted the master and looked in on them and wished them a Happy New Year, then let them get on with their jollification, but as to sitting down to a meal with them, he wouldn't have considered it the done thing. He was even more stiff than their father in this way, she thought, because she could remember years ago her father having the whole staff in the hall on New Year's morning for a drink and he being jolly. Strangely, it was the only memory she had of her father being jolly.

She did not think it strange that she'd had no invitations from outside this year, because those she'd received last year had come via James, she being his fiancée, and her mother's friends seemed to have faded away.

At seven o'clock Peggy brought her a light meal into the dining-room, and Agnes noted that this staid and dear friend of hers had an air of excitement about her, and she said to her, 'You are looking forward to the party, aren't you, Peggy?' And Peggy, joining her hands on the band of her white apron, nodded saying, 'I am, I am, because it's the first bit of jollification we've had for a long time. And Dave's a bit more himself these days, and oh I'm glad of that.' Her face taking on a more serious look now, she said, 'I was worried, for a time I was very worried about him.'

'Yes, I know, I know you were. I was too. Still, it's all over and forgotten.'

'Oh, me dear, I don't think it's forgotten, not

252

with Dave, it's still there. I see him brooding at times. But anyway, on the whole he's better. But . . . but he's still not sure of Robert . . . Bradley. If I could only get him to believe that that man is as close as a clam, for all his strange ways. Well, perhaps strange isn't the right word, unfitting ways would be better, because he'll never toe the line. As I said the day, things are changing, people are changing, you can't get people to bend their knee like they used to. I'm sorry, dear'—she put her hand on Agnes's shoulder—'but perhaps you understand what I mean.'

Yes, she understood what she meant all right, and part of her was even in sympathy with those who had to toe the line, but another tangent of thought said there must be servants and servants must be subject to masters. It wasn't only the rule in households but in factories and shipyards.

The thought of shipyards brought her mind firmly on to the man in question and she asked herself what the difference was in taking an order from Dave or any member of the household to that from a foreman in a workshop. At this moment she certainly couldn't see any difference; and after all what was it about service that Bradley should object to when a man like Dave and a woman like Peggy, forgetting the others, were happy in service and were very well off compared with many people round about, such as pitmen and their families. Here, they had good food and uniform and were housed well. Granted their wages weren't high, anything but. Still, were they in the outside world, they would have to pay for accommodation, food and working clothes. And that had to be taken into consideration, hadn't it? But a man like Robert . . .

253

Bradley . . . Why had she thought of him as Robert? Likely because Peggy used his Christian name now and again. Well, he must remain Bradley to her, that was definite.

Peggy now put her hand again on Agnes's shoulder and, bending down to her, she said, 'You feeling lonely, lass?'

It was on the point of her tongue to deny this, but looking up into the kindly face, she said, 'A bit, Peggy. It's the first time I've been alone at Christmas or New Year. Even when things weren't good, there was always someone here.'

'Those brothers of yours want somebody's tongue around them, especially Mr Stanley, he could have come back. Who are these people he's with anyway? He's never away from their house.'

'Oh, this isn't the Cunninghams', it's a friend of his from Oxford. I . . . I think they've got a good stable. That's the attraction.'

'Has he got sisters, the friend?'

Agnes smiled faintly as she said, 'Not that I know of; and even if he had I don't think they would have any pull compared to a horse. Oh'— she bowed her head—'that's a pun.'

Peggy didn't refer to the pun but said, 'How are things going, money-like, on the books?'

'Oh, not too bad, Peggy; in fact, much better than in previous years lately. Arnold has been quite generous, considering how he's got to spread the little money around. And I've got ideas for next year. I was thinking if we're able to develop the kitchen garden we could send some of the surplus to market.'

If she had expected an enthusiastic approval of this from Peggy she was disappointed, for Peggy

254

just stared at her: selling poultry and livestock was one thing, it was sort of farming, but selling surplus vegetables in the market, that was for small-holders and allotment keepers. Still, she supposed beggars couldn't be choosers and if Miss Agnes saw no let-down in doing it who was she to quibble. And so now she said, 'It's a thought. Aye, it's a thought.'

But not one that Peggy approved of, Agnes saw, and she smiled inwardly. People were odd, very odd. Everybody was odd, including herself, and she never felt more odd than she had done over the past few days, in fact since Christmas when Bradley had given her the copy of *Rural Rides*. The fact that he had chosen such a book and had already read it himself upset still further her ideas of what was right and proper. If one of her brothers had given her the book she would have thought nothing of it, but that a working man, a carpenter from a shipyard in Jarrow, had not only read this book but many others of greater depth, had set her mind questioning.

The conclusion she had come to so far was not one that classified Bradley, but one that showed herself to be ignorant, not only of literature but of life beyond the narrow confines of this estate. She had come to realize she had no conception of how people lived or thought, although she had accepted that she was more at home among those behind the green-baized doors than she was in the house and with those who had inhabited it. She was still very much aware that she was a lady, bred of a lady who could trace her ancestors back for four hundred years or more, and they had not depended on commerce for their existence as those belonging to her father had done.

'I'll go and bring Miss Millie down, if I can get her away from that puppy.' Peggy's interruption of her thoughts did not elicit a reply, but as the door closed on her, there arose in Agnes a deep protest and she cried inwardly, 'They shouldn't have left me here alone. It isn't fair. I'm becoming torn.' She did not go on to explain to herself why she was being torn, and about what, but, getting up, she walked rapidly down the drawing-room to the tall window that was bare to the night, and looking out on to the frost-rimmed hedge that bordered this side of the house, she again said, 'It isn't fair. What if I were to do something silly? What would happen then? They would come scurrying back quick enough then. Oh yes; yes, they would.'

But what could she do that was silly? She turned from the window and straightened her shoulders, at the same time bringing her chin up. She would never do anything silly; she knew her place, and had the power to keep others in theirs.


# CHAPTER FOUR

They had had their supper. It had been a splendid meal: a shoulder of lamb, roast potatoes, sprouts and turnip, and a suet pudding covered with rich gravy; then they had the choice of bacon and ham pie or pork pie; and to finish off they had the last of the Christmas puddings. Everybody had enjoyed it, most of all Millie who had caused a great deal of laughter at the table as she back-chatted with Robert.

Agnes had tried to stop her talking so much, but

when she realized that her chatter was raising laughter without embarrassment she ceased to reprimand her.

Bradley was sitting opposite to her. He looked very smart. That was another thing about him that was disturbing for, when out of his workday clothes, he dressed quite well, not as a gentleman would, but in good homespun cloth. Tonight he had on a grey tweed jacket and dark trousers; also he was wearing a collar and tie. His shirt was white and the tie a russet brown with a fleck in it. His hands, she noticed were squarish and his nails clean. And he looked happy: there was a gaiety about him that seemed to be affecting them all.

After the supper they had pushed back the tables and Bloom was now playing the accordion and Hubbard the mouth-organ, and very well they sounded together.

It was Dave Waters who surprisingly said to Maggie, 'Go on; you can give us a jig, girl.' And at this the players changed the tune to a rousing jig and Maggie took the floor and began to dance. Agnes had not seen her dance before and she found it fascinating, except she wondered why she held her body so stiffly, not moving her arms, while her feet, those big heavy feet seemed to have wings.

The dance ended, Maggie, almost doubled up with laughing, now said, ' 'Tis years since I did a proper one, I'm puffed.' Then in her exuberant way she cried, 'Come on! let's have the Lancers. Come on all of you's!' And she held out her hand towards Millie, but Millie, on the point of jumping up, was prevented by Agnes saying softly, 'No, no; you can't,' until a voice behind her said, 'Let her. There's no harm in it. Let her.'

She turned her head on her shoulder and looked up into Robert's face, and her lids began to blink rapidly and when he added still softly, 'And you, miss, come on, join in. 'Tis New Year's Eve, you can forget about it the morrow,' she felt her throat swell and the colour flushing over her face.

'Oh! come on, Aggie.' Millie was standing in front of her. 'Bradley will show us how to do it, won't you, Bradley? Oh! come on. I'd love to dance, I would, I would. Come on.'

What could she do when all the attention of those in the room seemed to be focused on her? But when she rose to her feet Dave Waters was standing before her with the look on his face telling her he wasn't at all pleased. It was as if he were saying, 'Don't do it; you'd be lowering yourself.'

The look didn't go unnoticed by Robert, who having taken Millie's hand in one of his, now extended his other to Betty Trollop, and, Betty laughing widely, they all three ran to the middle of the room and helped to form the ring, and when Agnes joined them she was flanked by both Dave and Peggy Waters.

It was immediately apparent that the only ones who knew anything about the Lancers were Mrs Bloom and Robert, for there was much laughter and much confusion as they wound in and out of each other, hands clasping. It should be strange that never once did Robert clasp Agnes's hand. He could have a number of times, but adroitly he appeared to avoid doing so.

Some while later when she sat down panting with the rest, she made herself smile while thinking, Why did he make it so obvious? There was no need; it would have been quite natural,

258

ordinary. Once he had deliberately swung round and turned his back on her. What did he mean by it? He was . . . he was a disturbing creature . . .

At five minutes to twelve they were all mingling in the hall. In one hand Robert was holding a piece of paper on which reposed a lump of coal, and in the other a flask of whisky and he laughed down into Peggy's face as she pulled the collar of his coat up about his ears, saying as she did so, 'It's enough to cut them off you out there tonight. Now get yourself away.' And she pushed him as she might have done a son, and amid varying cries, such as, 'Don't forget to pick up the luck as you are coming in,' and 'It's money I'm after, enough to set up house with.' This was from Greg as he glanced knowingly towards Maggie, and she, laughing loudly, called to Robert, ' 'Tis health I want an' an unworried mind.' And on Betty Trollop's request, 'A lad and a good job for me, Robert, that's all, a lad and a good job,' he turned his head and laughed back at her.

Millie, too, was about to call out something when Agnes admonished her, saying, 'No, no, Millie. Be quiet now, and stop jumping up and down.'

Millie, like a child, had been hopping in her excitement from one foot to the other and once caught the heel of her black slipper in the hem of her long velvet dress and nearly tripped. Her face was so painfully bright and happy as to make Agnes think: I doubt she's ever enjoyed herself like this in her life before; and the thought brought a feeling of sadness and guilt to her.

'Isn't it beautiful, Aggie?'

'What, dear?'

259

'Why, the party. It's a beautiful party. Isn't it, Dave?' She appealed to Dave Waters, and he, coming to her side, addressed her in the same manner as Agnes had done, saying, 'What's that, me dear?'

'It's a beautiful party. I said, it's a beautiful party.'

'Aye, it's quite good. You've enjoyed it, haven't you?'

'Oh, yes, Dave. Oh, yes. Could we have one every week?'

Dave Waters put his head back and laughed, saying, 'Not unless we have a New Year every week, an' that would be too much of a good thing. What do you say, Miss Agnes?'

'Yes, too much of a good thing, Dave.'

'For my part, I'm always glad when I get back to normal. But—' He moved to the side now and stood abreast of Agnes as he said under his breath, 'It's good to see her so happy.'

'It is indeed, Dave. The only thing is'—Agnes turned her head fully towards him now—'I hope it doesn't have any repercussions.'

'Oh, don't worry. As Peggy's always saying, you don't get sick on happiness.'

You don't get sick on happiness. There was a lot of truth in that. At the moment she felt so unhappy that were it to create its equal in sickness she felt she would be at death's door. Then once again she was chastising herself: What a silly thing to think. This time last year her idea of happiness would have been to be married or to be in this house without the presence of her father or any of her brothers, and now here she was, at least with her second wish fulfilled and she was more lonely and

260

unhappy than she had ever been in her life before.

There were the church bells ringing. Another year! Nineteen-fourteen. What would it bring? Would it bring any change to her life? She doubted it; she would be stuck here in this backwater while the world outside went by. Great things were happening in the world; and not unmixed with unrest, from what she read in the papers. But it wouldn't touch her or this house; she was here for life and the sooner she faced up to this the better for her health, both of body and mind. Yes, indeed.

'A happy New Year.'

'A happy New Year.'

'Many of them. Many of them.'

'Let me touch the coal.'

Robert had hammered on the front door and been admitted by Maggie. Then he was in the lobby among the little crowd shaking hands and all talking at once; and to Dave Waters he made a point of saying, 'It'll be a good year, you'll see.' And Dave had answered, 'God willing.'

And now he was standing in the hall proper in front of Millie and her, and Millie's eyes were like stars as she looked at him and cried in a high almost falsetto voice, 'A happy New Year! A happy New Year, Bradley!'

'And to you too, miss.' He now took hold of the two outstretched hands and when his own were shaken up and down he laughed as he said, 'It's going to be a splendid New Year for you.' And in answer she said, 'Is it, Bradley? Is it?' And he said, 'Sure thing, miss. Sure thing.'

And now he was standing opposite his mistress, but he didn't put his hand out towards her. He could not; if he touched her just once that would be

261

the beginning of the end, for end there must be.

'Happy New Year.' She had not added, Bradley.

He counted the seconds loud in his head before he lifted his arm and took the hand extended towards him. Her fingers were thin and cold, very like those of Millie's, and they were lost between his own and his palm. All of her being was in his hand. It passed up his arm and into his body. Weeks ago when she had forced herself into his mind, he had done his best to prevent it, but his mind was one thing, his body another.

'The same to you. And many of them.' It was the accepted reply that was issuing from thousands, tens of thousands of mouths at this very moment, but he had not added, miss.

She was on the point of withdrawing her fingers from his when Dave Waters came to her side. Whatever he meant to say, and from the look on his face it wouldn't have been exactly pleasant, was interrupted by a cry from the lobby.

Maggie, having run back to shut the front door, saw entering the drive what at first she took to be a carriage and then she recognized it was a trap, merely a trap. But a trap was enough to make her run back to the hall door and yell, ' 'Tis a visitor! 'Tis somebody coming to first-foot us. Isn't that grand now? ' 'Tis a visitor!' before scrambling back to the front door again.

'A visitor?' Agnes looked towards Peggy, then at Dave before saying further, 'Who can it be? Oh, perhaps it's Stanley. He's decided to come after all; he must have got the last train in.'

The voices had become subdued, because most of them knew that if it were guests that would mean Miss Agnes and Miss Millie wouldn't be staying for the rest of the party; it might even mean Dave and Ruthie would have to wait on in the drawing-room. But Maggie shattered their surmising for in what she took to be a whisper she said, ' 'Tis a stranger, an old man. He looks drunk.'

Dave and Peggy Waters followed Agnes through the lobby to the front door, where they all looked down through the sparse light shed by the trap lantern on to the man who was now pulling himself up the steps by the stone balustrade and who would have fallen if Dave Waters had not stepped forward and thrust his arm out, saying, 'What is it? Who do you want? Who are you?'

He could not make out the man's features for the upper part of his face was shadowed by his high hat and the lower part showed unkempt whiskers stiffened by frost.

'Robert Bradley. I want Robert Bradley.'

It was Agnes who recognized who the man was, although she had never seen him in her life before. She put out her hand to him and, taking his arm, she said, 'Are you his uncle?'

'Yes, yes, his uncle.' The man nodded his head slowly.

'Come in. Come in. Help him, Dave.'

Together they assisted him up the step and through the lobby and into the hall where Robert was standing, seemingly unable to believe his eyes, but only for a moment for, springing forward, he took hold of the old man, saying, 'What . . . what's the matter? Is it Aunt Alice?'

'No, no.' The head moved slowly; then to the amazement of them all John Bradley dropped on to his knees and, putting his hands up as if in prayer, he said, 'God has bidden me to come and

263

ask your forgiveness. He said I must not let the year begin—' the man now gasped and coughed, then went on, 'begin without begging your forgiveness. I . . . I besmirched your name as . . . as did my wife . . . and daughter. On her dying lips she . . . she told me the name of the man who had brought her to shame and . . . and God chastised me and . . .'

Before he could get any further Robert bent swiftly forward and, placing his arms under his uncle's, he attempted to lift him upwards. But John Bradley's body was limp, and Robert, looking towards the men who seemed to have become stupefied by the scene, cried, 'Give me a hand!'

Almost as one they crowded round and lifted the old man up. Then Robert turned and looked at Agnes as if to say, where will I put him? and she, reading his unspoken question, cried, 'Bring him into the drawing-room. He's frozen. Ruthie, build up the fire. Peggy, bring a hot water bottle and a hot shelf. Quickly now . . .'

During the next fifteen minutes there was much bustling to and fro. They laid John Bradley on the rug before the fire with a cushion under his head and placed an oven shelf under his feet and stone bottles to his sides. But when he did not soon regain consciousness Agnes, looking at Robert who was kneeling beside his uncle, said, 'Don't you think we should send for a doctor?'

'I don't know. Likely, it's just the cold that's got him. I know what would bring him round, some hot whisky.' He smiled wryly now, as he added, 'He wouldn't be so forgiving if he knew I'd introduced strong liquor into him.'

'He's not to know.' Robert looked at Peggy now

264

and said, 'That's true . . . could be medicine.'

Five minutes later they were spooning hot whisky down John Bradley's throat and had the satisfaction within minutes of hearing him cough and splutter. When presently he opened his eyes he looked at the faces hanging over him and muttered, 'Where . . . where?' And to this Robert said, 'You're all right. You're all right, Uncle. It's just the cold. Just get warm and you'll feel fine again.'

Robert realized that the incident had put a damper on the party and he looked up and around him, saying, 'Don't let it stop the jollification; I'll see to him.' Whereupon Peggy replied, 'Oh, we've had enough, anyway, if we never have any more. And they can have their drinks in the kitchen; they'll do as well there. Come along with you.' She now waved out Ruthie, Maggie, and Greg, and lastly her husband, but as she went to close the door on them Agnes called, 'Will you go up and see how Betty's coping?'

'I'll do that, but she can handle Miss Millie. And she'll surely sleep the night, she's never had so much excitement in her lifetime, poor dear.' She went out smiling.

Getting to his feet, Robert looked at Agnes and nipped at his lower lip before he said, 'I'm sorry about this.'

'There's nothing to be sorry for. I would think you should be glad that your name has been cleared.'

He looked down on his uncle, who now appeared as if he was sleeping, and, moving away from him he walked to where Agnes had seated herself in the wing chair to the side of the fire which was now blazing brightly and he said, 'No,

I'm not relieved, for it never really troubled me, me conscience was clear.'

'Don't you mind what other people think?'

'No; and I never have. If I get on with folks and they like me, well and good, if I don't get on with them I keep out of their way. What they think doesn't bother me.'

'But what if the people you like think the worse of you?'

'In that case, as far as I can see it, if they think the worse of me their manner towards me will change, and from liking they would show dislike, and so as I said, I would keep out of their way.'

'You seem to have an answer for everything.'

'Huh!' He turned his head to the side. 'I only wish I had. God, I only wish I had.'

It was noticeable to both of them that she was not addressing him as Bradley and nor was he using miss.

And now she asked him a very strange question: 'Have you ever been unhappy?' she said.

He turned and looked into her face. The firelight was playing on it, it looked flushed, it may have been the heat, and it was some seconds before he said, 'Not really; not until recently.'

'Recently?' She dare not ask how recently, and his mode of reply was to turn the question on her. 'What about you?' he said. 'Have you ever been unhappy?'

She moved her body in the chair and put her hands on the arms, her fingers over the end pressed into the leather, but she turned her gaze from him and towards the fire and stared into it before she answered him: 'If I were to speak the truth I would say I have never known what it is to be really

266

happy. I've experienced pleasure, but that's a different thing. I get pleasure from my playing; I get pleasure from looking at beautiful pictures; then again I get pleasure from walking in the wood. But as for happiness, there are so many grades of happiness; the little I know of it has always been threaded with pain.'

She was remembering the time when she thought she was in love with James: she had imagined she was happy even when the emotion was threaded with jealousy, and in spite of the feeling of inferiority he had the unfortunate knack of evoking from within her. But why were they talking like this? Who had begun it? . . . She had: she had wanted to know if he had ever been unhappy. If that wasn't a provocative question, she would like to know what was, so need she ask why they were talking like this? But she should recognize she had opened the way for him to take further liberties. What liberties? A conversation, the exchange of thoughts. She had never been able to have a conversation with any member of her family, not even with her mother. As for those outside, James or his family, James had wanted a good, adoring listener. That's all James had wanted, while his mother wanted someone to browbeat. But this man here, this man who was attracting her in a way that was frightening, terrifying, she found him compatible.

'What!'

The words that called forth the high demanding What! had been, 'You should be married.' She made to rise from the chair, then sat deeper into it. Her hands now in her lap, folded tightly together, and her face scarlet, she looked at him, right into

267

those dark brown eyes as she said, 'I shall never marry.'

'Never's a long time. Why are you so sure?'

'I know in my own mind. I am sure.'

She could not add, 'What chance have I to marry? Whom do I see outside the walls of this place?'

As if following her thought, he said, 'You should get out more, visit your friends. You are so young.'

'So young? I'm twenty-six.'

'Well'—he smiled now—'we're both of the same age, but you seem much younger than me in all ways. And'—his smile widened—'much prettier.'

This was too much, too much; he was taking advantage. She pulled herself from the chair and, going to the prostrate figure lying on the rug, she said, 'He . . . he should be put to bed.'

He was now standing at the other side of his uncle as he replied, 'If I know anything, my aunt will be distracted. But I can't move him like this. If it's all right with you, maybe he can lie here till daylight? Then I'll get him home. By the way the horse will be frozen out there, can I . . . ?'

'Oh, that's been seen to, Greg's stabled him.'

'Oh, thank you. Thank you.'

'I'll get someone to sit up with you.'

'Please don't, there's no need. And I feel I've done enough disrupting. It's a bad way to start the New Year.'

She made no reply, except to say, 'Good-night.' And he answered, 'Good-night.' And he still did not add, miss.

When she had gone he went and stood with his back to the fire, his hands behind him on his buttocks, and for a while he looked down at his uncle. Then his eyes lifted and he gazed around the room. New Year's morning, nineteen-fourteen, and he was standing in the drawing-room of this house as if he owned the place. Would he like to have a house like this? No, no, because along with it went responsibility and the governing of other people's lives and, made as he was, he was against being governed. So on principle he wouldn't want to govern; what he wanted out of life was to be his own boss.

Over the past weeks, among other things there had been the thought in his mind that he could rent a little back shop somewhere and start making furniture. However, before he could do that he would need cash behind him, and he certainly couldn't save much on what he was getting here. He had spent up at Christmas.

He looked down at his uncle again and he thought, Poor Carrie. She had been brave enough to come clean at the end . . . Yes, and now that he was vindicated in his uncle's eyes, couldn't he go back there? He supposed he could, but he wasn't going to, oh no: the fact that the man had come out on a night like this and on such an errand showed that he was still dominated by the fear of God and so would likely go on aiming to instil it into others, and he couldn't stand that, so there would be no going back to the workshop.

But he would have to go somewhere, and soon. Yes, he would, because tonight, after he had taken her hand he knew he had started to cross the open space between them and a few minutes gone, she had against her own judgement—oh yes, very much against her own judgement—come to meet him, even though she knew it wouldn't work, as he knew it wouldn't work, and so the best thing to do was to clear out.

Anyway, he wouldn't be strong enough to stand it, something would go pop inside him one of these days and he'd grab at her, and hold her, and squeeze the loneliness out of her eyes. God! he had never seen anyone look so lonely or in such need as she.

Under other circumstances they would have been married by now and he'd have had her in bed; but then, under other circumstances, he would never have met anybody like her. They didn't make them in her mould where he came from. Good women, aye, good lasses, aye, but not like her. She had something that he couldn't lay his finger on, something that drew him like steel filings to a magnet.

\*       \*       \*

She came down at seven o'clock the next morning fully dressed and she found him supporting his uncle's head as he endeavoured to get him to drink a cup of tea. The old man was now lying on the couch and Robert made a sort of an apology for it straightaway, saying, 'I got him on here in the middle of the night, he wasn't resting easy on the floor.'

'He should have been put to bed. How is he?'

'He's in a bad way, I think, starting a fever I should say. I'll . . . I'll have to get him home.'

'But how? He'll never be able to go in the trap in this state.'

'No, I've thought of that. I wonder if you would mind if I took a loan of the cart. It has high sides

270

and I could lay him in it. It would keep the wind off him.'

'Yes, yes, of course. And we'll put a mattress in it and cover him with blankets. Yes, yes; that's a good idea. By the way, did you have any rest?'

'Aye, I dozed.'

'Have you had anything to eat?'

'Ruthie's seen to it. They were all up early, they haven't had much sleep either. I'm sorry for the disturbance.'

'Oh, don't be silly.' She gave an impatient shake of her head, and on a different occasion her very ordinary response would have brought a twinkle to his eyes. But now he merely looked at her, then said quietly, 'I was thinking in the night, it's an odd thing about this house, it seems to create events. At least that's how it appears to me.'

She returned his look steadily, and then she said, 'I don't think it's the house, it's wherever you go, you yourself. Some people are made like that, they alter the atmosphere and create storms. However—' her tone changing now and her head moving in a brisk nod, she said, 'I will go and see about the preparing of the cart. And Hubbard can go in with you. He can drive the trap in and bring the cart back, and you must stay with your uncle until the doctor sees him, I'm sure your aunt will be glad of your presence in the house.' She waited a moment as if expecting some reply, but when he didn't speak, simply stared at her, she turned about and walked hastily from the room . . .

It took four of them to carry John Bradley out to the cart and lay him on the mattress. He made no protest whatever, seeming to be oblivious of what was going on. The women saw to it that he was well

271

happed up with blankets. They were white house blankets brought from the linen cupboard, satin bound and almost half an inch thick. It was one of the things that Robert noticed and thought: That's silly, they'll get messed up. He had never seen the like before and he guessed that neither Peggy, Ruthie, nor Maggie would have brought such quality down to be used on the back of a farm-cart.

As he drove the cart out of the yard and along the drive in front of the house, he saw her standing at the hall window. She was wearing a dark blue dress and in the white light of the frosty morning she stood out against the long pane as a painting in a frame.

He dragged his mind from her and to the business at hand. What if his uncle died? In a way that too would be laid at his door. A poor man coming out on such a night to ask his forgiveness, that's what they would say, not that he had been in the wrong in the first place: righteousness belonged to the dead in the minds of most folk. Oh, he wasn't such a bad old stick, some would say; yes, he had his faults, but then who hasn't?

He had heard it all before . . .

When they arrived in the yard and his aunt opened the back door, she remained for a moment as if petrified, and he had to call to her, 'It's all right. It's all right, Aunty.' When she came to the end of the cart and looked at her husband wrapped in blankets, only his eyes, nose and mouth visible, and these latter running with sweat, she said, 'Oh, dear God, where did you find him?'

'He came up to the house. Now don't worry, only get the bed ready.'

As she ran back into the house she called over

the yard, 'You there, Tim?' And when Tim appeared at the door of the workshop he too stood for a moment as if unable to take in the situation, until Robert shouted, 'Come and give us a hand.' And when Tim reached the cart he looked from Robert to Greg and back to Robert again, saying, 'He went after you then?' But Robert made no answer to this except to say, 'Give us a hand, we've got to get him to bed.'

It took the three of them all their time to get the still limp burden up the stairs; but once he was lying on the bed, Alice said, 'I'll see to him. I'll see to him.' And they all went out of the room and down the stairs, and there Robert, looking at Greg, said, 'When you're taking the cart back, will you go out of your way and call on the doctor? Tell him it's urgent.'

'Aye, I'll do that.' Greg nodded at him, then added, 'But it being New Year's morning I doubt if he's been long in bed, and he'll be like a bear with a sore skull. I wouldn't expect him to come running.'

'You tell him it's serious. Don't leave a message, see him yourself, will you?'

'Aye, I'll do that. Will you be back the night?'

'Yes, most likely.'

As both Greg and Tim went out of the back door, Nancy Parkin entered the kitchen and she stood for a moment looking at him before saying, 'Well, well, look what the New Year's brought in. You brought him back then. Where had he been?'

'For a walk.'

'Huh! You haven't changed, have you? She's nearly been out of her mind. Do you know that? He went after you, didn't he? Went to beg your pardon for putting the blame on you. Tim says he's

273

been yapping on about it for days, you and God.'

'Has he? Oh'—he raised his eyebrows at her—
'nice to know that I was linked with good company
for a change.'

'Are you stayin'?'

'I haven't made up me mind yet.' He stared at
her now through narrowed lids, asking himself how
on earth he had ever imagined her to be good
company.

'I'm gona be married.'

'Are you now? Well, I'm not surprised, you
would have to be married sooner or later, wouldn't
you? I'm sure your mother must be over the moon.
Mr Pendle it was, wasn't it? Mr Harry Pendle.'

'You can scoff. I can tell you this much, he's a
better man than you'll ever be.'

'I've got no doubt about that. I'm sure you
picked the best, although as I said before, Nancy, I
wasn't long in the running, was I? I mean, I was a
late starter, sort of pushed into the race, if you
know what I mean. I hadn't much option.' A grin
spread over his face now as he ended, 'Until I came
to the sticks, and then I baulked. Some horses are
born jumpers, others aren't.'

She flounced past him now on her way towards
the far kitchen door, where she turned and said,
'You think you're funny, don't you, smart-Aleck?
But I know this much, nobody's safe with you. You
would have taken me down, then skedaddled, as
me mother says. If you weren't responsible for poor
Carrie, it wasn't because you hadn't tried it on . . .'

The leap he took across the floor caused her to
squeal and with the flat of his hand he pushed her
against the door, hissing at her now, 'You mind
what you say, and tell your mother the same. I'm

telling you both, watch out or else you'll find yourself standing before the justice proving your words. A joke's one thing, banter's another, but you've got an evil tongue in your head. Now I'm warning you. You speak one more word against my character and the money for your wedding will go on a court case. *And I mean it.*'

And he did mean it, and showed it by grabbing at her by the shoulder and, swinging her back to the direction from which she had come and pushing her towards the back door, he said, 'As long as I'm here in this house, don't show your face. What's to be done I'll help me aunt.' And opening the door, he thrust her out and just prevented himself from banging it after her, only the thought of the man lying in the room above staying him. And he stood with his back to it, his teeth grinding, his hands clenched. They said men had mucky minds; by God! most of them only came second to some women. For months past, almost a year now he'd never been near a woman, not even for a cuddle. At times his body had burned and his mind had been a torment but he had worked and walked it off, because a new emotion had come into his life. He wouldn't have said he was a highly sexed man, he was though an ordinary fellow who had his needs, but like any priest he had sublimated them. Yet here was that bitch insinuating that, given a chance, he would have taken Carrie down.

As his body relaxed he told himself he had been a fool to get so angry. The trouble with Nancy was frustration and the fact that she preferred him to her future husband. Oh, he knew what was narking her.

He now went out of the room and up the stairs

and knocked on the bedroom door, and as he entered his aunt turned to him, saying, 'Give me a hand, will you, Robbie? It's getting this shirt on him. He came to himself a little while ago and helped me ease off his clothes, but now he seems gone again . . . he's in a fever.'

'Yes.' He nodded at her as he hoisted the limp form up and she pulled the nightshirt down her husband's back. 'It must have been the journey out last night, it was a bitter.'

'No, no.' She shook her head. 'He's spent days sitting in the workshop neither eating nor drinking; he was blaming himself but he should have been blaming me.'

'Oh no, Aunty, no.'

'Yes, Yes, Robbie. If I hadn't lied she would have likely been here today; he would have found solace in your company and you would have helped both me and Carrie to bear his censure. But all I could think of at the time was to stem his wrath.'

'I would have done the same; everybody wants to protect their own.'

'I wish I could think that.' She lifted up the corner of her white apron now and passed it over her face. Then coming round the bed, she looked at him as she said, 'Have you to hurry back?'

'No, no. There's no hurry. She . . . she told me to stay as long as was necessary.'

'You like it up there?'

'It's all right.'

'You've changed, you know, Robert.'

'Me changed? In what way?'

'Well, I don't know, I can't put me finger on it: something about you, it'll likely come to me when I least expect it.' She turned quickly to the bed now

276

as her husband groaned, and as she stroked the grey hairs back from his brow she murmured, 'I wish the doctor would hurry up.'

It was two hours later when the doctor arrived and looking as if he himself had just got out of bed, and the first thing he said to Alice was not, 'What's the matter with your husband?' but, 'Do you have any coffee in the house?' And when she said, 'Yes,' he said, 'Make it black and strong, will you?' Then he added, 'Why the devil do people take a New Year's day to get born and to die? I've been up since five o'clock.'

'I'm sorry.'

On the soft-spoken apology he smiled as he said, 'I'm glad you are. It's a change from my last patient, the man who died. He was blind drunk and he went out swearing, mostly at me. Walked under a horse, the idiot, and it wasn't standing still.'

He was speaking of a man dying.

The effect on Robert was to make him want to burst out laughing. Life was funny, odd: it was drama mixed up with comedy; scandal bred on lies; it was the joy of life escaping at intervals out of Miss Millie; most of all it was the loneliness in her eyes . . . Agnes's eyes. For the first time he gave her a name in the back of his mind.

The doctor said that John Bradley was in a high fever and that his resistance at the moment seemed to be very low. He would leave some pills and call later in the day when he would bring a bottle with him. 'In the meantime,' he said to Alice, 'keep his body sponged down. Don't change the sheets too often; it's his own sweat and it won't harm him as much as cold sheets against the skin.'

When he had gone Alice said with a note of

surprise in her voice, 'None of the Parkins have been in this morning. Nancy has been very good.'

He looked at her sheepishly, with a smile on his face as he now said, 'I'm afraid I gave her her marching orders.'

'Her marching . . . Whatever for, Robbie? You mean, you told her to get out . . . Nancy?'

'Yes. I told her as long as I'm here not to show her face.'

'But why?'

'Oh'—he turned away—'she said one or two things that annoyed me. I don't mind people telling me what I am if it's the truth, but if it isn't . . . well, I almost rough-handled her. After her dad comes home tonight I expect he'll pay me a visit.'

'Oh, Robbie.' She shook her head now, saying, 'Don't you understand? Whatever she said, it was out of jealousy. She was very sweet on you, you know. She's going to be married, but I don't think he's her first choice.'

'Well, Aunty, I gave her to understand from the first that I wasn't the marrying kind . . . but I'm sorry now that I acted as I did because you'll need her.'

'No, no. I was never one for neighbours popping in and out, and I must admit they're a nosy lot. I was glad when I heard a little while ago that he's thinking about leaving. Some of the lads are working in Newcastle now: one's a brass finisher, and another a dyer, and Mary Ellen has been taken on as apprentice milliner. But it's the travelling, especially in the winter. But for what he's asking for his house, I'm afraid they're going to be stuck there for some time. Three hundred pounds! Did you ever hear? It's only got three rooms and an

278

attic. It's got a decent bit of garden, but who's going to pay three hundred pounds for a place like that? Do you know what he paid for it twenty-six years ago? Fifty pounds. And now three hundred. Mr Bradley would have bought it off him, but not for that price. But—' She changed the subject now as she looked up into his face, saying, 'Now . . . how long do you think you can stay? I mean, how much leave can you take from up there?'

'Oh, a couple of days.' He nodded kindly at her. 'By that time the fever should be down, and then'—he put out his hand and patted her shoulder—'you can have Nancy back.'

'Oh! Robbie, Robbie. You know who I want back, don't you? Oh! Robbie.'

As the tears flowed down her face he drew her into his arms and as he patted her back he was forced to think wryly, Here I go again, comforting.


## CHAPTER FIVE

It was the fifth of January, he had been gone nearly five days. Two days ago she had sent Hubbard to see how Mr Bradley was faring. He had returned saying he was in a high fever and had been delirious, and that Robert had been up with him for the two nights. This had been related to her through Peggy who had gone on to say that Hubbard had said Robert looked asleep on his feet. Now another two days had almost passed and she'd had no word.

The place seemed different without him, bare of personality. Last night she had again confronted herself, and the knowledge that she was letting herself down by even thinking the way she did had again brought forth the rejoinder: what real harm could there be in thinking because all she would ever have of him were thoughts. She would never give herself away and so who was to know what she thought.

He already did.

At this she had gone to the mirror and stared at herself as she said to it, 'Well, he, like me, knows his place and he won't step out of it. Should he, he knows that he would be rebuked and strongly, and he's not the kind of man to lay himself open to that, because he has an opinion of himself and his own worth. Oh yes, that's evident in all he does and says.'

But that was last night. During the morning she said to Millie, 'Now I'm going into Newcastle to do some shopping. I . . . I want some material for a dress for you. Now you will be good, won't you?'

Millie hadn't asked if she might go with her, she had simply nodded her head while she brushed the poodle's coat, saying, 'Yes, of course, Aggie. And I'll see she doesn't do naughties on the carpet. I'll watch her, and put the paper down.'

Agnes had said, 'Better still, get Maggie or Ruthie to take you for a walk in the garden, so that lady can do her naughties there.'

'Yes, yes, I will.' Millie smiled; and then quite suddenly said, 'I have no one to talk to, Aggie.'

'What do you mean?' Agnes sat down beside her on the window seat and again she asked, 'What do you mean? You have no one to talk to.'

'Well, not since Bradley went away, and not since the party.'

280

'Don't be silly. You're talking to people all day. There's Dave and Peggy and Ruthie and Betty and of course Maggie; you chat with Maggie all the time; then outside, Hubbard and Bloom always have a word for you.'

Millie looked into Agnes's face now, but she did not speak, her large almond-shaped eyes looked filled with a deep want that Agnes recognized as being akin to the feeling that was within herself. She knew what her sister meant by having no one to speak to, while yet talking to everyone in the house. She rose from her seat now, saying, 'Be good.' And on leaving the room she saw Ruthie and said, 'I'm going into Newcastle to do some shopping. Keep an eye on Millie, please? Don't leave her alone. I won't be all that long gone. But run down now, will you, and tell your uncle that I want the trap.'

In the barn, Dave Waters looked at his daughter as he repeated, 'Trap? She's going into Newcastle? She's never gone into Newcastle on her own in the trap afore.'

'That's what she said, and she's getting ready.'

He pursed his thin lips and his short moustache seemed to bristle. 'Go and tell Greg to get it ready,' he said. Then he left the barn and went across the yard and into the kitchen where he found his wife alone, and he immediately began, 'She wants the trap, she's going into Newcastle she says to do shoppin'. She doesn't usually take the trap by herself; she doesn't like driving the trap. What's up?'

'Well, what can be up? She just wants to get out for a bit, I should think. And you're wrong, you know, she has taken the trap out on her own a

281

number of times.'

'Aye, but not into the city with the traffic as it is and them motor-cars flashing around. It isn't safe, for a start.'

'Why do you worry?' Peggy gazed at her husband in an almost pitying way. 'If it isn't one thing, it's another: it's the house, or it's Millie, or it's her. Look, she's a grown woman and she's not like Millie, you can't coddle her. And anyway, there's a change come over her of late. Ever since she broke off her engagement, she's been different.'

'Aye, she's different and I know who's the cause of it.'

Peggy's face was expressing honest inquiry as she said, 'You know who's the cause of it? What do you mean?'

'Just what I say. And I'll add this, you're blind, you're all blind.'

Exasperation in her voice now, she thrust her fists into her waist as she demanded, 'Well, tell me what it is I can't see . . . that we all can't see.'

'Bradley.'

'Bradley? . . . *Bradley?* You mean . . . ? Huh!' She turned her head to the side. 'You must be going out of your mind, man. Bradley and the Miss!'

'Aye well, perhaps I am goin' out of me mind, but I use me eyes and I've caught them.'

'*What do you say?* What do you mean, you've caught them?'

'Talkin'. Talkin'.'

'Oh, my God! she talks to us all. Look how she talks to you. You're not a servant to her, neither am I, we haven't been for years. She looks upon us more like parents.'

'Aye, that's just it, because I feel like a parent I

282

can read atween the lines and I know what's going on. He's a trouble-maker that fellow. Oh, I know, I know he saved me neck and I'm stuck with him, but he'll only try me so far. Let him lay a finger on her.'

'Dave. Dave.' She went up to him now and patted his arm; then raising her hand, she stroked his cheek, saying, 'It's in your mind, it's just because you think so much of them both, like I do myself. But Robert, he's one of the nicest fellows. You've got him all wrong. And he's changed, he's altered his town ways and he's fallen in with us.'

'Woman!' His voice was severe but quiet now as he looked into her face, 'I know what I know. I see beyond me eyes. It's likely because I do think the world of them both that I see like that, but I know there's something afoot.'

'Well, whatever you think, Dave, there's one thing I'll ask you: for God's sake keep it to yourself, because if she ever guessed you were thinking as you do about her . . . and him, I don't know what her reactions would be. Man'—she moved her head from side to side—'she's class; she mightn't have one penny to rub against the other, but it makes no difference, she's class. And what is Robert, after all? He's an odd-jobman. Aye, yes, he's got a skill at carpentry, but that doesn't give him a standin', a status like; he's still an ordinary working man. You could as soon think of . . . well, say one of the boys, Master Arnold or Stanley taking up with Ruthie. Come on, man, don't fret yourself any more, but think straight.'

His voice was still quiet as he said, 'I do think straight, and it's happened before where a man has married beneath him.'

'Oh, yes, yes.' She answered on a high note now.

'Admittedly from that end, yes: a man of class can stoop and take up a woman from beneath him, but never the other way round. You've never heard, and I've never heard of anybody like Miss Agnes lowering herself to seek a mate among the likes . . . well, let's face it, the likes of us. It doesn't work that way. As long as the man's superior, it's all right, and it happens, but not t'other way round. Never! Never!'

*      *      *

She did her shopping in Newcastle and in the main street. She had left the horse and trap on the outskirts and had come into the centre of the city by the tram-car. She bought the material for Millie's dress and fell to the temptation of buying herself a new hat.

It was all of three years since she'd had anything new except for the funeral outfit that had served both her father and her mother and which she had laid away and hoped that she would never use again, because she hated it.

The hat was of green velour: the brim at one side was turned slightly up, while across the front was a row of pink and mauve felt flowers. It had stood out in the middle of the plate-glass window and she had thought it would look most unsuitable on her, yet minutes later when she tried it on and the shop assistant who was an adroit saleswoman exclaimed with joined hands, 'It's exactly you, madam, and it's in tone with your coat, you couldn't have found a better match,' she agreed with her and parted with one pound, twelve shillings and sixpence, which was more money than had ever been spent on a hat for her in her life, she was sure of that.

She asked for her brown everyday felt to be packed in a bag and she went out from the store feeling slightly elated. Perhaps the elation showed in her face, because a number of heads were turned towards her as she walked down Northumberland Street.

Such was the effect of the hat that she had almost forgotten her main purpose in coming out, but as soon as she took her seat in the trap it returned to her and it tightened the feeling in her chest and she told herself there was nothing unusual about calling to see how the man was faring, for after all, Bradley was in her employ. He had been away five days now; she wished to ascertain whether he meant to return or not.

She was very thankful to leave the main road and to turn the horse into the quiet lane that led to Lamesley. When, having passed through the village, she eventually came to the hamlet her heart began to pump against her ribs and she chastised herself, saying, 'Don't be silly; there is nothing untoward in calling.'

Yet when she drew the horse to a stop at the side of the road and hitched the reins to a post in the railings and walked the few yards to the opening beyond which stood the house and the long appendage of a workshop running at right angles to it, she was trembling.

It was a pleasant looking house, built of stone and surprisingly large, she thought, for the home of a carpenter. Her hand shook slightly as she knocked on the front door, and it was almost a minute later when it was opened and there he stood looking at her, his face stretched in surprise which slowly melted into a smile as he said, 'Come in. Do come in.'

She went in without speaking and stood in the small hallway. He kept his eyes on her as he closed the door, then said, 'Come into the sitting-room; my aunt's upstairs.'

She went into the room, passing before him as he held the door open for her, and she noted with some surprise the comfort and homeliness of the room, and, unlike other cottages she had been in, that it was uncluttered, there were only a clock and two ornaments on the mantelpiece. The furniture looked solid, naturally because likely it was hand-made. But what she found most unusual was a large chintz-covered couch set straight before the fire, its cushions ruffled as if someone had been recently sitting there. This definitely wasn't the sort of set room favoured by most working-class.

He pointed to the couch, saying now, 'Come and warm yourself.'

It wasn't until she sat down that she found she was able to speak, when, looking up at him where he stood in front of her, she said, 'I really called to find out how your uncle is.'

'Oh, he's on the mend, thank goodness. It was touch and go for a time though. Anyway I was coming back today; in fact I was thinking of making me way about now.'

'You were?'

'Yes.' There was a short awkward silence until he said, 'Would you like a cup of tea? Look, I'll get my aunt; she'd like to meet you and for you to have something, it's still bitter out.'

'Oh, please, don't bother.' She made to rise but

he put his hand out towards her, the palm vertical as if he were pressing her down, and his tone changed now, as did the expression on his face, as he said, 'Now sit still, relax for a minute, I'll be back in a jiffy.'

When he left the room he left the door open and she saw him run the three or four steps towards the stairs, and the action reminded her of Millie. He looked light on his feet, yet his body for all his height was thickset and somewhat heavy . . . Sit still, relax for a minute, I'll be back in a jiffy. He had spoken to her like . . . like . . . How had he spoken to her? Like an equal. Yes, like an equal. She must be careful, she must, or things would get out of hand. She had been foolish to call here, utterly, utterly foolish. She was asking for trouble; she was giving him an inch and he would take a mile. No, no, he wouldn't. He knew the position as well as she did. Hadn't she been over this in her mind a thousand times?

When she saw the woman coming towards her, she rose to her feet and almost immediately she began to talk: 'I was passing and I wondered how your husband was. I'm . . . I'm so glad to know he's on the mend. It must have been very distressing.'

'It was. It was . . . Please sit down.' Alice extended her hand towards the couch, then went on, 'But I'm sure if he hadn't had the kind attention you gave to him in your home he wouldn't be here now. Robbie has told me how good you were. Would you care for a cup of tea?'

'Yes. Yes, thank you very much. It would be very acceptable.'

'Stay where you are.' Robert wagged his finger at his aunt, saying, 'I'll see to it.' And she smiled faintly at him before looking at Agnes and saying, 'He makes a good cup of tea.'

Left alone, they seated themselves each at an end of the couch. An awkward moment followed during which they looked away from each other and into the fire; then Agnes said, 'I would like you to know that I sympathize with you in your recent tragedy, Mrs Bradley.'

Alice continued to look into the fire for some time longer before she said, 'Tragedy is the right word.' And she added neither miss nor ma'am, which wasn't lost on Agnes but caused her to look deeper into the woman as she went on, 'I feel lost; the house is lonely. Of course, she was more Mr Bradley's than mine, always, yet she was still my daughter, and—' Alice now wetted her lips before going on, 'we became very close in the last months we were together, drawn no doubt by the wrong we had done to a certain party.' She turned now and looked at Agnes. ' 'Twas my fault. I put the blame on Robbie for a number of reasons. I thought it would lessen Mr Bradley's anger, but also because he was the kind of man I would have liked my daughter to marry. And last but not least, I liked him about the house, he was like a good son. We all wronged him . . . that was why my husband made the journey on New Year's Eve. But you know that by now.'

A quietness settled on the room; and again they sat looking towards the fire. Presently, Alice said, 'He's going back to you today,' which brought Agnes's head jerking towards her. But when Alice added, 'To his work; he says there's a lot to do,' Agnes realized it was an ordinary statement. But those words, he's going back to you today, made

288

her imagine for a moment that he had talked to this woman, about her. But of course that was ridiculous. Anyway, what could he say about her?

He came into the room carrying a tray on which was a china teapot with a milk jug and sugar basin to match together with three cups and saucers. The pattern was blue on an off-white background and rimmed with gold, and Agnes recognized the quality immediately and she exclaimed on it, saying, 'What a lovely set. It is old English Wedgwood, isn't it?'

'Yes, it is pretty old,' Alice nodded; 'it came from my husband's mother's family. It was her wedding present to us. It's an odd set: there were twelve cups and saucers, no plates. She said that years ago when, the gen . . . people had afternoon tea, that's all it used to be, just a cup of tea, no cakes or anything like that.'

She was right. Yes, she was right. She drank her tea. It was good tea, not at all a cheap blend. She knew about teas. That was one thing her mother had taught her. In the house they had a variety of Indian and China teas and just one particular kind for the kitchen, an inferior blend which she still ordered.

During the drinking of the tea she remarked on the room, how light it was, and how nice it was to have two large windows, and these to look out on to the garden beyond. And the paddock, was that theirs?

Oh yes. That and the other two that went down to the burn. Mr Bradley owned all of ten acres that took in the land to the back of the house and to the side, and all freehold. The fields were a nice stamping ground for the two horses.

As Agnes listened, she thought, two horses, ten acres and this comfortable house, this woman was better off than she was. Moreover, she had a business on the premises to support her and no worry about a staff and brothers who had to be educated and grounds that were like a jungle.

When she rose to take her leave, Alice thanked her for her visit, and she thanked Alice for the tea; then she looked at Robert and said, 'We can expect you today then?' And before he could answer Alice put in, 'He was just about to leave when you came. Another few minutes and you would likely have missed him.'

And now Robert put in quickly, 'I'll be along shortly.'

She stared at him as she said, 'Are you coming? By vehicle, I mean.'

'No, no; the walk is nothing.'

'Well, I'm on my way back now—' her voice had a business-like tone about it—'there's no reason why you should walk.'

He returned her look steadily before saying quietly, 'Thank you. I'll get my coat.'

There was no further conversation between Agnes and Alice while they awaited his return from upstairs, and when he was once again in the hall he bent and kissed his aunt, saying, 'Don't you worry now, I'll be over as often as I can until he's on his feet. And you've got no worry about the workshop, Tim'll see to that. As for inside help'—he pulled a face at her now—'the door won't be closed until our dear Nancy will be in.' Then he laughed as he added, 'Don't you let her say a word against me, mind.'

Alice smiled and, patting his arm now, she said,

'You're a naughty lad.' Then turning her eyes towards Agnes, she added, 'He's a tease.'

Agnes ignored this remark but again said a polite farewell.

He helped her up into the trap, then threw the brown paper parcel that he had been carrying on to the padded leather cushioned seat and in doing so dislodged a bulky brown paper bag which slid to the floor exposing as it did so the brim of a hat. About to take hold of the reins, Agnes turned in her seat and their eyes met.

'I'm sorry,' he said as he reached over and pushed the hat back into the bag and replaced it on the seat before taking his own place opposite her.

It wasn't until after she had set the horse in motion and they were approaching the Parkins' cottage that he realized they'd had a spectator: Nancy was standing by the gate and as they approached he could see the look on her face, the expression so tight that it aged her. He was on the offside to her but as the trap drove past her he leant slightly forward in front of Agnes and with an exaggerated gesture he touched his cap, then sat back with a tight grin on his own face.

It had been a stupid thing to do, he knew, but he had been unable to resist it, not after what had happened on the evening of New Year's day when she had sent her mother, not her father, in to him and he had then made sure that she left with a flea in her ear.

The meaning behind his exaggerated gesture had not been lost on Agnes. His last words to his aunt had referred to somebody called Nancy. This then was the person in question. Had she been another whom he had comforted? Oh! how stupid of her to have invited him to accompany her home. What if they were seen, as surely they would be? Well, he was a groom of sorts, and she was driving with her groom. That certainly wasn't an unusual procedure.

They had driven almost a mile in silence when he said, 'That was a silly thing to do, I know.'

She didn't say, 'What are you talking about?' Or, as she would more likely have put it the way she was feeling at the moment, 'To what are you referring?'

And he went on as if bent on defending himself now, 'She has a bitter tongue, that girl, and slanderous. I've had occasion to speak straight to her.'

Why couldn't she say something? But what could she say to such statements without becoming implicated? Without him taking advantage? Oh, for goodness sake! The warring being inside her screwed up its eyes and turned its head away, crying at her loudly, He'll take nothing that you don't give him.

Again they sat in silence until, his voice quiet and ordinary sounding, he said, 'May I say something?'

She gave a short laugh while looking straight ahead as she replied, 'I can't imagine anything or anyone stopping you from saying what you want to say.'

A stiffness showed in his voice now as he replied, 'There you are wrong. I can't say what I want to say. I can never say what I want to say. And when I make up my mind not to say something that's that. But in this case it was a simple thing I wanted to say, just this, that's a beautiful hat you're wearing.'

Her eyelids were blinking rapidly again. She felt silly inside. Why did she always make issues out of the simplest things? 'Thank you,' she said. 'That's what I thought when I saw it in the window. I couldn't resist it.'

'I wouldn't have thought many women could. Anyway, it's your colour, it's a lovely brown.'

'Brown?' Her mouth was wide as she now smiled at him. 'It's green.'

'Green?'

'Yes.'

She stared fixedly at him before saying, 'What colour is my coat?'

He looked at it from the top button that was half hidden by the small velvet collar down to where it fell round her feet before he said, 'It's brown too, but a different brown.'

'It's a bluey green. You . . . you must be colour-blind.'

'No. Me colour-blind? No!'

They were laughing together as she turned the trap into the drive. 'Haven't you ever thought about colours?' she asked him.

'No, I can't say I have. Things are black and white or brown and grey. You see I've dealt with wood mostly all my life, I see the trunk of a tree as different shades of brown, and the inside, the timber is off-white. Then there were the ships. Well, iron always looks a rusty brown.'

'What colour do you think these flowers are on the brim of my hat?' She pointed, at the same time putting her head to the side, and he, half raising himself, looked down and examined the felt flowers, saying, 'Some look a sort of dull white, not a pure white, and the others . . . well, I don't know

293

what name to put to them, except a kind of blue.'

'They are pink and mauve.'

'Pink and mauve?'

They were laughing again. 'Hadn't you any idea that you weren't seeing colours as they really are?'

'No, no idea at all. It's never come up. I've either picked a black or brown suit. The same with me shoes or boots. Oh . . . boots were always black. As for shirts, well, they were always white for best and a kind of dull colour, which my mother referred to as blue, for work.'

'Have you never been round an art gallery?'

'Yes. Yes, I have, in the city.'

'Well, didn't you notice the difference there? I mean some of the colours are so striking.'

'Yes, I suppose so, but I had nothing to go on. I enjoyed the shapes and the pictures. Anyway, when you go to the cinema . . . the pictures, they're all black and white. No, I've had nothing to go on. Well, fancy that'—he nodded his head now—'I'm colour-blind. I've had a defect all of my life and I haven't known it.'

He was laughing at it as if it was a joke, and she too was smiling as they entered the yard, and Peggy, happening to be looking out from the window saw them and brought out a startled 'My God! Eeh my God! he's right. And her talking of going to Newcastle; 'twas just an excuse. An' what's that she's got on her head? 'Tis a new hat. 'Tisn't her at all, she looks . . .' And she searched for a word to fit how she thought her mistress looked and when she found it she dismissed it with a neck cricking shake of her head because the word was wanton.

294

# CHAPTER SIX

The weeks passed. Spring came and moved into early summer, and it was the beginning of June before John Bradley came downstairs, for, following the fever, he had a slight stroke. He was a man now who would never work again. Most of the time he sat propped up in a chair in the sitting-room looking out of the window and waiting, as Alice said, for Robert's visits.

Practically every other night over the past months Robert had made his way to the house. He had now acquired a bicycle which got him over the three miles there and the three miles back in a very short space of time. He enjoyed the ride so much that he wondered why he hadn't taken it up years ago. Sometimes on his way back he would call in at The Bull. The feeling in the taproom against his uncle had changed: poor old devil, they said, to end up like that. And why, Billy Taggart had asked him, didn't he go back and take up his old job because he could be on a good thing there if anything happened to the old fellow.

He was all right where he was, he said, at least for the present.

Well he was daft. Was he still getting ten shillings a week?

And yes, at times he thought he must be daft for he was working twelve, sometimes fourteen hours a day now. The extra hours he put in were used to help bring to fruition the plans she had for restoring part of the kitchen garden to its old use and bringing the rose gardens back to a semblance of what they once were. What amazed him was how hard she herself could work in the garden. She certainly wasn't afraid of soiling her hands. And Miss Millie was in her element too. He had never seen that lass so happy, or so normal, as she had been these past months.

They had gone through a sort of standing still period, as he put it to himself. Whenever Arthur Bloom or Greg were absent, he talked to Millie, and if she was there she joined in. At other times, when the men were present, he just let Millie talk to him, and for most of the time she didn't need any answers.

But if everything was standing still between him and her, that certainly wasn't the case in the kitchen, for he knew he was under suspicion there right enough. At times old Waters would look at him as if he could throttle him. As for Peggy, her manner had changed too. Of them all, only Maggie remained the same. But Maggie was in a kind of seventh heaven, because she was going to marry Greg, and she hardly let an opportunity pass but she told him that it was all due to his manoeuvring.

He was happy for her. She was a grand soul, and Hubbard was a decent fellow.

On this particular July day, the sun was hot on his neck as he turned over a new patch of ground and he paused for a moment to wipe the sweat from around the collar of his open shirt with his handkerchief, then looked to the side to where Agnes and Millie were clearing the old straw away from between the strawberry plants. He smiled to himself as he recalled Bloom's reactions yesterday when she had wanted to put in the strawberry runners to make a new row. It was too early, he

296

said. But she had been reading about such things, she said. 'Aye, miss, you might,' he had replied; 'but reading and experience are two different things, and them that write them books for most part know nowt about what they are saying, they go on greenhouse growing or undercover things.'

He had won the day, and now she seemed to be content in just clearing up the beds.

She seemed happier these days, more content. Perhaps it was, he thought, because she had found an interest. And there was nothing like fresh air and working in it to ease the mind. He had found that out himself. But he also found out that there was no such similar palliative for night-time, other than getting yourself too tired to care or having a good drink. And he had been drinking more of late. He'd have to watch it. Aye, yes, he'd have to watch that, if only because he didn't want to become pot-bellied.

He saw young Betty come running round by the hedge and say something to her. Then he saw her hurrying away back towards the house, leaving Betty with Miss Millie. And Betty, coming up to him now, said, ' 'Tis a visitor, the Lady Emily Clinton-Smyth. Eeh! the way she's made up. Talk about a dog's dinner! By! I wouldn't like to work under her. You'd have to watch your p's and q's there.'

'Look,' he suddenly said to her, 'Millie's going after her. Bring her back and leave her with me; she'll be all right.'

Lady Emily Clinton-Smyth. That was the old girl who was at the funeral and who stayed till last. She hadn't been back here since. She was known as a character, that old girl! He wondered what she wanted; surely if she had been concerned for the Miss, she would have put in an appearance before now . . .

Agnes was thinking much the same thing as she hurried into the kitchen where, after washing her hands at the sink, she turned to Peggy, saying, 'Have you a comb handy, Peggy?'

Peggy went to the corner of the mantelpiece and, taking down a comb, she extracted loose hair from it before handing it to her mistress, saying, 'Tidy hair and clean hands are not going to do much for your dress, and you can't keep her waiting.'

'Well, I've been gardening, she'll understand. She should for she was keen on it herself at one time, so I heard.'

She handed the comb back to Peggy, then went hurriedly up the room, across the hall and into the drawing-room, to find Lady Emily sitting on a straight-backed chair to the side of the window and from where she had a good view of the drive. She turned her head as Agnes entered the room and started talking before she had hardly closed the door, saying, 'I see you've had the drive tidied up, not before time. Have you engaged more staff?'

'No; we have just the same men. How are you, Lady Emily?'

'Oh, just as you see me, I seem to have been like this for the last twenty years, and will likely remain the same for the next twenty. I've left word that I'm to be buried standing up and with all my clothes on.' There was a sign of an attempted smile at the corner of her mouth. Then looking Agnes up and down, she said, 'What have you been up to? Not very presentable.'

'I've been gardening. We're enlarging the
298

vegetable garden.'

'Well, well! gardening. Well, you could do worse. But it plays havoc with the hands and cripples your back, and what for? The annuals die and the others take years to grow and few people live long enough to have the pleasure of them. We have an avenue of trees that my great-great grandfather planted. What good did they do him I ask you? Life's a waste of time; I sometimes wonder why we've been put into it? For the glory of God, parsons tell you. Damn nonsense. Glory of God, indeed! We'll be very lucky if any of us see Him, that's my opinion. And we'll be very lucky if any of us are still alive this time next year. Do you know that, girl?'

Agnes now smiled gently as she said, 'Are you expecting a plague, Lady Emily?'

'No girl, I'm not expecting a plague, I'm expecting a war. The majority of people in this country are asleep, they can't see what's coming. Austria-Hungary and Serbia at each other's throats. You mark my words, there'll be an explosion shortly. And who'll set the fuse? That Kaiser of course. I've lived abroad half my life so I should know what I'm talking about. I've never liked the French, no sensible Englishman would, we are more akin to the Germans. Yet they are up to something, they always are, the Germans. That Mr Lloyd George standing with a foot on each boat, I know where he's going to land. It'll take Asquith to pull us out of this and Sir Edward Grey. That man's been doing his best to get those Germans to toe the line, but that Kaiser wants to goose-step it over everybody. Somebody wants to do to him what they did to poor Archduke Franz Ferdinand last month. Scandalous, scandalous. I

299

tell you, girl, we'll be lucky if we're alive next year. My remark about living twenty years ahead was simply prattle, I've no desire to live any longer. But I suppose I will have to go on as long as there's a duty to perform and that's why I'm here today, I'm killing two birds with one stone. I'm on my way to the castle . . . Ravensworth. You haven't been there lately, have you? No, no, of course not. Your mother used to go. Your mother was a lady, always remember that. Do you hear?'

'Yes, yes, Lady Emily, I hear.' Agnes's voice was flat. There was something coming. She didn't know what, but when someone like Lady Emily talked about doing her duty, she knew that it wouldn't be anything pleasant, and now again she was talking of duty.

'We have our duty, we of the upper class are bred for a purpose and the main point of that purpose is to show an example. We can be reduced to penury as you and your family have almost been, but nothing can take away your breeding. Your father was a weak man but he came of quite good stock, industrial perhaps, but then we all must get our money from somewhere. And those of us who have enough money to employ large staffs have a responsibility. Well, not only those with large staffs, those with any staff have a responsibility towards them, and, too, part of that responsibility consists in seeing that they maintain their place. Do you follow me?'

She now bent forward, her head bobbing so that her high hat which was perched on the top of her mass of white hair looked for the moment as if it was going to slip over her brow, but with an impatient sweep of her head she pushed it back;

300

then she ended, 'Oh, oh yes, miss, you do, you do. I can see by your face you do.'

Agnes felt faint. The purpose of this woman's visit was now clear to her, but she felt she wanted to get up and run, to hide her face and stuff her ears from what was coming.

'Now'—Lady Emily straightened up again and drew her pointed chin into the fleshy folds of her neck—'I'm known and feared among women of my own class. I have talked scandal and enjoyed listening to it all my life, again with my own class. There are liberties one can take, there are indiscretions one can commit, there are lengths to which one can go, great lengths, but within the borders of one's own class. But should one be so foolish or stupid as to step out of one's class, and down, even to the lower middle class, that is a great mistake, but to go further is a tragedy, a disaster, equal to that of cohabiting with someone of a different colour.'

Agues was trembling: her hands were joined on her lap and her nails were digging into each other. She told herself to speak, to put a stop to this, yet she wanted to know more, she wanted to know how this had come about. She had done nothing to merit these accusations, because what stooping she had done had been simply in her mind. But Lady Emily was talking again.

'As I said in the beginning, I've enjoyed talking scandal but since I've been acquainted with this matter that concerns you I have not mentioned it to anyone, because I am concerned for you. I am concerned that you have been burdened with the running of this establishment, and that your marriage to the Crockford man did not materialize.

Although that certainly wouldn't have had my blessing either, because he is a vain weak-kneed individual, and he certainly doesn't take after his mother. And I'm also sorry that you have brothers such as they are. Two to go off to Australia of all places. No gentleman would be found dead there. And then Stanley, he's never at home, is he? He spends his time at the Cunninghams. Oh yes'—she was nodding again—'I know all about the Cunninghams. He's got his eye on Diana. But he's barking up the wrong tree; she's got to marry money. Somebody's got to provide the cash to keep the stud going, they are all horse mad. But that won't stop either her or him enjoying themselves, for if I recall anything about that young lady she's away ahead of anything in their stable.'

When again she paused for breath, Agnes, getting to her feet, said, 'Have you finished, Lady Emily?'

'No, I haven't, not quite, girl. And sit down . . . do, do sit down, because, believe me, I'm here for your own good. You see, there's someone in your household, or out of it, I don't know, who seems to be very interested in your movements, as this letter indicates.' She now opened her long bead purse and from it withdrew a sheet of paper, and on the sight of it Agnes sat down again and watched the thin bony fingers open out the letter, then hand it towards her, as she said, 'Can you recognize that handwriting?'

Agnes, her breath now coming in gasps, looked down on the writing. She did not read what was on the paper, she only took in that the writing was very ill-formed. Lifting her head she looked at Lady Emily, saying, 'People who write anonymous letters usually disguise their hand I understand. But . . . but why should anyone write a letter about me? May I read it?'

'That's what I want you to do.' The old lady's head was bobbing again.

Agnes took the letter from Lady Emily's hand, but she had to blink her eyes to clear away the blur before she could read. The letter began simply:

Lady Emily,

You being a lady of quality and a friend of the Thorman family, I think you should know that Miss Agnes is in need of advice because she is being tempted into a situation that is lowering to her by a man in her employ. This man has a way with women. He has such a hold over her that she follows him about, and even works with him. It is a scandalous situation that a lady of her class should so lower herself. But it is not really her fault, as he is that kind of man. They meet in the wood under the pretext that they are looking for her sister. I feel you could do something about it, Lady Emily, as it is a disgrace.

I am, your Ladyship, a wellwisher.

'It isn't true. It isn't true.' The letter was shaking like a leaf in her hand and she repeated, 'It isn't true, I tell you. It isn't true, not a word of it. The man this letter refers to is *Mr Bradley* . . .'

'You call him Mr Bradley?'

'Yes, that is his name, Mr Bradley. Although I address him as Bradley, while those in . . . in the kitchen do so by his Christian name.'

'Well then, we'll call him Bradley. And you say that nothing in this letter is true?'

303

'One thing maybe, we have worked together in the garden. But Millie is always with us and most times Bloom . . . Arthur Bloom too. This letter is infamous.' Her lips were trembling, and now the tears spilled over from her eyes, and Lady Emily, bending forward, patted her knee, saying, 'There, there. I'll take your word for it. But why? Can you think why anyone should write such a letter to me, accusing you of such indiscretion?'

'Yes, yes, I can.' Agnes leant her head back against the wing of the chair. Yes, she knew who had written that letter. It was Dave. He had been acting strange for weeks now; he had even followed her when she had taken a walk in the garden. The time he referred to—her meeting with Bradley— was at the last full moon, when Millie had taken to wandering again. There had been other full moons that hadn't seemed to affect her, but on this night she had been missing and Bradley had gone out to look for her. But so had Maggie and Betty Trollop. It should happen that Bradley had found Millie and that just when she had come across them Dave had appeared on the scene. She remembered this very clearly for the following day he had almost been rude to her. She had put down the rudeness to the fact that it was Bradley who had found Millie and that Dave resented Millie's open affection for the man.

'Who is it then? Who wrote this letter?'

'It doesn't matter who wrote it, I can only assure you the contents are not true, all that has taken place between Bradley and myself is ordinary conversation.'

'You converse with the man then?'

'We've talked.'

'Why?'

'Perhaps because I have no one else to talk to.'

She had shouted; and now she was on her feet, her hand over her mouth and the tears raining from her eyes.

Lady Emily rose stiffly from the chair and, putting her arms out, she drew Agnes into her embrace, saying, 'There, there, my dear. There, there. These situations come about. Those brothers of yours should be shot. And me and my like round about are not blameless either; we should have called on you. But that sister of yours, you know, is something of an embarrassment and puts people off. I know the tales about her are quite exaggerated, I have said so. It is the common folk who start such things. Why, one of my maids was heard to say that when she got a hold of you she clawed at your hair like a bat. I told my maid Hewston to go and slap the wench's face. Millicent isn't sane, we all know that, but she is no maniac.'

Agnes withdrew herself from the embrace: she couldn't bear to listen to this, she couldn't bear to listen to any more; these tales about Millie were as wrong as those about herself, in fact, there was more truth in the accusations in this letter than those directed against Millie. She now crushed the letter in her hand, saying, 'I shall keep this, Lady Emily.'

'But it isn't addressed to you, my dear.'

'Nevertheless, I intend to keep it, and one day I will show it to the writer. He is a man who owes much to the man he is accusing.'

'So you think it is a man?'

'Yes, I know it is a man.'

'I wonder if I risk a guess in saying that it is your

old servant Waters. Would I be right?'

'I am not going to discuss who wrote the letter, Lady Emily.'

'No, no. Well, I can understand that, and Waters, if I remember rightly, valeted your grandfather, and then your father. When he was young he used to hob-nob with Gregory's man. That was when your grandfather came for the shoot. Now, my dear, I must go. I'm late as it is. One last word, and it is this: never marry out of your class. You may not be happy marrying in it, but you will still have friends to whom you can turn; marry out of it and you will be no better than an outcast. In my opinion, you may as well be dead.'

On this she turned about and walked with her stiff stately step down the drawing-room. Agnes had to force herself to move quickly in order to open the door, then she preceded her across the hall and through the lobby where, at the top of the steps, her coachman awaited her; but as if he weren't there she turned and had some last words for Agnes. 'Of course if the war comes,' she said, 'it will likely bring such changes, it may level everything out and Jack might feel as good as his master, and my God! that would be a nice state of affairs, wouldn't it? Well, I won't live to see it. Goodbye, my dear.'

Agnes mumbled words which she could scarcely hear herself and the old lady was hardly seated in her carriage before she returned indoors. She went straight up the stairs and made for her room where, once inside, she did not throw herself on the bed or even sit on its edge but paced the floor, at times biting on her thumbnail, at others beating her knuckles together until they hurt. Every fibre in her was crying to her to go downstairs and thrust this letter into Dave's face, then to tell him to go. But how could she do that to a man who had given his life in service to the house and those in it. And anyway, if he went so would Peggy, and she needed Peggy. Peggy had been her substitute mother; yet even she had been different of late. There was no change in the others, thank goodness; Ruthie, Maggie, and Betty were the same, as were Bloom and Hubbard; in fact, there was a kind of easy feeling outside the house, it was only inside that she felt the tension. But how was she to go on, knowing that she was being spied on? And Dave would of course realize the reason for Lady Emily's visit.

What should she do?

She now sat in a chair and, bending forward, she joined her hands together and, as she often did, she appealed to something within her when seeking an answer, and nearly always she received good advice as if from some inner being. She didn't always follow the advice, even though she knew the answers she got from deep within her were true. What shall I do? was her question. The answer came back firmly: nothing. Put on a bright face, act as if Lady Emily's visit had been pleasurable. This will baffle him. But if you were to acknowledge the letter it would give him an opening to approach you and reproach you, and he mustn't have the liberty, for then he could no longer remain in the house. Go on, go on now, while you know you can do it.

When she walked into the kitchen, as she expected Dave Waters was there talking to Peggy and he swung round and looked towards her. His face looked pinched and white, his eyes dark, he was like some man ready to do battle. She looked past him and addressed herself to Peggy as she said, 'Lady Emily is in her usual form, she's on her way to the castle. She's prophesying war and says that none of us will be here this time next year unless, as she suggests, we are under German rule. It seems now it's a good thing we are extending the vegetable garden, for if there is a scarcity of food we won't exactly starve.'

She made herself smile on them both, then she walked past them on her way to the yard and so to the garden. But outside her smile disappeared.

Should she tell him? Should she say to him, 'Bradley, will you please not talk to me in future, but take your orders entirely from Waters?' And what would he do then? She knew what he would do, he would leave. And then she would never see him again. Well, wouldn't that be best, best for both of them, because now she was in the open she knew exactly what her feelings were concerning him and also what his were concerning her. But as Lady Emily said, one might as well be dead if one stepped out of one's class.

## CHAPTER SEVEN

On the fourth of August war was declared. Midway through the next morning Stanley came back from the Cunninghams' in high excitement: he came into the house calling, 'Agnes! Agnes!' And so loud was his voice that she came running from the study into the hall, saying, 'What is it?'

'We are at war! We've declared war on Germany.'

'Oh well, it isn't such a great surprise, is it, after what's been happening these last few weeks?'

'But we are at war! Don't you understand? It's only been surmise up to now. But it's happened. They are devils those Germans, quite inhuman. The first news that's come in is of them slaughtering children by the hundreds.'

'They wouldn't do that, that's war gossip.'

'Wouldn't they?' he almost shouted as he leaned towards her; then he turned and swiftly crossed the hall to the drawing-room.

She followed him, and there watched him striding up and down, his face red with excitement. He was talking rapidly: 'There were two German fellows at Oxford. They were unbearable, arrogant, strutting about like peacocks, not only thought but said that theirs was the greatest country in the world.'

'Well, as far as I can understand it's what we've been saying about England for centuries.'

'But we are! We are. Look at our colonies. We are, and . . .'

'All right. All right. Let's take it as a fact. But tell me, what are you going to do?'

'Well, there's only one thing I can do, and want to do. I'm joining up. Nigel Cunningham has already gone. He's going into the infantry, but I'm for the artillery. Dick Weir's going into the artillery too. He says we could all be across there in the next two weeks.'

She stopped him in his tramping by asking, 'What about Arnold and Roland, will they be coming home?'

309

'I don't know.'

'Well, you hear from them more than I do'—her voice was sharp now—'you should know what their intentions are.'

'Don't be silly. How could I know what their intentions are with regard to a war? We didn't really expect it ourselves. Nigel, whose uncle's in the Lords, said that up till the last minute Parliament was divided, they didn't know what they were going to do. But this business about Belgium triggered it off because they are making for Paris, and then it's just a step across the channel and it could be us. It's unthinkable. So I suppose they'll come home . . . Yet—' He turned away and went to the window and stood looking up into the sky, his hands behind his back. It was a pose their father had often adopted and it irritated her, as also did his next words: 'They are doing so well out there. Arnold's got two cars, one's a racer. They've been thinking about taking a house on their own so it looks very much as if they were settled. Still, this is their country and . . .'

'I don't know about being settled. In the last letter I had from Roland he admitted he wasn't taken with the people, especially those in the factory.'

'Well, that's understandable, they're a raw crowd altogether and they've been given more licence than the workers over here. And'—he laughed— 'we mustn't forget their beginnings: it was a convict settlement, remember, and one would be foolish to expect cream in that situation. Anyway'—he swung round, rubbing his hands together now—'I'm going to change and go into Newcastle. I don't know when I'll be back. I might have to go straight in, I don't know the procedure yet. In any case, if . . . if they let me out'—he gave a high laugh—'I'll call in at the Cunninghams' on my way back, so I'll likely be late.'

'Stanley.' He was half-way out of the door when she checked him.

'Yes?' He looked over his shoulder.

'What about me?'

He turned fully around now and looked at her, repeating, 'What about you?'

'Just what I said, what about me, and this place?' She now spread her two hands shoulder high. 'In war they conscript labour, I understand.'

'Oh, I shouldn't worry about that. There's only one here who would be called up and that's Bradley. And he'll likely go in any case . . . of course, he will.'

Her throat was tight, her eyes wide and staring, but she kept her voice flat as she said, 'Hubbard and Maggie are to be married next week. I think Hubbard is for leaving and going in to the town. He hasn't said anything to me but Maggie has told her aunt that his brother who is employed in the Birtley Iron Works could get him a place and—' she paused now, then stressed her next words—'a decent wage, all of two pounds a week.'

'Well, if that's what he wants, let him go.'

'*Stanley!*' She bawled his name so loudly that he screwed up his face and came hurrying towards her, demanding, 'What's up with you? What do you expect me to do, chain them here? If they want to go they'll go.'

'Yes'—her voice was as loud as his now—'they'll go, and what have we left? Two old people in the house and one middle-aged woman, because . . .

311

because the excitement of war will lift Betty Trollop out of here, I know that. And outside, our staff will consist of one and of course me. Where is my place in this war? Tell me.'

'Where it has always been, here. Someone has got to stay and see to things. And look here, Agnes, have you asked yourself, if you weren't here where would you be?'

'I would be out in the world earning my living, as I can do with my music. I've told you that before. Here, I am treated no better than a servant by the three of you: you've never considered me for one minute. I've been used, I'm still being used. What if I were to up and go and take Millie with me?'

They glared at each other, for a moment cold dislike showing in their eyes before Stanley said, 'In that case, I would store the furniture and let the house to the military. The Cunninghams were saying only yesterday that there had been inquiries about Glen Manor that's been empty for the last six months, military inquiries. They were very interested in the fact that there are a large number of horse boxes there that would be suitable for the cavalry, I suppose. We have quite a number of horse boxes, haven't we? So that is the answer to your question, my dear sister: I would let the place tomorrow to the military, if they were interested.'

The words of retaliation were stuck in her throat, she couldn't speak, she only knew he meant what he said. Then from the look on her face he attempted to soften the blow by saying, 'You ask for trouble, Agnes. Anyway, I myself and the boys wouldn't want you to be homeless, you should know that; there's the lodge, you could always stay there.'

The lodge, three small rooms and a scullery and all so small. She had often wondered how anyone could bear to live in them. Yet when she was young, Pratt the groom and his wife and five children had lived there. All the children were born there, and they were in their twenties when they left.

She felt slightly sick and suddenly very empty. She turned away from him. Presently she heard him go down the room and close the door behind him.

They were at war. All young men would have to go . . . Robert, he would go. Of course he would go, he was that kind of man. And he was the kind of man that would put his whole heart into anything he was doing. Perhaps he would become an officer. Well, if he were to become an officer . . .

She swung round so quickly that her full skirt formed itself into a bell and as she marched from the room she asked herself, how ridiculous could one be; everyone knew they didn't take officers from the working-class.

An hour later she was amazed and not a little disappointed in some strange way when she spoke to Robert about the war. They were in the harness room. Millie was with them. She began by saying, 'Isn't the news terrible, we're at war.'

'Yes, so I understand,' he replied.

At the lack of enthusiasm in his voice she said, 'Everyone will be rushing to enlist. I suppose you won't be an exception?'

He straightened up from where he had been attending to a saddle laid over the horse bench and, his voice flat, he said, 'I'm not running to join in any war. As far as I understand from what I've read about wars, there's a lot of glory in it, created

313

so to speak by the dead, and they haven't much use for it. From what I've gathered there's no victors in wars because the winners have got to become jailors, and jailors in the end are always disliked, and when the prisoners riot there you go again, another war.'

'You like your metaphors, don't you?'

'Aye, it's a good way to get things over. The same as Christ used parables to make things plain to those who don't understand, or couldn't understand.'

'Thank you.'

'Oh.' His manner changed immediately. Turning his head slightly, yet keeping his eyes on her, he said, 'Now don't take it like that; you know what I meant and how I meant it.'

'I know what you meant, Bradley.'

The interruption caused them both to turn and look at Millie, and he said, 'Did you now, Miss Millie? And what do you think I meant?'

'Well, I think you meant that you're not going with Stanley to be a soldier.'

'Huh!' His laugh was louder now but his tone gentle as he looked towards her, saying, 'By! Miss Millie, you always hit the nail on the head. You're right, I'm not going with Mr Stanley to be a soldier, not until I'm forced to.'

'Are you what they call a pacifist?'

'No, not really.' He was looking at Agnes again and was shaking his head. 'No, if I've got to fight, I'll fight. Whether it's at a war or in a backyard, I'll fight, but not unless it's necessary, so I'll wait until the call-up comes. There'll be so many patriots rushing in this minute that they'll be trampling each other to death.'

314

They both turned and looked at Millie again for she was laughing now, her head back, her mouth wide open, and when Agnes cautioned her quietly, saying, 'Stop it. Stop it, dear. Stop it,' her laughter died away and, looking at Agnes, she said, 'I was laughing at Robert because he's funny. He says funny things, everybody rushing to the war and being trampled to death before they get there to be killed in the war.'

After a quick exchange of glances which each read as: If that isn't sensible thinking, I wonder what is? Agnes said, 'Come along, dear.' And without further words she left him.

She should, she told herself, feel elated, relieved that he wasn't running off with the rest to serve his country, but what she felt was disappointment. It had something to do with his character. She had imagined she knew him well enough to gauge his reactions to such a thing as war. But apparently she didn't know him at all, and she wasn't deceiving herself that his attitude was because he wanted to stay on in her employ. No, whatever his feelings were with regard to her, had he felt patriotic he would, even at this moment, have been about to join up in defence of his country.

He was a disturbing man. She had felt this from the first. And she felt an irritation rising in her towards him. It was a pity, she thought, he wasn't in some way being forced to join the army, for feeling as she did at this moment his absence would not have hurt her.

\*　　　\*　　　\*

It was during the third week of the war when

315

Stanley marched into the house in the uniform of an officer of the Sixteenth Battalion of the Durham Light Infantry. He looked very smart and was in high spirits. He was, he said, stationed just outside Newcastle, but he didn't expect to be there long. He was sure to be going overseas with another batch of the British Expeditionary Force. The beggars would be stopped in their massacre; they had been halted already in their drive for Paris. General Joffre, the French commander-in-chief, was the big noise over there. Some of the fellows didn't think that was right; it would have been much more sensible to have an English general at the top. These French were very emotional chaps. But then Kitchener was at the head of things so everything would turn out all right in the end.

On and on he went.

When Agnes could get a word in she said, 'I had a letter from the boys this morning. Of course they didn't guess when they sent it we would be at war now. Roland did suggest that with the apparent state of affairs that seemed to be galloping to a head over here, it might be better if he came home. But Arnold's for staying there.'

'Trust old Arny . . .' They were having lunch and he interrupted what he was saying to remark on the condition of the chicken: 'This bird's been run off its legs, hasn't it? It's as tough as leather.'

She made no reply, and he went on, 'Trust my eldest brother to stay where the dibs are. The last thing he said to me was, "I'll be a millionaire one day, you'll see." And I bet he will too, that is if he does escape the war. Is there any brandy left?'

'There's half a bottle; I . . . I keep it for medicinal purposes.'

316

'My God!' He wiped his mouth with his napkin before saying, 'As I've already said, the best thing for this place would be to let it, the army pay well. I'll put it to Arnold.'

'You'll do no such thing. In any case it'll take weeks and weeks before you'd get his authorization.'

'Now look here, Agnes, I . . .'

'Now you look here.' She leant across the table towards him; then, her tone changing, she said pleadingly, 'Leave things as they are for a while.'

'What if you're left here without help? There'll surely be conscription shortly and that fellow Bradley will have to go. I'm amazed he's still here. I spoke to him about it but he had his answers ready. He's too ready with his tongue altogether, that fellow, and I never took to him. Oh, and that reminds me, when I was at the Cunninghams' last week I met Lady Emily and she spoke about him. I wondered what she was getting at, but Jane came up and stopped the conversation. Lady Emily was asking if he was still here . . . Bradley. And then she got on about you. She said you needed looking after, you were lonely. She was about to upbraid me when, as I said, Jane came up. What was she meaning? Do you know?'

Oh, Lady Emily, Lady Emily, and her promise not to talk about the matter. The Cunninghams were a rowdy, busy-bodying lot and she knew from something that Roland had let drop the reason why Stanley was such a frequent visitor there, it wasn't only his love of horses. And Diana Cunningham was engaged to David Lecombe. The Lecombes were in steel and there was money in steel, especially during a war.

She stared at her brother. If he probed any deeper which might cause him to put two and two together, she would threaten what she would do about Diana Cunningham. She could write anonymous letters too. She would write to Mr David Lecombe. Yes, she would, she would . . .

Dear God, what was the matter with her, why didn't her mind shut itself off from such thinking? But most of all, why had Bradley come into her life? Why had she allowed her emotions to run riot where he was concerned? How could she go on living like this? . . .

'What's the matter? Aren't you well?'

'I'm all right.' She sat back in her chair. 'Hand me the water.'

He poured her out some water, and as she sipped it he said, 'You know, Agnes, in the long run you'd be better off without this place. You mightn't think we're concerned for you, but . . . but we are really. We've all said it's too much. And long before Mother died the indoors rested on your shoulders. Then, I know, you had a tough time with father. We all felt a bit guilty. And after he died, and you broke up with James, we wondered if it wouldn't be more fair to you to see that Millie was taken care of . . . in some way.'

'In an asylum?'

He nodded at her before saying quietly, 'Well, what else? What could we do?'

Yes, what could they have done? And it afforded her a little bit of comfort to know they had discussed her welfare, that they hadn't ignored her existence completely.

She looked at him now and said quietly, 'I'll be all right, if you'll just let things slide for a time.

Anyway, when you come back from France you'll want some place to come to, won't you? It can't be all that comfortable out there.'

'Yes, all right, we'll leave it until whenever Roland manages to get home, then we'll talk again. Well, now I must get back.' And he laughed as he rose from the table adding, 'I'm not my own master any more. Oh, the colonel! Boy! is he playing at war games. He thinks the enemy is in the backyard. It was funny yesterday. One of our fellows came dashing into the mess saying, "They're here, they're here, they're on the tennis courts!" Another wag said, "Does the colonel know?" And the fellow answered, "He's fighting them single-handed, forty love." They roared. It's a very nice place where we're billeted, it's on the outskirts of Newcastle. It used to belong to a shipowner; he's given it up for the war.'

Forty love. The colonel playing at war. They thought that was funny. Her brothers belonged to a world that she knew nothing of; but then she knew little of any world except the acres around this house, and although she had stressed she could earn her living there was part of her that doubted if she could ever do it.

Only recently she had been wishing for something to happen, a kind of explosion in her mind that would cause her to take definite steps in one way or the other. She would then know where she was, she would then know who she was, yes, who she was. Was she destined for a spinster lady living in the big crumbling house and on the charity of her brothers? Or was she somebody in her own right, somebody who would say: This is me, this is what I want to do. To hell with public opinion. To

319

hell with class . . . Ah, there it was, the stumbling block, there was the barrier, not something within herself, but something outside, an invisible something, yet as concrete and inflexible as the walls surrounding her, more so because they could be razed to the ground, but never the barrier of class.

## CHAPTER EIGHT

Robert was in The Bull and once again surprise had been apparent that he wasn't in uniform. And did he detect a little censure in his friends' manner towards him? Georgie Taggart had joined up, so had several of the young regulars, and there were those in the pits and on the farms whose work exempted them but who were declaring loudly against the injustice of being deprived of serving their country. In most cases the declarations were too loud to ring true; nevertheless people believed them.

After only a short stay in the bar he mounted his bike and pedalled slowly towards his uncle's. It was a lovely September evening. He stopped at a farm gate and, leaning his bike against it, stood with his elbows on the top bar and looked into the deepening twilight. The country stretching away below him looked soft, and gentle, yet relatively only a matter of miles away guns were blazing, men were dying, not by ones and twos but in thousands.

The scene before him suddenly changed and he saw only gory bodies, legless, headless, armless, bowelless bodies. They said that the Germans had massacred the Belgians, well now they were massacring the British. Yet the newspapers' headlines yelled: Our brave men have stemmed the German flow towards Paris. But at what a cost. All those young lives gone forever, all those mourning mothers and wives. What caused wars? Greed, the greed for expansion, for land, greed for power, for domination. He didn't like being dominated, he was against domination of any kind, so by his way of thinking he should be out there in France.

What was stopping him? Her? . . . No, he mustn't blame her. No, the truth was, he didn't like the sound of war, and all it conjured up. Forget about the glory; what glory was there in being dead? Why should men die or be maimed to satisfy the muddled thinking of elderly statesmen, men who no longer had the strength to fight or to reason calmly, only the power to sacrifice youth to gain their ends, the ends that began as dreams of power at the time the blood would have been coursing wildly through their veins?

And she was disappointed in a way that he hadn't joined up, he could see it in her eyes. She had been different of late, and he could trace the day of her change. It was after the visit of that old girl, Lady Smyth. She had come with a purpose, had that madam. Yet, change as she would, she still wanted to be near him. There were times when he willed her to come, and she came. It was uncanny.

And then there was old Waters. That old fellow hated him and not simply because Miss Millie sought him out to chat to. Oh no; he had taken to following his mistress about like a dog, in fact very like Millie's lapdog. Did he suspect anything? But what could he suspect? Except that they spoke to each other, mostly at arm's length. Of one thing he was sure, that old fellow had it in for him. And that was gratitude for you, after him saving his neck. Likely, part of the hate was fear, fear that he might talk. He had tried to assure him more than once that this would never happen, but apparently it hadn't got through to him.

What was he going to do? He could leave and get a job along with Greg for four times the money that he was getting now. Greg had fallen on his feet, and Maggie with him. Oh, he was glad for Maggie. By, that had been a fine wedding. Greg's cousin in Birtley had turned up trumps in letting them be married from his house. He had laid on a good table for the reception and they had all enjoyed it and the jollification afterwards. One thing had dimmed Maggie's wonderful day—and it had been a wonderful day for her, for never in her life had he seen anyone as happy—her mistress hadn't come to the wedding. Maggie had remained loyal: 'Well, Miss had to stay and see to Miss Millie,' she said, 'for everybody else was here.' He himself could have pointed out, but didn't, that her mistress could have brought Millie, if only to be present at the wedding ceremony.

Why hadn't she attended? Because she couldn't bear to see anybody married and happy? It was probable. But anyway Maggie had further said that her mistress had been most generous and given her all the linen to set up with from the linen cupboard and a case of their own cutlery. But then he had thought, one case wouldn't be missed, there must be a number of different sets of cutlery in that dining-room; he had seen the girls cleaning it often enough, for silver tarnished easily.

He left the gate and mounted the bicycle again, and rode for what he now called home. As he dismounted in the yard he looked towards the side of the house. The blinds were all drawn. Well, it was nearly dark. But there would be nobody in the bedrooms surely at this time, and the blinds there were all down too. He hurried into the kitchen and saw his aunt sitting by the fireside with Mr and Mrs Parkin sitting opposite her. And they were all three solemn faced.

Alice rose at once and, coming towards him, she raised her tear-stained face up to him as she said, 'Oh, I'm glad to see you, Robbie.'

The company too had risen to their feet, but there was no smile on their faces. It was Mrs Parkin who said, 'Well, we'll go, Alice. We'll look in later; we're always here when we are wanted.' She accompanied her last words with a look and a nod at Robert; but Mr Parkin said nothing, he just followed his wife.

And now Robert, looking down at his aunt, said, 'What is it? Is he worse?' even while knowing what her answer would be.

Shaking her head, Alice Bradley said, 'He . . . he went this afternoon, quietly, in his sleep. He just sat in his chair dozing; I . . . I was holding his hand and he went. He . . . he had been talking about you. Oh! Robbie. Robbie.' She fell against him and he put his arms around her, and as she sobbed he said, 'There, there, come on, sit down.'

He sat down beside her and, her eyes still flowing with tears, she muttered, 'He had his faults, God knows and He'll be his judge, but he had his good points too, and in a way he died happy. That's if he was ever happy. Aye—' she turned and looked

323

down the kitchen and repeated, 'if he was ever happy.' Then looking at him again, she said, 'He must have become a changed man when he lost your mother, because if he ever loved anybody it must have been her. He loved Carrie too, but in a different way: he expected Carrie to be spotless like an angel to make up for your mother's mistake. But'—she shook her head—'it wasn't a mistake on her part, she picked the right one for her . . . But I'm going to miss him. I'm going to miss him, Robbie, even his tyranny. I'll miss that. You know'—she looked downwards now—'I sometimes felt like one of those dogs that are beaten almost silly by their owners, yet keep following them, licking their hands. I became like that, in the end I would do anything for peace. Well, now it's over and I'll have all the peace I want, and I won't like it. Life's funny isn't it, dear?'

'Aye, Aunty'—his voice was soft—'Life's funny, it's a twisted thing.'

'Will you stay with me till after the funeral, Robbie?'

He had no hesitation in saying, 'Yes, yes, of course I will. I'll go back now and tell them.'

'Thank you. They're kind enough next door, but somehow I don't want to be beholden to them. Far better the devil you know, though, than the devil you don't know, because I don't know who we'll get next when he sells it. Mr Bradley'—she paused on the name now—'he offered him two hundred which I think is a fair price, but he wouldn't take it. Since the war started people think they can ask double for everything . . . You're still not going to join up? Are you, Robbie?'

'No, I'm not, Aunty. They can say what they like.

324

I'll go when I'm called and not afore; I've no desire to be a dead hero.'

She smiled faintly. 'You're sensible,' she said, 'but then you always were.'

*    *    *

She came downstairs in her dressing-gown to see him and she said immediately, 'Peggy's just told me. Oh, I am sorry. Yes, yes, of course you must go and stay with your aunt. When . . . when is the funeral to be?'

'I don't know, nothing's been settled yet, I wasn't in the house more than ten minutes. I came straight back.'

She walked towards the morning-room and he followed her, and when they were inside the room and the door closed she said, 'You won't be thinking of taking over the business, will you?'

'That hadn't crossed my mind. They've got a good man there and my aunt's very capable. Tim's been carrying on with an apprentice for some time now.'

'Oh. Oh, I see. I . . . I just thought . . . well—' she unbuttoned the top button of her dressing-gown then buttoned it again before she went on: 'You know how we are fixed here with Greg gone. It would be disastrous if there was no one but Bloom, because the years are telling on him.'

He was staring into her face now as he asked bluntly, 'What if I joined up?'

Her voice was now slightly stiff as she replied, 'But you didn't. If . . . if you had at the beginning I would have likely sorted things out by now.'

'You could again.'

325

He was being cruel. Where was her dignity? She should dismiss him with a word. Instead, she said, and now with lowered head, 'Yes, yes, I suppose you're right, I could again. And I likely will have to should you be called away to the army. Or'—she lifted her head—'if you should on second thoughts decide to take over your uncle's work.'

'I've no intention of taking over my uncle's work,' he said quietly. 'As for joining up, I'll go when they fetch me. Now, if you don't mind I'll be on my way. But I'll be back after the funeral.'

'Thank you.'

He didn't move, nor did she, there was only the span of an arm between them. What he did now was instinctive: putting out his hand, he took hers from where it was gripping the cord of her dressing- gown and, placing it within both of his, he held it tightly while he said, 'Don't worry. Things will pan out one way or another. They've got to. The way I see it is, at present I can't do anything and you mustn't. So let it bide. We know what we have, nobody can touch that.' He now brought her hand up and pressed it against his chest for a moment before turning abruptly and going out of the room.

She stood, her eyes closed, her mouth open, the hand he had held pressed tight against her throat with the other hand on top of it as if she were straining to print forever the impression of his fingers on her body. Then turning swiftly towards the empty fireplace, she put her forearm on the mantelpiece and laid her head on it, and as the tears soaked into the sleeve of her dressing-gown her lips mouthed his name, yet made no sound.

# CHAPTER NINE

Mrs Parkin was leading off in the kitchen. 'It's scandalous,' she said, 'the way the gentry have been going around buying up big quantities of tea and sugar, coffee and the rest. They even go in their carriages to the back street shops. But some grocers are wise to them and have put up notices: "Only regular customers served." That has shown them. It was the same the first week when war was declared and the shops ran out so quickly. The carriage lot seemed to get wind of new supplies coming in. Our Nancy said they were as brazen as brass walking into the shop and asking for four pounds of sugar and two pounds of tea, just as if they were regulars. She told them where they could get off. By! she did. It had gone on all day yesterday, she said, an' they'd only got the new stock in the night afore. Anyway, Mr Roberts let all the staff have first pick. He's good that way. So if you're short at all any time, Alice, you know where to come.'

Robert grinned, but it was a tight grin. He was standing in the hall just to the side of the open door leading into the kitchen. He was dressed ready for the road, the trap was in the yard. That woman had been nattering for the last half-hour.

Stepping briskly forward, he called down the room, 'Aunty, I think you'd better put a move on if you want to get back before dark.'

'Yes, Robbie, yes, I'm coming. I'm just going to lock the door. I'll be seeing you then, Betty. And thanks for all you've done.'

'Oh, that's all right. And thanks for what you've given me. But there was no need, I told you. I said . . .'

By, even sympathy has to be paid for, he thought. It was the same in Jarrow. You might have very good neighbours who wouldn't take a cent, but there were also those who would take your hand off for it. Like everything else, there were some and some.

'I'm sorry; I couldn't get rid of her.'

'It's all right. But she's so like her daughter that her voice gets on my nerves.' He smiled, and she returned the smile, saying, 'Poor Nancy.' And he repeated, 'Poor Nancy indeed! Now don't waste your sympathy on her. Come on, get up.'

As they drove out of the yard he said, 'I'd rather you went to the solicitor yourself, Aunty. I'll knock around until you come out.'

'Robbie, I haven't mentioned this before, but your presence is necessary at the solicitor's. I . . . I want you to hear the will read.'

He said nothing to this but his thoughts set him wondering if his uncle was going to leave him his tools as a peace offering. Well, that wouldn't be a bad thing, because there were some magnificent tools in that workshop, everything a carpenter dreamed of. There were some his uncle never allowed anyone to touch but himself. Well, whatever it was, he would have to show gratitude for it, just to please his aunt, because he was heart sorry for her. To lose two of them within months, it wasn't fair. She looked so lonely . . . So many people were lonely, and by the look of things there would be more in the future. The telegrams arriving daily: missing, believed killed . . . died for king and country. But loneliness, he thought, seemingly struck mostly at the women, and those in the upper class. Strange that, wasn't it? No, not when you came to think about it, because you couldn't be very dead lonely in a neighbourhood packed with people, where they'd walk into your kitchen without knocking, expecting to be offered a cup of tea, or bringing in one, or a loaf of new bread, or a scone or two. In any case most houses had their old folks who had been given a corner. They mightn't like the corner but it was better than living on your own, starving on your own. And then there were the bairns to see to. A working-class woman's loneliness would be felt mostly at night, when she wasn't too dead-beat to give vent to the gnawing ache.

But them in the upper class, even those who still had their menfolk, he sensed the want there. Of course, he was only judging on the few he had seen and the main one he was in contact with every day. Perhaps the reason was they weren't supposed to show their feeling in public; it wasn't the done thing. Being born into the upper class meant inheriting, besides other things, a facade, and they were expected to use it. Not for them the letting off of steam in public.

Would Agnes ever drop the facade, really drop it? Yet an understanding had come about between them. A week ago they had formed a pact: she had left her hand in his and her face had told him all he wanted to know, if he had ever doubted it before. Whatever might happen in the future it would be something to look back on . . .

The solicitor's office was dingy; it was one of six going off a corridor. He was surprised at the

329

shabbiness, having expected thick carpets and plush furniture. He was seated on a horsehair chair, the packing of which had been done some long, long time ago, for the springs were now forcing their way through it. Alice was sitting on a similar one. The solicitor, Mr Perrin, sat behind a desk in a black chair, his blue serge suit competing somewhat with the sheen on the leather chair. He now looked from one to the other before saying, 'The late Mr Bradley chose to draw up his will himself, but it's perfectly straightforward, nothing could be plainer, and properly witnessed. All I had to do was add a few lines in which he appointed me to act as the executor. Well now, it reads as follows:

"I, John James Bradley, of Elmdene House, near Lamesley in the county of Durham, declare I am of sound mind and from my estate do bequeath the sum of one thousand pounds to my wife Alice Caroline Bradley and fifty pounds to Timothy Yarrow provided he is still working for me at the time of my death. I leave all my other possessions to my nephew, Robert Bradley, which possessions consist of my house, land, and business, the furniture and effects in the said house, after the payment of any debts still outstanding all moneys in the bank and investments which stand roughly now at four thousand pounds, on condition that he allows my wife to bide in the house for the rest of her lifetime, where she shall be fed free of cost. Should my nephew decide to take up his residence there, I pray that my nephew will forgive me my misdeeds as I hope My Maker shall. Signed this seventeenth day of March, nineteen hundred and fourteen.

John James Bradley".'

Alice was looking at him with a gentle smile on her face. But there was no smile on his face as, shaking his head now, he said, 'No! No! 'Tisn't right. 'Tisn't right.'

She put her hand on to his knee and shook it firmly as she said, 'It's as he wanted. Right from when he recovered from the fever he said he wanted to do this and I agreed. He died happy because of it.'

'But I couldn't. I've done nothing. It's his life's work. Aunty'—he bent towards her—'it belongs to you, all of it. If Carrie had been alive it would have been hers. No. No.' And again he shook his head.

'I'm afraid you can't do much about it, sir'—the solicitor was looking up—'the property and money is yours. Throw it away if you must, but as things stand at the moment you own a house, a business, and a considerable amount of money. The old saying, don't look a gift horse . . .'

'You don't understand . . .'

'You will be amazed at what I understand, sir, and at this moment I understand that you feel quite unworthy to be a beneficiary, but I can assure you that will pass off. I have seen like cases before, though not one under these same pleasant circumstances in which all other parties are agreeable to the party who has received such a benefit.' He now looked at Alice, and then went on, 'You, madam, have been in agreement from the first with regard to your husband's wishes, and now that they are made absolute you are still in agreement. Is that not so?'

331

'Oh, yes, yes, sir; I couldn't be more pleased.'

'Then we're all pleased, or we should be pleased.' He rose to his feet, and they also rose; they exchanged handshakes and Mr Perrin, returning his attention to Robert, said, 'Should you want any advice about the stocks or any other matter, I'm at your disposal. Your aunt has a copy of the will. We hold here in safe keeping the freehold deeds of the property and land adjoining. Good-day to you, and I wish you happiness in your new estate.'

. . . He wished him happiness in his new estate, and by God, it was an estate: that house; that workshop with enough wood to keep half a dozen men going for two or three years; ten acres of land, and four thousand pounds. God! he was dreaming. But it still wasn't fair.

Outside he walked by Alice's side in silence. Then of a sudden he stopped and, putting his hands on her shoulders, he said, 'Why did you let him do it? 'Tisn't right or fair, it's yours. I expected his tools or something like that; even that seemed too much. Oh, Aunty.' He suddenly pulled her towards him, and as he did so a passer-by half stopped, and looked at them and with a wide smile on his face said, 'Don't worry, missis, he's doing it for his country, be proud of him.' Then the man looked amazed and indignant as the new recruit he imagined Robert to be turned round on him, saying, 'Go to hell!' before taking the woman by the arm and marching her off.

They had turned the corner of the street before they both stopped and Alice, looking at him, now began to laugh. Her body shook with her laughter; no sound came from her mouth because her hand was clasped tight against it, but her face was convulsed, and when he, too, began to laugh she leant towards him again, saying, 'Oh, Robbie, it was funny. If you had seen your face and that man's. Would he have believed it if you had told him you had just benefited from a will, because by the look on your face you could have just lost everything. And he thought you had joined up, and . . . and I was your mother.'

'Well, I wish you were.' He took her arm now and pulled it into his side, adding, 'From now on you will be. But let's get this straight: that's your house, that's your home, and so it will remain.' And she looked up at him tenderly as she said softly, 'I wouldn't mind to see it swarming with bairns.'

'Oh, Aunt Alice, don't set your heart on that; I'm afraid that's a vain hope.'

'Why not?' Her tone was alert now, her glance sharp. 'Don't talk silly. You're a young handsome fellow, you could get anybody you wanted. And you know you can. Oh yes, you do.'

'No, you're wrong there, Aunty, I can't get anybody I want.'

Her face twisted as she looked at him keenly and she asked quietly, 'You've got somebody in your eye?'

His gaze was directed ahead as he answered, 'Yes, you could say that. But that's where she'll have to remain, in me eye.'

Sharply she pulled him to a stop and round to face her, and her voice was now a whisper as she said, 'Not . . . not Miss Thorman?' And when he didn't answer but returned her stare, she said pityingly, 'Oh, lad, lad, fancy setting your sights in that direction. It's impossible.'

333

'Yes, I know that, Aunty, and she knows it.'

'She does?' Her eyes were wide.

'Oh yes.'

'You've talked it out?'

'No, no, we haven't talked it out, we just know.'

'Well, I never! Well, I never!' She turned from him and they walked on again, and now she said below her breath, 'To think of it. But you should have known from the first.'

'You don't know these things from the first, Aunty; you never know you've left the shallow end until you find you can't put your feet down.'

'You're going to continue working for her?' she asked.

It was some time before he answered, when he said, 'If it's all right with you. You see, there's only one other man left there because old Waters isn't any good any more and she'd be in a fix if I walked out now. But I tell you what, I'll make arrangements with her that I'll come . . . and . . . and it will be home'—he nodded towards her now—'I'll come home each night. I can get there in just over twenty minutes on me bike.'

'That . . . that'll be nice; I'll . . . I'll be grateful for that.'

So it was arranged.

*       *       *

It was pouring with rain when he rode in the next morning and so dark that when he arrived the lamp was still alight in the kitchen. On his entry Peggy turned from the stove, saying, 'You're back then?'

'Yes and very wet.' He took off his coat and then stepped back into the boot room and hung it up.

334

When he returned to the kitchen, Ruthie was coming down from the far end and, looking at him, she said, 'I thought you had gone and joined up.'

'No; they're going to call upon me when they're in a fix, they know how good I am at fixing fixes.'

She laughed and coming to the table she said, 'I'm glad you're back. Have you had any breakfast?'

'Yes, a mighty one before I left, but I could do with a cup of tea.' He grinned at her, then turned and looked at Peggy, saying, 'How are you, Peggy?'

'Same as usual.' Her face was straight. 'But I can't say that for many others. Betty's gone.'

'*Gone!* Gone where?'

'Munitions. After all we've done for Maggie, to entice her away. She says she hasn't. I went in yesterday and gave her the length of my tongue. She's changed, that girl, since she married, you wouldn't believe it. But she maintains she had nothing to do with Betty's goin'.'

'I don't think she had, Mam,' Ruthie put in quietly. 'But she saw Maggie's house and how nice she had got things, and she's young, is Betty. And she's been a good worker. You know that.'

'This damned war! It's turned people's heads. And now we haven't got a bit of sugar in the house.'

'Oh, I'll rectify that tomorrow; I'll bring you a couple of pounds.'

'Where will you get it?'

He looked at Ruthie. 'My aunt's always kept a good store cupboard. It's funny'—he laughed—'she doesn't make a song and dance about it, so people think she's got nothing and keep droppin' bits in.'

'That's sneaky.'

He looked at Peggy and said quietly, 'There's no sneaky about it. My aunt isn't that kind of person. Anyway'—he turned again to Ruthie—'is . . . is Miss Agnes down?'

'Yes; she's been down this hour or more. She's in the study.'

'Would you ask her if I could have a word with her?'

'You'll ask her nothing of the kind.' The voice came from behind him and he turned and saw Dave Waters glaring at his daughter. Then turning his infuriated gaze on to Robert, he said, 'I'll say whether you can see the Miss or not.'

'Oh, yes? Well let me tell you, Mr Waters, if I want to see the Miss I'll see her and not by asking you. Now Ruthie.' He turned once more to where Ruthie and her mother were standing close together now, their faces showing their concern, and he said, 'Either one of you go and ask your mistress if I can have a word with her. If you don't, I'll go and announce myself.'

'By God! you won't. You've gone far enough, let me tell you.'

As Dave Waters pushed past him Robert grabbed him by the arm and, glaring into his face, he said, 'Now let me tell you afore you go any further: you stop this witch hunt on me, or else there's going to be trouble for you. Now I've never threatened you or anybody else in my life, not in this way, but I'm telling you, Mr Waters, you get off my back, 'cos if you don't you'll find yourself lying flat on yours, as old as you are.' And with that he thrust him away; then turning towards the women, he said, 'Which one of you is going to tell her?'

'Go on.' Peggy thrust at her daughter, and

Ruthie ran up the room and out of the kitchen door. Dave Waters now stood facing the fire, his arms upstretched, gripping the high mantelpiece; Peggy stood by the table looking first at her husband's back and then pleadingly at Robert. No one spoke.

When Ruthie returned she remained standing at the top end of the kitchen near the door, calling down to him, 'She'll see you now.'

'Ta. Thanks,' he said stiffly as he then went out into the passage, through the second green-baized door and so into the hall. Here he paused for a moment, straightened his tie—he had purposely put on a collar and tie this morning—then made his way to the passage that led to the study.

After tapping on the door and hearing her say, 'Come in,' he entered. She wasn't sitting behind the desk but standing by the window looking straight towards him, and he forced himself to begin formally saying, 'Good-morning. The weather's a bit rough.'

'Yes, yes. It's been raining all night. There was a high wind with it at one time.' She swallowed, then said, 'I hope everything went off all right.'

'Yes. The funeral was quiet, just the people round about the hamlet and the members of the church. The parson spoke very nicely of him, which was only his due.'

She now walked round the end of her desk and sat down, then pointed to the seat opposite, and he too sat down, and when they were facing each other she said quietly, 'I'm . . . I'm glad to see you back. They've told you, I suppose, that Betty has gone.'

'Yes.'

'The sinking ship.'

'I wouldn't say so, I'd rather say the effects of war.'

'And you, have you made any new plans?'

He looked down towards the desk and, bending slightly forward, leant his forearm on it and tapped his fingers on the edge before he said, 'Strange things happen and nothing stranger, I fancy, than what I'm going to tell you now. I've'—a twisted smile came to the corner of his lips before he added, 'I've become a man of property.'

'Yes?' Her tone was quietly inquiring. 'Your uncle has left you something?'

'Everything, practically that is. Only one proviso, that my aunt stays in the house for her lifetime . . .'

'You mean, he has left you the house and . . . ?'

'Yes, the house and ten acres of freehold land, and his business, and, what is more surprising, a substantial sum of money, at least that's how it appears to me, a fortune, over four thousand pounds.'

Her face was showing her astonishment. Four thousand pounds, that was more than was left after they had sold the marine chandler business and the pictures, much more. And he had, too, a freehold property and business. Odd, the thing that had kept them apart before was class, but now what would irrevocably separate them was this legacy of a business that would have to be attended to, and an aunt that required his company. Well, what was the use, it didn't matter. Let things take their course; she was tired of it all, tired of thinking, tired of worrying, tired of hoping. Let Stanley pass the house over to the authorities; she would move into the lodge and take Millie with her. She would have

338

to fend for both of them. And Dave and Peggy would have to fend for themselves. She wasn't worried any more about Dave because Dave had changed. But she would always worry about Peggy. Still, everybody was crying out for labour of all kinds, and so they would find a position somewhere. As for Ruthie, she was able-bodied, she'd be grabbed at. Let everything take its course; and if day followed day and week followed week and she didn't see him, she'd forget him. She would live on memories.What memories? The two words were like an explosion to her mind. She had no memories except a handshake. Why hadn't she been like many women before her, if all she read was true, and had a liaison, then she would have had memories. But no, she had been afraid of stepping out of her class. And what would her class do for her for the rest of her life? As now; they wouldn't even come and visit her, she had nothing to offer, no horses to ride, no good cellar that they could swill down their throats, no expensive cigars, no tables supporting ten-course meals as this house had once seen; what it did have was a young daughter who should be put away, instead she was given freedom which embarrassed them, and an older daughter who had very little to say, and what she had to say was usually tart, especially since the breaking off of her engagement. There was really no incentive to visit.

'I thought if you wouldn't mind I would come in daily, and sleep at my aunt's place . . . I'll always think of the house as my aunt's.' He smiled at her, but all she said was, 'What . . . what did you say?'

He looked at her steadily for a moment before repeating, 'I said, if you didn't mind I would come in daily and sleep at my aunt's place. I have my bicycle; it's no distance. If I could start at eight and finish at six; that would suit me if it would suit you?'

'Oh, yes, yes. But . . . but the business that you've inherited. You can now . . . be your own master.'

'Oh, there's plenty of time for that. There's a good man there and a young boy, and if I can I'll get hold of another young lad to train up. Things will go along quite smoothly. Quite candidly'—he shook his head and smiled broadly now—'I don't know where I'm at at the moment. It was all such a surprise. There I sat expecting my uncle to leave me a few of his tools at the most, and he leaves me the lot. It came as a sort of shock. I'm not over it yet. I think it'll take a while.'

'Is it an old business?'

'Oh yes, yes. My father was brought up in it. My uncle was the elder. They had a disagreement about . . . well'—his chin jerked upwards—'over my mother, and they didn't speak for over twenty years, not until the day of her funeral in fact. But there's deeds and bills that go back to the late seventeen hundreds. One for a chair that was ordered for the castle. It was a large high-backed carved oak chair with a hide seat studded with brass heads, and it was fifteen shillings.' His smile widened now as he nodded at her and said, 'I think somebody over-charged on that one because it was for the castle.'

'The house has been there all that time?'

'Well, I understand it was only a two-roomed cottage to begin with. It has eight rooms now besides the workshop, and that has a long room above it that used to be mine, and still is. It's where

340

the wood is stored for late seasoning and the smell is good . . . What is it?' He half rose and bent over the table, then murmured, 'Oh, please, please.'

'It's all right.' She swallowed deeply, then raised her head, saying, 'I'm glad for you, that's all.'

He was still half standing bent towards her when there came a sharp knock on the door and after an exchange of glances she sat down and quickly picking up a pen, called, 'Come in.'

They both stared at Dave Waters while he, with a face that was almost purple, glared from one to the other before saying, 'I want a word with you . . . miss.'

'You can see I'm busy, Dave. I'll see you shortly.'

'It's all right.' Robert got to his feet. 'I . . . I think everything is straightforward now.'

'Yes, thank you.'

As Robert went towards the door, Dave Waters stepped quickly to the side as if to avoid being struck, then when Robert had passed through into the passage he closed the door, and none too gently, before coming to the desk where, without preamble, he began, 'I must have things out. It's either him or me. You've got to say. He's usurped my position. I'm nothing now, to you or to Miss Millie. He's taken Miss Millie, an' he's taken you. He's no good and you can't see . . .'

'Be quiet! Be quiet this minute! You forget yourself. I never thought that I would have to say that to you, but I say it now, you forget yourself. The only one who has usurped his position in this establishment is you. You have been given a free hand for years; you have taken advantage of it and what is more you are most ungrateful. That man who has just gone out saved you from appearing before a judge. Perhaps he saved your life. He certainly saved you a term of imprisonment. He has done nothing since he entered our service but be helpful. Do you know what I would do if I were he? Do you know what I would do?' She had now risen to her feet. 'I would send an anonymous letter to the police telling them exactly how your master died. The same kind of letter that you sent to Lady Clinton-Smyth about me . . . and him. Yes . . . yes, yes, you have a good right to turn pale.'

She restrained from putting her hand out to him when he clutched at the back of the chair facing the desk. And now with bowed head he muttered, 'I've . . . I've lived for you and Miss Millie. I've . . . I've given me life to this house, man and boy I've served it, it's been me life, I've thought of nothing else, only your welfare. And then . . . and then a stranger comes in, a townite, who doesn't know how to show respect, and what happens? He's looked up to. Miss Millie follows him about like a lapdog. And you'—he raised his eyes now—'you who I thought had so much sense, you fall for his glib talk, and the fact that he's read books.'

'Be quiet, Dave! You've said enough, more than enough. Stop it this minute.'

'I can't, miss, I can't. It's got to come out, and I'll say this; I'll see you dead afore he lays a finger on you. Your father never cared for you, or Miss Millie, well, I've cared for you both and I repeat what I said, if I catch him laying a finger on you I'll do for him, an' take what's comin'. So there . . . so there, you have it.'

She watched him almost stumble from the room before she herself dropped into a heap on to the chair. Dear, dear God. What was she going to do?

They thought Millie was not in her right mind. Millie was absolutely sane compared to Dave. The matter had turned his brain. She must be careful. No, no, it was Robert who must be careful, because that man was dangerous. She must talk to Peggy.

She reached out her hand and pressed the bell in the wall. That bell hadn't been rung since her father was last in the study—there wasn't enough staff in the house to keep running and answering bells—but after a moment Ruthie appeared in the doorway, and she said to her, 'Tell your mother I would like to speak to her.'

'Yes, miss.'

A few minutes later Peggy came into the study and Agnes, in an apologetic tone, said, 'I . . . I had to send for you, Peggy; I couldn't speak to you in the kitchen. I . . . I must say this to you, I'm . . . I'm afraid that Dave has become unbalanced.'

Peggy stared at her and said stiffly, 'No, lass . . . miss, he's not unbalanced, he's just full of concern for your welfare, as he always has been, and if you want the truth from me I think he's got a reason. All right, all right, I'm sayin' nothing against Bradley, he's a good enough fellow in his way, but that's all . . . in his way. In his way, as I see it, and Dave sees it, but it's not your way.'

'Peggy'—Agnes kept her voice level as she strained for patience—'do you realize that you are interfering with my life? And that if I wish to be friends with Bradley or anyone else in his position, that I'm quite at liberty to do so?'

'That's where you're wrong, miss, you're not. You've got a position to uphold. No matter what your father was, you're his daughter, but much more you're your mother's daughter and she was a lady, and you're a lady. And I say this to you now, if you were to take up with anyone such as Bradley, it would eventually be the death of you through shame. You were born into a different class, and breeding will out. Anyway, you'd be the talk of the county . . .'

Agnes stared at this woman who had been in her life since as far back as she could remember. She was right in all she was saying, if one went by the book, but the heart had nothing to do with books, feelings and emotions had nothing to do with the book. And would she know shame and misery if her life was shared permanently with Robert?

She waited for an answer but her mind gave her none. Her feelings had gagged her reason. But this she did know, no matter how she felt, no matter what course she might decide to take, she could not allow these two people, these two who had been very dear to her, to dictate to her in this manner, for they in a way were stepping out of their position as much as they suggested she was out of hers. And she put this to Peggy, saying, 'You consider that Bradley is taking liberties. Have you ever thought that you are doing the same, you and Dave? Granted you have cared for me all my life, and I have appreciated it, you know that, but when it comes to my personal behaviour, which up till now has warranted no such attack as I have received this morning from both you and Dave, I think you have gone too far, and presumed on your position. So that is all I've got to say . . . That will be all, Peggy.'

Never before had she dismissed Peggy. Now the older woman stared down at her while the muscles of her face worked as if they were being attacked by the tic; then she turned and almost ran from the room.

Agnes closed her eyes and lay back in the chair. Her hand was on the desk and touching the letter she had been reading when Ruthie had come to say that Robert was back and that he wanted to speak to her.

The letter was from Roland. He had joined up. He was still in Australia, training, and he sounded very excited for he was sure they were soon to embark for England, and he hoped he'd be able to come and see her. He often thought about the old home, and added, you never miss anything until you lose it. Arnold, he said, was doing well and was highly thought of, and so he didn't think he would leave Australia unless he was pushed. It was a pity poor Stanley had got himself stuck in a training section, but still she might find that a comfort, one of them being near.

Stanley a comfort. All Stanley could think of, ever thought of, was himself. Now strutting about in his second-lieutenant's uniform, he had taken the air of a general, at least to those whom he thought he could impress. Soon Roland would likely be in France where they were dying by the thousand. It was all glory with everyone at first. But the blood and gore were now seeping through. It was no comfort to the sorrowing mothers and wives to be told by the newspapers that their glorious dead had fought to a finish at Ypres. So many telegrams. She had heard yesterday that John Fraser had been killed and his brother Dick seriously wounded. They had only the two sons, the Frasers. And then there was Tom Stanmore; he had come home blinded, both eyes gone. People

345

were beginning to realize that war wasn't spruce soldiers marching behind a band, cheered on by screaming women.

And yet all this seemed secondary to the war that was going on in the house. It seemed ludicrous that people's personal troubles could, if not obliterate, push into the background the state of the nation and the world. She should be sorrowing for the crucifixion of youth, but what was she doing? She was sitting here fighting her private war, a small mean personal war. But was any personal war mean? It might be small in comparison but it was large in her heart. One thing she knew and that was, Robert Bradley was an outstanding man, someone who would have made his mark in any class. It was just unfortunate that he had been born into the working-class, and perhaps more unfortunate still that he had come to this house and that she'd had to meet him and come under his spell, because spell it was, for he was in her thoughts both night and day.

What was it about him that attracted her? She didn't know . . . so many things. She only knew that the feeling she had for him had no connection whatever with the feeling she'd had for James. That seemed now like a silly schoolgirl infatuation, so thin and ephemeral it wasn't worth looking back on. But the feeling she had for this man aroused something raw in her, some emotion she hadn't known she possessed, for she knew it would drive her to any lengths in order to keep him in her presence.

As long as she could see him, she knew she'd be able to carry on calmly . . . outwardly at least. And now he had come into money and business and a

346

home of his own it said something for his feelings that he was willing to forego his ownership in part so as to be near her.

But what was she to do about Dave and Peggy? One thing she was sure of was that Dave had become unbalanced. He had never been the same since the business concerning her father. But even before that, his protectiveness towards Millie hadn't, she knew now, been a normal thing. It was as deranged as Millie herself.

Where would it end? She would have to do something, but what? She wished, oh she wished she had someone to talk to.


## CHAPTER TEN

It was more than three weeks since he had been in The Bull. Each night he had made his way straight back to his aunt's, where there had been a good meal waiting for him, set on a bright cloth. And after they had eaten and talked about the doings of the day in both places, it had been well after seven o'clock, and he'd never felt up to getting changed and cycling to The Bull.

But tonight he thought he'd drop in before he went home. Apart from everything else, he was dying for a drink. Over the past weeks he had almost got used to being on the waggon, but for most of today he had been working in the barn, the tack room, and the swill house, where the boiler gave off dry stench from the coke fumes. His throat was parched; he wanted no more tea today, but he would like a long swill of cool ale.

347

The taproom wasn't full. The regulars were sitting in their usual places and there were two strangers at the bar, both in uniform, one a private and one a corporal. They looked at him as he entered, and he returned their stare. He was left standing by the counter for quite some minutes before Billy Taggart came along to take his order: 'Hello, there,' he said; 'I thought you had joined up and hadn't let us know.'

'No, not yet. I've been busy.'

'Aye, so I've heard. The same?'

'Yes, please.'

When Billy put the mug of beer on the counter he said with a half smile on his face, 'I thought you'd be going in for something harder, you know, wine and suchlike, brandy.'

'What makes you think that, Billy?'

'Oh, I hear you've come into a fortune, besides the house and business. 'Tis true, isn't it?'

'I don't know about a fortune, but 'tis true I've come into a house and a business.'

'You've fallen on your feet. By! some folks are born lucky.'

Strange now—wasn't it?—he thought ironically, the pleasure some people got out of knowing of another's bad fortune but rarely joyed with you about good. The saying, there's nowt so funny as folks was the truest one going. He would have sworn that Billy and Mary Taggart would have been happy over the luck that had come his way. Hadn't he repaid them well for his stay here? He had only recently given them another piece of his furniture, a low table with hand-turned legs. It had taken him weeks of nights to do those legs.

'Our Georgie's been sent over to France.'

348

'Has he? Oh, I'm sorry to hear that.'

'Well, somebody has to go, haven't they?'

Billy moved away to serve a customer; presently Mary came along, and she smiled at him as she said, 'Well now, you're a stranger. Thought you had transferred your custom since moving up in the world.'

'Ah, come off it, Mary. What's all this about, anyway? I've been left a house and a bit of a business and a few pounds. Does that make me different?'

'No'—her face straight now, she wiped the counter—'that doesn't make you different, Robert, but I'll tell you what does, those clothes you're wearing.' She nodded at him now. 'You must be the only able-bodied one out of uniform in these parts.'

'That's bloody nonsense. There's not a half a dozen fellows from round about that's joined up.'

'No, because they're either down the pit or working on a farm. But what are you doing? Yours is not a reserved occupation, you're free, you've got neither wife, nor chick, nor child, at least'—she paused—'not yet. What everybody's asking is, what's keepin' you up there? Now, now'—her voice was a whisper but she was pointing her finger at him—'don't get on your high horse 'cos everybody's got their lugs cocked. I'm just puttin' a word of advice in your way. People talk, things get about, you can't still people's tongues. Bloom keeps his ears open and his eyes and he talks to his wife, naturally, and his wife's got a loose lip. I'm just tellin' you.'

'Well, Mary'—his voice was as soft as hers now—'I don't thank you for telling me, because there's not a ha'p'orth of truth in what is being suggested.

349

Old Waters has got a bee in his bonnet, and not only where Miss Millie and Miss Agnes are concerned. I speak to them both and I get on well with them both, and that doesn't please the old fellow. But as for anything further, you can take it from me they're barking up the wrong tree. But by God! it's enough to make a fellow put some truth into their statements. Then what would they say? Oh, I told you so, it's been goin' on all along. How is it that I can't look at a woman but there's something made out of it, eh? Well, I'll have to see what I can do up there, put me charm to work. It's about time I deserved me reputation.'

Mary wagged her head now, and again wiped the counter down, smiling thinly as she said, 'I suppose it's the way you've got with them, and you know it and you work on it.'

He pulled himself back from the counter and surveyed her for a moment through narrowed lids; then he said, 'I'll be going, Mary. Oh, and by the way—' He had half turned from her, but looking at her again he added, 'I'll send for my bits and pieces one day next week, if that'll suit you?'

It was a moment before she said, 'Just as you please, they're yours, but they've been in storage some time.' It was his turn to pause before he said, 'You can send your bill in.' And on this he marched out of the taproom followed by covert glances.

He was angry. Talk about having friends. He had thought he could have sworn by Bill and Mary Taggart. Their attitude was all because their son was in uniform and he wasn't. If he himself had been in khaki they'd have never opened their mouths about the tittle-tattle except to laugh about it and egg him on. Well, that was the last time he would go to The Bull. What was happening to everybody? The war had turned not only the whole world topsy-turvy, but also his life . . .

He pushed his bicycle into the shed next to the workshop; then before going indoors he went into the workshop and stood looking round him for a moment. The whole place spelt peace, and there was that aroma, that scent that only wood gave off. What he should have done was to tell her that he was coming back here for good. Well, he still could . . . But could he? Could he look her in the face and say, 'You'll not be seeing me again and I won't be seeing you except on very rare occasions'? At the moment he couldn't; but he felt there would be a time soon when he would have to, when his body would no longer take heed of his head. It was having a hard enough struggle now. How he had restrained himself from pulling her into his arms before this he didn't know. Oh, yes he did . . . the barrier. It was made of glass and both of them could see through it, and she was standing firmly on the other side.

'There you are,' Alice said. 'Been working late?'

'No, Aunty.' He made himself grin as he added, 'I've taken to the beer again.'

'Oh.' She turned her head away from him, trying to hide her smile as she said, 'You're a naughty lad. Anyway, there's some roast lamb will help to sop it up. Come on, your dinner's ready.'

'I'll just wash first,' he said. 'How's your day been?'

'Oh, much the same as usual, but there's two new orders in. That's five this week. Tim's going on about not being able to cope. What do you think about getting another lad? The Wentworth boy

351

from the bottom cottage finished school last month. He's been set on in the brickyard but he doesn't like it, so his mother says. I think she was hinting. What do you think about it?'

'It's up to you, Aunty. You're running the business.' He didn't say he had been thinking along those lines.

'Yes, but I don't know much about boys. And Tim's funny. If they're a bit perky in answering back, he says they're cheeky, if they say nothing, he says they're dimwits.'

They both smiled now, and he said, 'Well, tell the boy to look in tomorrow night. I'll see what he's made of.'

He was drying his face on the towel when she said, 'I forgot. There's a letter for you. I left it on the sitting-room mantelpiece. I'll get it.'

'No, you get on carving up that lamb, woman. I'm starving.'

'Good.'

She was laughing gently. She was a changed woman; she was always bright-faced these days. Well, it was good to know he had made somebody happy. He went into the sitting-room and took the envelope from the mantelpiece. He looked at the hand-printed address which told him nothing, and he pursed his lips before slitting open the envelope. Then his whole body became still for, as if emerging from a shell, there appeared over the serrated edges of the paper the wispy ends of a white feather. Slowly he drew it out of the envelope, and took the piece of paper on which it had been lying. This he turned over and back again. It was blank.

There arose in him now a kind of fury. If he had

352

been out of doors in the yard he would have hurled something against the brick wall; he would have lifted his foot and kicked at the first object he came to; he would have taken his fist and battered it against the wall. He stood absolutely still, yet inside his innards seemed loose. It was as if the half a pint of beer he had taken earlier was working on them. He felt sick.

'Robert. Didn't you hear me?'

He shuddered and turned towards her, and at the sight of his face she hurried to him. He said nothing, but handed her the feather and the envelope. And she took them, saying, 'Oh, no! Now who would do that?'

'Aye. Who would do it?'

'Nancy?'

'Could be. But I've learned just the night that it could be others.'

'Those at the inn?' She cast her glance up at him.

'Aye.'

'I thought you said they were good people.'

He hesitated for a moment before answering, 'Yes, I did; and I suppose I could say they still are; but you see, when your only son's at the front, it colours your viewpoint.'

'Eeh! it's awful'—she shook her head— 'cowardly to do a thing like that.'

He took the feather and the envelope from her, saying, 'Well, that's the purpose of it they think, because I am cowardly.'

'You're no coward.'

The defensive note in her voice made him smile slightly as he said, 'Well, it'll soon prove it if I run off the morrow and join up.'

'You'll do no such thing . . . will you?'

'What do you think?'

'Come and get your dinner.' As they went from the room she added, 'You've got one consolation, you're not the only one that gets them. Philip Tyler got one on Saturday.'

'Him in the village? But he's on farm work.'

'Yes, but he only took it up after war was declared. His had a message with it. Get out of your bolthole, it said, and into a trench.'

'Well, I'm glad I've got company.'

They were half-way through the meal when Alice, laying down her knife and fork at each side of her plate and looking towards the window that showed beyond the side garden a fence that divided their land from that of the Parkins, said, 'She was in not half an hour ago, she had come straight from work, Nancy I mean. She was saying that somebody was coming to look over the house and she got on talking about you, why you were staying up at Foreshaw. Anyway, what do you think we should do about the house? Pay him what he asks, because I don't think we should let it slip through our fingers.'

'No, no, I don't think we should pay him what he asks. Hang on; nobody but a fool would pay three hundred for that place, especially when they see inside and what's to be done to it.'

'You think so?'

'I'm sure of it. And Aunty, the next time she comes, you refer her to me, will you?' The side of his mouth curled upwards. 'Tell her I'm the one that's doing the business; at least, tell her to tell her father that. But I'd like to come face to face with her; I would know immediately if she had anything

354

to do with that piece of white leghorn, because it's a chicken's feather, isn't it?'

'I wouldn't know. But anyway, I'll do that. Aye.' She smiled broadly at him now. 'I'll say quite calmly, Robert is dealing with all the business. The mere mention of your name narks her. Do you think I'm gettin' spiteful?'

'Aye, I do; and not afore time.' They exchanged smiles now, but then became silent because, as they both knew, it was no laughing matter getting a white feather.

## CHAPTER ELEVEN

'Are we going to have a party at Christmas, Bradley?'

'I don't think so, Miss Millie, not this year, with the war on.'

'The war's a funny thing, isn't it? Why do people fight each other? Will the Germans come here? Stanley says they have big birds that fly in the sky. He said it to frighten me, but I'm not frightened of anything that flies because I want to fly. I will fly some day. I hung out of the window last night and caught hold of the wisteria branch and it swayed back and forward like a bird . . .'

He pulled himself from under the dining-room table where he had been straightening a castor on one of the legs; then sitting back on his haunches, he looked up into the thin wraith-like figure as he said, 'Now Miss Millie, you promised me, didn't you, you wouldn't hang out of the window and touch that wisteria? Now you promised, because I

355

told you if you did it again I'd have to tell Miss Aggie, and then she would block the window up.'

'I only did it a little bit. You see, I forgot. Sometimes I forget things.' She walked from him towards the fireplace where some damp logs were smouldering and she said, 'I like it better when I forget things, Bradley; it's much nicer when I forget things. I want to forget about Stanley, because he shouts at Aggie when he comes. He looks very smart in his uniform, but he's not nice, and he upsets Aggie. Why is everybody upset, Bradley, and shouting? I don't like people shouting. Dave shouts a lot now. He shouted at Lady today and she was frightened and she ran away. I had to run after her and catch her and tell her that Dave didn't mean it and that he wasn't going to put her in the stable. Dave was vexed with me and said he wouldn't bring me any more lucky bags. But I think I'm too old for lucky bags, don't you, Bradley?'

'Yes, yes, you are, you are much too old for lucky bags. Young ladies should have chocolates.'

'Yes, they should.' She laughed now, her mouth wide, her eyes sparkling; then her head on one side, she asked, 'Do you like me with my hair up, Bradley?'

'I do. I do indeed, miss. I think it looks very smart, in fact it makes you into quite a young lady, a very beautiful young lady.'

'You think I am beautiful, Bradley?'

'Indeed I do, miss. But now I must get on with this other castor, else when you're having your Christmas dinner the table will tip up and— whoop!—the turkey will take wings.' He demonstrated with his hand in a swooping movement the turkey leaving the table, and she was

356

responding with a wide-mouthed laugh when the door burst open and there, like the avenging angel, stood Dave Waters. He was stooped at the shoulders as if about to spring forward; then coming up the room, he cried, 'Miss Millie! come away. Come away upstairs. Peggy's been looking for you. This is no place for you. And I've told you what will happen to that dog if you don't keep it off the chairs.' As he swooped towards the poodle that was curled up in a leather chair to the side of the fire, Millie also sprang and, grabbing the animal to her, she cried, 'You mustn't put her in the stable. She gets frightened, she doesn't like the dark. She . . . she told me she doesn't like the dark. He mustn't do it, must he?' She had turned appealingly to Robert, but he remained silent, staring at Dave Waters. And now Dave Waters hissed at him, 'This is your doing, putting her up to it. But wait, wait . . . just you wait till Mr Stanley comes. I'll empty me mouth. By God! I will.'

Robert walked up to him and with his face turned away from Millie's direction he muttered under his breath, 'You want to be careful that you don't get your mouth busted before you get the chance to open it.'

Dave Waters sprang back from him, crying, 'Now you've done it! That's your limit. I'm standing no more of you. I'll see Mr Stanley. He'll settle this once and for all. He's the master here, not her, not her.'

When the door had closed on them, Robert stood looking down at his open tool bag by the side of the table and, drawing in a long deep breath, he said, 'He's right, this is the limit. I can't put up with this any longer. I'll have to tell her as soon as she gets back.' She had gone into Birtley to do some shopping: he reckoned she should be here any time now. Well, once he saw her, it would be over and done with, final this time. He couldn't stand any more.

He grabbed up his tools and went out and up to the room above the stable. All he had up there now belonging to him was an overcoat and a pair of shoes which he now changed into to cycle home. This done, he rammed his boots on top of his tools, and put on his overcoat; then going to the window, he stood looking down into the yard waiting for the trap to arrive.

It was about half an hour later when he saw her enter the yard, and as she stepped down from the trap she saw him standing dressed ready for his journey home. It was only two o'clock in the afternoon and her eyes widened and as she made to come towards him he walked to the horse's head and led it into the stables. He unharnessed it and put it in the stall, the while she stood within the stables, saying, 'What is it? Please tell me.' Still he didn't speak but picked up the bits and pieces and again walked past her into the harness room. She followed him, and when he turned from the horse bench they stood looking at each other as she murmured, 'You're going. What's happened?'

'I can't stand any more. There'll be trouble and serious trouble with Waters, unless I get away. That man's mad.'

She shook her head now as she said, 'I'll . . . I'll talk to him.'

'Don't be silly.'

She took no offence at this, but now she gripped the front of her coat with her hands, saying, 'What

358

will I do? What can I do?'

'Nothing.' His voice was quiet. ' 'Tis better this way. You know it, and I know it. In fact everybody knows it, at least it appears so. We should have had sense from the beginning, at least I should, and know you can't climb mountains in your bare feet. Although'—he smiled a little sadly now—'I've had a damn good try, and would have gone on, just trying . . . well, just being near you. I might as well say it now. You've known it for a long time why I stayed on here, just to be near you. And I'm not mistaken, you wanted that, didn't you?'

Her head made an almost imperceivable movement downwards, and then she whispered, 'Yes, oh yes. And . . . and I don't know what I'll do now. I . . . I can't imagine what life will be like in the future. You've . . . you've shown me a new existence, what . . . what life could be like . . .'

He turned his head away for a moment as he said, 'That's perhaps a romantic view; you're lonely; I happened to be here. If there had been somebody of your own class around, a decent fellow, you wouldn't have noticed me . . .'

'Oh, yes I would. I . . . I met a number of men before I became engaged to James Crockford, but now I know they were all wanting. I never knew what it was really to feel for anyone un . . . until recently. And now for the remainder of my life all I'll know is that you are near, so near, yet so far away . . .'

'As for being near, that won't be for much longer. I would have to tell you sooner or later: I'm joining up. Three white feathers in two months has been a little too much.'

*You've had white feathers?'*

359

'Yes. The first one didn't seem to matter, it didn't leave any impression, except it got me mad a bit. But these things can wear you down. You don't know who's sending them. In my case, I think it's my one-time so-called friends. Anyway, I'd have been makin' a move soon; this is just a little earlier.'

He watched her close her eyes tightly and when the tears squeezed themselves from underneath her lashes he put his hands out and caught hers, saying, 'Don't. Oh don't. That'll finish me.'

She opened her eyes, her lids blinking, but he made no attempt to draw her close. There was a distance of both their forearms between them when she said, 'Robert, will you . . . will you please—' he watched her throat swell before she finished, 'kiss me, just . . . just once.'

God! This was it, the powder to the keg; she didn't know what she was asking because once he kissed her . . . well . . .

Of a sudden she was in his arms, his lips hard on hers, her body pressed tight to him. Whatever she expected the kiss to be like, it had been nothing like this, this hot fierceness; but something in her responded to him and she clung to him and held him almost as fiercely as he did her.

So lost were they in each other that when the door burst open and they were wrenched apart they fell back blinking like bewildered children while they stared at the khaki-clad figure bristling with indignation.

'How dare you lay your hands on my sister! You low lout, you!'

As the crop was raised to come down across his face, Robert ducked to his left, at the same time swinging his right fist across Stanley's chin. And when the spruce lieutenant staggered against the horse saddle-tree, Robert's hands went around his throat and, dragging him upwards, he now thrust him against the wall of the tack room. And what he might not have achieved in a moment or so had not Agnes torn at him, crying, 'Don't! Don't, for God's sake! Oh, please don't.'

When they were separated, Stanley, holding his neck, and his face now suffused with rage, gasped, 'You'll suffer for this. I'll have you behind bars before long. Get out!'

'I'll go when I'm ready.'

*'You! You . . . !'*

'You come out with one more insult an' before God I'll finish you off. What are you, anyway? What have you ever been but a gutless nowt.' Robert now straightened his coat, picked up his cap from where it had fallen on the floor, then, after one long look at Agnes, he went out.

She stood, her hands now cupping her face, her hat awry on her head, her breath coming in large shuddering waves from deep within her, and when of a sudden she turned and ran towards the door Stanley grabbed her arm, saying, 'No, you don't. What's come over you anyway, acting like a slut? You're as much to blame as him, but by God! he'll suffer for this. You'll see if he doesn't. I'll have the police along there before he sleeps tonight.'

'Oh no, you won't.' She wrenched herself from him.

'Who's going to stop me?'

'I am. You lift one finger against him . . . Anyway, I would swear blind you were lying. But apart from that, you try to harm him in any way

361

and I'll explode your little world with that Diana Cunningham, or Mrs Lecombe as she is now. But her husband's in the fighting line, isn't he? And so are you and her.'

She knew she wasn't only putting two and two together from the bits of gossip that Lady Emily had dropped, but she was using the fact that her brother on the few times he called in had not once since he had joined up passed a night in this house, and she knew that he had had week-end leaves.

'You're a bitch, do you know that? You're a loose bitch.'

'Then Mrs Lecombe and I are in the same boat, aren't we? But I'm warning you, Stanley, and I mean it. You try to harm Bradley in any way and I'll try my hand at anonymous letter writing, just like Waters did about me to Lady Emily.'

'Well, Waters was right. He's right in everything he said. He's just told me what's been going on. You're brazen. All right, whatever I'm up to, I'm up to with my own class, I don't step out of line. You've delved into the gutter. And there's something else I'll tell you. You've always talked about being free, well the way's open to you now, and Millie with you, because I've heard from Arnold. He's been in touch with the solicitors, the place is to be sold. The army didn't take up the offer, not as yet anyway, so it's on the market and open to a buyer, and that includes the lodge too. So that should give you something to think about, shouldn't it, dear sister? Perhaps your odd-jobman will take you on, and Millie too.'

'Perhaps he will at that.'

'Don't you dare.' He advanced towards her. 'If I thought you would let the house down by going to him, I'd shoot you both.'

'Oh, brave brave boy. But it's the uniform talking, Stanley. As Robert said, you're gutless. You're like Father, all talk. Maggie used to have a saying, full of wind and watter, and that's you. Now get out of my way before I try to finish off what Bradley started.'

There was something in her face that deterred him from reaching out towards her again as he was about to do. And now she went out into the yard; but there was no sign of Robert.

She did not enter the house by the kitchen, she could not trust herself to meet Dave or Peggy Waters because Dave had assuredly been spying on her and told Stanley that she was in the tack-room with Robert. Well, with the latest news, there was one thing sure, she'd soon be rid of them all. But what was she going to do? If she had only herself to think about, she knew what she would do. But there was Millie. Oh, dear God, if she had only someone to go to, someone to talk to, some woman to talk to. There had been Peggy, but Peggy was no longer on her side.

As she passed Millie's door she heard Ruthie talking to Millie, and so she went into her own room and having taken off her outdoor things she sluiced her face in cold water, then sat down by the window.

She had to think, think what she must do. Yet her mind wouldn't take her along this road, it went back to a short while ago when for the first time in her life she had been really kissed, held in a man's arms, and really loved. For the first time in her life she knew what it was to want someone heart and soul and that that person wanted her too. It had been the most beautiful experience, exquisite, for a moment that is, because then it had been dirtied. And that fight. Robert would have killed him. Both had been in a rage, but Robert's was a terrifying rage. Would the men in her class have fought like that over a woman? Well, Stanley had. But no, he wasn't really fighting over her, he was fighting because he imagined she had let her side down.

As she sat it came to her that there were facets to Robert she knew nothing of. He was proud, and she had never imagined working-class people to be proud. Then she had imagined so little, she had never looked to far horizons outside, or to character inside, her world had been tight, circumspect . . . and she was tired of it. Oh God, yes she had been tired of it for a long time now.

And he was going to enlist. She might never see him again; in a short while he'd likely be lying like thousands of others, mangled dead. Oh, what was she thinking?

She got up and paced the room . . .

It was around four o'clock when a tap came on the door and when she said, 'Come in,' she was surprised to see Stanley enter the room. His face was stiff and his lip and jaw were discoloured, but his look was no longer aggressive. He stood in the middle of the room staring towards her where she was sitting once again by the window, and he said, 'I've . . . I've got to be off now. I'm on duty tonight.'

Her mind taking a skittish turn, she almost said, 'Well, don't keep her waiting,' but what she did was turn her gaze from him and look out of the window again.

'Look.' He took a step towards her now. 'I . . . I want to say I'm sorry about all this. I understand

364

. . . well, that you might have been lonely and you'd forgotten yourself.'

She swung round on her seat, crying at him now, 'I did not forget myself.'

She watched him grit his teeth before he said, 'Well then, more shame you.' It was still evident he was trying to control himself because now he beat one hand against the other as he said, 'You know you can't do this, Agnes. It's fatal to step out of your class and you know it. If you must go off the rails, there's plenty of chaps who would be only too glad to . . .'

He actually stepped back as she jumped up from the seat, crying, 'Glad to service me, eh? That's what you're saying, isn't it? Well, if that's the case, why haven't you brought them here before and lined them up for me to choose from? Have you ever brought any of your friends here? No, you haven't had time, you've been busy elsewhere. Anyway, it's a thought. You could ask Mrs Lecombe to send me a few of her cast-offs. I understand it's the thing today to pass them around, the men I mean, because they are coming in short supply, the best ones being out at the front, or dead.'

They stared at each other in hostility; then he preceded his next words with a long sigh: 'It's no use talking to you, not in this mood. Anyway, I've been seeing to business. I've told Waters what the situation is. They are not too old that they won't be able to find employment, people are wanted for all kinds of things these days. Arnold says I'm to arrange for the storage of the best pieces of furniture and sell the rest and out of that you are to have your allowance doubled. Myself, I'll be glad to

365

be rid of the responsibility . . . Well, I'm off, and Agnes, please . . . please promise me you won't do anything silly. I mean . . .'

'Yes, what do you mean?'

'Oh, it's no use going on. You know what I mean . . . don't let yourself down, remember who you are. Goodbye.'

Remember who you are. Could she ever forget who she was? She wished she could. Oh how she wished she could forget that she had been born in this house, that she had had the benefit of nursemaids and nannies, that she had listened as a child to the revelry downstairs, that from the nursery windows she had watched the coaches coming and going, that the nursemaid had pointed out Lady so-and-so's carriage and Lord so-and-so's landau. If she could only forget that Millie had been born and that from that time things had gradually changed, slowed down and down and down, until at this moment here she was sitting longing to take to her heels and run through the park and down the road to the hamlet and into that house with the comfortable sitting-room and into his arms. Yes, into his arms. But she couldn't do that.

Don't let yourself down, remember who you are. She had forgotten who she was a short while ago and she had let herself down, and she had known happiness for the first time in her life. But she was wise enough to know that that kind of happiness couldn't last, not at that pitch of intensity and between two people, two opposites as they were, with a barrier of different worlds between them. Everything was against it.

But she must put her mind to this new situation.

The question was, how much longer would she have in the house? And if she was to set up on her own . . . with Millie, then she must have some suitable furniture. It didn't matter about the antique pieces, she wanted none of them, odd things from the spare rooms would do. But what she must do first was go down and face them in the kitchen; and she must keep her dignity.

She went out of the room to meet Ruthie carrying a tray towards Millie's room, and Ruthie said, 'She's awake now; she had a good sleep after you gave her her drops.' And when Agnes said to her, 'I'll come and take over in a minute until you've had your tea,' Ruthie replied, 'Oh . . . I've had it, miss. Mam came up for a while.'

As Agnes went down the stairs she thought, Peggy was up here and didn't look in on me. What a change had come over the house. For years, like a mother hen, Peggy had been in the habit of tapping on her door, putting her head round and saying, 'You all right?' It had been a comforting habit.

She found them both sitting at tea in the kitchen and it was noticeable that neither of them made any effort to get to their feet. Before this, had they done so, she would always have stopped them.

Looking from one to the other now, she said formally, 'I'm sorry I'm interrupting your meal, but I understand that Mr Stanley has told you of the arrangements.' She found it difficult to go on, this was awful, really awful. These two people who had for years been so dear to her were now like strangers. No, worse, enemies. She had to force herself to continue, 'I don't know when you will want to leave, but . . . if I can . . .'

She got no further, for Dave Waters's chair

367

scraped against the stone floor and the thrust he gave it toppled it backwards, and he now cried at her, 'You stand there and say that, as cool as a cucumber. I was here afore you were born, we were both here afore you were born. We've brought you up, an' the young one, we brought all of you up, and you can stand there and tell us to go.'

'I'm . . . I'm not telling you to go, it isn't my fault.'

' 'Tis your fault. Of course it's your fault. Lettin' yourself, down, degradin' yourself. Master Arnold must have heard of it, that's what put the idea into his head, to sell the place.'

'That's nonsense . . . Peggy'—she turned to the woman who was sitting now with her head down looking towards her plate—'tell him, make him see reason. You know that isn't right.'

'She knows as well as I know, we both know, it's because of you and your philanderin' with the scum of the earth, because that's all he is, the scum of the earth. And now since he's come into money, nothing'll hold him. Dared to lay hands on you an' you let him. And now he's thinking of buying the place. *Him! Him!* I heard him.'

She stared at him wide-eyed and now she said quietly, 'You must be mad.'

'I'm not mad. I heard the both of you in the library t'other day, I've got ears. I heard him say about the alterations he'd make when he bought it.'

Dear Lord! Dear Lord! Robert had spoken about the cottage next door to his house and said that his aunt was thinking it would be a good thing if they were to buy it. He couldn't see the reason for it himself as their house was big enough, and the cottage would need a lot of money spent on it

368

to make it into a comfortable place. Dave must have been listening to all this, and in his twisted mind it had made him imagine that Robert was talking about this house. Oh, dear Lord. What next? What next?

What next startled her; for now he said, 'Anyway he'll get his deserts the night. Master Stanley'll see to that. He's going to put the polis on him for attacking him.'

'He can't do that.'

'Oh, can't he? He's got a bruised face to show for it. And he's an officer, an' you know what happens when you attack an officer. I'd like to see him swing . . .'

At this, all idea of dignity left her and she cried at him, 'You're a thankless creature. As for swinging, he saved you from swinging, you seem to forget that. And what if he opens his mouth to the police? Have you thought of that?'

It was evident from the look on his face that he hadn't and this proved to Agnes that he had become really deranged. But she saw that Peggy realized this for now she got to her feet and, going to her husband, she said, 'Sit down, calm yourself. Now calm yourself.'

'Calm meself! Calm meself you say'—he pushed her off—'an' that bastard coming here, be master of this house?'

Peggy now turned and looked at her, and in her eyes too was the recognition of what had happened to her husband, and for a moment she felt herself consumed with pity. But this feeling was soon overridden by fear: he was dangerous. What if he should become violent? There wasn't a soul in the place. Bloom hadn't been in today nor yesterday, he was suffering from a chill. A short time ago it hadn't seemed to matter to her how few there were outside as long as Robert was there, for he seemed to be able to fill all capacities. He had been a bulwark. Now there was no one to turn to. Why hadn't Stanley stayed? He could have. She didn't believe his tale of having to be on duty. He would now be at the Cunninghams' . . . Or perhaps he wasn't. Perhaps he had imagined that she wouldn't carry out her threat. He must have said something to Dave before he left regarding Robert or else why should Dave have said that about Robert ending up in prison?

She turned swiftly now away from them and hurried up the room, but before she had reached the green-baized door, Dave Waters called after her, 'You've ruined this house.'

In the hall she stood and pressed her hand to her head asking herself what she must do. But she had known the answer before asking the question, and now she was running up the stairs, and when she reached Millie's room she pushed the door open and beckoned to Ruthie. 'I'm going out,' she whispered. 'I may be gone a couple of hours. You'll see to her, won't you?'

'Yes, aye, of course.' Ruthie nodded at her, then added, 'What's wrong, miss?'

'Everything, Ruthie, everything. And your father, he's . . .'

Ruthie nodded at her now and, her voice a whisper, she said, 'I think he's going round the bend. He's got it in for Robert, but I've tried to tell him it's all imagination what he thinks. The trouble is'—she jerked her head backwards—'Miss Millie, 'cos she took to him, I mean to Robert. It's ever

370

since that. Sure you're all right, miss?'

'Yes, Ruthie. Only see to her, won't you? And if your father comes up, I . . . I shouldn't let him in. And if you have to go out, lock the door.'

'I will, miss, I will. And miss'—she put out her hand as Agnes, about to move away, paused—'I'd like to say this, whatever you do, I don't blame you. They don't understand. People get so old and kizzened up in their own minds, they forget they were ever young.' Agnes now pressed Ruthie's arm before turning away and hurrying into her room. It was a comfort to know that somebody was on your side, that somebody understood.

She quickly got into her outdoor things again, but she didn't put a hat on, she merely wound a woollen scarf around her head; then she hurried out.

She did not see Waters entering the hall as she left. It wouldn't, however, have mattered to her at this moment if she had. But the sight of her dressed for outside and his guessing her destination snapped the last threads of reason in the man's mind.

She ran through the gardens, then took the path through the wood that Robert had travelled since he first came to the house. The night air was cutting at her face and she was panting when she reached the road, but on fairly level ground now, she began to run again and she didn't stop until she saw a swaying light coming towards her in the distance. As it neared her she made out that it was attached to the side of a cart, and when she came abreast of it the driver peered down at her and called, 'Evening.'

'Good-evening.' Her answer sounded like a frog

371

croak and she felt rather than saw the driver turn in his seat as he went past. The next encounter made her embarrassed, but in no way frightened her. A half-dozen pitmen coming off their shift stopped as she came up to them where the road narrowed and one of them, swinging his lantern in her face, said, 'Ah-ha! who have we here? A lass out on her own. You a German spy, eh?' There was a ripple of laughter from the men at this, and when the speaker, getting bolder, said, 'Haven't seen you around afore. Where's a bonny lass like you been hidin'?' she said, 'Would you allow me to pass!'

The tone of her voice and her words brought a silence to the men, and the spokesman, after peering at her closely, stood aside, and she went on, her legs feeling as if they didn't belong to her.

She was feeling almost on the point of exhaustion when she came to the outlying cottages of the hamlet, each one of them showing the reflection of gaslight behind paper blinds or drawn curtains.

There were no lights showing in the front of Elmdene House and for a panic-filled second she thought, They're out! He's gone. He's gone already. Stanley's done what he said. But when she came to the open gate and then passed into the yard she saw a bright glow showing from two windows.

Before she knocked on the back door she supported herself with one hand against the stanchion, for her heart was beating so rapidly that she felt she would collapse at any moment. But when the door opened and she saw the woman standing there, she said, 'I'm . . . I'm Miss Thorman. I'm . . .'

Almost in a kind of daze she watched the woman turn and call quietly, 'Robbie!' before stretching out her hand and saying, 'Come in. Come in.'

She walked into the room and the light and the heat blurred her vision and for a moment made her feel faint. She put out her hand and felt it grasped, and then his voice said, 'What's the matter? What's happened to you? Come and sit down, come . . . Is there any tea in that pot? Get her a fresh cup, Aunty, will you?'

It was only after she was sitting down that she saw his face clearly. Putting out her hand, she touched it, saying, 'You all right?'

'Of course my dear, I'm all right. But what brought you, and in this state?'

'Has anybody been? I mean, the police?'

'The police? No.' He smiled at her, shaking his head now.

'Dave said that Stanley meant to . . . to go and tell them.'

'Huh!' He laughed, then dropping on to his hunkers before her he said, 'And what would be the charge? That I'd hit him and his evidence a bruised chin? And what proof would he have, because you know'—he now put up his hand and unwound the scarf from her head, then stroked her hair back from her brow as he finished—'you wouldn't bear false witness against me, would you?'

He was smiling, he was happy.

'Here, my dear, drink that up, a nice hot cup of tea. Now we were just going to have a meal, you'll have a bite?'

'No. No, thank you, just the tea. I've . . . I've got to get back.' She turned her gaze down on Robert now, saying, 'It's . . . it's Dave, he's become

373

demented. I'm . . . I'm afraid. He . . . he's got the idea that you are going to buy the house.'

He pulled himself upwards and, his head back, he let out a deep laugh, then said, 'Never! Never!'

'Oh, yes.' She nodded up at him. 'He imagines you are going to live there.'

He turned and looked at Alice and, the laughter sliding from his face, he said, 'Can you imagine it, anyone being as mad as that? All because I used to talk to Miss Millie.'

Yes, Alice thought to herself, she could imagine it; she had lived with a man for years who had been obsessed by his daughter. But what had turned Mr Waters's brain was not only the love for the young deranged girl but for this one here too. Apparently from what Robbie had already said the old man and his wife had not only run the house for years, but had brought the two lasses up, and in a way she could understand the man's feelings when the apple of his eye, so to speak, stepped out of her class. And there was no doubt about it, she was stepping out of her class. But then that wasn't to say it was going to harm her, or that she would sink under it. No, not since she had picked a man like Robbie. But again that wasn't to say that life was going to run smoothly for them. Oh no. And now here she was, pleading with Robbie to go back with her, and only an hour or so ago her own heart had practically sung when he had come home and said he was here to stay, at least until he joined up. That white feather business had got him down an' all. Eeh! that was terrible.

She listened now to the lass saying, 'It will only be for a short time until I can make arrangements and get Millie away. I'm afraid he's quite insane,

374

it's in his eyes. For years they've dubbed poor Millie as someone out of her mind, and I was right when I wouldn't have any of it, for when I looked at Dave just a little while ago I saw insanity in all its darkness, and I knew I was right about Millie and always had been. Odd she may be, but not insane.'

'Would you excuse me a minute?' Alice didn't wait for an answer but left them together, and as she went into the dining-room the thought that was niggling at her was, if the lass got settled, would he go with her?

Settled? She stood looking towards the bright fire and again said to herself, settled? This was his home, this was where he would settle. They could come here, her and the young lass, she wouldn't mind that, oh no, because once that was done he'd be here for life, she would never lose him again . . . except through the war. Yes, there was that. But if the lass came here, she'd be company, they'd be company for each other . . .

Robert was saying much the same thing as he sat on the settle close to her, her hands tightly clasped in his. 'Look,' he was saying, 'don't worry about having any place to go, if you could face it, you're right here. I know me aunt. Well, I've got to say it, what I want, she wants. She's as lonely as you are, or once was. There's plenty of room and I've got the place next door now. Why, we could house a staff here.' He drew her hands tightly up against his chest, and solemnly he looked into her face as he said, 'There'd be no strings. I'd be away. I'm going in tomorrow and that'll fix it.' And now he allowed a grin to come to his face as he ended, 'A bright lad like me, they'll grab me up and send me over afore I've hardly got me uniform on.'

'Oh! Robert. Robert.'

'Now, now. Don't start to cry again; you know what happened last time. I'll go back with you. We'll take the trap and bring what is necessary for both of you. Then tomorrow you can get in touch with that brother of yours. Huh!'—he jerked his chin upwards—'I'd better not be here, had I, when he sees what you've come down to?'

'Robert.'

'Yes, my dear.'

'Robert.'

He nodded at her. 'Yes, yes, what is it?'

'Will you marry me, Mr Bradley?'

His eyes were wide. Then he shut his lids for a moment tightly, his teeth pressed down on his lip and after a moment of silence he said, 'You know what you're saying, Miss Thorman?'

She responded in like manner, saying, 'Yes, Mr Bradley, I know what I'm saying.'

'You know it'll be tough for you?'

'I don't know any such thing.'

'Well, I do. You will be shunned by your own kind, ostracized is the word, isn't it?' He gave a mirthless smile. 'You'll have to mix with my kind, an' the majority of them won't be to your taste. Then there are those brothers of yours. I could bet once I'm in the army they'll see I'm in the front of the front line.'

'Are you refusing me?'

'Oh, Aggie!' Again she was in his arms, again his lips were hard on hers.

When finally they drew apart he held her face between his hands as he said, 'There may be minutes in my life happier than these, but I can't imagine them, and the honest truth is, I never knew what would come out of this, but even in my wildest dreams I didn't think . . . well—' He swallowed deeply, then stroking her cheek he said, 'The first time I saw you in the wood, in the moonlight, I thought, There's a madam if ever there was, a haughty upper-class piece.' He laughed now and hugged her to him. 'And you know something? When I came to work for you, I couldn't stand you, at least that's what I told meself. And then the day I picked you up from the ground I asked myself who I was kidding. I knew then I loved you. It was my first real experience of love . . . real love, and since then, Aggie, and I'll always call you Aggie, not Agnes—' He bent forward and touched her lips lightly now before going on, 'As I said, since then I've never known a moment's peace, not till this minute. And yes, Miss Thorman, I will accept your proposal to marry you. *Let anybody try to stop me.*'

Once again they were enfolded, and only parted on the sound of coughing coming from the hallway. They both turned and looked towards Alice; and now Robert, getting to his feet pulled Agnes up with him and, his arm about her, he looked towards his aunt and said, 'Well, you'll not be surprised. You know what?' His face was alight now, a deep twinkle in his eye. 'She's asked me to marry her. Cheeky monkey, isn't she?' He hugged Agnes towards him and her head fell on his shoulder, and Alice came up to them, holding out her hands and saying softly, 'I'll give you me blessing but only on one condition, that you settle here for life.'

'We accept that condition, Mrs Bradley.' He nodded at her, then looked at Agnes, and she, too full to speak, listened to him now saying, 'We had to buy that place next door, hadn't we? When I'm

377

finished with it, it will rival any manor house. Might be smaller, but wait till you see the inside. And I'll make every piece of that furniture with me own hands. I'll strip that place down and panel it and it will be for you, just yours.' He looked down into her face, his own unsmiling now, and he added, 'I mean that, a place of your own, where you can be by yourself, and even I'll have to knock on the door afore I can come in.'

'Oh, Robert. Oh, Mrs Bradley.' Her tears were now flowing down her face as she turned to Alice, saying, 'You . . . you don't know what this means to me; you can have no conception of the joy and relief that I have some place to come to, and someone to come to'—she cast her glance at Robert—'someone who will accept Millie. I hope you will like Millie, Mrs Bradley. She's a sweet, sweet child. That's all she is, she's nearly nineteen years old but she's still a child.'

'Nobody could help but like Millie, and you'll see when you first meet her.' Robert was nodding at Alice. 'Anyway, we'll go and get it over with. They can have my room tonight, eh, that'll be all right? And I'll go back among the sawdust. I liked it up there anyway.'

'You'll do no such thing. I'll have the other room ready for you as soon as you get back. Now get yourselves away. But wrap up well, dear.' She handed the scarf to Agnes but Robert took it from her and, putting it over Agnes's head, he pushed her back towards the settee, saying, 'Stay there a minute until I get the trap out; it's no use coming out in the cold.'

Left together, they looked at each other; then Alice, sitting down beside Agnes, said, ' 'Tis a big step you're taking and I know you'll feel strange, but for my part, I'll do me best to ease things.'

'Oh, Mrs Bradley. If you only knew how grateful I am. Please don't think that I am leaving something marvellous, it is the opposite way about. I've led a lonely, narrow harassed life. I cannot remember knowing any real happiness until this last half-hour. No matter what happens in the future, and I am sensible enough to know there will be difficulties, but I can assure you they won't arise because, to use a phrase that has been thrown at me so much of late, I'm stepping out of my class; to my mind at this moment the step is upwards, and for my part I will try and do my very best not to intrude on you'—she paused—'well, your routine and your way of life.'

'Oh, my dear, don't worry about that. If you only knew how grateful I am to have someone round the house again. Since I lost my daughter and then my husband my life has been empty. I don't know what I would have done if I hadn't had Robert. But . . . but I didn't have enough of him.' She smiled now, then added soberly, 'Oh, if it wasn't for this awful war and he hadn't to go away, life would . . . well, be perfect.'

'You ready, dear?'

She rose from the settee and took his outstretched hand; then they all went into the yard where the trap was waiting and when the two of them had mounted it, Alice, looking at them, smiled and said, 'Hurry back. I'll have a good supper waiting for you. And just tell yourselves'— she nodded from one to the other—'this is the last time you'll have to make that journey.'

# CHAPTER TWELVE

Peggy Waters had for a long time realized that her husband was nearing the border of insanity, but now she knew he had crossed it when he came tearing into the kitchen shouting at her, 'She's gone! She's gone to him. She'll bring him back. 'Tis not to be borne. I tell you, woman, 'tis not to be borne. I won't stand it. No, never, him in the master's bedroom. That was his father's afore him. I served them both. Gentlemen. Gentlemen. And now this scum comin' into this house. Well, I'll put a stop to that.'

As he now ran towards the back door she clutched at him, trying to hold him, beseeching him, 'Dave! Dave! Have sense, he can't buy this place, he wouldn't have the money. Whatever the carpenter left it would be nothing like the money to buy this place.'

'Leave go, woman! I know what he's up to. Right from the minute he stepped into this house, I saw it in his face. He followed her about, he mesmerized her, like he did the child. He's a devil. His uncle tried to kill him, his uncle knew what he was.'

'Give over. Give over. You know his uncle came and explained. You remember . . . you remember, New Year's Day.'

'I remember his every move was to get her. And look what he's done to her, a lady like her, brought her down, dragged her into the gutter. But he won't do it in this house. Oh no, he won't do it in this house.' With a twist of his arm he thrust her from him and rushed out into the yard; and now as quickly she rushed back up the kitchen, through the hall, across the gallery and to Millie's room and, pushing open the door, she cried to Ruthie, 'Come! Come quickly and give me a hand with your father. He's gone clean mad.' She paused, then jumped aside as the poodle sprang past her, and Millie cried, 'Oh, look! Look! Lady's gone. Let me get her. Let me get her.'

Together they restrained her, but gently, pressing her back into the room, and it was Ruthie who said, ' 'Tis all right, Miss Millie, 'tis all right. I'll get her. Now you stay there, I'll get her. Now don't move. Be a good girl. I'll be back in a minute.' And she pressed Millie on to the foot of the bed. Then both she and Peggy ran towards the door, where Ruthie took the precaution of turning the key in the lock before following her mother at a run down the stairs.

Left alone, Millie sat picking at the threads of the eiderdown between her finger and thumb, talking as she did so: 'She'll get lost. She doesn't know her way without me, she'll get lost. She's never been out in the dark. But then it won't be very dark, the moon's coming up. But it isn't very bright yet. You're naughty, Lady, you're very naughty you know.' She went on picking at the threads. 'They won't be able to find you, you'll be lost, lost.'

Of a sudden she got up from the bed and went to the door, and when she found she couldn't open it she rattled the handle. Then turning about, she walked back to the middle of the room saying, 'They shouldn't do that, they know I don't like to be locked in. Aggie! Aggie!' She ran back to the door and beat on it with her fists, calling all the

381

while, 'Aggie! Aggie! Lady's out! Open the door, please. Please, Aggie, open the door, I must get Lady. I must find her. She gets frightened.'

When her hand began to ache she turned round again, and now she went to the window. It was closed and the sneck was locked. She brought a chair and stood on it and pulled the sneck loose. It was very stiff and it hurt her fingers. And now, putting each hand under the metal lips attached to the bottom frame, she slowly eased it upwards. It seemed much heavier tonight than it had done when last she had opened it and shaken the branches of the wisteria.

A cold wind blew on her face and made her shiver. She went to the bedrail and picked up her woolly dressing-gown and put it on, and she had just returned to the window and looked downwards when she saw a small white dot running along the terrace below. And now leaning forward, she called, 'Lady! Lady! Come back! Come back!' But Lady disappeared around the side of the house. Dear oh dear! if she got into the wood, she might run until she got on to the road, and they weren't allowed to go on the road. She had told her that she mustn't go on the road. Oh, Lady. Lady.

She leant well out of the window and gripped the thick old gnarled branch of the wisteria. She had never yet climbed down it, but she had many times imagined doing so, and now the door being locked, she knew she couldn't get out except through the window.

She knelt on the broad sill, then reaching out through the window to the side of the wall, she gripped a stout old shoot whose tentacles were embedded in the stone and so pulled herself on to the outer sill. Then gripping the shoot with both hands she lifted one foot and placed it on a branch. Then she giggled. It was easy, like a ladder. She was clinging now with both hands to the main shoot of the wisteria and her right foot was groping for another hold. When it found it, she began her descent and all thought of the dog went out of her mind as she hung in mid-air. It was lovely, like flying. She knew she would fly one day. She wouldn't tell them that she could fly, not even Aggie, because Aggie would be vexed and shut the window permanently. When she was more than half-way down her dressing-gown got caught on a branch and she had to release one hand to disentangle it. But she laughed as she was doing it. It was so exciting. The night air was blowing through her hair making her feel cool, light. She would like to hang on here forever. But then there was Lady. Oh yes, that's what she had come down for, Lady.

When her feet touched the ground she stood for a moment looking up into the sky. There was a moon shining somewhere, but it was behind the clouds. Yet the clouds were light . . . Everything was light, her feet were light. She now ran in the direction she had seen the dog go and as soon as she turned the corner of the house, she saw her. She was sniffing round the rain barrel, and she called to her softly, 'Lady. Lady. You're a naughty girl. Yes, you are.'

The dog remained still while Millie picked her up; then when it licked her face she gurgled happily and hugging it to her, she said, 'You're cold. You will catch a cold. We must go indoors. You're a very, very naughty doggie.'

She went towards the door that led on to the back staircase. This door was rarely used and, like the other doors of the house, was never locked. The staircase was dark and she had to grope her way up. The landing formed the beginning of a long passage that opened out on to a small hallway and the door leading from this led into the extreme end of the gallery that ended in the north wing. As she went to open the door she heard excited voices on the landing and she closed it again. That was Peggy and Ruthie. They would be vexed with her and tell Aggie, and Aggie would scold her. She would wait here until they were gone.

There was a pale light coming through the landing window and she went and sat on the edge of the narrow sill and waited, all the time talking to the poodle in an undertone . . .

In the kitchen his deranged mind was telling Dave Waters that if he wasn't careful, cute, they'd stop him in his purpose, and so when he saw his wife and daughter coming towards him he said in a voice that was so calm it took the wind out of their sails, 'Now let's talk things over sensibly as I can the way I'm feeling. She's gone to him, hasn't she?' He looked from one to the other. 'And we've got our marching orders. Well, what are we going to do about it?'

The mother and daughter looked at each other; then Peggy said, 'We could go to Maggie's. We'd be welcome there. And . . . and Ruthie can get a job anywhere.'

'Yes, I can that, yes.' Ruthie was nodding at her father now, at the same time wondering what had caused her mother to panic in the way she had.

'Well then, that being so, what's going to happen

384

to the young one?'

'Miss Millie?' Peggy screwed up her face as she said, 'Well, she'll take her along with her.'

'What!' He laughed a strange high laugh now. 'That fellow only used Millie as a tool to get at the other one.' It seemed he could no longer refer to Agnes by name. 'Do you think he'd put up with her? Not on your life. Anyway, she's always been with us, we brought her up, and I could always get work, they are taking the lame and the blind now.' He made a deep sound in his throat before going on, 'The best thing to do is to ask her, bring her down and ask her who she'd like to live with.'

'No, no.' Ruthie shook her head. 'No, Dad, she's pretty near one of her states, and Miss Agnes gave her some drops this afternoon. She's . . . she's a bit dopey.'

'Go on, bring her down.' There was a change in his tone now, and the two women looked at each other and when Peggy made a motion with her head Ruthie left the room. But she seemed to be gone only seconds before she came tearing back again, crying, 'She's gone! She's gone! She must have got out of the window.'

'She's fallen?' Peggy's voice was a loud cry now, and Ruthie said, 'No, no! She must have climbed down. I looked out and there's nobody lying there.'

'Oh my God! We only needed this. She's on the rampage again. It's that dog. It got out, she'll be in the wood after it.'

They all ran into the boot room now and both Peggy and Ruthie pulled coats off the hooks and dragged them on before running out in the yard. And it was Peggy who cried, 'You take the rose garden, Ruthie. I'll go towards the lodge. Your

385

dad'll make for the water.'

It was understood that Dave Waters would make for the water on these occasions because nearly always that was where Millie eventually wound up after she had been on one of her rambles.

But tonight Dave Waters didn't run as he usually did through the alleyway and sprint down the vegetable garden and around by the greenhouses and so into the wood; instead, he remained standing until he saw his wife and daughter disappear. Then the way was clear for him. There were four cans of paraffin oil in the tack room, and he brought out two and placed them on the kitchen table. The other two he carried at a run through the kitchen, then through the hall and up the stairs, and in the corridor, putting one down, he unscrewed the top off the other.

Starting at the end of the corridor, he kicked open the doors and began sprinkling paraffin here and there. In Millie's room he saturated the bed. When the first can was empty he made a zigzag trail with the other along the gallery, throwing it up the curtains that hung on the long windows, spraying it over the balustrades; and when that too was empty he ran down the stairs into the kitchen and picked up the other cans.

In the drawing-room, he did a thorough job, spraying the curtains and the furniture. He was sparing with the dining-room but in the library he emptied the can with great sweeps of his arm over the bookcases. This done, he ran into the kitchen and, taking several pieces of kindling wood from a basket, he thrust them into the fire and when they were alight he ran back up the kitchen, along the passage and into the hall, then to the drawing-room, through this and into the library. It was here he threw his first stick. As he ran back through the drawing-room he hurled one towards the bottom of the curtains and another on to the hair rug before the fireplace. Back through the hall again he went into the dining-room, and lastly he opened the lobby doors before turning and looking up towards the stairs. Already there was a smell of burning in his nostrils and he drew it in and, lifting his arm, he hurled the two remaining sticks towards the bottom of the stairs . . . These he stood watching for a full minute, because although they themselves were burning the stair carpet had not caught alight, nor yet the stanchion post, and he had made sure to soak that.

He was about to move forward when there was a burst of flame, and he stepped back. Then he walked backwards through the lobby until he reached the front door, and as he opened this the fresh draught made the flames flare up and illuminate the entire hall.

The smell of the smoke had brought both Peggy and Ruthie scurrying back, and they stood aghast at the head of the drive not believing their eyes. The whole lower floor of the house was ablaze and there in the light of it on the gravel stood the husband and father.

*'What have you done? What have you done? You madman.'*

Dave Waters turned and looked calmly at Peggy, saying now, 'I've done what I've intended. He'll not come and rule the roost here. And what money he's got won't rebuild it.'

'Dad! Dad! You're mad. And we can't find Miss Millie.'

'What's that?' He turned on her. 'She's in the wood.'

'She's not in the wood; at least we can't find her.'

'She'll be down by the water.'

'We've been round there.'

'The dog.'

'There's no sign of the dog.'

'No, no.' His eyes were wide now, his mouth agape; his hands stretched upwards as if in supplication and, his voice a scream now, he ran towards the front door yelling, 'Millie! Me dear. Me dear. Millie!'

They reached him as he stood choking in front of the main doorway and they dragged him back on to the terrace. On the drive they were grouped together tightly when Peggy, gasping and choking, raised her head, then cried, 'Oh my God! Look!' And they looked and there at one of the gallery windows, with a dull glow behind it, was silhouetted the poodle. It was at this moment that the trap came at a gallop on to the drive; a farm cart closely followed, and behind this some men were running.

Transfixed by the sight, Robert and Agnes sat for a moment staring at the house. All the ground floor was ablaze. Windows were cracking and smoke and flames were pouring out. The smoke was coming in great gusts from the front door and behind all the upstairs windows fronting the drive there was now a bright pink glow.

When they reached the group on the lawn, Agnes shouted, 'Millie! Where's Millie?'

'Oh! miss. Miss. We thought she was in the wood. She got out, she climbed down the wisteria. We thought she was in the wood, we went looking. But look! there's . . . there's the dog up there.'

388

'You've done this. You've done this.' Dave Waters now sprang at Robert, only to be knocked back by Robert's forearm as he shouted, 'You bloody madman! You'll be locked up. God! you will, if somebody doesn't kill you. He's done this, hasn't he?' He was yelling at Peggy and she, her face convulsed, cried, 'He's not in his right mind. He's not in his right mind.'

There were voices all about them, crying, 'Where's the water? Get some buckets.'

As Robert ran towards the front door, he knew that buckets would be useless here. But he wanted something over his head. He whipped off his coat and half buried his head in it and, bent double, he ran forward. But he got no further than the far doors of the lobby for there the whole place looked like one sheet of flame.

When he staggered out on to the terrace again, Agnes caught hold of him and, both coughing and spluttering, they went down the steps. But then pulling himself from her hold, he cried, 'Get a ladder, somebody. Get a ladder. Bring it this way!' He was already running round the corner of the house towards Millie's window.

Dave Waters was standing alone now, seemingly oblivious of the people running backwards and forwards to the yard tap with buckets. But of a sudden he almost jumped from the ground as he cried, 'He won't get her! He won't get her!' And he turned about and ran in the opposite direction towards the back door through which only a short time ago Millie had gone. The stairs were full of smoke, but he reached the landing. The door to the gallery was open; the rooms off it were full of smoke but not alight. It was the gallery curtains

389

that were ablaze and the staircase. He went towards the staircase but here he was met by a sheet of flame. Choking, his lungs burning, he turned round several times and lost all sense of direction. He was crawling on his knees now as he fought his way back towards the staircase door, but when he gripped the iron leg of a bed he knew he had entered one of the rooms. When he again found the opening to the doorway his lungs were on the point of bursting. He could see the red glow of the curtains now and he knew that the window was beyond. In one last effort to gain it he put his hand out; it gripped the flaming material and the whole thing fell around him. His struggle now was one of suffocation, not of burning, and he was dead before his clothes really caught alight . . .

Robert found it comparatively easy to climb the wisteria and just as easy to get into the room through the open window. But now he was checked by the smoke. He groped his way towards the bed, fully expecting Millie to be lying there suffocated. But there was no one on it. He had patted the coverlet and his hand came away damp, and he knew before he smelt it what it was. He crawled round the room now, feeling for her; and when he was sure she wasn't there he wriggled on his belly towards the landing.

The landing was full of smoke but not yet ablaze, but the gallery, what he could see of it, looked one great sheet of flame, and he was about to turn back into the room when he heard a whining cry. He could see nothing, but he moved towards it. It seemed to come from the end of the bedroom corridor, and then he felt it before he saw it. It was the dog, and as his hand moved over its back he touched the hand that was holding it, the fingers embedded in its wool. Choking and spluttering, he felt along the arm to the body. It was round the corner on the gallery and it was alight. This fact was borne home by the searing pain that shot through his hand, that hand that had patted the eiderdown that was covered with paraffin, for now his hand was ablaze. In the moment he paid no attention to it but dragged the figure around and into the corridor. The dog was quiet now as it too was dragged along.

Once he managed to get her into the bedroom he thrust his foot out and pushed the door closed; then he beat at her with his hands. The dressing-gown was alight in parts but being wool it was slow to burn. Not so her nightdress, which had already burned up to the bottom of the dressing gown.

When he attempted to rip the dressing-gown off her he was obstructed by the buttons. These undone, he tore at the garment and at her now smouldering nightdress, banging at it with his hands. But when he saw a flicker of light streak up it, he tore it off her, then looked round for something with which to cover her. His hand went out towards the bed then stopped: it only needed that and they'd both be alight.

He took up his coat which had dropped to the floor and put it over her and was about to drag her to the window when a voice came from that direction, shouting, 'You there? You there?'

'Aye,' he croaked. 'Give her a hand.'

When the man entered the room he coughed and spluttered and Robert gasped at him, 'When I get through, lift her over.'

'You . . . you'll never manage her on your own.'

'It's the only way. Two of us can't go down together. Anyway, she's no weight.'

He now crawled out of the window and put his feet on the rung of the ladder and the man lifted Millie up as if she was a baby, and as he put her into the support of Robert's arm the ladder moved and the man yelled, 'I told you. I told you.'

'It's all right, just hang on to it. I'll be down in no time. And . . . and fetch the dog.'

'Dog?'

'Aye,' he called up between gasps; 'it's on the floor.'

Agnes attempted to take Millie from him, but was pushed aside. The place seemed swarming with people now and he was not surprised to hear Doctor Miller's voice saying, 'That's it, cover her up.' He stood now bent double coughing as if he would bring his heart up, and he didn't straighten his back until he heard the man who had come up the ladder saying, 'It's done for. Put it out of its misery, hit it on the neck.'

'No, no!' Robert reached out now and grabbed the dog from the man's hand. The wool all round its haunches was singed, as was that on its ears and its top knot, but its heart was still beating, and he looked at the man now and said, 'She prized it. She'll want it later.'

Somewhere a voice said, 'I doubt if there'll be any later for her, poor soul.'

Doctor Miller was standing by him now turning his hands over. 'You're going to have trouble here,' he said. 'They'll have to be cleaned up. You'd better get on the cart with Agnes. Apparently she knows where she's going. They've laid Millie in it. How in the name of God did this start?'

'Waters set it alight.'

*'Waters? No!'*

'Yes. He's been going off his head for some time and this is the result. The place was going to be sold and he couldn't stand it, that among other things.'

'Where is he now?'

'I don't know.' Robert looked about him. People had stopped running backwards and forwards with buckets, they just stood in groups gazing at the blaze that was now consuming the whole house. 'I hope he's dead,' he said, 'because if he's not, he'll very shortly wish he was when he's put away.'

'Don't say that, man. Don't say that.'

They were now walking towards the cart which seemed to be surrounded by more people when Robert stopped and said quietly, 'You knew there was something fishy about Mr Thorman's death, didn't you?' The doctor said nothing. 'Well, I can tell you this much, doctor, if anything happens to Miss Millie and Waters is still alive, I'll tell you all I know of that incident. I want to make sure that he'll be put where he can do no more harm, because such is his mind at the moment, it will be Agnes next.'

Doctor Miller showed no surprise at Robert's mention of Agnes rather than of Miss Agnes; he was usually the first one to hear scandal and gossip. 'Go along,' he said; 'I'll be following on. And don't touch those hands until I see them. And get Millie into bed. That's all. I shall be with you as quick as I can.'

Robert went to the cart. Millie lay stretched out, hardly discernible under a number of sacks. Agnes sat by her side, her whole body shivering, her face

393

white, her eyes staring. She looked at him but they didn't speak. 'I'll follow in the trap,' he said. 'But here, take her dog.' He stood aside while a man placed the animal on her lap.

The cart was driven away, and someone brought the trap, but when he tried to mount it the agony in his hands was so great that he bent his head forward. 'Here, let me,' one of the men said, then added, 'Give me a hand.' And the two men now hoisted him up into the seat. But seeing Robert couldn't pick up the reins the younger man jumped up beside him and, grabbing the reins, shouted, 'Gee up! there.'

Thus he made his way back home, and as he drove the young fellow talked: 'Never seen a blaze like that in years,' he said. 'Aye, he did a good job. They say it was old Waters. Went off his head. By, it was a brave thing you did to go up that ivy stuff and get the lass down. But I don't suppose you'll get any medals for it, you have to be in khaki these days afore people cheer you. I'm in the pits, so I'm all right, but me brother, he's a clerk, white collar you know, because he had T.B., but you can't shout that out, so he got a white feather last week. By God, if I found out who did that I'd have stuck it in one end of them and pulled it out the other. And so would our Lance. He's me elder brother. A hewer he is. He's the one that went up the ladder and helped you down. Strong as a horse he is, doesn't look it, wiry. All our lot are wiry. What are you?'

It took a great effort for Robert to say, 'A carpenter.' He felt sick; he'd never experienced such pain. Looking back he knew he'd never before really experienced any pain at all, not physical pain.

394

He'd had a tooth out once. He had thought that was bad because he had put up with toothache for three weeks as he was afraid to go to the dentist. But this was . . . he hadn't a name to put to this pain, it was driving him mad.

He told himself it was only his hands that were burnt, yet his whole body seemed to be consumed with pain. He wanted to cry out against it. And poor Millie. He hoped her legs hadn't caught it much, not if she was to suffer like this. But that poor dog, it must be in agony. He should have let it be put down.

'A carpenter? Now that's funny, I wanted to be a carpenter. I do a lot of whittling, make things like, you know. Where do you work?'

'I have my own business.' And he had. Yes he had a fine business, a fine house, and he was going to marry a fine splendid beautiful woman, and he was going to build her a house, and he was going to line it with wood and make all the furniture. That's what he had said. It was as if he had flown in the face of providence. Had he been religious he would have thought that God was checking him for his pride, for would he ever be able to use his hands again? The little finger and the one next to it on his right hand looked stuck together. Perhaps it was only the dirt and the skin.

He held them up as if the cold night air would ease the agony of them, and the young man said, 'They're gona handicap you for a time.'

Yes, they would handicap him for a time; but as long as it was only for a time.

As they turned into the yard his companion said, 'Oh, is this your place? I've passed it now and again. 'Tis a nice house. I knew it was a carpenter's

395

shop, it's quite famous around. It's been here a long time, hasn't it? Did you know them up at the house? I mean is that why you're bringing them here?'

'Yes. Yes, I knew them up at the house.'

'Did work for them likely?'

'I did work for them.' God! if only he would shut up.

'Well, I wouldn't expect much thanks by what I've heard of them up there. Poor as church mice and still lording it, the men anyway. And one of the daughters letting herself down with some workman. Me mother's always said educated ladies get frustrated and then they get brazen, they'll take anything. They say the fellow worked up there and he had it off with her, and of course she was only using him. He must have been gullible if he thought anything would come of it. They never step out of their class, not that lot.' His voice trailed off as he looked into his companion's smoke-grimed face, the eyes blazing at him now, and it dawned on him too late to whom he had been opening his big mouth. His mother said he always chattered too much. He spluttered now, 'Can . . . can I help you down?' And Robert growled, 'No, you can't. You've helped me enough.' Then sliding from the seat, he dug his elbows on to the back of the trap, swung himself round and jumped to the ground. The jerk sent waves of pain through his body that made him feel faint, but he gave the young fellow one last deadly look before he followed the men carrying Millie into the house, where Alice was wringing her hands, crying, 'Dear Lord! Dear Lord! What is this? What's happened?'

When she saw Robert, his hands held away from

his sides, she again cried, 'What's happened?'

'A fire; the place is burnt down. Waters did it. Will you see to her . . . them? Doctor Miller will be here in a minute . . . But Aunty.'

'Yes, my dear? Yes, my dear?' She was looking up at him. 'Would . . . would you mind if . . . if I send somebody for a drink? A bottle of brandy or whisky, anything?'

'No, dear, no. And don't you bother, I'll do it. Go and sit down, go into the sitting-room. I'll do it. I'll do it now. Yes. One of the Parkins will go; they've got bikes.'

She ran from the room and he sank into a chair, and for a moment he forgot about the pain in his hand, he could only think of the chatter of that fellow and how dirty people could make life. How they could stain a beautiful thing, and once stained by slander it was indelible, it was there for always. Was he right in letting her take the final step?

Right. Right. His right hand. What good would he be with only one hand? God! he wasn't going to pass out, was he?


## CHAPTER THIRTEEN

The house burnt itself out. The only articles saved were crockery and kitchen utensils. These had been thrown into the barn on the night of the fire, but on the following morning there wasn't an article left.

It was not until the debris that had fallen from the first floor down into the hall was cleared, that they came across the charred body of Dave Waters. The news was brought to Alice by one of the two boys working in the shop, and she took it up to the bedroom where Robert and Agnes were sitting by Millie's bedside. It was Agnes she motioned out of the room. Quietly she said to her, 'They found Mr Waters's body.'

Agnes remained silent for a moment. Then looking into the pleasant face before her she said, 'This news should bring me deep sorrow, Mrs Bradley, but the only feeling I have is one of relief, because I've thought for nights past he may be wandering somewhere, or be in hiding, because no one saw him go into the house. It's as well. Yet I'm sorry for Peggy . . . his wife.'

'Yes, it's always those who are left who suffer; the dead can't feel. Will you tell him?'

'Yes, presently.'

'There's a bite ready for you when you feel like it. I'll come up and sit with her at the time you both have it.'

'Thank you.'

She went back into the room and Robert's eyes questioned her across the bed, and in answer she said, 'Later, I'll tell you later.' Then when Millie moaned and moved restlessly, she bent over her and stroked her hair back from her brow, saying, 'There, there, dear. There, there.'

Millie was recovering as much as she would ever recover, according to Doctor Miller, for her heart which had never been good, as he said, had now undergone such a strain, what with the smoke and the burns on her legs, that it was very tired. But, he said, with care it could go on ticking for a week, or a month, or even a year; but not to be surprised if it stopped at any moment.

As for the condition of Robert's hands, his

398

manner after he had dressed them the first time had been grave, when he said, 'This, I'm afraid, is going to be a hospital job. Those two end ones are almost burnt to the bone. It's a pity they're on the right hand. And the pad of your left is in not much better state. But they're very good at grafting these days, they've had plenty of experience of it over the past months. You can visit the Royal Victoria in Newcastle as an outpatient until they can do the job. Then you'll likely have to go in. The main thing is to try to move your fingers. Oh yes, yes,'— he had nodded—'at the moment you feel that you will never move them again, and when you do start you'll know about it too.'

When he had asked in a tentative voice, 'Will . . . will I be able to carry on my work?' the doctor's answer had been, 'I don't see why not after a time. Men manage with half hands, some with no hands at all. I shouldn't worry about that, just give yourself time. But in between don't let us hoodwink ourselves: you are going to feel them, for they are in a bad way.'

And that, Robert had thought during the next forty-eight hours, was an understatement. The first night he drank three large whiskies, but still couldn't close his eyes; nor could he do anything for himself, not lift a cup or a glass to his lips. It was some weeks before he could laugh at the memory of his aunt who had lived so teetotal a life that not even ginger beer had crossed her lips pouring whisky down his throat at intervals . . .

They were both downstairs now and Agnes, after cutting up his meat and vegetables, lifted forkful after forkful to his mouth, and he groaned in between bites the while she chided him, saying,

399

'Don't be silly, eat it up.'

'Oh, Lord'—he shook his head—'that it's come to this.'

'Yes, that it's come to this,' she repeated. 'And I've never done anything that has given me more pleasure.'

'You're easily pleased.' He gulped on a mouthful of food.

'There you are mistaken.' She took up a napkin now and wiped round his mouth. And, his head down now, he said, 'It's humiliating.'

'Would you rather a nurse in hospital did it?'

'Yes, yes, I would.'

'Well then'—she went round the table and began on her own meal—'we'll see about it. I'll see Doctor Miller when he comes this afternoon and tell him you want to be taken into hospital.'

'You do if you dare.' They smiled at each other now, and he asked, 'What did Aunty want?' But she continued eating for some seconds before telling him. 'They found Dave.'

He waited, he too had wondered if the old man was hiding somewhere and so could strike again at any moment.

'He must have burnt to death.'

He looked away from her. Well, it wasn't a good way to go, he'd likely have died from suffocation before being burnt. But whichever way he went, he was glad he was gone, for now he felt he could breathe again.

'Do you think you should go and see Peggy?' he said.

'Yes, I do. It will be very awkward, dreadful. Yet I feel she must be relieved too for she had known what was happening to him.'

He looked down at his hands now where they rested on the table, two big white bandaged lumps. It wasn't two years since he had come to this part of the country, he thought, yet his presence right from the beginning seemed to have wrought havoc: meeting Millie by the lake; arousing the animosity of Nancy Parkin; the business of Carrie and the knife throwing—that could have done him in—then going to Foreshaw; the moment when he first touched her as he lifted her from the ground; the killing of the master; his uncle coming out on that bitter night to ask his forgiveness, and never recovering from it, the only bright thing being the will and the feeling of independence it had brought him. But that brightness had been dimmed, for day after day Waters had trailed him; he couldn't move but he knew that the man was watching him.

Then that moment in the tack room when he first kissed her. That was never to be forgotten, that was the beginning of the change. Yet how did it end? By him almost strangling her brother. Then again the emergence into brightness, into joy: 'Will you marry me, Mr Bradley?' Oh, she was wonderful, wonderful. He looked at her. Would there ever come a time when she would stop loving him, when she saw him for what he was, just an ordinary fellow? But he had never pretended to her to be anything else and he doubted if he could change. He didn't want to change, except in a way: learn more, be more knowledgeable. Yes, that would please her and he would do it. And she would help him, she was like that. If only he knew that his hands were going to be all right. Anyway, there was one thing they had done for him, they had delayed his enlisting for a time, if not for altogether, and he wasn't sorry. Oh no, by God, he wasn't sorry. He wanted to be no hero. A live carpenter was better than a dead V.C. any day in the week.

'What are you thinking?'

He smiled at her. 'I was thinking of you,' he said; 'I'm always thinking of you.'

'When shall we be married?'

Oh, God, she was funny. He put his head back and managed to laugh. Say, Polly Hinton or Nancy Parkin or any other girl of his acquaintance had said to him, 'When shall we be married?' he would have shied like any nervous colt and said, 'Look here, hold your hand a bit, miss. Who said anything about marriage?' Cheeky monkeys, the lot of them. Yet, here she was, this lady, because in his mind that's how he'd always think of her, a lady, saying coolly to him, 'When shall we be married?'

For the moment he forgot the constant searing pain in his hands and arms and, pulling a face, he said, 'Well now, about that, I've been thinking I might change me mind.'

So much had she altered in the last few days, which seemed to have taken on the pattern of years, that she calmly cut into a piece of steak and chewed on it before saying, 'If I were you, sir, I'd think again. It's either marriage or breach of promise.'

She was so pleased to see him laugh, knowing what he must be suffering and what he had gone through during the past days. She looked across the table now, love showing unashamedly in her eyes as she asked herself, would she ever get tired of this man? Would there come a time when she would say to herself, they had been right, oil and water

402

don't mix? *No, never.* This oil and water had already merged one into the other.

He said now, quietly, 'How can it be done, quickly I mean?'

'By special licence, I understand, or as soon as you are capable of putting the ring on my finger.'

'Huh!' He gave a quiet chuckle. 'Good.' He nodded his head once. 'So be it. Are you going to inform your brothers?'

'No. It is none of their business.'

'I can see Second-Lieutenant Stanley making it his.'

'Well, once it's done, it's done. So I think the sooner the better. If that meets with your approval, Mr Bradley?' She was smiling primly at him now, and he answered in the same vein, 'Quite, Miss Thorman. Quite.'

She now rose from the table and came hurrying round to him and, standing behind him, she put her arms around his neck and, bending over, she kissed him; then said, 'I've never been so happy in my life . . . If only Millie,' she said to herself.

He turned his head up to her. 'You know nothing yet, woman, not the half of it.'

The twinkle in his eye she knew to be naughty, and she tapped his cheek as she said, 'I am willing to learn.'

'Oh, Aggie.' He swung round in his chair and his arms went about her. His hands stuck straight out behind her back but his elbows squeezed her tightly and, looking into her eyes, he said, 'What would I have done if I hadn't met you?' And she answered soberly, 'The question is, what would I have done, Robert? Yes, what would I have done with my life if I hadn't met you? I'll thank God for you until the day I die.'

*      *      *

It was two days following Dave Waters's funeral when she went into Birtley and knocked on Maggie's door. It was opened by Ruthie whose mouth fell into a slight gape before she turned her head and looked into the room, evidently used as kitchen and living-room combined, and to her mother who was sitting by the table which was set amid a clutter of furniture. But she didn't speak.

'May I come in, Ruthie?' Agnes asked.

'Oh, yes, miss. Yes, miss. Mam, here's . . .'

'I know who it is.' Peggy had risen from the table and was staring at Agnes.

'I thought I would come and see how you are faring, Peggy,' Agnes said, feeling very embarrassed.

'See how I was faring? Nice of you, miss, very nice of you to make the time. Sorry you couldn't make some time to come to Dave's passing.'

'I . . . I couldn't bring myself to do that. I'm . . . I'm very sorry. I . . . I thought you would understand.'

'Yes, yes, I understand, miss. I understand that some people are very unforgiving and that others can give their whole life to a family, as he did, and be thought nothing of. He had his faults. Yes, his main fault was too much caring. He cared too much for you both, and for you in particular. And you goin' downhill upset him so much. Oh yes, it did. Yes, it did.' She was nodding her head now at Agnes. 'He wouldn't have gone the way he did, his mind wouldn't have turned if you hadn't let your

404

side down, so to speak. That just finished him. Huh!' She turned and walked the two paces to the open fireplace where, grinding a black kettle into the heart of the fire, she said, 'I still don't know how you can do it, you brought up as you were, to lower yourself . . .'

'I'm not lowering myself, Peggy. I'm going to marry a man who is a good honest man, an equal, if not better than some, of the so-called gentlemen I have met.'

'Aye.' She watched Peggy's head fall back on her shoulders as she appealed to the ceiling. 'I never thought my ears would hear such things, never in me life. It's a wonder I don't lose me reason an' all, after all I've done for you.'

'You did for me what you wanted to do.' Agnes's voice was harsh now. 'You and Dave ran the house as if it were your own. Now we are speaking plainly let me tell you that you took liberties that no other servant would dare to have taken. You were treated as one of the family and, let me tell you also, you didn't treat those under you with the same consideration as you yourselves received, never, neither you nor he. Well, I came to see if I could be of any assistance to you, but I see I can't. Good-day.'

She turned on her heel and walked from the room and she was half-way down the bank on which the two-roomed houses stood when she heard Ruthie call, 'Miss! Miss!'

She stopped and faced her, and Ruthie, her voice tearful now, said, 'Don't take any notice, miss, she's not herself. She's gone sour, and on me an' all. Oh, miss'—she shook her head—'I don't like this life. I don't like this life. I don't like this

405

place. It's Maggie's house. She's out working full time now and she's carrying, you know, she's gona have a bairn, and Mam's all for her, I don't count any more. Miss, can I ask you something?'

Her breathing easier, Agnes said, 'Yes, yes, of course, Ruthie.'

'It's just this. Do you want anybody? I mean to help with the chores and where you are now with Miss Millie? I'll come gladly. I'll do anything to get out of here. She won't miss me. Anyway, I've always known that she preferred Maggie to me, ever since Maggie came on the scene. Maggie butters her up, I never could. And then there's Greg. He's not very civil at times with both of us there. I think, well I know, he'll put up with Mam, but he wants me out. You see, there's only two rooms and it's awkward. I sleep on a mat on a shaky down. Oh, miss, life's so different now.'

Agnes now put out her hand and patted Ruthie on the arm, saying, 'I'm . . . I'm sure we could do with some help, but I'll have to talk it over with'— she paused again—'with Robert and . . . and his aunt. There's going to be a new house built at the side and that will mean more work. Anyway, I tell you what. Give me a couple of days; come over on Friday. But are you sure your mother won't be more upset?'

'Vexed or pleased, it doesn't matter, I've got to get out. I could go into munitions but then I'd have to find lodgings, and I don't like lodgings, I've never been used to them.'

'All right, Ruthie, I'll try to fix up something. Goodbye now, and don't worry; it'll be all right.'

'Goodbye, miss. And thank you, thank you.'

Agnes walked down to the bottom of the hill

where she had left the trap in the care of a boy. She gave him a threepenny piece and mounted and turned the horse for home, thinking as she did so. Well, that's the end, nothing more can happen. But something did.

\*  \*  \*

The following morning she had a letter from Stanley. It contained a threat that brought a cynical smile to her face. It started briefly,

Dear Agnes,
    I hear that you intend to marry that fellow. Should you do so, I am warning you that, acting in place of Arnold as head of the family, I have the authority to remove Millie to an Institution, and this I shall do immediately should you take the step that you have so blatantly advertised . . .

She sat down and wrote the following,

Dear Stanley,
    You are at liberty to take any step with regard to Millie that you feel might be for her benefit. Just ask Doctor Miller when she can be removed from here.

She signed herself briefly, Agnes.

It was well into the New Year when she received another letter from Stanley. Ruthie brought the letter to her as she sat in the sitting-room massaging Robert's fingers. His left hand was without bandages now. The skin of it looked cracked and brittle and there seemed to be no pad below his thumb. Two fingers of his right hand were still bandaged, but the others, like the left hand, were stiff and scarred. She took the letter from Ruthie, saying, 'Thanks, Ruthie;' then added, 'Would you like to make a pot of tea? I'm as dry as a fish.' Ruthie smiled widely. 'Certainly, ma'am,' she said. 'It'll be there in a minute.'

Agnes now smiled down on Robert, and he returned the smile. It was the first time she had been addressed as ma'am, and he said, ' 'Tis ma'am now. Well! Well!'

As she slit open the envelope she said to him, 'Open those fingers, keep moving them.' And to this he answered, 'Why should I when I've got you to move them for me.'

She gave an almost flighty toss of the head, then read the letter. It was again from Stanley, briefer this time and more polite.

Dear Agnes,
   Will you please meet me in the stable yard tomorrow, Thursday, at three o'clock, if that is convenient for you.

Yours, Stanley.

She raised her eyebrows, then turned the letter round and held it in front of Robert's face, repeating the last words, 'if that is convenient for you.'

'Are you going?'

'Yes, yes, I'm going; and I'm going to take pleasure in the meeting.'

'I wish I could come with you.'

'You will be, in spirit.' And now her voice

408

dropped and she bent forward and put her fingers on his lips as she said, 'Ever and always.'

*       *       *

The following afternoon she drove the trap on to the drive. It was the first time she had seen the place since the night she left it, all the windows burning brightly, the fire illuminating the sky. There was nothing left of it now but blackened and charred stone walls. It would seem that locusts who ate only wood had stormed over it, because there weren't even any charred window frames left. No doors as far as she could see. The sight saddened her. She drove the trap round the corner into the stable yard, there to see Stanley leaning against one of the horse boxes.

He came immediately towards her and helped her down on to the yard, and they stood looking at each other. After all, she thought, they were brother and sister, and so she said, 'It's a terrible sight, isn't it?'

'Dreadful.'

Turning, they walked slowly to the front of the house, and there were almost tears in his voice now as he said, 'Not a stick of furniture saved, not one stick, and not a penny insurance.' He turned and faced her now and, his voice changing, he said, 'Why didn't you see to it?'

'What do you mean, why didn't I see to it? You mean, keep up the premiums on the insurance?'

'Yes, I mean just that.'

'Stanley'—she shook her head—'was there ever a time when I had any say in the money matters of that house?' She pointed her arm straight out now,

409

her finger extended. 'It's only the last year that I've had a dress allowance. Arnold left you in charge. You're the one who should have seen to the insurance. You had the money with which to pay the staff. You had the money to meet the bills. Did you ever once say to me, there's so much cash, you can see to them?'

'You should have reminded me.'

'Remind you!' Her voice had risen now. 'Remember once when I yelled at you, as I yelled at father, that the insurance on the house wouldn't have been paid, only the solicitors saw to it because of the mortgage?'

'I still maintain that you knew more about these things than I did. You should have.'

'Shut up! Don't you put the blame on me, you've done it for too long, all of you.'

'I will put the blame on you. Women should see to these things. Do you know that there's nothing left, nothing, only the ground. And what's that worth? And because of the state of things, Arnold . . . Arnold has cut off my allowance, and yours too.'

'Oh, but that doesn't matter to me.' She laughed now.

'No? Well, I'll tell you something else. He's writing to you and as head of the family he forbids you to marry that fellow. He says if you do, he's finished with you. We'll all be finished with you. You're letting us down. We may not have any money left, but we've still got our name to think about.'

'You may have, Stanley, and so may Arnold and Roland, but I changed my name yesterday.' She watched his mouth open wide and his eyes blaze as

410

he muttered, 'You what? You can't! You wouldn't.'

'I can, and I did, Stanley. I am now Missis Robert Bradley.'

'We . . . we could have it stopped, we . . .'

'Don't be silly. You're acting like a Victorian father. Why don't you say you'll horsewhip him.'

'By God! I will at that.'

'I'd like to see you try. He could wipe the floor with you, Stanley, with one hand burnt almost to the bone as it is. And why don't you go the whole hog and say you'll have it annulled. That's what they used to say, wasn't it? My daughter's made a mistake, my sister's made a mistake, it must be annulled, it was never consummated. But let me tell you, Stanley, it was, and beautifully.'

'My God! I can't believe it. You're . . . you're indecent.'

The words were a muttered growl from between his clenched teeth and for a moment they stung her as, head in the air, she turned quickly from him and walked back into the yard and mounted the trap.

When she turned the horse and came on to the drive he moved quickly towards her, and as the trap came abreast of him he grabbed its side and yelled up at her, 'I never want to see you again. Do you hear? I disown you, and so will everyone that ever knew you.'

She drew up the horse for a second as she looked down at him and said, 'I know that, Stanley. Oh yes, I know that. And it's a wonderful feeling to have sunk as low as I have. Goodbye, Stanley. Give my regards to Diana Cunningham.'

But when she reached the road all bravado had left her. That was the last time she would pass through those grounds. That was the last time she

411

would look on her brother, or on any of them. He had meant what he said; they would cut her out of their lives; as would all their friends. She was now married to a carpenter. She had, as it were, let the side down, and she knew that there was a penalty to pay for letting the side down. In some cases it would mean loneliness, degradation, but not in hers. No. She straightened her back, flapped the reins and said, 'Get up! there.' And as the horse went into a sharp trot she thought, Not in mine, no. Whatever lay ahead, and the path would not be always smooth, she was well aware of that, but on it, over all the ruts and the sudden potholes, there he would be, the carpenter Bradley.

Her beloved Bradley.